The Grace Allendale Series:

Hush Hush

TICK TOCK

Mel Sherratt is the author of thirteen crime novels, all of which have become bestsellers. For the past four years, she has been named as one of her home town of Stoke-on-Trent's top 100 influential people. She also works alongside the National Literary Trust as an ambassador on The Literary Project, to support their ongoing work in the city to raise literacy levels. She lives in Stoke-on-Trent, Staffordshire, with her husband and terrier, Dexter.

MEL SHERRATT
TICK
TOCK

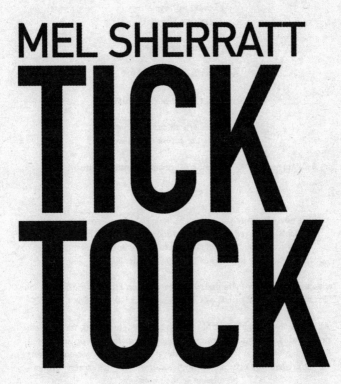

avon.

Published by AVON
A division of HarperCollins*Publishers* Ltd
1 London Bridge Street
London SE1 9GF

www.harpercollins.co.uk

A Paperback Original 2019
3
Copyright © Mel Sherratt 2019

Mel Sherratt asserts the moral right to be
identified as the author of this work.

A catalogue copy of this book is available from the British Library.

ISBN: 978-0-00-827107-7

Typeset in Minion by Palimpsest Book Production Ltd, Falkirk, Stirlingshire
Printed and bound in UK by CPI Group (UK) Ltd, Croydon CR0 4YY

MIX
Paper from
responsible sources
FSC™ C007454

This book is produced from independently certified FSC™ paper
to ensure responsible forest management.

For more information visit: www.harpercollins.co.uk/green

ACKNOWLEDGEMENTS

I can hardly believe that *Tick Tock* is my thirteenth crime novel. It feels like it was only yesterday when I was tentatively publishing my first and hoping that one or two people might like it.

Thanks must go first to my fabulous agent, Madeleine Milburn, and her ever growing team! I found a fantastic business partner six years ago when we met but more importantly I gained a very special friend. Thank you for coffee, cake, Pimm's, pick-me-ups and general cheerleading. Thanks to Team Avon – Helen, Rachel, Oli, Sabah, Anna, Dom and Elke – who have been a pleasure to work with on the next stage of my journey. Particular thanks must also go to the close trio of friends I am very lucky to have – Alison Niebiezczanski, Caroline Mitchell and Talli Roland. Finally, thanks to a certain gang of CSers, who brighten my day with their chat about anything and everything. You're such a bunch of cockblankets.

I want to say a huge thank you to anyone who has read my books, sent me emails, messages, engaged with me on social media or come to see me at various events over the country. Without you behind me, this wouldn't be half as much fun. I love what I do and hope you continue to enjoy my books. Likewise, my thanks go out to all the wonderful book bloggers and enthusiasts who have read my stories and taken the time out of their busy lives to write such amazing reviews, I am grateful to all of you.

And then, my Chris. Without your support, I know I wouldn't have got this far. Love you to bits, fella.

2014

Melissa Wyatt ran along the lane, down towards the field she would cut across for the next part of her journey. She was in training for the London Marathon, only a few days away now. It was her first attempt, the furthest she'd ever run, but she knew she had the strength inside her to complete it.

She was now a firm believer that she could do anything once she put her mind to it. Even two years ago when she'd become a mum at thirty-one, she would never have thought it possible that she could run three miles, let alone twenty-six.

She'd started off slowly, a ruse to lose the baby fat. At first every session had been torture, but eventually her puffing and panting had ceased, and she'd begun to get into an even rhythm. It had only taken three months before she'd been hooked. Now there was no stopping her, because as well as keeping her fit, it had given her a new lease of life. It had lowered her stress levels, giving her a sense of peace.

When she was running, her mind could switch off from all the daily hassles. She could be herself again. Her son, Joshua, wouldn't be throwing a tantrum because his TV programme had finished and there wasn't time to watch another. Her husband Lloyd wouldn't nag her because he couldn't find something that he'd lost after putting it down somewhere 'safe'. She wasn't at the beck and call of staff and clients ready to interrupt her in a flash, unlike her day-to-day life as a customer services manager at the local building society. She was plain and simply Melissa.

At the bottom of the lane, she climbed over the stile at the side of the gate and ran into a small wooded area. She loved going through here. It was dark and somewhat eerie at this time in the morning.

As she clambered up the man-made steps and out into the open field, she wondered what to cook for tea. Maybe shepherd's pie, if she remembered to get some mince out of the freezer. There would be no time to nip into the butcher's to buy some fresh. It was going to be a late evening because she had staff training for an hour once the branch closed at five.

She was now coming into a hilly field, empty except for her. It was early; most people were still asleep. Melissa much preferred to run in the mornings than the evenings. There were fewer people about, and fewer cars too, which was good because the lanes were narrow. A creature of habit, she covered the same route for a few months before switching up to ensure her body became challenged.

At the top of the hill, she took a moment to catch her breath. Up here, she could see for miles. High-rise flats, factories intermingled with the odd strip of green, but mostly built up row upon row of houses. Manchester was a place she'd always call home.

After a minute's rest, she began to run again. With a bit of luck, she'd be home before anyone in her household was awake. Oh, to have a coffee in peace before Josh was out of bed.

She was nearly at the other side of the field when she heard someone. Turning slightly as she ran, she saw a man running

2

behind her. She slowed and stepped to one side to let him pass, and he drew level on the worn-down grass pathway.

When he threw a punch at her, she was taken by surprise. She gasped as he hit her again, stumbling backwards with the force and landing heavily on the ground.

Almost immediately the man was straddling her and his hands were around her neck.

She tried to push him off, but he was too strong.

She scratched at his hands, but he only squeezed harder. Struggling was useless, but she had to try. He seemed possessed, his face creased with rage.

As the light began to fade from the world, she wondered why she'd been singled out. What had she done to deserve death? Because he was killing her, wasn't he? And she could do nothing about it.

ONE

Five Years Later

Tuesday

'What makes you think he likes you?' Courtney Piggott asked her friend Lauren Ansell as they walked across the field behind their school. 'Just because he looked at you a certain way doesn't mean anything.'

'Of course it does!' Lauren replied. 'And I've fancied him for ages, so that *look* means he's mine for the taking.'

'You're so weird,' Courtney's twin sister, Caitlin, said. 'If you believe that, then—'

'Girls!'

The three of them froze as they heard their PE teacher, Mr Carmichael, shouting to them.

'I wish you'd exercise your feet as much as your mouths,' he continued. 'Hurry up now. Get a move on!'

The girls picked up their pace, jogging a few feet across the field until the teacher turned away from them again.

'I hate cross-country.' Caitlin came to a halt with a groan. 'There should be laws against making us do this. It's not cool – at all.'

Lauren tripped over her shoelace as they walked, almost falling but managing to right herself in time. 'I'll catch you up in a minute,' she said, shooing her friends away before bending down to tie the laces again.

The twins continued through the gap in the hedge and out onto the lane.

'I wish there was a short cut back to the school,' Caitlin said as they walked.

In front of them were the rest of the class, in twos and threes, only the odd pupil running alone. They were the last of the group by a good minute or so, but neither of them was bothered about hurrying to catch up. Instead, they dawdled as they waited for Lauren.

'Or a magic portal. If there was, we could sneak back and watch everyone else coming in.' Courtney laughed.

'Or Doctor Who's TARDIS!' Caitlin laughed back.

In front of them, their teacher beckoned them to hurry up as he disappeared around a corner, but still they went at their own pace. They had run this lane many times during their five years at Dunwood Academy. There was nothing to see but a high hedge either side, a space for one car to drive past at a time, which was why it was safe for students to run down, as not many drivers used it.

Ahead of them the twins could see the roof of the school buildings, the railings around it coming into view opposite a row of council bungalows for the elderly.

'Where's Lauren?' Courtney shivered as a gust of wind came up the lane. 'We'll be in trouble if we're not back soon.'

'I thought she was behind us.' Caitlin swivelled round, but they were on their own.

'She can't have got very far, Cait,' Courtney told her sister. 'I bet she's found a quicker way back and has left us.'

'She'd better let us in on it if she has.'

They carried on for a few more steps and then Courtney stopped again.

'We should go back for her.'

'But we'll get into trouble if we don't finish soon.'

'She should have caught up by now. It will only take a minute.'

With a heavy sigh, Caitlin followed her sister back into the field. They ran towards where they'd last seen Lauren, across the field and around the corner of trees.

Not noticing that her sister had stopped, Caitlin almost bumped into the back of her.

Courtney was pointing at a figure lying in the grass. 'There's something wrong.'

'What do you mean?'

Caitlin followed behind her as they ran to their friend. The wind picking up across the open ground was the only thing they could hear. They drew level, their eyes widening with fear. Lauren was lying on her back, her blonde hair fanned out around her head.

'She's having us on, isn't she?' Caitlin said.

'I don't know,' Courtney whispered. 'Lauren?'

She prodded Lauren's leg gently with her toes. Maybe that would make Lauren giggle if she was winding them up. But she didn't move.

'Lauren?' Caitlin dropped to her knees. 'Are you okay?'

It was then she noticed the glazed look in her friend's eyes.

TWO

Leaving her home in Manchester hadn't been as gut-wrenching as DS Grace Allendale had thought it was going to be. It had been more of a relief as she'd closed the door for the final time and handed the keys in at the estate agent's. The house had begun to depress her. It never seemed to remind her of what she'd had, only of what she had lost. Starting afresh was what she'd needed.

Moving back to her hometown of Stoke-on-Trent had turned out in her favour, too. Despite her first case being personal, she'd settled into life at Bethesda Police Station. She was getting to know everyone eight months on, as well as the good and the bad of the area.

Stoke-on-Trent was a city of two halves in every meaning of the term. There were beautiful areas of vast countryside alongside barren inner-city areas that had been set for regeneration and then forgotten about. Abandoned factories of years gone by close to others that flourished, staying in the game by welcoming visitors and embracing social media coverage. It had several large housing estates owned by the city council and lanes with affluent property owners, their gardens stretching to acres. Empty shops in local towns sat next to family firms that had been in business for decades. Rough alongside smooth: wealth alongside poverty.

Grace never went with the adage that the wealthy were any better than the ones scraping around for pennies. She firmly believed there were shades of polite and ugly in every level of society. She'd seen compassion from a drug user at the lowest ebb of his life; she'd seen injuries of domestic abuse caused by a high-ranking politician. So much went on behind closed doors regardless of class.

Arriving back from a meeting with Allie Shenton, a colleague who oversaw six local community intelligence teams, she felt a buzz of activity as soon as she opened the door to the office where her team was located. Her phone went off and she slipped a hand inside her jacket pocket to retrieve it. It was her boss, DI Nick Carter.

Grace could see him sitting in his office. She raised her hand to show him she was here as she walked across to him. Something must have come in while she'd been out. Adrenaline began to pump through her, as had become natural.

'We've had a call of a suspicious death at Dunwood Academy, over in Norton,' Nick told her. 'Female, sixteen years of age. Out on a cross-country run, got left behind. First thoughts were she'd had some kind of seizure. Two pupils found her; one ran to get help. By the time their teacher got to her, bruising had started to appear around her neck.'

Grace pulled a face. 'Do they suspect foul play from anyone there? The teachers, or the pupils?'

'I'm not sure. Can you task someone with getting everything ready here and then we can go in five?'

'Will do.' She headed back to her desk.

Perry Wright, one of two detective constables on her team, was sitting opposite her.

9

'I've grabbed a pool car, Sarge,' he said as she approached.

Grace nodded her appreciation. 'Sam, are you okay setting up the incident room for us, please?'

'Sure thing.' DC Sam Markham nodded.

Since she'd first arrived at the station, Grace had learned that the staff in her team had jobs they preferred. Wanting to be in the thick of it all, it was usually Perry who came out to the enquiries with her. Grace liked that she had someone solid by her side. Although, while Perry was fit and bulky to Sam's small and nimble, Sam could still pull a suspect down in a rugby tackle whenever necessary. At thirty-eight, she was two years older than Grace, and she came into her own as office manager: sorting things out, getting the details down, doing the minute things that could make or break a case. It worked, and Grace hadn't felt a need to change things.

'Tell me about the school,' Grace said to Perry as he drove them north to the scene of the crime. She relied on her team for their local knowledge, even though she was learning the different patches and area.

'Dunwood Academy? A bit of a dive before government intervention. Certain kids were always getting into trouble and the school was underperforming on grades. But it's doing much better at the moment. Plus, it's on the edge of the Bennett Estate.'

'Ah.' Grace nodded. Perry didn't need to say any more.

The Bennett Estate was the second largest estate in Stoke-on-Trent. Like a lot of social housing, it had a reputation for trouble and unruly tenants but, more often than not, Grace found that rumours were just that. This area, however, did live up to its status as a sink estate. She wasn't being unkind when she reckoned 90 per cent of its residents didn't work, 70 per cent were single parents and most of them were probably bringing up the next generation of crooks.

The school was on the edge of the city, meaning that it backed onto a considerable amount of countryside. But driving up to the block itself, you wouldn't have reason to believe that. It was a deftly overpopulated area with homes on every available piece of land. Built in the mid-1940s, the estate was past its sell-by date in terms of today's standards. Cars were parked everywhere owing to lack of space, on already narrow roads, which were a rat run for car chases.

Grace and Perry pulled into the already crowded car park. As they stepped out of the vehicle, there seemed to be orderly chaos everywhere Grace looked. Teachers were herding pupils into a main hallway. Parents had started to turn up, no doubt having been rung by frantic children wondering what was going on.

They passed a woman she assumed to be a member of staff trying to explain to a man that he needed to wait until his child's name was crossed off her list and then someone would go and fetch him; Grace presumed this was to ensure they had a record of who was on the premises. Another woman was trying to stop a worried parent from barging through.

A uniformed officer was marking down names of people who were going into the school as part of their investigation. Grace knew they could contain the crime scene as it was away from the school site, but it would be handy in the days to come to show who had been where and doing what here as well.

Nick caught up with Grace and Perry after parking next to them.

'I think we'll go and see her first,' he said. 'Then we can speak to the girls who found her, the teachers who took the class and the headmaster. Eyes are on us.'

Grace nodded. A small crowd was gathering across the road from the entrance gate, a row of bungalows behind them.

Already, there were a few either speaking into or tapping away at their phones.

Nick pointed to a lane at the side of the school. It had been blocked by a marked vehicle parked horizontally across the tarmac, its lights flashing.

'She's a five-minute walk from here,' he said. 'Let's go.'

THREE

Grace, Nick and Perry presented their warrant cards to another uniformed officer with a clipboard and, once he'd noted them down, began the sombre walk to the body. The school was at the end of a road that led to a single access lane. With hedges on both sides, and knowing what she was about to look at, Grace couldn't help feeling claustrophobic. It was eerily quiet too, once they'd left behind the noise of the school. Grace shivered, even though the April day was mild.

After a steep incline, the entrance to the field loomed at them. There was another police car parked, its tailgate open. Inside were the items they were required to put on before going to the crime scene, to avoid contamination and help them catch only their killer's DNA and vital evidence – forensic white suits and shoe covers, latex gloves and masks to cover their mouths.

They each dressed in the appropriate gear and turned off the lane, through a gap in the hedge. Grace looked in front of her; there were a few bushes scattered across the grassy landscape and a large hedge around the perimeter. To her left, she had a clear view across some of the city, seeing rows of houses and gardens, and a large football playing field with a changing hut.

If this death was suspicious, Grace mused, it would be the second murder investigation in Stoke-on-Trent since she'd arrived. Back in September, she had helped to catch a serial killer. The timing couldn't have been more poignant, but then again, the killer was someone she had known, so it was no coincidence that their rampage coincided with her return to her birth town.

Since then, the city had been fairly quiet. There had been the usual assaults, domestics and some low-level crime, but nothing as big as her first case with her team.

They reached the tent. In the far distance, Grace could see a row of gardens from properties that backed onto the field. She doubted any surveillance would scope this far, but made a mental note to send someone to contact their owners anyway. Then she took a deep breath before following Nick.

It was unprofessional, she knew, but she couldn't stop the tears welling in her eyes as she took in the young girl at her feet. She had long blonde hair and a heavy fringe. Her head was partly facing away from them, her eyes open and thankfully looking in the opposite direction.

The bruising around her neck was prominent now, popping up from above the collar of her sweatshirt. The uniform of leggings and long sleeves was different from the one Grace remembered from her school days: T-shirts and short skirts, and the mottled legs that weren't a nice look when it was cold.

She seemed a pretty girl. Grace wondered if she had been popular at school.

'She would have been so full of life until this morning.' Her voice was low. 'Why would anyone take that away from her?'

'Are you okay?' Nick asked.

'Something in my eye.' Grace blinked profusely, not caring who saw her in distress. 'Although if I didn't have any emotion, I couldn't do this job.'

'Whereas I have to switch mine off to do it,' Dave Barnett, the senior crime scene investigating officer said, acknowledging them at the same time. 'I wouldn't survive a week if I didn't.'

'I think it's good to have feelings,' Grace said. 'What happened to her, Dave?'

'On first thoughts, she's been asphyxiated.' Dave pointed to the bruising on the victim's neck. 'But it could be a case of a murder not quite there. Either someone cocked up and didn't finish the job, or they knew what they were looking for and left her to die.'

'I don't follow,' Grace said.

'You can strangle someone until they stop breathing altogether, or if you press on the carotid artery in the right place, the heart will slow down and a victim will lose consciousness quite quickly, usually in seconds. If left that way without being revived, it takes no more than five minutes to die, depending on the age and health of the victim.'

'So you suspect she was still alive when the girls ran for help?' Grace swallowed.

'I think our killer either panicked or ran out of time.' Dave nodded.

'Based on several statements, it would seem it was a time issue. And everyone thought she'd had a seizure at first, until the bruises started to appear,' Nick explained.

'How did she get singled out?' Perry questioned. 'She would have been in a class of, what, thirty?'

'It could be someone who is close to our victim, who knows her routine,' Grace suggested.

'Any sexual assault?' Nick asked Dave.

Grace found herself holding her breath as she waited for an answer.

'It's not looking likely,' Dave said. 'Maybe your killer was disturbed when the other girls came back to look for her. Poor kids will be traumatised, no doubt.'

'If they had nothing to do with it.' Grace nodded, knowing they'd be talking to their witnesses very soon.

'We need to check out any known offenders in the area, regardless,' Nick continued.

Grace moved closer to the victim. 'Are we looking at an opportunist?' she asked. 'We're in the middle of a field. Our killer might have seen the pupils out on a run, else how would someone have known she'd fall behind? And there would only have been a matter of minutes to pounce.'

'It's a tricky one.' Nick paused. 'We'll inform the parents after talking to the headmaster. And we'll have to be quick as I bet it's already broken out on social media.'

'But she was ID'd by her teacher,' Perry said, 'as well as the girls who found her.'

Grace finally stepped out of the tent and breathed in heavily. It always got to her when she first saw a victim's body – the heaviness, the sadness, the sheer callousness of these acts. She wondered how Dave coped with it all the time.

Alongside Nick and Perry, she removed her forensic clothing and placed everything carefully into evidence bags. Then they began the walk back to the school. All around her was that feeling of bleakness, a sense of desolation. Glancing back, she reflected again on the pointless loss of life.

Once on the lane, she took out her phone. She wanted to see who was saying what about their dead girl. Like most cops, Grace had a love-hate relationship with social media. Sometimes it was great for their intelligence, getting to the root of things, because some people are more likely to be honest online than to the police. Other times, it was macabre, reporting on real-time crimes before victims' families had been notified.

She clicked onto Twitter and typed in the girl's name. Nothing there yet, thankfully, but she saw the hashtag #deadgirlatDun-wood was trending in the local area. Next, she tracked down Lauren Ansell on Facebook, the image of the girl startling her as she popped up so full of life on her page. Despite her age, Lauren didn't have a closed profile, so it was all over that feed.

Posts were coming through, even though her status hadn't been updated since nine thirty the night before, which could mean that some of the pupils' parents would know by now as the rumour mill exploded.

Are you okay?

I've heard something's happened at your school. Message me!

This can't be true. Not Lauren. This is a wind-up!

'It's all over Twitter and Facebook that something's going on at the school.' Grace showed Nick the screen. 'Some are already sensationalising it. I do hope we can get to her next of kin in time.'

'I just pray she isn't friends with her own parents,' Nick added. 'We'd better get over there as soon as we can.'

FOUR

Dunwood Academy was an L-shaped two-storey building. It had been rebuilt on the grounds of a previous high school and then given a different name as well as a complete make-over. Everything about it was modern and new, markings still fresh outside on the tarmac and painted white walls inside with hardly a scuff. But today it had an eerie sense of shock, an undertone of fear that made it seem duller than it was.

As Nick went back to his car to make some calls, a man at the entrance gave them directions to the headmaster's office, checking first via his phone that the head was there. Grace walked by Perry's side, along two empty corridors and up a flight of stairs. The school secretary's office was the first on the left. Nathan Stiller was in there waiting for them.

Nathan was in his early forties. Grace couldn't help feeling she was stereotyping him, but he was fashion model material. Discreetly, she clocked his choppy dark hair, short but tidy beard and navy-blue suit with slim-fit trousers and waistcoat. His black brogues were shiny, his shirt the proverbial crisp white. Not at all what you'd expect from a schoolteacher.

But his demeanour was forlorn. All this would come down on him, Grace assumed. He would most likely blame himself too, as much as the teacher who had taken the PE lesson.

After introducing themselves, Grace and Perry were shown into his office. Grace glanced around before they all sat down. On the wall were certificates for qualifications Stiller had taken, an award for the school itself and a few photos of pupils gathered together. One she spotted was a clip from *Stoke News*. Several pupils were holding up a giant cheque for £2,000 for local charity Douglas Macmillan Hospice.

'I can't believe this has happened,' Nathan said. 'It's such a shock. I've been the head at this school for five years, so I've known Lauren since she first came here in Year 7.'

'Obviously, we need to contact her parents as a matter of urgency, Mr Stiller,' Grace said.

'Please, call me Nathan. They're divorced. I wasn't sure whether to contact her mother or not until I'd spoken to you – she lives locally. In the end, I felt I had to ask her to come to the school. But her phone went to voicemail. I left a message about half an hour ago.'

'Do you have any other details?' Grace asked. 'Does she work? What about Lauren's father?'

'Yes. I've got them up onscreen.' Nathan sat down at his desk and wiggled the mouse to wake up his computer. 'Mrs Ansell remarried and is named Gillespie now. She works at Mintons Solicitors in Newcastle-under-Lyme. Her ex-husband lives in Derby.'

'Does the class take cross-country every week at the same time?' she asked.

'No.' Nathan wrote down details before looking up again. 'It's as and when the weather permits and never more than once a month. Robert sorts it out so that each year has a lesson.'

'Robert?' Perry queried.

'Robert Carmichael. He's the PE teacher. The classes get very competitive and it gives the pupils a good workout in the fresh air.'

'Who owns the field where Lauren was found?' Grace questioned.

'Arthur Barrett and his family – a local farming generation. The school have been using it with their permission for over twenty years.' Nathan shook his head in disbelief. 'I hope I don't have to suspend Robert for not watching them all.'

'He can't have eyes in the back of his head,' Perry said.

'I guess. But it only takes one person to blame him. And me.' Nathan ran a hand through his hair and swallowed. 'Although, according to some of the pupils, he shouted at them to hurry up a few times.'

'We need a list of the pupils who took his class, too,' Grace said. 'We'll have to speak to them all over the course of the next day or two. If there aren't enough teachers spare to sit with the pupils, or if any parents or guardians specifically want to be with their children when we speak to them, we'll arrange appointments. Whatever happens, everything will be dealt with in a sensitive manner.'

Nathan nodded his understanding.

'What's the school like?' she asked next. 'Any problems you're aware of?'

'Dunwood Academy is doing well this year.' Grace heard pride in his voice as he continued. 'There used to be two high schools until we joined forces, covering a wider area. There was initially concern about the number of its pupils, and special measures being in place at one of the two previous schools. It could have gone either way. One could have brought the other down to their level, but it didn't. The academy's performing well now.'

'There was never any tension between the students from each school?' she asked.

'There was, but not for a long time.'

'We'll require a register of both staff and pupils – who is present and also who is absent today, please,' Grace said. 'Likewise, we have your CCTV to check, especially with the lack of surveillance equipment and witnesses in the lane.'

'I've already arranged for that to be done.' Nathan gave a loud sigh. 'I only found out when Robert called me after he'd requested an ambulance. When I saw Lauren, that was when I called the police.'

'What's Robert like?' Grace asked.

'He's a good man. I've known him for five years, since I started here.' Nathan lowered his voice. 'And there was no . . . sexual assault?'

'It's too early to say.' Perry was non-committal. 'But we'll keep you informed.'

Nathan's face paled as his thoughts went into overdrive.

'It's highly unlikely, seeing as the whole incident could have only lasted a few minutes according to the timeline of the Piggott twins,' Grace said, hoping to pacify him. 'We like to keep an open mind until we have forensic evidence, though.'

Grace thought back to her last case. She'd kept an open mind then but had been totally shocked at the end result. Relocating to Stoke after the murder of her estranged father earlier that year had left her vulnerable. The shock of her first murder case being on her family's grounds was immense, and after her half-sister had been apprehended as the killer, things could have turned out worse for Grace, but her team had stood by her. She wouldn't take any chances or make any assumptions this time.

Jade Steele was in prison now, awaiting trial for murdering

four people and assaulting her brother Leon. It would stay with Grace for the rest of her life what Jade had been capable of, but she also believed it was only because of Jade's upbringing. Jade had been abused for most of her life by their father and his friends, and she was taking revenge on a group of men who had been grooming young women. It had been hard to police – Grace herself got away from the man when she was twelve. Could she have gone down a similar path if she hadn't? But it had also been thrilling when she'd been involved in solving the case.

'Well, you have my full cooperation to do whatever's necessary,' Nathan said. 'Also, if there's anything you require while you're here, be sure to let me know.'

'We'll need to set up a mobile police unit in your car park,' Grace said, 'and we could do with somewhere to use to speak to people.'

'I've made the decision to close the school for lessons. It won't be popular with everyone, but I thought it was the right thing to do. We can arrange counselling sessions from tomorrow. Most pupils will be collected as soon as possible, but we do have some who will need to stay here until parents can pick them up at the end of the day. You can use any of the class-rooms.' Nathan paused as if he were gathering his emotions. 'We'll look after everyone as best we can. I'll assemble them in the large hall. It serves as a school canteen during lunch break. We can hand out drinks and food where necessary. I think it will do the students good to sit together.'

'Yes, it's going to affect a lot of them,' Grace replied.

When there were no more questions, Grace turned to Nathan. 'Can you see if Courtney and Caitlin are still here, please?' she said. 'We need to have a chat with them.'

'Yes, of course.' Nathan nodded. 'I'll get in touch with their form teachers.' His phone went off and he quickly read the message. 'Robert's in the medical room when you need him. He was feeling sick, well, after seeing the body.'

Grace nodded. 'Can you bring him to us?'

'Yes. You can use my classroom, too.'

FIVE

Grace was startled by all the images on the walls when they were shown into the classroom. It seemed as if she had walked into a set from *Game of Thrones*. She assumed they were in a history room and, even though the novels were fantasy, Nathan Stiller was using the popular series to encourage the pupils to learn about darker times.

She tried not to stare at an almost life-size image of the actor Sean Bean at the back of the room, looking all caveman rough-and-ready. To her right, fictional character Daenerys Targaryen, the Mother of Dragons, was looking just as tempting. It was quite some show, as were the books themselves. Grace had been bereft when the seventh series had finished on a cliff-hanger after binge-watching all of them. Grace had been bereft when the seventh series had finished on a cliff-hanger after binge-watching all of them. She looked forward to watching the final season, if she ever had time.

Robert Carmichael was sitting at the desk at the front of the room. He was of average build with dark brown hair. His face was as white as chalk, the smell of vomit lingering around him. He wore grey tracksuit trousers and a black T-shirt that was in need of an iron, obviously a spare. Grace knew that he would have changed out of his clothes regardless. Forensics would have bagged them up after he left the crime scene.

After introductions, Grace asked him to run through what had happened that morning.

'It was another lesson, nothing out of the ordinary,' Robert began. 'Most of the pupils were in front of me, with only the lane to run. There was a supply teacher helping me out at the front.'

'Name of?' she asked.

'Sarah Flynn. She's only been with us a few weeks at the most.'

Grace wrote down the woman's name for future reference.

'There were a few girls at the back of the group who I'd had to cajole to finish,' Robert added.

'How many are in the class?' Perry asked.

'Thirty-one.'

'So twenty-eight on the lane and three left in the field?'

Robert nodded. He held a hand over his mouth as he swallowed quickly a few times.

'Are you okay?' Grace asked, wondering if he was going to be sick. 'Would you like a glass of water?'

Robert shook his head, faltering before speaking again. 'I should have kept an eye on them.' Tears welled in his eyes. 'But when I looked behind me, I could see them on the lane, so I kept on going. I now realise there must have been only two of them. I was almost back at the school when Courtney came running down to fetch me.'

'Courtney's one of the girls who found her?' Grace queried.

'Yes, Courtney Piggott. She said that Lauren had collapsed in the field and that Courtney's sister, Caitlin, was with her. She said I needed to hurry, as she didn't think Lauren was breathing. I told her to go back to the school and let the head-

25

master know what had happened, but she was hysterical, so I rang Nathan on my phone while I ran back up the lane. When I got to Lauren, I realised that Courtney had followed me. The rest of the class had gone back inside the school, luckily.'

'Did you notice anyone else around?' she asked.

'Not that I recall, but then I was worried about Lauren.' He took a deep breath before looking at them. 'When I got to her, I could see she wasn't breathing, so I called for an ambulance. I know basic first aid, so I tried to resuscitate her. All the while the twins were crying by my side.' He swallowed. 'I tried for such a long time, but in the end, I knew I'd lost her. That's when I noticed the marks coming out around her neck.'

Grace noted he was pointing at the floor, as if the body were at their feet. She couldn't help but feel for the teacher. He was doing his job and this would probably scar him for the rest of his life. People would look at him differently, despite him doing nothing wrong.

Lots of people had regrets after things like this happened. It only took a second or two for something drastic to occur, for lives to be ruined: the child who wriggled out of its father's grip and ran out into a busy road; the woman who decided to walk through a dark alley rather than the long way around; someone driving too fast because they were late for an appointment. While they weren't in the right, Grace had sympathy.

'I waited until Nathan arrived and he confirmed what I knew. The paramedics came quickly after, and they worked on her too, but we all knew she was dead. Then the police arrived and declared it a crime scene.' Robert put his head in his hands and wept unashamedly. 'It was my fault. I should have checked again to see there was no one lagging behind.'

Once Robert had gathered himself, he left the room. Grace turned to Perry and sighed loudly.

'That poor man's going to be haunted by this. He's going to

torture himself for not being there, for having his eye on most of the class rather than all of them; though how he was supposed to do that is beyond me. He's going to think he could have stopped her death if he was behind them.'

'He can't see everything.'

'Try telling him that when he wakes up covered in sweat after a nightmare in which he sees Lauren running and then being grabbed, and there's nothing he can do about it.'

'That's a bit dramatic,' Perry added.

'I'll bet it's what happens. Carmichael didn't do anything wrong and yet we both know he's going to be made into a scapegoat until we catch the killer.' Grace checked her phone for messages. 'We need to move fast on questioning the twins,' she confirmed. 'First up on our list will be to find out if Lauren had a boyfriend.'

'You think she might have been killed by another pupil?' Perry frowned. 'I mean, I'm not ruling it out. It could have happened, but really?'

'Assuming that Lauren knew her killer, I'd say we need to rule out jealous peers first.' Grace shrugged. 'Maybe Caitlin or Courtney Piggott had a grudge to bear. Twins might cover up for each other, too.'

Perry pulled a face. 'It's a possibility – gruesome though.'

Although she'd seen some similarly awful things in the past, Grace shuddered at the thought.

'I'd say anything is game at the moment, with no witnesses or camera footage to go on.' Grace's phone beeped and she retrieved the message that had been sent. 'Nick's after me. He wants you to speak to the Piggott twins while I go with him to inform Lauren's mum and dad.'

SIX

After talking to Perry about what to say to the Piggott sisters, Grace rejoined Nick and they left the school. She then spent an uncomfortable few minutes speaking to Lauren Ansell's father on the phone.

'That wasn't nice,' she said after disconnecting the call. 'The local police had already informed him. I could hear him crying, taking deep breaths to calm himself.'

'What did he say?'

'He passed the phone to a police sergeant. A Mick Attwood – he told me Mr Ansell was in a meeting at the time of the attack and for most of the morning, too. So we can rule him out; although living so far away, he'd hardly be a suspect anyway. What a way to learn your only child's been murdered.'

'I'm glad Nathan Stiller's phone call to our victim's mother went through to her voicemail,' Grace added as they travelled along the D road towards Newcastle. 'I hate the thought of an accident happening as relatives rush to wherever they need to be in a state of disbelief. I've seen it too many times, and I get that they're questioning what they've been told because they want it to be untrue, but even so.'

'I'll need to get ready for the press conference,' Nick said. 'I'll be giving a statement at four p.m. to camera. I'm not sure whether to do it outside the school gates or up in the quiet of the lane.'

'I think you know the answer to that one.' Grace knew that press wouldn't be allowed anywhere near the lane, even if the field was a good five-minute walk from the general public. 'Although for the viewing figures, they'll want the cameras accessing as much as they can. Funny how they say that's so the general public might be of more use, spot more, give us a lead. It's always for their advantage, really.'

'I hope some of them don't try to go in to the field via the other entrance.'

'All covered,' Grace told him. 'The search team are there, too. No one will get through. It does seem a bit audacious, though.'

'Go on.' Nick kept his eyes on the road.

'Well, most murders are associated with dark alleys late at night. There's something sinister about how out in the open this one is. It was bold, daring, and it had to be quick with so many chances of being caught.'

'Meaning?'

'Meaning we may not have a lot to go on unless anyone saw it happen. Which is both likely given the crime took place in broad daylight, but unlikely given how big the space is.'

Nick nodded his reply.

Twenty minutes later, he drew into the tiny car park at the front of a row of new-build offices. Mintons Solicitors was in the second shop from the right, alongside a hairdresser's, a sandwich bar and several vacant spaces.

'I hope she hasn't had time to answer her calls yet,' Grace said as they walked into an airy reception room and across to a desk with two women behind it. 'Even though I dislike doing this, it's much better for the family.'

The receptionist made a phone call and less than a minute later, a woman came out of a side door. Grace and Nick glanced at each other surreptitiously. She had the same looks and build as their victim.

It was clear from the laughter following her that she didn't know what had happened. The smile dropped from her face as Nick held up his warrant card. Grace followed suit.

'Mrs Emma Gillespie? I'm DI Carter and this is DS Allendale. May we speak to you for a moment, somewhere in private?'

'Something's happened, hasn't it?' Emma's hand clutched her chest at the same time as she moved aside for them to pass. 'Is it Alan? Lauren? Are they okay?'

She opened the door to a vacant side office and they all went inside. Grace steered her towards a chair, pointedly looking at it until Emma sat down.

'Is this your daughter, Lauren?' Nick showed Mrs Gillespie a photo that had been printed off from the school computer.

'Yes.' Worried blue eyes flicked from one to the other.

Grace pulled a chair over and took Mrs Gillespie's hands in her own as Nick began to speak.

'I'm afraid we have some very bad news,' he started. 'This morning, the body of a young girl was found on a field near to Dunwood Academy. We have reason to believe that person is Lauren. I'm so sorry to tell you that she's been killed.'

'Lauren?' Emma shook her head. 'No, she's at school. I dropped her there myself this morning.' She looked at Nick for confirmation. 'There must be a mistake. It can't be her.'

'I know there's a lot to take in, Mrs Gillespie. We'll ask you to make a formal identification of the body, later this evening or tomorrow, if you're able.'

'No, this can't be right.' Emma shook her head in denial. 'What happened to her?'

'We're treating Lauren's death as suspicious,' Nick said. 'We believe the injuries she'd sustained were caused by someone else.'

'What do you mean?'

Grace watched as the first few tears began to trickle down Mrs Gillespie's face, the news finally beginning to sink in. When she turned towards Grace, willing her to say that Nick had got it all wrong, it almost broke Grace's heart.

Emma crumpled and began wailing loudly. 'Where is she?' she managed between gasps.

'She's still at the crime scene. We have officers—'

'The field!' Emma's voice grew hard. 'You've left my daughter lying dead in a field!'

Grace could see she needed someone to blame, but Nick explained what he could of the situation amid her gasps of disbelief.

'I dropped her off at school! She should have been safe.' Emma stood up. 'I want to see her.'

'You can.' Nick nodded. 'Once she's away from the crime scene.'

'No, I want to see her now.'

'I'm sorry.' Nick's tone was insistent.

Emma gasped. 'Please tell me she wasn't raped.'

'We don't think so.' As she began to cry again, Nick continued, 'Is there anyone we can call for you? You mentioned Alan.'

'He's my husband. Lauren's father Richard needs to know, too. We're divorced.' She looked at Grace.

'We informed him on our way to see you,' she said. 'We're here to do as much as we can. Later, there will be a family liaison officer to help.'

Emma gave another loud sob. 'Please. It can't be her,' she cried. 'Not my Lauren.'

As Grace left the room to inform Mrs Gillespie's colleagues that she'd be leaving with them, she wondered how she would have coped if it were her daughter. Lauren was an only child. It meant their family had been wiped out in one hit. It was beyond cruel. But then when had a murderer ever been bothered with that?

As she explained what had happened to the receptionist, watching her go to pieces too, Grace realised that keeping this under wraps was going to be hard. There were already so many people who knew what had happened. But even if there had been no official identification, everyone knew they had the right person.

Lauren Ansell had been strangled and Grace was going to find out who had done it.

SEVEN

She stood in her tiny kitchen looking out of the window. There were three boys playing football on the green down in front of her, two jumpers on the grass to mark the goal. Their shouts didn't bother her, but she'd only give them a few more minutes before someone came out and moved them on. She remembered that feeling well – a sense of no one wanting you around, not fitting in anywhere but having nowhere else to go.

The flat she was in was her fifth rental since she'd left home at sixteen, and it felt right. It was a maisonette really, upstairs in a block of four. Two up and two down, with tiny shared gardens back and front, and her own front door at the side. This had been one of the better places she'd stayed in over the years. The wallpaper wasn't peeling from the walls. The carpets didn't stick to her feet – hell, even having carpets had been a bonus. The furnishing wasn't too old-fashioned and there was no scratching as a result of bed bugs in the mattress.

The tenant downstairs was Arnie Jerold. He was in his eighties and apart from having his TV on full blast most evenings, she had no complaints. Arnie also looked after the garden and didn't mind sharing it with her.

Last summer, she'd drunk many a glass of something cold with him as well, to pass the time. She liked him and the tales he told her of his family. He didn't have many visitors, but his two sons came once a fortnight and for that he was grateful. They took him out for Sunday lunch with the family. It was enough, he'd tell her.

He'd asked about her life and she'd told him all of it, knowing he wouldn't believe her. He'd smirked and she'd laughed, and then she'd told him a whole bunch of lies about a happier, made-up life. Arnie seemed to like her but he only saw the woman that she wanted him to see and not who she really was.

After the boys on the green had scored five goals, she poured another glass of wine, congratulating herself on fooling people again. She was so good at it now – a player, she liked to call herself. So far, everything was working out to plan – even better, actually. She'd chosen him well and he was like putty in her hands. He was turning into a great disciple. It had taken time to find him, but after several aborted attempts she had found the right one.

She remembered a few of the men she had tried to lure into her game. Trevor Wilde had lived up to his name, been willing to do a lot with her sexually, but after she'd tried to asphyxiate him once, she'd never seen him again. He'd turned white and practically ran out of the flat, even though she had told him what she was about to do and he'd agreed.

Then there was Lester Baker. Now, he was really weird and she hadn't liked him at all, but had gone through with everything in case he was the one. In the end, he'd turned out not to be.

But this one? He had stayed the test of time. She'd been able to mould him, manipulate him into what she wanted. So far, so good. And her man had been pleased, too.

She logged onto the website with anticipation. She had found 'All Talk' three years ago and it had been perfect for her to recruit *from.* It was a website for people who wanted more sex in their lives by fantasising and talking about it online.

She'd lurked in the background while she got to know who to concentrate on. She'd read comments before joining in with the better conversations. Then after a while she'd been invited into some of the secret forums and message boards, where eventually she'd been able to plant seeds of her own.

She wondered if it was too late in the day to chat to WildWoman73. And she doubted NightRider24 would be online now. Timing was out for both of them.

But there would be others online, she was sure.

EIGHT

Perry made his way to the headmaster's office. The quiet corridor reminded him of how many times he'd done that as a teenager in between lessons. He'd often been a nuisance at school, wanting to be one of the popular kids and mixing with the troublemakers. Luckily for him, he'd left them all behind at the gates on his leaving day and had gone to college.

Although he'd never told anyone back then, he'd been caught with a stolen bicycle and received a caution from a man who'd inspired him to do something with his life before it was too late. From that moment on, he'd wanted to join the police. The job suited him, even if he did have to investigate and see some dark things. At least he had a chance to make a difference. Lots of his school friends were either out of work or in prison.

In the headmaster's office, Perry asked Stiller where he would find the girls.

'I'll fetch them for you. You can use my office. My classroom's being used by some of your officers now.'

Perry nodded his thanks. As he waited, he looked around. There was a small table that they could sit at. Perry was glad:

at least it wouldn't feel as formal as sitting across the headmaster's desk.

Nathan led the girls into the room, looks of fear shooting between them. They had clearly been crying, both of them bunching tissues in their hands. As soon as Perry looked at them, one of them started again. The other wrapped her arms around her sister for comfort.

Procedurally, he wasn't supposed to interview them together. He needed to speak to them one by one. They were the last people to see their victim alive. For all he knew, it could have been one of them and the other was covering. It was hard to imagine, but not impossible.

As well, he knew the longer they stayed together, the more they could get their story straight if they were lying. However, he could also see how upset they were and it probably would be more distressing to split them up right now.

As this was a preliminary talk before they were questioned with their parents present, he decided to keep them together and play good cop. Only time would tell if his plan would work but, similarly, he was sure he'd know if they were lying. He decided to chance it and continue.

'Girls, I'm sorry for your loss.' Perry pointed to the table. 'But as you know, it's important that we get as many details as possible about what happened this morning.'

Everyone sat down; Nathan next to him, the girls opposite. Perry smiled, hoping he looked approachable. Both girls would feed off each other and he wanted them to open up.

'I'm DC Wright – you can call me Perry, if you like.' His tone was soft. 'Mr Stiller will stay with us throughout the conversation, so I hope that puts you at ease. Now, I know everything going on around you is a terrible shock, but I wanted to ask you some questions. Is that okay?'

Both girls nodded, one wiping away tears that had fallen.

'Before we start, do you want to ask me anything?' Perry smiled again. 'Actually, first you'd better tell me who is who.'

'I'm Caitlin,' the girl on the right said. She pointed to her sister. 'She's Courtney.'

The twins were both thin and had long blonde hair, straightened, with a block fringe. Their faces were red and blotchy, black smudges around their eyes from the make-up he presumed they shouldn't be wearing to school. Both had wide brown eyes and high cheekbones.

Perry started his questioning.

'Can either of you remember seeing anyone hanging around when you were finishing your run?'

Both girls shook their heads in unison.

'Not anyone in the distance?'

Heads shook again.

'Okay,' Perry said. 'Sometimes we remember things better at the time of impact, but often we can recall details at a later date. If that does happen, you can always let your teacher or Mr Stiller know and they will contact me. Okay?'

It was getting tedious as they nodded again. But Perry reasoned they'd had a terrible shock, losing a friend. The whole class would be affected, let alone those closest to Lauren Ansell. Some of them would be feeling guilty because they'd got away.

'Is there anything you can tell me about Lauren?' Perry said next. 'Something you might want to talk to me about. Or ask me?'

Silence greeted him again. Perry kept his eyes on them, hoping they would talk to him, but neither of them obliged.

'Does she have a boyfriend?' he tried.

'She's been seeing Thomas Riley,' Caitlin told him.

Perry made a note in his pad before looking up again. What he saw were two terrified faces.

'Look,' he said. 'I have to find out as much as I can about Lauren. If there are any rumours about her, we need to know. I'll be speaking to Thomas later, but is there anything else? Was she having problems with anyone?'

'She didn't like her step-dad much,' Caitlin said.

'Did she tell you this?' Perry asked.

Caitlin nodded. 'She was always saying he was rude to her, begrudged her being around as he wanted to spend time with her mum on his own.'

'Did you visit Lauren at home?'

They both nodded.

'Did you get the feeling he didn't like her?'

Caitlin shrugged. 'I'm not sure I noticed either way.'

'Could Lauren have been hiding something? Perhaps feeling people wouldn't believe her.'

'We *always* believed Lauren,' Courtney spoke this time. 'And she'd tell us, wouldn't she, Cait? If anything was bothering her.'

Caitlin nodded fervently.

Perry held in a sigh, annoyed with himself for insinuating that Lauren was keeping something from them. Perhaps he would have been better waiting for their parents to arrive. As silence filled the room again, he sat forwards in readiness to stand.

'If there's anything you can think of—'

'She liked chatting to Jason at the youth club,' Courtney blurted out.

'Courtney!' Caitlin cried. 'There's nothing wrong with that.'

'Well, he flirts with us all.' Courtney looked at the table for a moment before her eyes came up again. 'He could easily have run up the lane after us and been hiding.'

'He wouldn't do that!' Caitlin insisted.

Perry raised his hand as they began to babble, but Nathan, who'd stayed quiet until this point, piped in.

39

'By Jason, do you mean Mr Tranter?' When Caitlin nodded, he turned to Perry. 'Mr Tranter is a teacher here.'

Perry instantly thought back to the previous murder case they had worked on. One of the murdered men had been a lecturer at Staffordshire College and had groomed several of his female students for sex. He hoped this wasn't going to be a repeat of that. Trying to hide a frown, he made a note to look into Tranter further after the meeting.

'He gets on well with you all?' he asked the girls.

Courtney nodded, but she wouldn't look at Perry. By now, it was clear to him which twin had the most influence over the other.

'Was Jason friendly with anyone else?' he asked.

'He's friendly with *everyone*,' Caitlin said, folding her arms.

Perry paused for a moment. 'Do you think Lauren had a crush on him?'

'She was going out with Thomas!' Courtney cried. 'She's not a tart.'

'And Jason's lovely,' Caitlin insisted. 'He's supportive and looks out for us all.'

'Looks out for *you*, you mean,' Courtney muttered.

'No, he looks out for *everyone*!' Caitlin repeated.

'Well, you can't take your eyes off him and you knew Lauren liked him!'

'Girls, please!' Nathan held up a hand.

Perry threw the headmaster a faint smile. These were tactics to stop the twins talking about their friend; perhaps they would be worried about getting into trouble regardless of if they had or hadn't been involved. It was human nature to stress.

He stood up. He hadn't come out of the conversation any the wiser and they needed to question them more diligently with another adult besides Nathan. He'd wait to speak to them individually when their parents arrived.

As he left the room, he spotted Simon Cole in the car park. Simon was the senior crime reporter on the local newspaper and, more recently, he and Grace had become an item. He wandered over to him. Perhaps Simon could put something in tonight's edition of the *Stoke News* that could warn everyone to stay vigilant for now, but not enough to alarm.

What a thin line to tread.

NINE

Grace was back in Nick's car. Emma Gillespie had left hers at work and he was driving them to the family home. Grace tried to drown out the sobs of the woman sitting behind her.

In the picturesque village of Stanley, they turned into Puddy Lane. Nick slowed down to pass two riders on horses and then pulled into the garden of a cottage-style dormer bungalow that seemed to have undergone a huge renovation. Benefitting from cream rendering and sage-coloured windows, it looked a quirky place to call home. A terrace at the front overlooked fields, sheep frolicking in the one next to them making Grace envious. She wanted to marvel and say what a lovely place to live, but it wasn't the time.

A man she assumed to be Alan Gillespie was waiting in the doorway. He ran out of the house as soon as they arrived. Emma fell into his arms and sobbed.

Grace found herself looking away for a moment. Things like this still upset her, making her think of her own loss. As well as losing her mother in 2017, she had been a widow for two years when she'd arrived in Stoke-on-Trent. Her husband, Matt, had been diagnosed with acute myeloid leukaemia in 2013, and although nearly three years had passed since his death in 2016, she was still getting over it. She was *still* grieving for him, but with her new partner's help, she'd been healing the gap left behind.

Nick and Grace gave the couple time to comfort each other and then followed them inside. Emma had dropped to her knees at the foot of the stairs. In her arms, she clutched a hooded jumper that had been hanging on a coat hook.

'She was my baby,' she sobbed. 'Why would anyone do that to her?'

'Let's get you seated in the living room,' Alan said, wiping his cheeks. 'We need to be strong now, give the police as much information as they need to catch the bastard that . . .'. His voice broke as he helped Emma to her feet.

Once everyone was seated, Nick began to question them.

'Are you aware of anyone who might have wanted to harm your daughter?' he asked. 'Was she having any problems? Maybe her friends, or a boyfriend?'

Emma shook her head. 'She seemed happy. I don't think anything was bothering her.'

'Did she get on with her father?'

'Yes. She visited him every other Friday and stayed over until Saturday evening. We had quite an amicable split. We'd just grown apart. He's a good man.'

'Could we have a look around her room?' Nick asked eventually after covering everything necessary.

'She isn't hiding anything,' Emma told him. 'She hasn't even experimented with drugs, nor had a cigarette.'

'To our knowledge,' Alan admitted. 'She's a good girl, but like any of us at that age, she could be telling us one thing but doing something completely different.'

'What's that supposed to mean?' said Emma.

'Nothing.' Alan looked sheepish. 'I'm trying to understand

what's happened. Lauren went to school. She should have been safe there! I want to see the headmaster, demand an enquiry.'

'All in good time,' Grace tried to appease him. 'You need someone to blame – I understand that. But please, you also need to stay strong for each other.'

'What do you know?' Emma snapped. 'You can't even tell us who killed her!'

'We're gathering evidence as quickly as possible.' Nick nodded at Grace, who took it as her cue to stand up.

'Her room, Mrs Gillespie?'

'It's the second door on the right upstairs,' she replied. 'I . . . I don't want to go in there just yet.'

Grace shook her head. 'You don't have to. I promise I will be careful.'

Lauren Ansell's bedroom was fitted out in silver, white and purple. Lilac curtains were half open, as if she'd left in a rush that morning, the duvet on the bed pulled back haphazardly. There was a pile of clothes on a chair underneath the window and a stack of shoes by the skirting board. The air was full of the scent of deodorant and perfume.

A lilac laptop stood open on a small desk in front of the window. Slipping on latex gloves, Grace tapped a key to see if the screen would wake up, but it was switched off. She'd take it with her to see if there was anything on there. Social media platforms – Twitter, Facebook, Snapchat, WhatsApp, Instagram – might tell them what they needed. So, too, would Lauren's phone, which had been found in her school bag. She would set Sam on them both once they were all back at the station.

Next, she went over to a set of drawers. Gently pushing aside the clothing, she rummaged around, checking the tops and bottoms to see if anything had been taped down, but there was nothing.

She skimmed her eyes over the dressing table, inside the

make-up bag. She flicked through a pile of magazines and several books, but nothing dropped out.

Across the room, the wardrobe was crammed with clothes fighting for space. Grace rifled through pockets, but there was nothing hidden away there, either.

The final place she looked was under the mattress, for a diary. She'd left it until last because it was the obvious place and as a teenager, she'd hidden hers everywhere but there. Always less risk of someone else discovering it.

There was nothing.

'What happened to you?' she whispered.

Standing in the middle of the room, she had a sense that Lauren was a loved and happy teenager. She bet she had the odd row with her parents about pushing boundary lines, but there seemed no obvious signs of neglect. Lauren had a lot of the latest fashion in clothes and accessories; she didn't seem to want for anything. Grace had a feeling she'd be missed dearly.

Spotting photos around the dressing table mirror, Grace leaned forwards to see. They were mostly of Lauren. A few with her in a group of girls, all of them with long blonde hair. And there was one of Lauren with twins. Grace frowned as she looked closer.

'She was a popular girl,' a voice said behind her. 'I've known her since she was six.'

Grace turned to see Alan Gillespie.

'They were always making a lot of noise.' He pointed to the photo. 'They used to come here often. I think Emma let her have a bit more freedom than was necessary.'

'Indoors?'

'Yes.'

'I think that's much better than giving her freedom outdoors,' Grace acknowledged. 'It means she was at least safe, even if you did have to tell her to pipe down every now and then. Do you know the names of these girls?'

He took the photo from her. 'The twins are Courtney and Caitlin Piggott, although I never know which one is which.' He pointed to another girl. 'Sophie – Sophie Bishop. The one at the end is Teagan Cole.'

Grace had already recognised Teagan and knew she was going to be upset. Come to think of it, she might have met Lauren herself, albeit briefly, when she'd given her and Teagan a lift back to Teagan's house with her father, Simon. Losing a friend at such a young age would leave a gap.

She spotted another photo of Lauren with a boy. She pulled it towards her and the sticky tape on the back of it gave way. Looking closer, she saw he was about the same age as Lauren and wondered if he went to Dunwood Academy, too.

She turned to ask Alan, but he was no longer there. When she could find nothing else, she took the laptop and the photos downstairs.

'Who's this with Lauren?' She held it up so that both parents could see it.

'Dylan Corden,' Emma told them. 'He was a boy she met on holiday in Greece last year. He lives in Leeds.'

'Was Lauren in contact with him?'

'Only online. We haven't seen him or his family since. As far as I know, it was a holiday romance.'

'Did she still talk about him?'

Alan shook his head. 'Not since she started dating Tom.'

'Tom?'

'Thomas Riley. I haven't heard her mention Dylan in a long time.'

'Does Thomas attend Dunwood Academy, too?'

Alan nodded. 'He's been here a few times as well. Seemed okay to me – even though you worry about them at that age.'

Grace made a note of his name to check with Perry.

'May we take these photos?' she asked. 'I promise you they will be returned as soon as we're able.'

'Take anything you need,' Emma replied.

'Do you have a recent one of Lauren, too?'

Grace could see Alan was holding back tears as Emma rummaged around in the sideboard. When she turned back and handed them a photo, her shoulders shook as she cried again.

'I don't know who would want to hurt her.' Emma looked at them both in turn. 'You have to find out who it was – and why!'

'We will do everything we can,' Nick promised.

Once outside the family home and on the way back to the school, Grace turned to Nick.

'I need to tell you something. There's a photo of five girls on Lauren's mirror. One of them is Simon's daughter, Teagan. I'm letting you know because in no way do I want this brought up later. This won't be another conflict of interest.'

'Hey, lighten up,' Nick replied. 'It would only become that if she was in a group that had either attacked Lauren or had been injured.'

'Well, I just wanted to—'

'Grace, sometimes I'm rather impulsive and I pushed you too far on Operation Wedgwood last year. I did it for my own purposes, as I really wanted to break up the Steele family. I was wrong to put it all on you.'

Grace was shocked. It had taken him six months to say that, and their working relationship had soured because of it. Her predecessor, Allie Shenton, had said Nick was one of the good guys, but until now he had yet to prove it to her. He *had* pushed her too far, even though they'd caught and charged the killer.

'I get that you're worried,' Nick continued, 'but I'd say what was more important is that if Lauren is part of a group, then perhaps we need to warn them all to be vigilant. This might be an isolated incident but until we gather more evidence everyone is a suspect, even those twin girls for now. You're staying on the case, understood?'

'Understood.' Grace nodded, glad that was cleared up. She'd wanted to come clean, but there was no way she was going to be under the threat of being removed again.

TEN

In an empty classroom, Perry was sitting across from sixteen-year-old Thomas Riley. Thomas was in the same year as their victim but in a different set of classes.

Nathan Stiller sat next to him. At Perry's suggestion, he'd placed three chairs in a triangle without a table between them. Although everything he said would be written down, Perry didn't want Thomas to think he was being interviewed. Thomas could be placed in a chemistry lesson with his fellow pupils and teacher at the time the murder took place, so the less stress Perry caused the better.

'Do you know what's happened, Thomas?' Perry started, knowing that rumours were bound to be going around the school.

'It's Tom,' the boy replied. 'Is it true that Lauren's dead?'

'We believe so,' Perry replied.

'You *believe* so?' Tom looked confused. 'Don't you know?'

'There has to be an official identification of the body, but we think it's her.'

Tom's face became stern as he bit his bottom lip. Perry could see he was wrestling with his emotions, trying to keep his grief hidden.

'I can't go into detail, but I do need to ask you a few questions, Tom.' Perry rested his elbows on his knees, clasping his hands together as he leaned forwards. 'You're not in any trouble. Can you tell me when you last saw Lauren?'

'This morning, a few minutes before classes started.'

'Did you meet at school or before?'

'At school. She lives in the opposite direction to me and gets a lift in. Her mum drops her off.'

Perry noted he was still speaking of Lauren in the present tense. 'And was she okay?'

'She seemed fine.' Tom nodded fervently. 'She came rushing over like her usual self. She was always late, so we never got a lot of time together in the mornings. It was just to say hello, you know?'

Perry smiled: he could recall a few times he'd had illicit kisses before the bell went off for lessons to start.

'Do you know if she'd fallen out with any of her friends? Had there been any arguments lately?'

'I don't think so.'

'Had she many close friends?'

'She was always with the twins – Courtney and Caitlin.'

'Piggott,' Nathan added.

Thomas nodded. 'Teagan Cole and Sophie Bishop, too.'

Perry wondered if Grace knew about Teagan. He made a mental note to check.

'We were talking about going to the cinema this weekend, what we wanted to watch,' Thomas continued. 'That was the last thing we spoke about.'

'So you don't know of anything that had been troubling her?' Perry asked one last time. 'She hadn't mentioned any problems at home, or at school?'

'She didn't like her step-dad much, but he seemed okay to me.'

'What did she say about him?'

'Just that he was always watching her.'

'Was she worried?' Perry's senses went on to alert.

'I don't think so, but she said he was a bit strict. I think she missed her dad. She kept saying he didn't tell her what to do all the time like Alan did.'

Perry relaxed a little then. 'How long had you been seeing each other?'

'About three months.'

'Did you visit each other's homes?'

'Yes.'

'And you didn't see anything to worry about?'

Thomas shook his head.

'Okay, Tom, that's all for now.' Perry backed off, seeing the lad's hands had started to shake.

The door opened and a man marched into the room. He was in his mid-forties, with the demeanour of a warrior ready to battle.

Tom got to his feet and rushed into his arms. 'Dad, she's dead.' He burst into tears. 'Lauren's dead.'

'It's true?' The man glared at Perry over his son's head.

'And you are?' Perry asked, avoiding answering his question.

'Oliver Riley. And you have no right to question my son without me being present.'

Perry nodded. 'I agree, but we weren't questioning him, and the headmaster was present too.'

'The detective has been asking Thomas questions about Lauren, nothing more, Mr Riley,' Nathan started, 'and I was—'

'I don't care whether you were here or not. You still have no right.' He let go of Tom. 'Come on, we're going home.' He took out a business card and threw it on the table. 'If you need anything else, contact me and I'll bring along my lawyer.'

'Mr Riley!' Nathan followed Thomas and his father as they left the room.

Perry chewed his lip. He knew the anger from Mr Riley was reasonable. It was fear that made some people respond that way. Most fathers would be wary of their son getting the blame for something they didn't do. He might be fearful they were going to stitch him up – people still thought the police did things like that. Plus Perry guessed that, despite his harsh demeanour, even Mr Riley could be feeling guilty that his son was okay and another child had been murdered. It was all reflexes.

Nathan came back into the room after a few minutes.

'That was dreadful!' he exclaimed, sitting down with a thump. 'I'm sorry he was so sharp. He shouldn't have been so rude.'

'It's understandable.' Perry waved away his comment. 'It's a hard thing to get your head around.'

'Especially when she was so young, with her whole life ahead of her. And you have no idea who it might be?'

'We'll have lots to go on soon.' Perry wouldn't be drawn.

They sat in silence for a moment.

'Do you see many crimes like this one?' Nathan asked quietly.

'Thankfully, no.'

'So terribly sad.' Nathan stood up quickly. 'I need to find something to do. Someone will want my help somewhere, I'm sure.'

Once Nathan had left the room, Perry sighed. So many ways to deal with grief. Keeping busy was one of them. It helped until the quiet set in, when everything came rushing back. It couldn't stay away for long.

Nathan turned to Perry as he got to the door. 'You will catch whoever did this, won't you?' He spoke in a distressed tone.

'We're on to it.' Perry looked at him with as much reassurance as he could muster.

ELEVEN

When Grace returned to Dunwood Academy, it was just after two p.m. Nick dropped her off and went back to the station, while she went in search of Perry to see what he'd found. Whenever anything like this happened, she was reminded that he was a good second-in-command, getting everyone to come to him with details of what had been said, seen, suggested. She could imagine how upset he'd been when she'd pipped him to the post for the sergeant's job last year. He would no doubt be promoted soon.

It was at times like this she remembered her team back in Manchester. DS Gus Banks, her line manager then, and the formidable DC Sandy Princeton, who she'd worked alongside. Sandy's nickname was the Oracle, as she had a memory that could recall anything from cases gone by.

Grace could see both Sandy and Gus in Sam and Perry; she felt very lucky to work with them. She could have ended up with a lot of backstabbing and prejudice after what had happened last year when the truth had come out about her relationship with the Steele family. Things could have been so much worse, but instead, most of the team had stood by her.

They'd lost one colleague when DC Alex Challinor had gone rogue on them and this now left them a man down. Sadly, Alex hadn't been replaced owing to budget cuts, so they were always begging uniform to help out.

'Anything new?' she asked when she found Perry grabbing a quick coffee in the hall that was now serving as a canteen. It had been set up to accommodate both the public and the emergency services.

Perry shook his head. 'No one from the class seems to have seen anything – at all.'

'I guess our killer depended on that,' Grace acknowledged. 'It was a brave move to attack our girl in such an open space. Let's hope the press release brings us something.'

Perry told her about Lauren's friends and about speaking to Thomas Riley.

'Did you see Teagan Cole?' she asked.

'Yes, I spoke to her earlier. Sophie Bishop, too. They were all close friends.'

'What did Teagan say?'

'That she and Sophie were back in school when they heard about what had happened.'

Grace updated him on seeing Teagan on one of Lauren's photographs.

'It's a coincidence,' he reassured her. 'Not someone out to get you.'

She glanced at him over her paper cup as she took a sip of tea that she'd been given. 'I hope so.'

They sat in silence, each with their own thoughts. At the next table, a group of uniformed officers had come in for a break. Their heads were as low as their voices as they huddled close together, rather than upset anyone around them with a badly placed comment or observation.

'So, are we looking for a killer with a motive?' Grace asked after a few moments. 'Or someone who's out for a bit of fun with us?'

'What do you mean?'

'Someone playing a deadly game.'

'Nothing would surprise me in this job,' Perry admitted.

The mobile police unit had been set up outside and Sam had come over to help coordinate all the people they needed to speak to. Grace discovered that Sam had booked lots of appointments for the following day too, to wrap up anyone they'd missed. It was a tedious exercise, not only because there were a lot of kids, but also because most of them would know nothing. Yet *someone* somewhere might have noticed something suspicious and they didn't want to miss anything that could be right under their noses.

The next three hours were taken up with speaking to staff and the pupils who had stayed behind to talk to them until parents had arrived, collating any of the house-to-house information for further action and responding to the general public as speculation about Lauren Ansell grew. Grace was hoping it would be possible that the formal identification would take place that evening, although that would very much depend on forensics.

Finally, after a press release had gone out, they were ready to go back to the station around five p.m. There was nothing more that could be done at the school that day and it was only fair to let the teaching staff go home. They needed rest. They would be devastated and it would be a long day for them tomorrow. All media attention would be on them and their school. Grace hoped there were no hidden secrets that were going to crop up and take them away from the real investigation. The public were always quick to assume the worst, and all kinds of dirty laundry might be aired, however irrelevant.

As she left the school grounds with Perry, Grace could see her partner, Simon, hovering around by the gate.

Even though their relationship was new, they seemed to have a non-spoken agreement to be mutually respectful of each other's roles. They talked about ongoing cases, but there was nothing to push either of them to answer questions that they didn't want to. Each had a job to do, maintaining a professional standard as well as keeping their relationship healthy. Grace hoped it continued, as she thought a lot of Simon.

From the look of him, he was finding this distressing, too. His shirt had sweat patches under the arms despite the cool day, his tie was askew and his choppy blond hair even messier than usual.

'Thanks for the tip-off this morning,' he said, taking her arm as they moved away from the crowds. 'I couldn't believe it. Even more harrowing when I knew the victim.'

She gave a faint smile. 'How's Teagan?'

Grace had only managed to have a very quick chat with his daughter when his ex-wife had turned up to collect her.

'Still devastated, but at least she's at home now.'

Since she and Simon had become an item, Grace hadn't gelled with his daughter at all. Each time they met was a little harder than she'd anticipated, despite her best efforts. Teagan seemed to blame Grace for her parents splitting up, but Simon and his wife had been separated long before she'd met him. Even so, Grace was the first woman he'd formed a relationship with and that made her, in his daughter's eyes, the spawn of the devil.

Simon ran a hand over his chin, stubble already forming since his morning's shave. 'I can't believe Lauren's dead, Grace. I've known her since she was five years old. She and Teagan met at nursery school.'

'I'm so sorry,' she appeased. 'It's going to affect a lot of people, even if they didn't know her. No one wants to send their child to school and not have them return.'

'Worse, I can't stop thinking that it might have been Teagan. She was in one of the other groups of girls to come down the lane.'

'Hey now,' Grace soothed, giving his hand a quick squeeze. She wanted desperately to kiss him and allay his fears, but she couldn't do either here.

'They're having a meet-up in the youth club this evening,' Simon said. 'Teagan asked if it was okay to go along. When I said I'd prefer her to be at home with her mum, she accused me of putting my job first.' He gave a half-smile. 'I'll be on call for a while now this has happened. It can't be helped.'

'You have to make people aware. Whereas *we* need to catch whoever did this so they don't do it again.'

In the background, Grace could see Perry waving for her attention.

'Time for me to skedaddle,' she added. 'We're going back to the station for team briefing. Do you need a lift?'

'No, I'm in my car. But I'll stick around here for a while longer. See you this evening, at your place?'

'Let yourself in if you get there first.' She nodded. 'It's going to be a late one.'

TWELVE

Teagan Cole was in the kitchen having a standoff with her mum, Natalie.

'But everyone will be there except me,' she whined, pulling a face.

'I don't care about that. I just want you home with me tonight.'

Natalie walked across to her daughter and held out her arms, but Teagan rebuffed her, wriggling from her mother's embrace.

'I want to hang out with my friends. I'll be fine inside the youth club. Cait and Court's mum will collect and drop me off. I won't be alone any time and I—'

'No means no, Teagan, and that's my final word.' Natalie shook her head. 'It's not much to ask that you stay where I know you're safe.'

'You'd humiliate me by not letting me go?'

'Oh, don't be so dramatic.'

'Pot. Kettle!'

Natalie threw her a warning look.

'The twins need me,' she tried once more.

'*I* need you here.'

Teagan stormed out of the kitchen. Upstairs in her room,

she flung herself lengthways onto her bed and located her iPad. Earlier, she'd sent a text message to Caitlin. Though she wasn't allowed out, she had to speak to the twins. Caitlin had replied to say she'd call her in a few minutes.

Teagan was upset that she couldn't go to the youth club with them. Everyone who mattered would be there and she'd really been looking forward to seeing Lewis because she wanted a hug from him. And it was the first major thing to happen like this in her life, so she wanted to be with her friends again, talk about what had happened.

Lauren had died and on top of that she'd had to be civil to Grace. As a person she was fine, but as someone who her dad was going out with, Teagan didn't like that at all. Maybe if she hadn't come sniffing around him, her parents might have got together again.

She rolled over onto her back and sighed. She was wise enough to know that her parents hadn't been happy for a while, even staying together for her sake until she was older. She knew they were destined to stay apart and she didn't blame Grace for it really. But it was hard to switch allegiances and she didn't want to upset her mum, despite her seeing Adrian now.

She quite liked Adrian, although she would never admit it. Still, she'd be annoyed if he wanted to move in with them, and she suspected that would be the next move. She was only the daughter, after all. She had no say in who lived where, and it was only fair her mum and dad were happy, too. But she liked making their lives hell by comparing one against the other.

All of a sudden, guilt crept in and her eyes filled with tears. How could she be thinking of herself after what had happened to Lauren? Her friend was dead – murdered. What a selfish brat she must seem.

Her iPad alerted her to a FaceTime connection. She tapped the button to connect.

'Hey,' a Piggott twin said. 'Courtney's in the shower. She won't be a minute. Your eyes look red. How are you, babes?'

'I'm okay,' Teagan acknowledged. 'I can't believe she's dead. Earlier I was watching stuff about Lauren on the news . . .'

'Me too.'

'It seems weird to see our school on the TV. There are tons of flowers outside the railings.'

'Yeah, we have some to bring with us this evening.'

'I've got some here, but I can't put them down until tomorrow afternoon. Mum wants to come with me.'

'Well, I'll take a photo of where we put ours and you can put yours next to them then.'

'I can't believe you can go to the youth club and I can't,' Teagan said, forgetting her earlier thoughts of remorse.

'Don't worry. I'll call you when we're there. You can hear all about it.' Caitlin flicked her hair back. 'Did you see the male detective this morning? Perry something.'

'Yes. Sophie did, too. He said it was because we were all close friends with Lauren.'

'We had a quick chat as soon as we got back to school after, you know. Then we waited for our olds to come before he spoke to us again. He was really nice, put us at ease.'

'Well he would – you didn't do anything!' Teagan rolled her eyes.

'But,' Caitlin leaned forward and whispered, 'apart from her killer, we were the last people to see Lauren alive, weren't we, Court?'

'Yes, we were.' Courtney sat down on the bed next to her sister. She was wearing a pink fluffy dressing gown with a purple towel wrapped around her hair.

Teagan watched as Caitlin shuffled across the bed to make way for her sister.

'Hey, babes.' Courtney waved at Teagan.

'Hey yourself.' Teagan waved back. 'I wish I could come out with you two tonight.'

'I know.' Courtney sighed. 'I wish you could, too. It's going to be weird enough without Lauren.' She held in a sob as her sister gave her a hug.

Teagan heard a voice yelling in the background. 'Who's that?'

'Gotta go, Tee,' Caitlin said. 'Mum's shouting us. We'll speak to you laters, yeah?'

'Suppose so.' Teagan tried not to feel dejected. 'Do you both want to come around here tomorrow – Sophie, too? Now school's closed . . .'

'Yeah, we could do.' Courtney nodded.

'Laters, babe.' Caitlin blew her a kiss and the screen went blank.

Teagan huffed. It wasn't fair that she couldn't go to the youth club with her friends. Of course it would be safe after what had happened this morning.

But when she realised that one of their group would be missing, she burst into tears again. What were they going to do without Lauren?

THIRTEEN

Bethesda Police Station was situated in the lower part of Hanley, in the city's Cultural Quarter. It sat alongside the Potteries Museum and Art Gallery, the City Central Library, the Magistrates Court, the *Stoke News*, where Simon was based, and Chimneys, the station's local pub. Work had also started on an apartment block, next to the two Smithfield buildings situated behind it. For the past few years, it had always been a hive of activity, noise and fanfare.

Like Dunwood Academy, Bethesda Police Station was an L-shaped building, but it was over three floors. Grace's team was on floor one, a large open-plan office with several other teams in operation besides Major Crimes. Luckily, she sat at a bank of desks in the far corner, which meant slightly less noise.

She was in the incident room at that moment. She rubbed at her neck, trying to ease the pressure. It was just before six that evening and she was waiting for an early team briefing to start. The crime was the first of its kind to be connected to a school in the city and the national press as well as the *Stoke News* were already all over it. TV cameras were outside both the school and the police station. Grace resented their intrusion as much as she welcomed it, in terms of its necessity for information sharing and gathering.

Nick had given another brief statement on camera and they had a team waiting to man the phones, hoping the public might ring in and give them a lead. All it took was someone remembering something from earlier that morning. Jogging a memory, recalling anything different.

On the whiteboard in front of them was the recent photograph Grace had commandeered from Lauren Ansell's parents. The schoolgirl's face stared back at them, so full of life. It was hard to think she was dead.

Conversation was going on around her as people piled into the room.

'I spoke to so many girls today who are going to be scarred by the death,' Sam said to Grace. She had been at the school most of the afternoon in the mobile unit. 'I know once I get home this evening I'll be giving Emily a cuddle, even if I have to wake her up. I need to feel her beating heart next to me, hold her in my arms.'

Sam's daughter, Emily, was eight years old. Sam was divorced from Emily's father, but living with a new partner, Craig. Grace knew lots of parents would struggle with the death of a child – she certainly would have if she'd had any. It brought home to people how this sort of thing could happen to anyone.

Even having no children of her own, it made her think of her half-niece, Megan Steele, who she hadn't seen since her mother's arrest. Megan was the same age as their victim, although thankfully not a pupil at Dunwood Academy. Not for the first time, Grace wondered whether or not it was appropriate to get in touch with her but, as usual, she decided it wasn't.

She glanced across at Perry, who was deep in conversation with another officer.

'Frankie, you're back with us!' Grace said, her smile wide as she addressed the keen and eager young man in uniform. She'd asked for him as soon as the investigation had started, knowing there would be long hours and few staff to spare.

'I am indeed, Grace!'

Frankie was otherwise known as PC Mick Higgins. Mick was drafted in to help whenever they were busy, but as it often became confusing with their DI being named Nick, after their last murder investigation had finished she'd asked if he had a nickname.

Mick had grinned. 'They call me Frank.'

'Frank?'

'It's not because I'm a boring old fart,' he insisted, 'but because I'm a chip off the old block. My granddad, Frank, was a beat bobby for thirty years.'

'Would you mind if we called you that? Or, better still, Frankie?'

It had stuck immediately. Grace was glad he was on their team again. She would have liked him permanently after Alex had been sacked last year. One day she was sure Frankie would make a great detective, but for now, she'd settle with getting him on the larger cases they dealt with.

'Okay, everyone,' Nick said as he came into the room and sat down at the head of the table. 'Welcome to Operation Middleport. Just to let you know, we've not yet had positive identification that our victim is Lauren Ansell, but I will be visiting the morgue later this evening to confirm this. Let's see what we have so far. Grace, do you want to start us off?'

Grace cleared her throat. 'Lauren was sixteen years old. Found strangled in a field near to her school. She was with a class, out cross-country running. According to her friends, twins Caitlin and Courtney Piggott, she'd lagged behind to tie her shoelace and they'd carried on walking. When she hadn't rejoined them, they'd doubled back and found her unconscious, possibly dead by this time. We can't be certain.'

'Neither twin is known to us,' Nick said. 'But *do* you think it's something they could have done and are covering up? Maybe an argument over a boy, or something silly.'

'We can't rule it out entirely until forensics are back.' Grace shook her head. 'Perry spoke to Caitlin and Courtney Piggott.'

'I don't think they had anything to do with the murder, because their teacher saw them come around the corner without Lauren,' Perry said. 'There wouldn't have been much time to hurt her before or after that. They all have clean slates, too. Pleasant girls according to their headmaster and the teachers I spoke to. Lauren seems to be well liked, no obvious signs of being a loner.'

'There were a fair share of teens outpouring their grief and there are flowers galore outside the school gates on the railings,' Grace added.

'Caitlin mentioned another teacher's name, Jason Tranter,' Perry continued. 'Said that Lauren had a crush on him. I spoke to him briefly, asked him about it – he was quite embarrassed.'

'How old?' asked Nick.

'Mid-thirties. He's a good-looking fella; I reckon lots of the girls might like him. He also runs the school youth club.'

'Okay, thanks, Perry. What else do we know about the parents?' Nick looked at Grace.

'They divorced nine years ago when Lauren was six. Her father, Richard Ansell, lives in Derby. I spoke to him first on the phone when I informed him of the death. He was in a meeting with several people at the time of the murder.' She checked over her notes. 'Lauren lived in Stanley with her mum, who has since remarried. Alan Gillespie. No more children.'

'Did she visit her father?' asked Sam.

'Yes.' Grace nodded. 'She went regularly every other Friday.

Everyone seemed to think everything was going okay for Lauren. She was doing well at school, had lots of friends and a happy home life.'

'Both the twins and Thomas Riley suggested that Lauren didn't get on with her step-dad,' Perry said. 'Should we look into it?'

Nick nodded. 'And we have no CCTV outside the school?'

'No,' Sam replied. 'Neither the lane nor the fields are covered. I'm going through the footage from the school cameras, but it's very doubtful that our suspect would walk past the school to get to the fields, unless brazen or stupid. Although it has been known.'

'They could have come on foot from any number of places,' Perry added. 'We're searching out home CCTV from surrounding houses that back onto that field, seeing if anyone has any personal footage.'

'The search team will widen their area tomorrow to cover the surrounding fields where Lauren Ansell was found,' Nick continued. 'They're due to go across the lane and search the field opposite. Our killer could have run quickly across the lane and in the opposite direction.'

'They could have run along the hedge in the field where Lauren was found, too,' Perry noted, 'and then come out on the lane further up.'

'We spoke to the farmer who owned the field,' Frankie piped in. 'He hasn't seen anyone hanging around lately, but he did say that lots of runners use it, walkers too, even though it's private property, so he probably wouldn't have noticed anyway.'

'Unless he happened on the class, our killer must have got the information from someone.' Nick nodded. 'We don't have much to go on yet, except a load of statements from teens who were running ahead of them.'

66

'Where does the lane lead to?' Grace pushed back her chair and got up to look at the map of Stoke-on-Trent that was on the wall by the side of the whiteboard.

Perry joined her, standing at her side.

'It goes for about half a mile with farmland either side of it and then it comes to a T-junction.' He tapped a finger on it. 'There's barely a handful of properties up there – the rest is green.'

'And none of them saw anyone lurking around in the area?' Nick questioned.

'Nothing yet,' Grace told him, checking through her notes. 'We have more people to interview, though. There were so many of them – a lot were upset and some were picked up early. It will take most of tomorrow to speak to them all. Also, who would know about the cross-country run?' she pondered. 'Another pupil? Another teacher? Another regular runner? Or could it be a parent of one of the children who'd let it be known they were doing cross-country?'

'I hated cross-country.' Sam pointed at Grace. 'I don't know how anyone wants to run full stop.'

Grace smiled. She knew lots of her friends felt the same, but she loved the freedom of running. She couldn't *not* run now. She enjoyed the quiet it gave her mind to work things out, the discipline to train to improve, pushing herself to aim higher with each session. It was frustrating that she still suffered from insomnia, something that no one in the team knew she had, but secretly she was pleased it gave her more time to run.

Insomnia was something left over from the days of Matt's illness. The amount of times she'd lain by his side in the middle of the night, afraid to go to sleep in case he wasn't alive the next day. The days that turned into nights at the end of his life, where she didn't know dark from light. The weeks, months and now years that she'd failed to get into a regular sleep pattern

67

again, more to do with her loneliness and grief. It was getting better now that she was with Simon, but at times it was as bad as those earlier days.

'Sam's keeping an eye on anything coming in from the press release and I expect we'll be doing a further update this afternoon.' Nick turned to look at Grace. 'Keep the pressure up on speaking to people today. We need to build as big a picture as we can about Lauren, plus get a timeline of her movements before she died. The post-mortem should be with us early in the morning, hopefully.'

'We'll be going back to the school first thing too,' Grace continued.

'It's staying open?' Frankie frowned.

'Only for us,' Nick enlightened him. 'Now that the mobile unit is set up, we can take first statements there and bring anyone into the station if we need to question them further.'

'The youth club is still being held this evening,' Grace added. 'It doesn't seem very respectful, but I can understand. The kids might need someone to talk to.'

'They might open up if they're all together on their own,' Nick agreed.

'They might. But there is the danger that they'll hear things from others that they didn't really see and then take those ideas as their own.' Grace paused. 'Do you think I should be in attendance? Or do you think I'm best having a word with Jason Tranter in the morning, see if he overheard anything, or was told something useful?' She looked to Nick for advice. 'How's it best to play it, do you think?'

'Difficult to tell.' Nick ran a hand over his chin. 'If we wade in, he might clam up. Maybe we should see what he gets out of the pupils first.'

Grace nodded. 'I'll let him know. How long has he worked at the school, Perry?'

'Five years. He's a local, too.'

'What does he teach?' Nick questioned.

'Art. He seems okay, had the kids' welfare at heart, but I'm keeping an open mind.'

'As long as it's not a cover-up like the Soham murders,' Nick almost growled. 'Seemed as though Ian Huntley had the kids' interests at heart and look how that ended.'

Grace shuddered involuntarily, knowing she wouldn't have liked to work on that case. Then she paused, feeling an overwhelming need to do whatever it took to bring down the person or persons who had done this.

'On second thoughts, sir, I'd like to go to the youth club this evening.'

FOURTEEN

It was half past seven at night when Grace arrived back at Dunwood Academy. News had got around throughout the day, and now there were people of all ages gathering both in and around the school gates.

Grace always liked to step into the community when she could. See who was saying what and about whom. Often a snippet of conversation could turn into a nugget of information. Sometimes that's all it took. So that's why going to the youth club was a necessity. Besides, she wanted to help if she could. She knew what it was like to suffer the loss of someone close.

She passed bouquets and single flowers, propped up next to each other on the railings. Candles had been lit and scattered around, in between a few teddy bears. But it was the handmade cards and messages that brought a lump to Grace's throat. Some of these children would never forget this incident in their lifetime. Especially the ones who were closest to Lauren Ansell.

So many flowers in a row reminded her of Matt's funeral. Even though they'd asked for donations for the local hospice he'd been taken to for his last days, there had still been lots of tributes. Because he was so young and dying of a terminal illness, it had been quite a big crowd. A lot of people had known him when he'd passed away.

Matt had wanted everyone, including herself, to wear his favourite football team's shirt or red T-shirts and to take lots of selfies with Grace. It had made for some happier memories of a sad day.

Pushing thoughts of Matt to the back of her mind, she tried to put herself into the students' position. What it must be like to lose a classmate, a friend at sixteen years old. Long-term friendships were made at that delicate age. She could remember being the new girl when she and her mum had left Stoke when she was twelve. Everyone had already paired off with a best mate or groups to hang around in. She didn't fit in anywhere. Of course she'd made friends eventually, but not any special ones. She was often guarded, never wanting to get close to anyone. She supposed that was owing to her background, having had a very abusive childhood.

Yet, even though there would be people milling around tomorrow, the next week, the following month, Grace realised that most of the people in the crowd – particularly the ones who weren't close to Lauren Ansell – would have forgotten her soon and gone back to their normal lives. Just that in itself showed how precious life was, that it could be taken from you in an instant, and the world ticked on regardless. But you could still become a star for a day because of how you'd died.

Grace stepped around a woman hugging a teenager to her chest as the girl sobbed. There were two other girls next to her, crying silently as they stooped down to read the messages. Ahead, a lone male stood back, an angry expression on his face.

Was her killer amongst the people watching? Some suspects liked to be near to the scene of the crime afterwards; others wanted to be as far away as possible, only looking on from a distance via social media channels and the TV.

She glanced around, taking everyone in as she walked, hands in pockets, hoping not to stand out as a cop. She'd worn her hair down and had ditched her suit jacket for the denim one that was always in the boot of the car. She'd freshened up her make-up, too.

Finally at the gates, she paused for a moment. Hands behind her back, she stood in silence looking at the images of Lauren Ansell. One photograph showed a young woman who had everything to look forward to. Her eyes were smiling, dancing even, and there was a mischievous grin on her face. It wasn't the usual school photo. It had been taken when she was somewhere hot. Grace could see a beach in the background, lights shining on the sea. Lauren was tanned, happy and smiling. She hoped her parents remembered her like that once the grief had gone.

'You're the cop I saw this morning, aren't you?' a voice said behind her.

Grace turned to see a teenage boy, tall, short dark hair, with an array of spots on his forehead. His wary eyes were flitting around before they finally landed on her.

'Yes, I was here earlier,' she replied. 'And you are?'

'Lewis Granger.'

'Did you know Lauren?'

'We were in the same class.' He looked down the road and then thrust his hands in his pockets as he turned back. 'I'm going to miss her.'

'I'm sorry to hear that. Did she get on with everyone?'

'Yeah, she was good company. We hung around together.'

'She seemed very popular from what I've seen.' Grace threw a thumb over her shoulder. 'I'm going to the youth club. Is that where you're heading?'

He nodded. 'I'm waiting for my mate to turn up.'

'I'll see you in there.'

As she walked off, he spoke again.

'It seems weird, someone I know dying.'

She turned back to him. 'There will be counselling available from the school when it reopens. It's going to be tough for a while.'

Grace waited for him to speak again but when he stayed silent she walked away. She wondered if he'd searched her out for a reason, or maybe he'd noticed her arrival.

With her mind working overtime, she went inside.

FIFTEEN

The youth club was being held in a large hall, a pool table at one end. Next to it was an old sideboard with a coffee machine and stacks of paper cups in a pile. Music was playing low, the sounds of a recent chart-topper Grace knew some of the words to. She wondered if it was a favourite of Lauren's or a track that was being played regardless.

Sitting in a huddle on a small settee were three girls. Several people stood in twos. A group of mixed teens sat around a large table. All of them seemed subdued, unsure what to do. The atmosphere was tense.

Grace moved towards two girls who were trying to comfort each other.

'Excuse me, where will I find Mr Tranter?' she asked, deciding not to show her warrant card. There was no need for such formality here.

One of the girls pointed to a room in the far corner.

'Thanks.'

Grace followed the direction of the girl's finger. Arriving at the room, she saw the door was open. There was a man inside, sitting at a desk. He had a thick sheen of dark hair and sultry blue eyes, and was casually dressed in jeans and a black woollen jumper.

'Jason Tranter?' This time Grace did get out her warrant card. 'DS Allendale.'

'Hi. I assumed someone might show up this evening. Come on in.' He moved a pile of papers from a chair.

Grace sat down. 'I thought I'd drop by. I'm not here to question anyone in particular.' She thought it better to be economical with the truth rather than unfriendly. Of course she was there to gather information from as many people as possible, but she still needed to keep them at ease. 'It will give me a feel of how well liked Lauren was, and also the chance to listen to her friends and their thoughts.'

'Their thoughts?' Jason frowned.

'Sometimes people give themselves away when they least expect it.' She held up a hand as he sat forwards to protest. 'I don't mean anything other than information that someone might think isn't important and then turns out to be quite the opposite. I doubt they'll open up to me as a police officer, but I hope I can rely on you to see what you can find out?'

Jason nodded. 'Sure.'

'How long have you been working at the youth club?' she asked, looking around the room and spotting a corkboard crammed with photos of pupils.

'A couple of years,' Jason told her. 'It's voluntary. I love teaching during the day, but I don't really like being stuck in a classroom. So this is another outlet for me. It's only a few hours a week.'

'So you know the pupils out there quite well.' Grace paused. 'Do any of them give you problems?'

'They all do at one time or another. They're teens. Hormones galore. The boys fight, the girls argue. They make up or they don't in some cases.'

'Anyone not made up at the moment that you know of?' Grace pushed. 'Any big arguments lately?'

'Nothing comes to mind.' He shook his head.

'I'm just trying to get the layout of Lauren and her friends. If she's been hanging out with different ones we've yet to find out about, it could be important.'

'It's Robert I pity. It wasn't his fault, but it happened on his watch and I know he'll blame himself. I would have done the same in his position. The girls were lagging behind, they were a minute out of his sight, and there had been three of them. Who would have thought that something like that could happen?'

'How many pupils attend the youth club?' Grace asked next, wondering why he had chosen to change the subject.

'It has about seventy kids in total who use it every now and then. They don't have to attend the school to be a member, though. We take anyone who will behave themselves.' He smiled. 'Some turn up every week, on the two nights we open.'

'Which are?' Grace asked.

'Tuesdays and Thursdays. Others appear sporadically. They pay a pound subs and sign in. It covers the cost of the school being open late, and the drinks we provide. I won't collect any money tonight. It doesn't seem right. Do you want to see the signing-in book later?'

Grace nodded. 'Was Lauren a regular?'

'She came most weeks, twice sometimes. Her and her friends. There's a group of about five of them, all girls. We offer a safe place for the kids to hang out, and also keep out of trouble in the local area.'

'Did you get on well with her?'

'Yes. She was a good kid. It will be weird not to see her around.'

Grace noticed he didn't stir at the question. As Perry had

76

mentioned earlier in team brief, he didn't seem fazed by the fact that a murdered girl had a crush on him.

'Tougher for the kids than me, I guess.' Jason sighed before standing. 'Can I grab you a coffee, perhaps introduce you to some of the members?'

'That would be great.'

'Nathan's around, too. He's been popping in and out. It's not often we have the headmaster here.' Jason paused. 'I must admit, I hadn't been too sure about opening the youth club this evening. For starters, why would any of the parents want their children out of their sight after one of the pupils at the school had been murdered? But Nathan insisted, saying it would be a good place for the kids to have time to be with each other and grieve.'

'I expect he won't be able to stay away.' Grace knew how much pressure Stiller would be under right now.

A cry rang out and they all turned. One of the girls who'd arrived had burst into tears and dropped into the arms of another.

'That's Katie Davies,' Jason explained. 'Sophie Bishop is comforting her, with a Piggott twin. I can never tell them apart. They were all close friends of Lauren's.'

Over the course of the next hour, Grace chatted to lots of the teenagers. Nathan Stiller did indeed come and go, joining in conversations as the students reminisced about Lauren. Some of the teenagers laughed openly about her when sharing anecdotes; others, Grace could tell, felt guilty if they did. But she knew as well as anyone how much better it was to remember the good times. Be comforted by them. Bury them deep within to be resurrected whenever necessary.

Because she'd done the same when Matt had died. It hadn't lessened the pain, but it had made the days seem more bearable.

She was still struggling with the nights.

SIXTEEN

At the youth club, Sophie Bishop had been messing with her phone all evening. She'd been doing it under the pretence of looking for what people were saying about Lauren on social media. But really she was waiting.

Finally, a text message came in:

Meet me behind the sheds in two minutes?

She glanced around the youth club until she caught his eye. Her stomach flipped like it did every time he looked at her. She nodded her reply and turned to Courtney and Caitlin, who she was sitting with.

'I'm going to grab a bit of fresh air.' She stood, acting casual, even though her heart was pumping fast. 'I feel like I need some space.'

'Want me to come with you?' Courtney asked with a look of concern.

Sophie shook her head. 'No, you stay here. I won't be long.'

'Okay, babes. Message me if you want me and I'll come out to you.'

Sophie nodded to her friend. Once outside, she let out a breath. Her dad hadn't been too impressed when she'd said she was going out, but eventually she'd persuaded him that she needed to be with her friends. Teagan hadn't been allowed to come, which was annoying, but at least she had the twins. She'd told her dad she was being picked up and brought home by Mrs Piggott. Luckily, he'd been okay with that.

She gulped down a sob. She was going to miss Lauren so much. They'd known each other since junior school and even though Sophie never usually cried in public, she hadn't been able to stop the tears all day. Her eyes were red and sore, but there was no point in trying to make herself look presentable again now. He'd have to take her as he found her. One of them was missing, gone forever, not coming back. How were they supposed to cope with that?

After dropping them off at school, Mrs Piggott had told them she'd be waiting at half past eight, which is why Sophie knew time was of the essence. But as well as being there for the rest of the girls, she wanted to see him. She wanted to be comforted, too.

Finally, her phone beeped:

I'm here.

It was quiet back there but, even so, Sophie glanced around to see if anyone was watching. When she felt it was safe, she ran across to the outbuildings behind the sports hall. As she reached the first shed, he popped his head out and disappeared again. Around the corner, out of view, she ran into his arms.

'I thought I wouldn't be able to see you,' she cried as she held on tight to him.

He rubbed a hand over her hair. 'I'm glad that we've found

time.' He tilted her chin towards him and kissed her. 'How are you?'

'I'm okay, but it's such a shock.' She wiped away tears that had fallen. 'I can't stop crying. She was one of my closest friends.'

'I know.' He drew her into his arms again. 'I feel like I don't want to let you go. I don't want anything to happen to you. I care about you too much.'

'I care about you, too,' Sophie replied, although she wasn't really sure. Was he talking about love? She didn't feel as if they'd been together long enough for that. But then, how would she know? She'd never been in love before.

They'd been meeting for nearly six weeks but she hadn't told anyone. She'd sneaked out to see him two or three times a week. Knowing that people wouldn't understand why she was seeing him, she'd fibbed to her dad, saying she was over at the twins' house, and she'd lied to the twins, saying she was staying in. So far, it had worked out fine. Except when things like this happened and she wanted to see him but couldn't.

'I wonder who the killer could be,' she said. 'It's hard to know that someone is still out there.'

'I guess. But the police will catch whoever did it,' he said.

She paused for a moment in honour of her friend, then flipped the talk back to herself as only a teenager could.

'When will I be able to see you again?'

'Soon.'

'I hope so.'

She breathed in the scent of him, the tang of his aftershave. She really wished they had somewhere they could be alone together. She wanted his hands all over her.

He kissed her gently on the lips this time. 'I need to remember you until we can be together.'

Sophie almost laughed – she couldn't help it. He was trying to be romantic, but it sounded like a line out of a bad movie.

'I can get out tomorrow, if you can?' he questioned.

'I'll try.'

'When will you know?'

'Probably tomorrow afternoon. I'll text you.' She glanced at her watch. 'I have to go. Don't want to blow my cover.'

He pulled her close, his lips crushing down on hers. It was passionate, something that made Sophie's heart soar. She broke away with regret.

'I *need* to leave.' She moved away from him reluctantly.

He held on to her hand until he had to let it go.

Sophie blew him a kiss before running back to the youth club.

When she got to the entrance, she breathed a sigh of relief. Neither the twins, nor their mother's car, were anywhere to be seen. She'd got away with it.

She slipped back inside the hall. Courtney and Caitlin hadn't moved. They both had their heads down looking at their phones.

'How are you now, babes?' Courtney asked as Sophie sat down again.

'Slightly better.' She felt a blush rising to her cheeks and she got out her phone again. There was a text message from him already:

Can't wait to see you again. xx

She tapped the phone to her bottom lip, trying desperately hard not to smile.

SEVENTEEN

After leaving the youth club just before nine p.m., Grace went back to the station for an hour. The phones had finally calmed down a little after the press release, only the odd call coming in. Officers and civilians were typing out details they'd pass over to Grace and her team. She would delegate cross-referencing them in the morning.

Nick had gone with Lauren Ansell's parents to identify the body. She sat at her desk, thinking of Lauren – sixteen years old and murdered. That poor child who wouldn't be going back to her bed that night. Her family who were mourning her loss. Her friends at school who'd miss her dearly. It seemed such a waste.

Finally, she texted Simon to say she was on her way home. He'd contacted her a few times during the day, letting her know when he'd be finishing and any developments with the *Stoke News*. Apparently, there had been lots of messages of condolence, but nothing much of anything else.

Simon would always check in on her somehow – either speaking to her on the phone or texting her first to see where she was. She liked that he cared enough, though she knew he hated living in his tiny house that he'd been in since the break-up of his marriage.

Grace was glad to see the living room light on when she pulled into the drive. It was comforting – much better than coming home to a dark, empty house. Simon never called uninvited, but she'd given him a set of his own keys as a silly stocking filler that Christmas.

Just as she was about to get out of her car, a text message came in. She read it before going into the house.

'Hey.' She sat down on the arm of the settee, leaning down to kiss him.

'Hey.' He smiled faintly. 'Anything else come in?'

'I've had a text from Nick to confirm formal identification has taken place, but other than that, nothing more than we knew this morning.'

Grace rubbed at her neck, feeling the tension in her shoulders. Suddenly, she realised that Simon was crying.

She slid down next to him and took him in her arms, pulling him close.

'It could have been Teagan, Grace. She was only a few feet in front of Lauren,' he said. 'Every time I saw Emma Gillespie cry, I felt guilty for being glad my own daughter was alive. I can't seem to get it out of my head. They must be going through hell right now.'

She let him cry until he lifted his head. Then she wiped a tear from his cheek, no need for words.

'Sorry,' he said.

'You don't have to apologise. How's Teagan?'

'Upset. We decided against her going to the youth club. I felt like the Big Bad Wolf, even though Natalie had agreed. I know Teagan wanted to be with her friends, but I needed to know she was safe, too. I called to see her this evening, not that it's any consolation.' He wiped at his eyes, a faint smile forming. 'She kept ringing her friends. I was tired of hearing "babes".'

Grace giggled. It wasn't her favourite word, either.

'I'm glad she stayed away,' she soothed. Despite what people might expect, Grace didn't feel an ounce of jealousy that he'd been with his ex-wife. Simon's divorce had come through two months ago. 'I know it will be hard for her, but you're right, until we apprehend our suspect, she's better at home.'

'Do you have any leads?'

'We have some things to look into. We're going back to the school tomorrow. It's closed, thankfully.'

Simon nodded. 'Kettle's boiled. Want a brew?'

'I need a shower first. I'll be ten minutes.'

Simon turned back to the television as Grace went upstairs. She smiled to herself, glad he'd cried in front of her. They were comfortable together. But that was all she could give him for now. She needed to see if their roles would get in the way of any big cases; if they'd be okay under the scrutiny. They had to work together, but not seem to be. To the outside world, they were always a threat. The cop and the journo. She hoped to prove everyone wrong. She was loyal to her team, as well as Simon, but she wouldn't allow either one to be put to the test by the other.

Showered and changed, she joined Simon in the kitchen when she heard him getting cups out. He took her into his arms and she relished how tightly he held on to her.

'I don't know how you do your job when the victims are so young.' He spoke softly against her hair. 'Is she your youngest?'

'No. We had a five-month-old boy who was shaken to death by his mother. She tried to cover it up by saying she had been asleep and he'd suffocated. That's the worst I've dealt with yet.'

'Ouch.' Simon squeezed her to his chest. 'And I thought reporting the aftermath was harrowing.'

Grace moved across the room. Even though she liked having Simon around, it was at times like this that she missed just being able to get on her treadmill and run the emotion of the day away. She wouldn't sleep much that night; she never did after she'd seen a life taken. Everything would be going around inside her head for a while yet.

There was so little to get her teeth into on this case. No motive, no witnesses, no CCTV; no one had seen anything, but it was early days. She hoped they'd be able to find Lauren Ansell's killer and that this case wouldn't remain unsolved. Or worse, that the killer would attack again.

'I read your piece just before team brief. You did some great coverage,' she told him as he handed her a hot drink and a plate of buttered toast.

Her stomach growled, making her realise she'd hardly had anything to eat all day again.

'Thanks.' Simon hid a yawn with his hand. 'It was kind of the Gillespies to offer to work with me so soon because I knew Lauren; her mum only wanted me to cover it in the *Stoke News* to see if it encouraged people to come forward with information. Yet, it was equally as easy as it was hard to write.'

Grace half-smiled. 'Perhaps someone will remember something and come to us in the morning. It only takes one lead.'

'I hope so.' Simon kissed her on the forehead as he passed her. 'I'm going up the wooden hill. Don't be too long.'

She nodded, a mouthful of toast making her unable to speak.

'Promise?' He gave her a knowing look.

She nodded again vehemently and swallowed. 'Just finishing my drink. I need some kip.'

Alone in the kitchen, she sat down at the table. She really

did hope someone might know something tomorrow. Either that or forensics would come back with some clues. She tried not to picture the lifeless body as it had lain out in the field.

Grace didn't want the girl to die without the case being solved.

EIGHTEEN

She hadn't been in long from work. Her feet were killing her; she'd been standing behind the till for most of the evening. Even though she had a monthly allowance sent to the bank from her mother, it still didn't buy her everything, especially when she was paying rent at the moment. The allowance had come in handy, however, on the occasions she hadn't been able to withdraw it from the bank and keep it safe, and it had built up nicely for her as a safety net. And besides, after all the time spent on the streets, it pleased her that she could hold down a job. Still, now was her downtime. She could relax for a while.

She smiled at him seductively. It wasn't very romantic at her flat, but he respected it was her safe place. His, too, on several occasions now. It was nearly half past ten, an hour since he'd arrived. They'd been watching the news clips about the murdered schoolgirl.

She removed her underwear in a tantalising manner and then hopped onto the bed. In one quick move, she straddled him, relishing the way his eyes roamed around her naked body.

His arms were already outstretched above his head in anticipation of what was to come.

'I can't wait,' he said as she tied his right wrist to the head-board.

She kissed him deeply before reaching across his bare chest and up to his left hand. 'Remember the last time?' Then she tied that wrist securely to the headboard, too.

'I do!'

She laughed. 'You couldn't get enough of me.'

He nodded, a wicked grin on his face.

She kissed him again, running her hands over his taut body. Then she placed both hands on his chest and stared at him. Even though he knew her well, she could tell he felt vulnerable. She liked having the power to do whatever she wanted with him.

'So, are you ready?' She gave him her best alluring smile this time.

'As ever.' He glanced down his body. 'Can you see how much?'

She licked her lips in anticipation. It was great to have him so infatuated by her: she had him begging for more every time he saw her. She'd taught him so much over the past few months, but he always liked this trick the most.

She lowered herself onto him and placed her hands around his neck. Gently, she moved up and down on him, at the same time squeezing her fingers.

'Close your eyes.'

'I want to see you,' he whispered, his voice husky.

'Close your eyes.'

He left them open defiantly.

'Close your fucking eyes!'

He did as he was told this time. At first she could feel his resistance, but then he relaxed a little and she knew he wanted more. She moved up and down again, over and over, getting into a gentle rhythm. Her fingers pressed firmer on his neck, and she could feel his urgency building.

A moan escaped his lips and she rode him faster, with each

thrust squeezing his neck a little tighter. Knowing exactly where to place her thumbs – gently did it. She didn't want him to pass out too quickly; she needed her pleasure, too.

Her orgasm began to build and she pressed harder on his neck. As he tried to thrust into her, she pinned him down by squeezing her thighs tighter. She was the one in control here.

'You're mine, do you hear me?' She began to moan as she orgasmed, her muscles going into spasm. 'No one else's. Mine.'

His eyes opened for a moment as he reached his peak. His face contorted and she loosened her grip slightly as he moaned loudly, over and over. The look on his face was one of pure pleasure, disorientated but truly alive. A wild glint in his eyes. His smile lazy as she gazed down at him.

'Good?'

He nodded, unable to speak. This time his eyes closed through exhaustion. She untied his hands and snuggled up in the crook of his arm. He held her close while their breathing slowed.

'That was amazing,' he said. 'Can I do it to you soon?'

'Only if you're very good.' She laughed inwardly, knowing full well that she would never let him. She couldn't trust him, nor did she want to. It was a dangerous game, one she'd played many times, but always being the one in control.

There had only ever been one man who she'd allowed to do it to her, and she would never let another.

Some memories were too precious to taint.

NINETEEN

Wednesday

Teagan had arranged for some of her friends to come round. They were due to get to her home about half past nine that morning. Her mum and Adrian didn't know anyone else was coming except the girls, but she wanted to see her friends, be part of the mourning for Lauren. It seemed macabre, but she didn't feel a part of it at all and she needed her mates.

Even though she missed her dad, Teagan liked that she got on with her mum so well. She was proud as well to bring her friends round to her home. She knew she was lucky to live in such a big place with her own room and belongings. Lewis, for instance, said he had the tiniest of bedrooms. Her friend Joel, too, bunked up with his brother Dean. There were some perks to being an only child.

She made everyone coffee as they arrived, showing them through to the back of the house. The large kitchen led onto an even bigger conservatory and there were six of her friends sat there together. Courtney and Caitlin had arrived first, quickly followed by Sophie. The boys – Lewis, Joel and Tom – had come as a group half an hour later.

Teagan knew she'd have to remember to wash all the mugs rather than put them in the dishwasher to get rid of the evidence before her mum came home from work, but it wasn't as if she was having a party with loud music and plenty of booze. Not that it would matter much – she was trustworthy and they weren't all about to jump into bed with each other. They were friends, that's all. Well, apart from how she was starting to feel about Lewis. Things were definitely beginning to change between them.

A blush came to her cheeks in spite of the guilt she felt when really she was supposed to be consoling Tom with the others. Although, none of them really knew what to say to him.

'Do you have any biscuits, Tee?' Sophie shouted through. She was sitting on the settee next to Joel and Caitlin. 'Only, I've had no breakfast so if not, can we have some toast?'

'I've done nothing but make drinks for the past half-hour,' Teagan replied. 'Come and get something yourself. There's a packet of chocolate digestives in the cupboard.'

Sophie sighed loudly.

'I'll get them for you,' Joel offered.

Teagan gave him a half-smile. Out of all the boys in their group of friends, she liked Joel most. Well, apart from Lewis, of course. Joel was easy to get on with, he didn't want to rock the boat and he never did any of the childish things that the other boys often did. As he drew level with her, she reached out and handed the packet to him. 'Give them to milady, won't you?'

'How are you?' he asked before moving.

Teagan's eyes welled at his concern. Someone only had to mention Lauren's name or ask how she was feeling and she would dissolve in tears.

'It seems weird without her,' she said. 'She should be here with us today.'

'If she was, we'd be at school,' Joel attempted to joke with her.

Sophie joined them and hoisted herself up onto a high stool at the island in the middle of the kitchen. She twirled around in the seat.

'I'm starving.'

'You're always hungry.' Teagan handed her the biscuits. 'Have you thought what to do for Lauren's memorial yet?'

As soon as they'd all got together, it had been the first thing they had discussed. Doing something to remember Lauren by would be good for them all. They'd talked about the usual things like planting a tree, or having a place in the school as a garden of remembrance. Lewis had suggested they all look out their best photos and chip in for a book to be made up. But after looking into the cost they had ruled it out, so they were back to square one.

Sophie shook her head, tears forming in her eyes. Teagan crossed to her and gave her a hug.

'I miss her, Tee,' Sophie said quietly.

'Me too,' Teagan replied. 'When it's been cleared, shall we all visit the field and lay some flowers together?'

'I don't want to go anywhere near the place!'

'It will be ages until the police let anyone see that, anyway,' Joel calmed. 'It's a great thing for us to do, though.'

'We can wait.' Teagan nodded, tears rolling down her cheeks now. 'Even if it's a few weeks' time, we can all go together. Just our group. To say goodbye.'

'Looks like I came in at the right time.' Lewis joined them and walked over to Teagan, putting his arm around her and holding her close for a moment. She felt safe in his embrace as she breathed in the scent of him.

'Come on, Tee,' he said. 'She wouldn't want you to cry all the time for her.'

Teagan said nothing. She wasn't crying now, but she was feeling guilty because she felt happy.

Really, she wasn't sure *how* she should feel. Lauren was dead – nothing would alter that fact. But that didn't mean she couldn't be pleased that *she* was still alive, did it?

A knock on the kitchen window startled all of them. Teagan turned around to see her father. She moved away from Lewis as if she'd been burnt.

'Shit, my dad's here,' she told everyone as she raced to the back door.

'Dad!' she cried, jumping into his arms. 'Why didn't you knock on the front door?'

Simon hugged his daughter. 'Thought I'd surprise you, and I hate using the front door now. Your favourite room's always the conservatory. Hadn't expected to see so many friends with you, though. Are you okay?'

'Yeah,' Teagan sniffed. 'They've come for coffee. You won't tell Mum, will you?'

'As long as everyone's behaving themselves, no.'

'Dad! We're not having an orgy. We're just chatting about Lauren. We still can't take in the news.'

When Simon went through to the kitchen, he raised a hand to the group of teenagers who were sitting to attention in the conservatory.

'Hey, guys, relax. I'm only here to see how Teagan is. How are you all doing?' He perched on the end of the settee next to Thomas.

'We're coping, Mr C,' Sophie said, sounding so grown up. 'But it's so hard to take in that she's gone.'

'It will be for a while, I expect. It's hard for me, too. I've known her since she was a small girl.'

'Do you want a coffee, Dad?' Teagan asked.

Simon smiled inwardly. What she really meant by that was how long was he planning on stopping. He was obviously cramping her style. Even so, he didn't want to be with her friends, just his daughter. He'd thought she would need cheering up but, being grown up about things, she was handling it in her own way. They all seemed to be.

'No, thanks,' he replied. 'I called on the off-chance you were in, to see how you were doing.'

He stayed chatting to Teagan in the kitchen for a few minutes before going on his way. Lauren's death was affecting him more than he was letting on to her. He'd wanted to come and see her as soon as he could, hold her and ensure she was safe, especially after chatting to Lauren's parents yesterday and feeling guilty for writing about it.

But he'd had a job to do. Lauren had merited a good write-up, and the people of Stoke had deserved to hear the news. Even if it had been hard to report it this time.

TWENTY

It was nearing midday when Grace arrived at Dunwood Academy. Apart from it being confirmed that Lauren Ansell had been formally identified by her parents, team briefing had been very much a repeat of the night before. They'd all been tasked to do more of the same until they got the result they wanted. Closing in, battening down, tightening the screw. That was what they were good at.

She wasn't even fully out of her car when she heard someone behind her.

'Excuse me, miss!' a voice shouted. 'Yoo-hoo!'

She turned to see an elderly woman waving as she made her way down the path towards her. Behind was a row of bungalows for as far as Grace could see. Sam had told her the properties were council-owned, housing single elderly tenants or married couples. They were in groups of four, a lawned area in front of them, which she guessed was perfect for shooing off kids playing football. The area was pleasant, well kept, with flowers starting to bloom as spring was upon them.

As the woman drew level with her, Grace could see she was determined to make the most of what she'd got. Her hair was short and pink-rinsed, not a curl out of place, blue eyes shining beneath hooded lids, and there was a layer of lipstick almost lost on thin lips.

'I wondered if I could have a quiet word with you.' The woman put a hand on Grace's arm. 'I think I may have seen something.'

If there was one thing Grace had learned as a police officer, it was that neighbours were always good for potential leads. Often, even after uniformed officers had spoken to them, they were the ones who remembered the gems of information that could move cases forward.

Grace followed the lady down the path and stepped into a homely living room, crammed with memories of years gone by. From a row of dolls in glass domes, to a collection of teapots, a cabinet full of pottery thimbles and a mountain of different-coloured scattered cushions, everything had a place.

'It might be something and nothing,' the lady said as she pointed to the settee.

Grace sat down and waited patiently for her to do the same.

'I might look good on my pins, duck, but oh the pain when I sit back down again.' She smiled. 'I'm Alma, by the way. Alma Warrington.'

Grace took out her notepad and wrote down Alma's name.

'Have you lived here long?' she asked in readiness of less personal questions once she had gained her trust.

'Twenty-seven years, ever since my Bill passed away.' Alma pointed to a photo on the wall in front of them, over the fireplace. 'That's us on our wedding day.'

Grace smiled, checking out the couple in the middle of the frame. They barely looked out of their teens, the small row of friends and family standing behind them all with huge smiles. They looked very happy. It was sad to see it had been stripped away because he'd died so long ago. Like Matt and her, they'd never had the chance to grow old together.

'But I bet you don't want to hear all about me,' Alma said. 'I wasn't sure whether to say anything, but it's played on my mind all night. I know I'm an early bird and rise at half five every day without fail, but this morning I was up at half past four!' She stopped for breath and leaned forwards with an excited look on her face. 'I saw that girl who was murdered talking to a man in a car the day before she was killed.'

That had Grace's attention. 'When was this?' she asked.

'They park outside here, you see,' Alma continued, deaf to Grace's question. 'All the parents who collect their children. Why on earth some of them have to be picked up by car is beyond me. We used to walk miles each day when I was a young girl, rain or shine.'

'So you saw Lauren Ansell?' Grace tried to keep her on track.

'Yes.' Alma put her hands in her lap with a thump. 'She was arguing with him.'

'How old would you say he was?'

'About forty.'

'And where were you when you saw him?'

Alma pointed to the bay window, the table in front of it set out as if she were expecting someone for dinner.

'I was coming back from the shops and was on the pavement. She didn't want to get in the car. She said she was staying with her friends, and that he was embarrassing her.'

'Did he say anything, Alma?'

'He told her to get in or there would be consequences.'

'Consequences?' Grace frowned.

'Exactly.' Alma touched her nose knowingly. 'I think he has something to do with the girl going missing. I think she upset him and he hit out at her – only by accident, mind. And then he . . .'

Grace wanted to put up a hand for the woman to stop; she knew she was going off-key now. No one had gone missing and no one had hit out at Lauren Ansell. The girl had been strangled. But it was important that a witness was listened to regardless, so she let her continue.

And she would be checking out the man Lauren was seen arguing with.

'Can you remember what he looked like?' she queried. 'Or the car that he was in?'

'It was some sort of 4x4 – a big thing, high up off the ground. But aren't they always? I can't tell you the model but it was navy blue. I've seen him picking her up a few times before, but she's never been so hostile. He grabbed her by the arm eventually, opened the door and shoved her inside. He said something to her, but I couldn't hear what. But –' she clapped her hands together in glee '– I did get the registration number, if you'd like it.'

Grace couldn't help but grin. 'Yes, please.'

She waited for the woman to get out of the settee and over to the sideboard, then search out what she was after. Finally, Alma turned and handed a piece of paper to her.

'Thank you ever so much.' Grace stood up and moved to the door. 'You've been most helpful.'

Alma beamed at her. 'You'll let me know if anything comes of it?' she said as she opened the front door.

'Yes, I will.'

Grace thanked her again and as soon as she was out of hearing range, she rang the control room and asked for a vehicle PNC on the registration number. A minute later, she had her answer. The car was registered to Alan Gillespie, Lauren's step-father.

Grace checked her watch. Lauren's parents were due to arrive in an hour. Maybe Alan Gillespie would be with them. She could ask him about it then. It could be nothing – just part of being her guardian. Or it could be something . . .

Grace found Perry next and they went to locate Jason Tranter. They found a classroom where they could ask him a few questions.

From his hunched demeanour and the pallor of his skin, Grace could see that Tranter was worried.

'Any news?' he asked, eyebrows raised.

Grace shook her head. 'Sit down, please.' Grace pointed to a chair. 'In light of our enquiries, we'd like to ask you a few questions.'

'Yes, of course.'

Grace stood in front of him and perched on the desk, Perry standing next to her.

Jason clasped his hands together and put them on the desk. He looked up at them and swallowed. Grace wondered if he was nervous about something other than the fact they wanted to talk to him again. Some people were unnerved by the police whether they had done anything wrong or not. It was the authority figure. Plus the caution they dished out to everyone before speaking to them.

'My colleague, DC Wright, spoke to twins Courtney and Caitlin Piggott yesterday,' Grace said, 'along with a few of the other pupils. Some of them mentioned that Lauren Ansell had a bit of a crush on you. Can you enlighten me on that?'

A look of embarrassment shot across Jason's face. 'It was hormones, nothing more.'

'You're sure about that?'

'Of course! Just because I'm a teacher and mix with young people, you think I'm a *pervert*?'

'I never said that.' Grace looked at him. 'I have to look at every eventuality with open eyes.'

'Then don't look this way with them! I had nothing to do with—'

'Do you always get this angry so quickly?' Grace asked.

'Yes, when I'm being accused of doing something that I haven't done. And don't give me all that psychobabble that if I get angry now, I must have got angry talking to Lauren and strangled her!' He got up from the desk so quickly that his chair screeched across the floor. 'You saw how those kids were with me last night and, more to the point, how I interacted with them.'

'I saw you disappearing for about ten minutes.'

'I went out to my car! And then I came back in – did you see me then if you were keeping such a close eye on me?'

Grace stared at him. 'I wasn't watching you all evening,' she said. 'There might have been things I missed.'

'Let's cool it a little,' Perry jumped in. 'No one's accusing you of anything, Jason.'

Jason stood for a moment, letting the steam settle. Then he bit his lip as he looked through the window.

'I haven't harmed anyone, okay? Lauren was a sweet girl and yes, she might have had a crush on me but it was all one-sided. It has to be in my role.'

Grace raised her shoulders and dropped them dramatically again. 'Okay,' she said, satisfied for now. 'I'll get someone to take a statement from you later today.'

Once Jason had left, she threw an apologetic look Perry's way. Even though she was trying hard not to show her emotion, she was jumping to conclusions way too early.

She mustn't let the case impact on her so much.

TWENTY-ONE

It was just before one p.m. and Grace and Perry were hastily eating sandwiches in the fresh air of the school playground. The mobile unit was in full swing. Already, Grace had seen someone go in and come back out again, followed by a young boy with what looked to be a parent. Even without going inside, she could picture Sam beavering away, getting to know everyone and collating information.

She was about to chat to Perry, when she spotted the vehicle with the registration number that Alma Warrington had given her that morning coming into the car park.

'Here are the Gillespies,' she told him, nodding her head in their direction. 'I hope the press behave themselves.'

'I'm not looking forward to this.' Perry screwed up his wrapper and shoved it in his pocket. 'This job is more heart-breaking when kids are involved. Everything changed for me when I had Alfie. You don't realise how much until you have a child of your own.' He balked. 'Sorry, that was insensitive.'

Grace gave him a faint smile of understanding, knowing she might never have that feeling now. Even though she and Matt had wanted children before his diagnosis, she wasn't sure if she would have any the older she got, nor was she settled enough with Simon even to consider it.

They both watched as Alan Gillespie parked up. He got out of the car, Lauren's mother following suit. Out of the back seat came Richard Ansell, Lauren's biological father. Even from far away, he looked beaten.

Grace wiped her hands and mouth quickly with a paper napkin before walking over to them.

After finding out about his alleged altercation with Lauren, plus the conflict that Perry mentioned after his chats to the Piggott twins yesterday, Grace had tasked Sam with doing a more thorough check on Alan Gillespie's background. They knew that Gillespie worked for the NatWest Bank as a business relations manager and from his profile online she'd found out he was a keen golfer, often joining in local charity events. But nothing else had come back on him so far. Grace would need to find the right time, but she'd have to speak to him alone as soon as she could.

Still, she was glad not to have to go to their home today. Even more so because she assumed the press would be camped outside by now, as the story had gone national. And she knew that DCI Jenny Brindley, who had been present at the team briefing that morning, would be keen to get another press release and short reel out as soon as possible.

Grace had addressed a few journalists in front of the school again since arriving, but nothing in an official capacity. Simon had stayed in the middle of the crowd, listening but not cajoling her to speak. She'd answered the group very sparingly, with lots of talk about an ongoing investigation and being unable to comment further.

'Do you have any more updates?' Richard Ansell asked after she'd introduced herself.

Close to, she could tell where Lauren got her colouring from.

Richard had pale skin and short blond hair; his daughter also had his eyes.

'We're looking into so many things at the moment, Mr Ansell. But I'll tell you as and when we find something.' Grace pointed to the railings. 'Are you up to seeing the tributes for Lauren?' She looked at them all in turn.

'I want to see where she died,' Emma said, her tone quiet.

'I don't think that's a good idea, duck.' Alan took her hand in his own.

But Emma wasn't perturbed. 'She died all alone, Alan, and I . . . I just need to see where.'

'I can get someone to take you.' Grace nodded, understanding her needs. 'If you're sure.'

Emma had a determined look on her face. She wore a tiny bit of make-up, but she still looked pale. A splash of lilac popped out from underneath her black jacket. After seeing Lauren's bedroom decor, Grace wondered if it was her daughter's favourite colour.

'I'd like to see too, please,' Richard said.

'I'll stay here.' Alan thrust his hands in his pockets, looking like a lost soul.

Once Perry had led them away, Grace had the opportunity she needed. As soon as Emma and Richard were out of hearing range, she turned to him.

'I'd like to talk to you.' Grace pointed to the school building. In the canteen, she sourced drinks for them both.

'Is that one of the parents?' the woman behind the counter asked.

Grace looked up, to see she was in her fifties at a push. She'd been there the day before, too. A name badge on her right lapel said Susan.

When Grace didn't confirm or deny, the woman continued as she poured tea into two paper cups.

'It's such a shame. I hope nothing happens to the school.'

'Like what?' Grace asked curiously.

'Well, I hope they don't close it down because of the tragedy. The headmaster's getting some great results now and it would be terrible for the pupils.'

'I'm sure it won't come to that,' Grace said.

At least the woman wasn't worrying about herself and her job.

'Have you worked here long?'

'Several years now. I like it. It keeps me young, so to speak.' Susan smiled as she wiped the counter. 'It's good watching them start here in Year 7 and grow up, too.'

'So the school has a good vibe?' Grace probed.

'Yes, since Nathan . . . Mr Stiller arrived, it's really changed. I'm so shocked at what's happened, though. Do you have any idea who it might have been?'

'We're working on it.' Grace gave one of many stock answers.

She rejoined Alan and took him through to the *Game of Thrones* classroom, which was empty at the moment. She sat down at a desk across from him.

'Alan, I want to ask you about Lauren,' she started. 'She's your step-daughter, isn't she?'

'Yes,' he replied.

'Did you get on well?'

'Yes, I thought so. Is something wrong?'

'I wondered if there had been any arguments or disputes between you and Lauren lately?'

'Oh, all the time.'

Grace saw tears well up in his eyes and he looked away for a moment.

'Lauren was a lively spirit, quite determined but level-headed,' he continued once he'd turned back to her. 'She always dug her heels in when it came to getting her own way. But I suppose we fell out no more than any normal father and daughter.'

'She called you that?' Grace asked.

'No, she called me Alan, but she was like a daughter to me. Lauren and I have great respect for Richard. I would never want to take his place and I wouldn't want her to think I was doing that. Richard and Emma are her parents, but I tried hard to get right what I could. I thought we got on well.'

'There's nothing you want to tell me?'

'Should there be?' He sat forwards now. 'Am I under suspicion?'

'We had a report of a man fitting your description arguing with Lauren outside on Monday afternoon, the day before she died. Can you tell me what happened?'

'Ah. I'd had twenty pounds go missing from my wallet that morning. It wasn't the first time it had happened and I was annoyed.' Alan shook his head. 'I had finished work early – a meeting I'd attended hadn't gone on as long as planned. On the way home, I decided to pick Lauren up from school, confront her about it in private rather than when Emma was present. But she started mouthing off at me, so I told her to get in the car. She said I'd embarrassed her in front of her friends and refused to go with me. So I made her get in the passenger seat.'

'You *made* her?'

'I – I wasn't that forceful. I just took her by the arm and opened the door for her to get in.'

'Has she stolen from you before?'

He nodded. 'A few times. I wanted to put an end to it and as you know, her mum doted on her, so I tried to sort it out myself before confiding in Emma.' He looked up at Grace. 'I understand that you have to question me, but I can assure you, I had nothing to do with Lauren's death. She's . . . she was a great kid. I was proud to know her.'

Grace sat for a moment, watching him. He seemed genuinely upset. He was talking about Lauren and not himself, looking out for his wife's feelings, and had been trying to keep Lauren out of trouble. If it was all true.

Satisfied for now, but still keeping an open mind, she let him go. Once the team had looked into his background more, they might be able to rule him out, but for now, with no witnesses other than Alma Warrington to back up what he was saying, he would remain a person of interest.

TWENTY-TWO

After another afternoon of talking to people and collating evidence, Grace's phone went off. She scrambled for it and saw it was a call from Simon.

'Hi, Grace, where are you?'

'Hey. I'm just heading back to work. Do you need a lift?'

Grace always offered, as did he, even though they had a vehicle each. Sometimes it was easier to car share and often she would be in a pool car.

'No, thanks. I'm at home. I've picked up some oatcakes for Teagan and me. If it's not too early for you to call in, I can make you two to take away? Crispy bacon as you like it?'

Grace smiled. If anything would warm her heart, it was the mention of the Staffordshire delicacy.

She ended the call saying she could join them for half an hour before she went back to the station for team briefing. She could discreetly check in on how Teagan was faring. Perry had spoken to her yesterday to get a witness statement and she'd been inconsolable. Losing one of her best friends must be having a dramatic effect on her, even though she wasn't willing to share any of it with Grace.

She let herself into Simon's house with her key. The smell of bacon came to her and she sniffed, her mouth watering in anticipation as she went through to the kitchen. Simon was drying his hands on a tea towel. He looked freshly showered, wearing her favourite outfit of his: white shirt and faded jeans.

'You sure do know the way to a woman's heart.' She pressed her lips to his. 'Now, where are my oatcakes?'

'I'm plating them up. Do you have time to join us?'

She nodded. 'As long as it comes with a cup of tea.'

He smiled, pointing to a mug.

'Ooh, you spoil me!'

Grace picked it up and went through to the living room. Simon's home was really basic and gave her the sense he wanted to spend as little time as possible there. The furniture was flat-pack and sparse, just the essentials. A coffee table, one large settee and a small dining table.

'Hi, Teagan.' Grace smiled. 'How are you doing today?'

'Okay, thanks.' Teagan gave her a faint smile but immediately turned back to the TV.

To her relief, Teagan looked as relaxed as her father. But still, Grace had to say something rather than stand there like a lemon.

'Things must be hard for you at the moment?' she asked with genuine concern.

'Am I under caution?' Teagan snapped.

'Tee, come on now.' Simon rolled his eyes discreetly at Grace as he brought in two plates of food and popped them down on the table by the front window.

'I was wondering how things are,' Grace continued, determined not to be put out.

'They'll be much better when you catch the lunatic who murdered my friend!' Teagan burst into tears.

Simon opened his arms and she ran into them for a hug.

Grace grimaced over her head as Simon rubbed his daughter's back.

'I'm really sorry for your loss, Teagan,' Grace said, unsure of what else to say that wouldn't antagonise her.

'Thanks.' Teagan sat back down again.

Simon held up a finger, disappeared into the kitchen for a second and came back into the room with a plate for himself.

'I think you need to be more vigilant for now, Tee.' He sat down across from his daughter. 'We all know how vulnerable teenagers can be, especially being exploited on social media. Just be careful who you're friending and talking to at the moment.'

'Well, I'm confined to the house.' She sighed. 'Which isn't fun. At all.'

'You're safer indoors,' Simon stated.

'Dad, lighten up, will you!' Teagan reached for the sauce bottle. 'I'm here, and I'm safe, aren't I? You should worry more about me when I'm *in* school after what happened to Lauren.'

'I worry about you all the time, actually.'

'That's because you report the news. You have way too much imagination.'

Grace couldn't help but stifle her laughter. 'I'm sorry, but you two are so alike,' she said to explain her outburst, hoping to ease the tension.

Simon grinned but Teagan didn't.

They ate their food, Simon joking every now and again.

'These are delicious.' Grace spoke between mouthfuls. 'Teagan, do you like spaghetti bolognese? I'd love to—'

'That's what this is all about, isn't it? This impromptu visit.' Teagan put down her cutlery and gasped. 'Please tell me you're not moving in together.'

109

'Of course not!' Grace cried.

'Although,' Simon replied, 'I wouldn't rule it out for the future.'

Teagan scraped her chair on the flooring. She picked up her plate. 'I think I'll eat mine in the kitchen.'

'Sit down, Teagan!' Simon said.

'I don't want to spend time with *her* – is it that hard to see?'

'But—'

Grace put a hand on his arm and shook her head.

When Teagan had left the room, Simon exploded.

'She has no right to be so rude,' he cried, almost slamming down his cutlery. 'I really am embarrassed to call her my daughter at times.'

'She's going through a difficult patch at the moment. She's lost her dad and now one of her friends.'

'I'm not dead.' Simon smiled at his own joke.

'You know what I mean.' Grace put down her cutlery, too. 'I don't know how to win her over,' she admitted. 'But I won't give up trying. Is that okay?'

He reached across and gave her hand a squeeze. 'It's fine by me.'

'I'm not trying to scare her, but she does need to be aware. She's street savvy, I know. And you two do a great job of looking after her. But we have a murdered girl and it gets to me, that's all. Teenagers think they're invincible.'

'Most of them don't stick to the rules. I know I didn't.'

'I guess you're right. Still, I didn't do a very good job with Teagan then.'

'That's because she wants me all to herself.' Simon grinned. 'I can't help being irresistible to women.'

'Don't flatter yourself!'

Grace's phone went off. It was only a message coming in but it signalled her break was over.

'I'd better be going.'

Simon leaned over and took her hand. 'Just catch the bastard who did this.'

Teagan was in her bedroom talking to Sophie on FaceTime.

'I can't stand her creeping around my dad,' she whispered, knowing the walls were paper-thin. 'I don't ever want her to move in with him.'

'Chill out, Tee, she's not that bad,' Sophie replied.

Teagan's eyes widened in disbelief. 'You have no idea what I have to put up with.'

'Like what?'

'Like . . . like . . .' Teagan groaned, realising she was over-reacting. She sat on the bed. 'So, what are you up to this evening? Still being all secretive?'

'I might be.'

She sighed. 'You're going out, aren't you?'

A slight giggle. 'I might be.'

'Where are you going?'

'I can't tell you.'

'Why? Are you ashamed of who you're seeing?'

'No!'

'Then tell me who he is! Please.'

'All in my own time.'

Teagan huffed, knowing when she was beat.

'I still can't believe Lauren's dead, Tee.'

'Don't change the subject! But you're right, I can't either.'

'Have you seen the vigil on Facebook? Caitlin set up an event for it. There's going to be tons of people there.'

'I'd better be able to go to that!' Teagan cried, then realised how childish she was being and lowered her voice. 'I dread looking at Lauren's Facebook page now, but I hope her olds don't take it down.'

'They might, I guess.'

'Did you see some of the photos that Lewis and Joel were sharing? We were on a lot of them, too.'

'Yeah, I saved some of them.'

'Me too.' Teagan frowned. 'What are you doing?'

'Getting ready.'

'Well, stand still when I'm talking to you. You're making me feel dizzy walking around.'

'Sorry, but I'm so excited.'

'Can't you tell me his name?'

'No!'

Teagan heard a door go in the hall outside. 'I've got to go, Soph. I'll WhatsApp you later and see you tomorrow.'

'Laters, babe.' Sophie blew her a kiss and disconnected the call.

Teagan put down her iPad and lay back on the bed. There was a knock on her door and her dad opened it.

'You don't have to be so rude to Grace, Tee,' Simon said as he stood in the doorway. 'You have to get used to the idea that one day she and I might become more of an item – and if not her, then someone else. Your mum's moved on, too.'

Teagan felt sheepish. She knew he was right but one thing was certain. She didn't want to put off any boys because her dad was seeing a cop, and she wasn't going to tell him *that*.

Simon smiled at her. 'I know it's tough, but try a bit harder next time she's here. For me?'

'Okay, Dad,' Teagan said, knowing full well she would do nothing of the sort, but at least it made him happy.

TWENTY-THREE

Diane Waybridge switched off the computer and removed her jacket from the back of the chair.

'That's me done for the night,' she told her colleague, Rita.

'Do you have anything nice planned for the rest of this evening?' Rita asked as she continued to tap away at her keyboard.

'I have a mountain of ironing to do. What I would give to be able to sit down with a glass of wine and watch some trashy TV.' Diane rolled her eyes. 'No rest for the wicked, I suppose.'

'My boys were in their teens when I was your age.' Rita leaned around her monitor so she could see Diane. 'Mind, I'm not sure if they were more trouble then or now! It's still "Mum this" and "Mum that" and "Mum, can I have?"'

Diane grinned. 'We love it really.'

'No, we really don't.'

Diane reached for her handbag, popped in her mobile phone and stood up. Her hand on her car keys in her jacket pocket, she said a collective goodnight to everyone and made her way out of the building.

Diane had been working at Smithfield Insurance Brokers

ever since she'd returned to work after the birth of her twins, who were now four. She'd thought she'd always be a stay-at-home mum, prided herself on it, but by the time they were twelve months old, she was missing company, routine, and she wanted something more. So she'd started doing the twilight shift: three nights a week from four p.m. until nine p.m. and all day every third Saturday.

It was enough to keep her mind active, and she enjoyed the banter as well as the routine. The people she worked with for the most part were great and she had a laugh. In fact, the only downside she'd found was the masses of cakes she had to consume as there were so many birthdays.

She crossed the road and started her journey out of Hanley to find her car. It was on spare ground down off Century Street in a makeshift car park, so that she didn't have to fork out on charges every day. It wasn't ideal, but the walk did her good.

She turned off the beaten track and headed down the road, grinning as she remembered her conversation with Rita. She was grateful she had a lot of help from her parents who lived close by. Her twins were growing up so fast.

She knew she was lucky to get to spend so much time with them, even if they often tried her patience. Some parents never saw their children much as they were always busy working to provide for them. With her husband Steve being a regional manager of a large computer chain, they had a good standard of living, even though she didn't see as much of him as she'd like.

She felt a blush on her skin as she remembered what they had been up to the night before. They'd shared a bottle of wine and one thing had led to another. Before she could protest, he had dragged her out into their back garden and they had made love on the lawn. It had been freezing and damp, and they'd laughed a lot as they'd tried to be quiet and stay hidden from the neighbours.

She got to her car and opened the boot. As she was putting her shopping inside, she heard someone shout from behind.

'Excuse me. I'm after Festival Park?'

'Yes, you need to . . .'

There was a noise to her right. Diane turned her head to see someone coming at her wearing a balaclava. The person grabbed her arm.

'Hey,' she protested, trying to shrug their grip.

'Shut the fuck up.' A hand sliced across her face.

Diane cried out as she was pulled towards her car, but a punch to the nose had her seeing stars. Blood gushed into her mouth and she retched. Before she had time to react, she'd been pushed into the boot, the lid crashing down as her face hit the rough carpet.

The smell of blood was all around her, its taste in her mouth making her want to vomit. There wasn't enough room to turn round, so she banged on the floor of the boot. She heard the car door open, then the car dipped and, in seconds, it raced off.

Diane continued to bang. 'Help! Please! Let me out!'

But over the roar of the engine, no one heard her.

TWENTY-FOUR

Grace was sitting at her desk. It was after nine p.m. and despite the appeal in the media, nothing concrete had come up over Lauren Ansell's death. She didn't want to let her team know how frustrated she was that there were no leads at all about the girl's murder.

Lauren seemed to be a well-liked teenager. Her last known movements had been at school with lots of other people. The group of girls she hung around with seemed pretty harmless, too, and the boy in the photo who she'd had a fling with one holiday had been out of the country at the time of the murder.

Who would want to kill her?

Grace hadn't been surprised to see Teagan was one of Lauren's friends. Despite she and Teagan not getting on well, sometimes she saw a spark of the girl Teagan could be when she wasn't in Grace's company. She'd catch her laughing with Simon, sharing a joke, watching a silly video on her phone. She'd see her waving frantically when she was being picked up by her mum.

Grace hoped Teagan would accept her one day, although that wasn't going to be soon. Teagan didn't usually go out of her way to make nasty comments like she had earlier, and she didn't ignore Grace when she spoke to her. But Teagan didn't ever speak to her first, ask how she was, ask if *she* wanted to watch the silly video on her phone. It stung, but she smiled and let it go. Grace didn't see her enough for it to be a problem at the moment, nor would she make an issue of it. So long as it didn't bother Simon.

Her team were still busy around her, a babble of conversation on phones and between themselves. Perry and Frankie were going through things to action in the morning while Sam was collating information with the tech team from Lauren's phone now it had been unlocked, hoping to find something.

She stood up and collected cups, then looked over to see Nick in his office.

'Cuppa, Nick?' she shouted over.

He raised a thumb in the air without taking his eyes from the screen. Grace knew he was putting together the last words for his next press release, which was due in the morning.

'Anything come in I should know about?' he asked as she plonked a mug on his desk a few minutes later.

'Nothing yet.'

Nick sighed. 'I can't get that poor girl out of my head. I haven't been affected by a case like this for a long time.'

'It's probably her age,' Grace surmised. 'Sixteen, so young.'

'And worrying, too.' Nick pointed to a framed photo of two girls on his desk. It was of his grandchildren, Rose and Lucy. 'I know they're only eleven and ten, but if anything was to happen to either of them, I'd never forgive myself.'

Grace picked up the photo. They were beautiful girls and it wasn't the time to smirk, but they were doing that silly trout pout that she knew they'd regret in years to come. They could pass as twins, they were so alike. Far too much make-up for that age, though.

'Remind me where they live in the city?' Grace asked, putting the frame down on his desk again.

'They moved to Stafford two years ago.' An email pinged in and Nick sat forwards. 'Nathan Stiller. There's going to be a vigil for Lauren tomorrow evening at seven. Also, the school's reopening tomorrow afternoon. He'd like someone to join in a special assembly.'

Grace grinned. 'Those will be my jobs, then?'

'The assembly, yes.' Nick didn't even look up from his screen. 'I want you all at the vigil.'

Diane Waybridge pummelled her fist on the side of the car as they travelled along roads she couldn't see. Whenever the vehicle slowed, she banged at double speed.

'Help!' she screamed. 'Help me!'

But the music in the car was turned up sharply until they moved off again. She sobbed. No one could hear her. It was hopeless.

Panic bubbled inside her, the claustrophobic atmosphere getting to her as she started to question who they were and what they might want. She had only seen one of them, but she was certain there were two people. Had she been shoved into her own car at random? Had they been waiting at the spare ground for anyone to come back and it just so happened that it was her?

Or had she been kidnapped for a ransom of some sort? Her husband's pay was above average for the area, but still, they weren't rich. Yet, she'd let them take every penny they had if she could be reunited with her family again.

Were they going to harm her? Had Steve done something to upset someone? Because she was sure she hadn't.

All these questions ran through her head as they continued the journey. She lost track of time – had they been going a

118

minute, five, half an hour? Was time slipping by slowly or was the clock ticking for her?

She tried not to think of where they were taking her, what they'd do to her when the car stopped.

Should she jump out all fists flying? She wasn't a fighter, but she would defend herself if she could. But two against one gave her a disadvantage. They could both lay into her in the boot and she'd be unable to get out.

Stop it!

She was freaking herself out. How she wished she'd paid more attention to any self-defence articles she'd read over the years. She had to stay alert until she knew what was happening.

The road underneath her became extremely bumpy. She banged her head as the wheel dipped into a hole and back up onto even ground again. Then the car stopped. There was a moment's silence as she held her breath, listening. She could hear nothing.

Was there any point in screaming until she could see what she was up against? They might drive away if she made too much noise.

She decided to stay quiet, her body racked with shivers as her nerves kicked in. She said a silent prayer as the tailgate went up. It took a few seconds for her eyes to adjust to the fact that it had turned darker outside, too.

She found herself in the middle of a wood.

She didn't recognise anything about it.

Standing over her were two figures, both wearing balaclavas – one a few inches taller than the other. They were dressed in black.

'What do you want?' she asked, her teeth chattering as she spoke. 'I can get you money.'

The nearest one to her grabbed her by the wrist, pulled her out and threw her roughly to the ground.

119

'Come on, wild woman, surely you can put up a better fight than that?'

Diane knew she was in real trouble when they both burst into laughter. Loud and raucous, at her expense. Her eyes flitted from one to the other, then at her feet as she wondered if there was anything she could use as a weapon.

On all fours, she scrambled to where she could see a pile of house bricks. But one of her kidnappers pulled her by her feet and turned her over onto her back. She balled her hands up into fists and punched out, kicking her legs frantically. But her arms were seized and one of them straddled her, pinning her down.

As gloved hands went around her throat, she couldn't stop the tears that poured down her face.

Silently, she prayed she'd see her family again. Secretly, she knew she wouldn't.

TWENTY-FIVE

It was late in the evening. She looked down at him as he lay on her bed, trying to keep her emotion in check.

'I bottled out.' She cursed loudly. 'I don't believe it!' Angry tears pricked at her eyes.

He rested a hand on her leg. 'Are you okay?'

'I'm fine.' She wiped at her face as tears fell. 'I'm annoyed with myself, that's all. I'm sorry. I've let you down.'

'No, it's fine.' He pulled her naked body into his arms. 'You'll do it next time. It's easy after you've experienced it.'

'I suppose.'

'And at least you tried.' He tilted her chin so that she could look into his eyes.

She smiled. 'I can't wait to try again.'

He pulled away from her with a frown. 'It's my turn next.'

'Are you sure?'

'Oh, yes.'

She pulled him on top of her and kissed him, pushing her tongue deep into his mouth.

'I want you. Now,' she whispered afterwards, her hands moving lower.

She looked deep into his eyes – seeing excitement intermingled with danger. They matched the way she felt.

She kissed him again, knowing she had him exactly where she wanted him. Inwardly, she laughed: it really was like taking candy from a baby.

TWENTY-SIX

Friday

It was five thirty a.m. Grace was running on her treadmill, pushing herself to finish a three-mile run. She hadn't been able to sleep again, her overactive mind asking all sorts of questions as she got ready for the day ahead.

Operation Middleport would take her back to the school today. After staying closed since Tuesday, they were opening again at one p.m. Nathan Stiller thought it best to open Friday afternoon, and then the week after they could begin to get back to routine, no matter how hard or how brutal that seemed. Besides, the school had a lot of single parents and under-average earnings, some having to work long hours. He believed their children needed to be there.

It sounded a strange thing to say, but Grace understood its importance. With normality came regime. It would help everyone to forget what was going on while they were in their lessons.

She slowed the machine and squeezed her eyes shut tightly to blot out the image that had flashed before her. Lauren's face, eyes dead, gazing into nothing. The girl would never experience going to work or university, her wedding day, holding her first child. Not even her eighteenth birthday. It was heartbreaking that her life had been taken so early. Grace couldn't help herself. It made it more personal, more crucial for them to nail the bastard who had taken Lauren's hopes and dreams away from both her family and herself.

She kept thinking back to conversations with Alan Gillespie and Jason Tranter. There was something about both of the men that she didn't particularly gel with, but that didn't mean they were killers. Gut feelings were all well and good, but there had to be some substance behind them. Plus, they both had alibis for the time Lauren was murdered. But she was still keeping an open mind that they could be hiding something else.

She stepped off the treadmill and wiped herself down with a towel. Grace lived in a quiet cul-de-sac in Caverswall, located in the south of the city, and now that the weather was getting better, she was hoping to get across to Park Hall Country Park and start doing some outside running. Given the opportunity she would always run in the fresh air, but her work demanded long hours. The time she should be in bed was when she used the treadmill and she wasn't about to go out in the dead of night while the city was sleeping except for its oddballs.

Yet, was it an oddball who had murdered Lauren Ansell? she wondered as she picked up a hand weight.

As she began a set of bicep curls, the dead girl's image came back to her again. Unsettled, she tried instead to recall the school photo Emma Gillespie had given them, with the image of a bright and happy sixteen-year-old.

'We'll find your killer, Lauren,' she said between breaths. 'I promise you.'

Grace was heading out to work when her phone rang just after seven. She scrambled to retrieve it from her pocket as she locked the front door at the same time. Nick's name flashed up on the screen.

'I'm on my way in,' she told him before he had a chance to speak.

'We have another body, Grace.'

'Male or female?' She held her breath as she waited for his response.

'Female, young, blonde. Mid-to-late twenties.'

'Ah, no.' Her shoulders drooped as she pinched the bridge of her nose.

'Dog walker reported her. She was found on the outskirts of Central Park, about thirty minutes ago.'

'I'll be with you as soon as I can.'

Grace disconnected the phone and rushed to her car, her heart beating rapidly at the thought of another victim. She'd wanted to ask Nick all the details, but equally knew she needed to see for herself as quickly as possible. Central Park was nearly six miles away. She could be there in about twenty minutes if the traffic wasn't too bad.

As she reversed out of her drive and then popped the car into first gear, she shuddered as if someone had walked over her grave. Two murders in less than a week was not good.

Not good at all.

TWENTY-SEVEN

Central Park is a vast area of open land in the heart of the city. On the outskirts of Hanley, it is favoured by dog walkers, skateboarders, cyclists, young children feeding the ducks around the small lake with their parents and walkers in general. Today, the entrance on Hanley Road was cordoned off, police vehicles present, officers on foot and crime scene tape flapping in the distance.

Grace showed her warrant card to the uniformed officer, who was logging down who came in and out. The barrier was lifted and she drove in. She recognised Nick's car straight away. Perry had beaten her in, too; his parked by its side.

An ambulance was on standby, no doubt to be relieved of its duty soon. A middle-aged man sat on its steps, a black-and-white border collie curled up at his feet. The person who found the body, Grace assumed, as she watched him clutch his chest and bow his head in disbelief. If she thought it was hard to see murder victims as part of her job, she couldn't begin to imagine what it would be like to find one as a member of the general public. She'd had guidance to deal with these types of things – even if the training never fully prepared you for every eventuality.

And things were different with the age of the victim. The younger they were, the more it stung. The more brutal the attack, the more it got to her.

She dressed in forensic gear, all the time wondering what had happened to this woman. Then she took off in the direction of the crime scene tape she'd spotted earlier.

Questions were tumbling through her mind even before she saw the body. Why another murder so soon after the last one? Why had the killer made no attempt to hide the body whatsoever? And were they looking for one killer, or someone who had copied their first murderer after hearing the details of Lauren Ansell's death? Could it be possible there had been two attacks in the city by different people? The odds suggested not, but nothing would surprise her.

Whatever they found out, Grace knew they would have to bring in more staff to stop the panic when the news got out that another female had been killed. And to warn people, because two could very well lead to three, especially so quick in succession.

She stepped inside the tent to find several of her colleagues there.

'Morning, Grace.' Dave Barnett gave her a smile as he tended to the body.

'Hi, Dave,' she replied. 'Morning, everyone. What do we have?'

'Take a look for yourself.' Nick stepped to one side so she could stand next to him.

Their victim was lying on a rug. She'd been rolled into a ditch, piles of rubbish on either side of her. Thoughts of what might have happened to her began to invade Grace's mind, but she drove them away quickly. She needed to wait till they knew more – speculation was pointless.

'Do we have a name?' she asked. 'Any ID on her?'

'Nothing,' Nick replied. 'Bruises to her face and neck only. No signs of sexual assault.'

'Oh,' Grace said, surprised. 'That's significant, don't you think?'

'I think so.'

'Time of death?'

Grace glanced at Dave for confirmation as she stooped to get a closer look. A good ten hours by her reckoning.

'I'd say between 21.00 hours and midnight last night.' Dave moved for the forensic photographer to take a photo. 'I'm thinking she was killed somewhere else and then brought here. People don't often go far without a mobile phone and at least a bit of money or a card. They must have been discarded somewhere.'

'Do we have any missing persons reported?' Nick asked.

'I'm just checking,' Perry told him.

It was only then that Grace noticed he was on the phone. She waved in acknowledgement.

There was a commotion outside the tent and then Frankie appeared. He held up an evidence bag with something pink inside.

'Uniform have found a mobile phone.' Frankie passed it to the DI, who took it from the bag.

Nick checked the inside of the leather cover, where there was a pocket. Inside was a photograph. With a grimace, he showed it to Grace.

'Ugh.' Grace cringed.

The photo was of two young children, possibly twins, both laughing as they clung to each other. If this was a photo of their victim's children, this was going to be a tough one to police.

'Get on to the tech team for a name and address,' Grace told Frankie.

'No need. We have a woman reported missing,' Perry told them. 'Diane Waybridge – twenty-nine and the mother of four-year-old twins. Finished work in Hanley at nine p.m. last night and never returned home. Husband reported her missing at 22.09 when he found the spare ground empty where she usually parked her car. I'm taking a bet it will be her.'

Grace emerged from the tent, standing for a moment to breathe in the day's air. In the distance, she could see the city centre. To her left were two large hills she might enjoy climbing one day if she ever got a quiet moment. Behind them, the main road was taking workers and school children to their destinations.

It was busy both ways. Rush hour was approaching. They were near a vastly populated urban area, surrounded by terraced and semi-detached properties, with another row of council-owned bungalows.

There would be plenty for uniform to do that day going house-to-house and getting statements. Lots of open ground to search, too. Everyone was going to be working at full pelt to solve two murders, especially with the possibility they were linked.

But this was so different from the field where Lauren Ansell had been found. It wasn't out in the open, so less chance of being seen. Diane Waybridge must have been kidnapped, and the bruising appearing on her body suggested she'd put up a fight.

Someone *had* to have seen something this time.

What they needed to ascertain as quickly as possible was how the body had got there and whether, as Dave had suggested, their victim had been killed at the murder scene, or killed and then brought here afterwards.

She shouted over to a uniformed officer. 'Can you start the house-to-house with the council-owned bungalows, please?

Maybe one of the tenants saw someone using that entrance in the dead of the night.'

'Will do, Sarge.'

As he walked away, Grace ran through what she knew: two women strangled in three days, both with no apparent sexual assault. It could mean that their killer was one of three things she could think of: impotent, female, or someone who was killing for fun.

To her mind, she couldn't decide which was worse.

Before she left, she would take a walk over to the main drag herself, get a sense of what could be seen from Hanley Road.

Perry came up beside her. 'We're going to have to up our game.'

'As if we ever let it slip.' She gave a faint smile, even though she knew time was now of the essence. 'Potentially we have another serial killer, who could strike again at any time.'

TWENTY-EIGHT

Still on site by Hanley Road, Grace was talking to Frankie when she was waved over by Perry.

'Uniform have been to visit a garage in Sneyd Street. They've caught something on CCTV.'

'Sneyd Street?' Grace pointed in the distance. 'Is that behind us here?'

Perry nodded. 'It's quite a busy road – a cut-through from Sneyd Green to Festival Park.'

'And it housed the infamous Ryders Row?' Grace said.

Grace had read up on local businessman Terry Ryder, who had been convicted of murdering his wife in 2011. Ryders Row was a line of twenty-two terraced houses. Ryder owned all of them and rented them out, making a good profit on the takings.

'It did, and probably will again once he comes out of prison.' Perry joined in step as they walked together towards the garage. 'There's always someone keeping an eye on it for him. We try to keep track, but it's a case of him swapping things round to suit. Or some of the watchers getting murdered themselves.'

'Oh?' Grace was intrigued.

'When he went inside, he had brothers Jordan and Ryan

Johnson taking care of his business empire. They were looking after his daughter, too. Kirstie Ryder was only eighteen when he was taken into custody, so she stayed in the home, but she was causing a lot of trouble. In the end, we think Ryder told Jordan to move into the house.

'The two of them, Ryan and Kirstie, concocted a plan to get rid of Jordan. But then Jordan was beaten to death and someone murdered Ryan – shot in the house. Never caught the killer for that one. Haunts me to this day.'

'I remember Allie telling me about that case. Haunts her too, she says.'

Perry nodded. 'Ryder had a mighty crush on our Allie.'

'She didn't tell me that.' Grace grinned.

They came to the end of the park entrance and turned right into Sneyd Street. Reynolds Garage was a couple of minutes' walk away. There were cars and vans parked everywhere. The sound of a radio was fighting with the noise of an engine revving from a car on a ramp. Grace breathed in the smell of petrol and diesel as they were shown into a room at the back of the building. She held up her warrant card to a man in his fifties with a long grey ponytail and a leather waistcoat over a thick jumper. The man introduced himself as Dan Spencer, the owner of the garage.

'As soon as I heard what had happened, I checked the cameras at the front and back of the building. We have a good security system because we kept getting burgled,' he explained, pressing a few buttons. 'I can email this to you afterwards, but I thought someone might want to look at it quickly while you were on site, too.'

Perry and Grace stood behind him as Dan pointed to the screen.

'There you go. This was at half past eleven last night.'

Grace watched as a small, dark-coloured hatchback pulled

up. A person got out of the passenger seat and went around to the boot.

'Does that look like a male to you?' she asked Perry, moving closer to see.

Perry nodded. 'By stance, yeah, but I can't be sure.'

They watched as the figure lifted the boot of the car. Then they both froze as someone else got out of the driver's seat and helped the other person to remove a roll of carpet. As they walked away, struggling to carry it, Grace realised what had happened.

'She was in there?' Grace shook her head in disgust. 'That poor woman. And no one saw or heard anything?'

'We have a real problem with fly-tippers,' Dan explained. 'They dump stuff there all the time, so I guess it mustn't be hard. No one seems to see anything at the time. It's mainly businesses here though.'

'Do we have a number plate anywhere?' she asked.

'Yes, I have it written down.' Dan held up a piece of paper and Grace took it from him.

Dan pressed play again and they watched as the two figures carried the body along the path until it disappeared from view.

'Did you catch them coming out?' Grace asked.

Dan nodded and pressed fast-forward: two figures ran along the path and into the car.

'Forty-two minutes?' Perry noted the time at the top of the screen. 'What were they doing for that length of time?'

'You'd think they'd want to get in there and out again as quickly as possible so there's less chance of them being seen,' Grace muttered. 'Is Sneyd Street busy during the evening, Dan?'

'Not as much as during the day,' he replied. 'My son lives in the flat above the garage, but he didn't hear or see a thing last night.'

Grace left her contact card with him, and she and Perry walked back to the crime scene. She rang through for a vehicle registration check.

'So Dave was right. She was killed off-site,' Grace said to Perry as they walked.

'I thought she'd been dumped on carpet that had been fly-tipped. At least it hasn't been there long enough to be contaminated by much outside. But how the hell didn't anyone see them do this?' Perry ran a hand over his head. 'I know it's dark but—'

'I wonder if she *was* alive and killed on-site, and that's why it took so long.' Grace's face darkened.

'It's possible. She could have been unconscious, or drugged. Or she could have been dead. Either way she was heavy, and she didn't walk herself.'

Details came over the radio. The vehicle belonged to their victim.

'But that doesn't make sense,' Perry said afterwards.

'She could have been driven away in her own car, killed off-site and brought here afterwards.'

'*That* doesn't make sense, either.'

Grace shook her head, trying to rid it of the images that were popping up of Diane Waybridge's last moments, the woman fighting for her life. What must have been going through her mind as she knew she wasn't going to get away? 'We need to find her car. There will be forensics inside the boot as well as in the front seats. I'll get someone from uniform to locate any more cameras in situ.'

'And perhaps figure out where that rug came from, too.'

Grace nodded. 'We also need to think about there being an accomplice or if we're looking at two killers.'

They had almost reached the crime scene again when, suddenly, there was a commotion in front of them. Grace and

Perry looked over to where a man was trying to push his way through, two officers holding him back.

'Shit, I wonder if that is our victim's husband.' Grace was running before the sentence was finished. Perry too.

'Hey!' Grace shouted.

'Is it her?' The man turned to them.

'Mr Waybridge?' Grace queried, aware the fact that she knew his name would set him up to hear the bad news.

'Yes.' He stopped struggling and looked at her. Then he began to shake his head. 'No . . . no!' he cried. 'Please tell me it isn't her.'

'Mr Waybridge, we've found a body that we believe may be your wife,' she told him.

Grace stooped beside him as his legs gave way and he dropped to the ground.

'No!' he cried.

'We'll need to make a formal identification, but for now, you have to move away from the scene of the crime.'

'Can I see her?'

'I'm sorry.' Her tone was defiant as she shook her head, her eyes not leaving his. 'Not like this.'

'I have to!' His words were quieter now between the sobs.

Grace reached for his arm. 'Let's take you somewhere quieter.'

TWENTY-NINE

With Perry's help, Grace escorted Mr Waybridge over to a police van. They got in the back, the tinted windows giving them privacy.

'Can you tell me when you last saw your wife?' Grace asked once the doors were shut.

'Yesterday morning. I went to work for eight a.m. and I got home just after six in the evening. Diane starts work at four o'clock, so my mother-in-law looks after the kids until I get home, or they go to stay with her if I'm working out of the area. When Diane wasn't back by half nine, I rang her, but there was no reply. I called her office, but they said she'd left at her usual time and that's when I began to worry.' He caught his breath for a moment before continuing. 'I rang my mother-in-law to ask her to look after the kids again while I drove the way she would have come home. I thought that maybe she'd broken down or something, even though I knew she'd call me if that had happened. I couldn't find her, nor her car, anywhere, so I went home and called the police.' His face wore a pained expression. 'But that doesn't explain how she got here. It isn't anywhere we come to. It isn't near our home.'

'Which is?'

'Hanford.'

'Which is?' Grace looked at Perry, still not as knowledgeable about the local town as her colleague.

'Five miles or so from here,' Perry replied.

'So on a normal evening she'd have been home about nine thirty?' Grace asked Steve.

'Yes.' A sob escaped him.

'And there was nothing troubling Diane that you know of?'

'Nothing.' His eyes darted around the van for a moment, unable to look at her. 'We keep ourselves to ourselves. Our friendship circle is small, but it's a close one. Everyone's going to be devastated when I tell them.'

'We'll allocate a family liaison officer as soon as we can,' Grace informed him. 'They can help you with things like that. So as far as you know, this morning everything was fine when you went to work?'

'Yes.'

'Nothing hinted at?' Perry queried.

'Nothing!'

Grace nodded. 'We're trying to get a picture of her last known movements. Who she would have seen, spoken to, been with.'

'That's just it. She went to work, she left at her normal finishing time and then no one knows what happened to her. But something did!'

He sobbed again and Grace let him release his grief for a moment before asking any more questions. It was at times like this she hated the process, but equally she knew how important it was.

'Diane didn't have a bag on her,' she said, once she had given him a moment. 'We did find her phone nearby.'

'But that's ridiculous.' He shook his head. 'I don't understand.'

Grace had already tasked Sam with retrieving city CCTV to

trace the woman's last steps. Maybe that could throw some light on where she went and with whom after she had finished her shift.

'I didn't go to bed last night.' Steve spoke to no one in particular. 'Every time I closed my eyes to sleep, I saw her lying injured somewhere. Calling out for me. But I . . . I never expected this to happen. She was my life. What am I going to do without her?'

'Steve, I know this is hard, but does Diane have any distinguishing marks or tattoos we can recognise her by?' Grace questioned.

'She has two angels on her left shoulder.' Steve patted his own as he spoke. 'Good and bad. And she has a scar on her right lower leg where she broke it and had to have a plate put in.'

Grace nodded her thanks. Even though she was certain their victim was Diane Waybridge, those details alone would definitely determine things once checked out.

'You need to go home,' she told him. 'It isn't good for you to be around here.'

'But she's lying there!' He pointed out of a window towards where they could see the crime scene tape. 'She's been there alone all night. I don't want to leave her.'

'She's gone, Mr Waybridge. I'm so sorry for your loss, but you would be better off in your own surroundings, giving those children of yours a big hug. They're going to need you now more than ever. Was that a recent photograph of them in her phone holder?'

He nodded. 'They're four years old – Isla and Raffie.'

'I don't suppose you know the password to unlock her phone?' Perry asked.

Steve shook his head this time. 'Can I see it?'

'Why?'

'I . . . I just want to be sure.'

Grace held her breath for a moment, knowing how much grief it would cause. But she understood his need, more to cling on to the fact that it couldn't be his wife until he had tangible evidence. Even though she'd held Matt's hand as he'd passed away, it still hadn't sunk in that he was dead for some time. It had only hit her when she had registered his death.

She nodded. 'Fetch it for me, Perry, please,' she instructed.

The door to the van slid open and closed, the noise from the outside bursting into the silence for a moment. Grace could sense an urgency as people were rushing about. Now there were two victims, it wasn't just a one-off. Their thoughts were turning to the possibility of a number three. What kind of a sick individual did this?

The door to the van opened again and Perry appeared with the evidence bag. Grace showed it to Steve. He didn't need to say anything, as he broke down in tears again. Grace was glad when he nodded through them, though.

'You could try our wedding anniversary date, or maybe the twins' birthday for the unlock code.'

Grace took them from him before standing. 'Let's get you away from here,' she said.

It wasn't good for him to be here. He might overhear a remark or see something that would haunt him. And they had a job to do, for both him and his wife.

Grace allocated someone in uniform to see that Mr Waybridge got home, instructing them to stay at his address until a family liaison officer was assigned. Then she went back to the rest of the team in Central Park. Nick had returned to the police station, and it was nearly time for her to go to Dunwood Academy.

Spying a shop, she purchased food and coffee then went to find Frankie. She found him inside the work hut by the entrance.

'How's it going?' she asked, breaking into her sandwich.

It felt grim to eat while on duty there, but she had to keep her energy up or she would be of no use to anyone.

'Slowly. There are a lot of streets to cover around the perimeter – Sneyd Street, Hanley Road. The streets off them are mainly terraced properties, too. And a ton of passing traffic. It's going to take a while.'

'Anything useful come up so far?'

'A woman on Sneyd Street noticed a small hatchback going past her front window several times around 23.30, but she didn't get a make, model or registration number. Just said it was a dark colour.'

'That's *so* helpful – not.'

Even though she didn't feel hungry, Grace bit into her sandwich and gazed out onto the park, the white tent in the distance.

Officers in uniform searched in a line, taking tiny steps. She spotted the *Stoke News* van, knew Simon would be around somewhere, but she couldn't see him. They'd sent a few text messages back and forth this morning, but she hadn't got time to speak to him now.

'I have to go to the school this afternoon and address the kids at a special assembly,' she told Frankie.

'I might head back to the station. I've done all I can here.'

Grace nodded, seeing Perry running towards them. 'We can catch up at team briefing this evening, if not before. What's up, Perry?'

'Uniform have found Diane Waybridge's car. It's parked a couple of streets from here.'

THIRTY

Diane Waybridge's car had been left blocking the drive of a semi-detached house in Kelvin Avenue. Grace was told it was a few streets away. As she needed to leave for Dunwood Academy, she dropped Perry off to look over the vehicle before it went to forensics. She arrived back at the school with minutes to spare before the assembly started at one p.m.

In the corridor, she spotted Jason Tranter talking to Nathan Stiller. Well, they weren't talking insomuch as they were having a heated exchange about something.

They both stopped speaking as she drew level. The first thing she noticed was that Jason was sporting a black eye.

'What happened to you?' She pointed at it.

'Just a misunderstanding,' he muttered before walking off.

Grace waited until he was out of range before asking the head what was going on.

'He wouldn't say,' Nathan told her. 'But we weren't talking about that. I've closed the youth club until further notice and he's not happy about it.'

'I think that's wise,' Grace said. 'I know he has the children's welfare at heart, and perhaps thinks they need somewhere to offload, but we have to be mindful of the family's feelings, too. They might see something like that as insensitive.'

Nathan nodded and then gave her a serious look. 'The murder on the news this morning. There are suggestions of a woman being strangled.'

Grace nodded.

'Does it have anything to do with Lauren?'

'I can't confirm anything until we have more details. As soon as we do, I'll let you know.'

They both went into the main hall. Grace stood to the side and Nathan went to stand at the front. The pupils filed in and sat down, teachers and staff standing around the edges. Grace noticed the women from the canteen and the caretaker. Simon was there, too. He nodded at her when she caught his eye.

'Right then, boys and girls.' Nathan clapped his hands for quiet and the murmuring stopped. 'As you know, Dunwood Academy has been closed since Tuesday following the tragic death of one of our own, Lauren Ansell. Some of you will have known Lauren and most of you will know her through the media now. It's a tragedy to lose someone so young and under such difficult circumstances, and I know you might have lots of questions. So I've brought along Detective Sergeant Allendale to speak to you all.' Nathan looked Grace's way. 'Detective Sergeant?'

Grace walked to stand next to Nathan. Seeing the stage behind her, she was reminded of a happier time after she had won a prize for coming first in a history exam, when she'd gone up to collect it. This time it was tinged with sadness. Little had she known then that she would be speaking about the murder of a young girl in a school twenty-five years later.

She glanced along the rows until her eyes fell on Teagan. She smiled at her, but Teagan pretended not to see. Still, Grace was pleased to see so many pupils had returned. It had been a tough decision to open the school again three days after the murder, but she liked Stiller's reasoning that he wanted them to come in this afternoon and then resume normal lessons the week after.

'Thank you.' Grace cleared her throat and began. 'As Mr Stiller mentioned, we're investigating the death of a pupil, Lauren Ansell, who was in her final year here. If any of you want to speak to me, or any of my colleagues, about anything – no matter how small it is, no matter how unimportant you may feel it is – please come forward. We're here to speak to you.'

A hand shot up. Grace glanced at the head teacher, who nodded.

'Yes?' she said.

A boy stood up, three rows back, two seats in. Grace recognised him as Lewis Granger, the teenager who she had spoken to on Tuesday evening before she'd gone inside the youth club. His shirt was unfastened at the neck, his tie hanging down more than she assumed it should, but at least he had come in uniform.

'How long does it take to die when you're strangled?' Lewis asked.

A murmur went out around the hall.

'Quiet, everyone!' Nathan bellowed.

'That's not the kind of question I was thinking about,' Grace said. 'It's also something I'm not qualified to answer.'

She looked at Lewis with raised eyebrows. Of course, she understood how he might be curious; it was a macabre murder. It would no doubt fascinate them all as much as frighten them.

'But there was another woman found this morning, wasn't there?' Lewis continued. 'It's on Twitter. Has she been strangled, too? Is it the same killer?'

'We can't say at this moment in time,' Grace answered.

'But—' the boy sitting next to him began.

'Either say something sensible or sit down!' Nathan shouted at them.

'Lauren was our friend!' Lewis answered.

'Enough!' Nathan warned.

Grace held up a hand. 'I'm sure you must understand that family has to be informed first and then a formal identification of the body will take place before we can reveal any further details.'

'Well, if it is, it's your fault that it happened.' Lewis's tone was accusatory. 'You should have protected them.'

Whispering erupted again.

'Enough!' Nathan yelled. 'Granger, if you don't have anything important to say, then I suggest you sit down. DS Allendale is extremely busy, working on the case, so . . .'

Lewis shrugged and did as he was told, but he glared at Grace. She felt her skin colouring. This was worse than facing the mob of the press.

'We very much hope this is an isolated case.' Grace addressed the room once more. 'But if any of you have information, then let someone know and we'll speak to you.'

Grace waited until all the pupils had left the hall before joining Nathan again.

'I'm sorry about Lewis Granger and Joel Nicholls,' he started. 'Granger can be a real troublemaker.'

Grace put up a hand for him to stop. 'They're bound to be curious. Half of them will want to know; the other half will be scared to find out. It's human nature. I get that all the time, no matter how old the audience is.'

'It doesn't excuse his outburst though,' Nathan said before another teacher waved from down the hall and he nodded Grace goodbye.

Grace watched as he walked away from her. She couldn't

help feeling sorry for him, the weight of responsibility still boring down on him.

Out in the playground, she spotted Perry and he beckoned her over.

'Did they go easy on you, copper?' he joked.

She smirked. 'It was okay. There were a couple of lads giving me a bit of grief.'

Perry held up a hand as he took out his phone. He swiped and pressed it a few times, turning it round to show her. It was a piece from today's *Stoke News*.

'Have you seen this yet?'

The Stoke Strangler – two females dead.

'Oh, for . . .' Grace groaned loudly.

She strode over to Simon, who was chatting to a woman she presumed was a local resident or a parent. Simon was looking attentive, notepad in hand and nodding in all the right places.

'It's shocking, isn't it,' the woman was saying, 'how something like this can happen on your own doorstep. And now there are two of them – what are the police doing about it? I daren't go out at—'

'A word?' Grace prodded Simon's arm and nodded to a spot a few feet away.

Simon held up a finger to the woman. 'I'll be one minute.'

The woman rolled her eyes and folded her arms but stayed put. Grace couldn't help but glower at her. She was only after a moment of glory. A line where she could say she had made the news. So many things were exaggerated as so-called witnesses became excited. Most of the time it did more harm than good.

'The Stoke Strangler?' Grace seethed when they were out of earshot. 'Really?'

145

Simon had the decency to look uncomfortable. 'Well, that's what everyone will be calling him, so I thought I'd get in first.'

'What makes you so sure it's a him?'

'I . . . I don't know, but strangling is so close and personal, and two women who look the same. Isn't it obvious?'

'That's why you'll never make a copper,' she snapped. 'You jump to conclusions.'

'Excuse me.' His tone was just as angry.

'You're scaremongering and we're trying to keep things calm.'

'Two women have been murdered. I'm not the one who's doing the scaremongering.' He shook his head in frustration. 'Oh, I see. While you can do your job to the best of your abilities, I can't do mine?'

'You could show some compassion,' she replied.

'I have! There's an interview with the headmaster in there too, about Lauren's potential, if you happened to look past the headline.'

Grace coloured with embarrassment.

'Whatever you say, local people need to know,' Simon insisted. 'There's also an appeal number and email in there. I thought it might help.'

'You should have asked first,' she noted, calmer now. 'My job—'

'Is no more important than mine in our relationship.'

It was her turn to throw him an icy look. Was he being serious?

'Glad to know where I stand,' she threw back childishly.

Simon shook his head in exasperation. People were looking over at them. He took a step back and scowled at her.

'You wouldn't have a job to do if some bastard hadn't murdered two females,' he said. 'So how about I report the news as I see fit and you catch the killer? That would make a brilliant headline, don't you think?'

Grace opened her mouth to speak, but Simon had already walked away. The woman he'd been interviewing had waited, so with a wide smile and a 'sorry about that' he was soon back in journalist mode.

Grace walked away, head held high. If he thought he could use her for information one minute and then play silly games with her the next, he had another think coming.

THIRTY-ONE

Her phone rang. She reached across for it, smiling when she saw it was him calling.

'Hey,' she said.

'Hey, how are you?'

'Good, thanks. You?'

'Yeah. I can't wait to see you again!'

She could hear the excitement in his voice as she lay back on the bed. 'Patience, my love!'

'Okay. I'll see you soon though, won't I?'

'Of course. Tomorrow, like we said.'

'Great. I can't wait. I'm horny thinking about it!'

She laughed. 'Stop it! You're so naughty.'

After disconnecting the call, she started to fantasise about what she'd do to him the following evening. It was her favourite pastime, especially when she did a choker on him. She loved the danger, the way it made her feel totally in control.

After the first time she'd done it to him, she remembered how he'd told her that he'd been checking out the procedure online. His research had shown there had been quite a few celebrities who had died of erotic asphyxiation. He said he wanted to do it to her, learn the mechanics of stopping at the crucial time.

Good old YouTube. You could find a clip about anything on there; although sometimes they didn't stay online too long. There were some weird and wonderful things on the Net. Like the website All Talk. She'd lurked in the background there for ages, reading other people's posts and messages on the forum before plucking up the courage to join as a member. From there, it had taken a week before she had started to chat to him on the forum and then in private messages. And then they'd met up.

She had let him speak and then smiled at him. He couldn't get enough of her, but she would never let him do it to her, never let him experience what she did.

She reached for her laptop, opened the browser and logged into All Talk. It was such a shame WildWoman73 wouldn't be around to talk to any more.

THIRTY-TWO

After battling with rush-hour traffic, Grace joined evening team briefing to find everyone already sitting down. Some kind soul had saved her a seat and she took it gratefully. It had been a taxing day and there was so much to do that she knew it was going to be a long and draining evening. She doubted she'd sleep that night, if she ever got to her bed. She would find it hard to switch off, especially with the argument with Simon still on her mind.

DCI Jenny Brindley had joined them and she sat next to Nick at the head of the table. Several officers, including Frankie, were stood around the edge of the room. This was the first briefing since Diane Waybridge's body had been found that morning.

Although Jenny was present, it was Nick who started. He got to his feet and went to the whiteboard, pointing to the image of the woman next to Lauren Ansell.

'Our second victim, something I was hoping not to say. Just to recap, ma'am.' He looked at Jenny as he talked her through what had happened to Diane Waybridge. 'So –' he moved to a map of the city on the wall and pointed again '– what happened before Diane was killed and her body was left in Central Park?'

'Cameras cover her until she gets to Century Street,' Sam told them, pressing a button on her laptop that brought up images of Diane Waybridge on the big screen.

They all watched as their victim walked through the streets for a couple of minutes.

'Then she goes out of range and we don't know what happened to her from there on. But her handbag and a carrier bag full of shopping were found in the boot of her car.'

Nick looked around the room again. 'Who's been speaking to her friends? Do they know of anything going on?'

'Me and Frankie have been doing that,' Perry said. 'Nothing came up from anyone where she works, although we've only spoken to everyone in a group so far. She seemed well liked from what we've gathered.'

'Everyone gave us the impression she doted on her family too,' Frankie added.

'We have yet to determine if she got in the car of her own free will, or if she was bundled into it,' Nick said. 'Owing to the time lapse before the CCTV footage from the garage, we believe she either went or was taken somewhere before her body was dumped in the park. But where?'

'Also the footage shows our two suspects dropping off the body, rolled in a carpet,' Grace updated them. 'The time was 11.45 p.m. So what were they doing in the park before they returned to the car?'

'I tell you one thing sickos like this might have been doing: getting off,' Perry said in a snide tone.

'Don't be absurd,' cried Sam, shuddering at the thought.

'Maybe it isn't such a ridiculous suggestion.' Grace gave it some consideration. 'There are no signs of sexual assault, perhaps because they're getting their kicks in other ways.'

'So do we think both of them carried out the murder?' Nick threw out to the room.

They all began to speak at once until he raised his hand for silence.

'Has time of death been ascertained yet?' Jenny asked.

'Approximately between ten p.m.,' Grace told her, 'and the time we saw the body being left at the park, ma'am.'

'And we don't know what was happening for the forty-two minutes that the two suspects were out of their car and in the park with the body?' Jenny frowned.

'Not yet,' Grace replied. 'But we do know that the rug she was wrapped in was from Next. A popular one and a snip at seventy pounds, but discontinued now. It will be a needle in a haystack trying to trace who has them in Stoke, even *if* our suspects come from Stoke, but I've asked them for a list of customers who bought it before it became obsolete. Not sure they'll be able to provide it though, under data protection and GDPR – not to mention people who paid in cash.'

'We have a sixteen-year-old victim, strangled but no sexual assault,' Nick said, 'and two days later, a woman strangled and also no sexual assault. All the same, who's looking into local sex offenders?'

'I am, sir.' Sam sat forward. 'I'm making a list for us to visit. Although most of them are on the Sex Offender Registry because of child pornography, our youngest female victim is sixteen.'

'Maybe someone's doing this to get turned on, but is impotent at the crucial moment – hence no sexual assault,' Nick added. 'We need to establish how they're linked to the same killer. The women don't know each other?'

'Not to our knowledge,' Grace said. 'They don't even live in the same area. And we're still working through a lot of people. Then there's the vigil this evening.'

'Okay, can you go to the morgue with Mr Waybridge afterwards?'

Grace nodded at Nick.

'We'll talk to the press again in the morning, once our victim has been formally identified, and get the public's help on sightings of her, too.' Nick clapped his hands. 'Okay, great work everyone. You all know what to do this evening and it's going to be a late one for us all, I'm afraid. We'll catch up again in the morning.'

THIRTY-THREE

After team briefing, Grace popped downstairs in the station for a shower and to change into casual gear: jeans and a black jumper, Converse boots. She tied her hair back and added a beanie hat. People would know who she was, especially as she'd be with her team, but it might keep her blended in a little so that she could use her ears and eyes on the crowd. Even a snatch of information at this stage could lead them to the killer. She needed to know what was being said.

Grace wasn't looking forward to the vigil but knew the importance of it, both for them and for the community. Originally it had been for Lauren Ansell, but now news was leaking out of Diane Waybridge's murder, it was likely to be even more widely attended. It was imperative that a discreet police presence was there to alleviate fear, while everyone else available was working on Diane's case. It was a necessity for intelligence. Someone amongst the crowd might be their killer.

But she also knew that the crowd might get hostile with them. In some eyes, they had let two women die, despite them working on Lauren's murder and having no idea that another female was going to be strangled so soon. There had been no

154

warning signs that another attack was imminent. The police were on their own – strategising, thinking, working things out. Everything took time. Their investigations had to start somewhere.

She took Sam with her back to Dunwood Academy. Sam had changed, too, and was dressed similarly in jeans, trainers and a jacket. Scarves and hats were a given – there was a cold wind blowing and rain in the air.

'I can't believe there have been two murders so quickly,' Sam said as she buckled up. 'I was trying to think it out, but it doesn't make sense. It's a shame our killer didn't leave some sort of calling card so we would connect the meaning of them quicker. Although, that's probably why they didn't, I suppose.'

'What makes you think the killer wants to be identified?'

'Well, the bodies aren't being hidden, are they? It's as if they're deliberately being left on display to taunt us. Right under our noses, so to speak.'

'I guess, but maybe they think there's enough similarities in the two females.' Grace pulled out into the traffic again.

A lot of serial killers liked to tag their victims or leave something with the body as a signature for the murder. Others liked to take things with them for souvenirs. So this killer appearing to do neither seemed strange.

Unable to get near to the school when they arrived, Grace parked up two streets back and they joined the crowd walking towards the school gates. There was going to be a short remembrance service and some of the pupils from the school were going to say a few words. Until then, she and her team would stay in the background.

Grace and Sam split up and she scanned the crowd, looking for Simon as well as Perry and Frankie. Simon had said he was coming with Natalie and Teagan. Instead, she turned as she felt someone staring at her. Her half-brother, Eddie, was visible through the throng of bodies. He nodded when he caught her eye.

She groaned under her breath, knowing she wanted to go over to see how Megan was but equally knowing she didn't want to talk to him. She pushed down her annoyance and as they drew level, she realised Kathleen Steele, the woman her estranged father remarried after she and her mother escaped his clutches, was standing next to him.

'I wasn't expecting to see you here,' Grace said to them both.

'It was Megan's idea,' Eddie explained. 'And my son Charlie wanted to come, too.'

Grace looked around, half-expecting Leon, Eddie's brother and Grace's other half-sibling, to be with them but she couldn't see him.

'Leon's in Spain,' Eddie added pointedly. 'He's on holiday.'

Grace tried to hide her surprise that he had practically read her mind.

'Charlie's around with his friends, but Megan's over there.' Kathleen pointed to a group of teenagers. 'None of them knew the murdered girl, but they were all so shocked by what happened that they wanted to be here.'

Grace had yet to meet Charlie, still hell-bent on keeping her distance. But she turned to the group, spotting a glimpse of her half-niece in the middle of them, surrounded by her friends. Megan Steele seemed a popular girl, self-assured, which she was pleased to see.

She felt Kathleen's hand on her arm.

'Actually, I was wondering if I could have a quiet word with you,' she enquired.

'Oh?' Grace had questioned if there would be more to it than Megan wanting to be there. 'About what?'

'I can't speak here. Would you call in to see me, please?'

'I'm not sure I'll find the time. As you can imagine—'

156

'Please,' Kathleen begged. 'I need your help.'

'It might be a while before I—'

'I won't keep you more than a few minutes. Can you call tomorrow on your way into work?'

'It will be too early.'

'Later, then.' Kathleen squeezed her arm gently. 'Please.'

'I'll let you know if I have time.' Grace nodded, although already knowing she would have to visit, even to put her own mind at ease. Curiosity killed the cat and all that. 'I'll text you to let you know I'm on my way.'

'Thank you.'

She turned away from Kathleen and bumped straight into Simon's boss, crime editor of the *Stoke News*, Phil Thurston. Grace cursed inwardly: the night was going from bad to worse.

Phil had been the main culprit in outing her in the press last year, letting everyone know her connection to the Steele family, and there had been bad blood between them ever since. He hadn't liked how she'd stood up for herself. She hadn't liked how he held it against her and went out of his way to get her into trouble with her team and the general public by printing things about her whenever he could. And she knew he pushed Simon for info. Simon had told her how he'd refused to help him on several occasions now. But she also had to try to stay on his good side. Phil was more powerful than her in terms of damage they could cause each other.

'Grace! How lovely to see you!' Phil chirped. 'It's been a while.'

'Hasn't it just,' she replied. 'Sadly, not long enough for me though.'

'Ouch, your tongue is razor-sharp.' He laughed, pulling back his head and revealing a mouthful of fillings.

He wasn't anything to look at, middle age being unkind to him. He'd lost most of his hair and gained too much weight around his waist. Grace was glad she didn't have to wake up to him every morning. Ugh, the thought.

'I was after Simon,' she said, for want of something to say.

'Ah, the other thorn in my side.'

Even though she was still annoyed with Simon from earlier in the day, Grace was cross on his behalf. She wasn't going to mention that headline, though.

'Simon's good at what he does,' she told him. 'You might not like it, but we make a good team.'

'With you being a Steele, I guess you do. Catching up back there, were you?'

'Excuse me?' Grace queried, her back already up at his reference to her family connection. 'You can never let things rest, can you?'

Phil glared at her. 'You're the one who moans I print things you don't like.'

'That's because you want to cause a reaction by sensationalising. You must have a very sad home life to want to vilify mine all the time.'

'Don't flatter yourself. I only wrote about you because the people of Stoke deserve to know the truth, no matter how painful that is to the individual involved.'

She rolled her eyes in an exaggerated manner: she wasn't going to get in an argument with him now.

'I have work to do.'

She pushed past him, cursing under her breath to make her feel better. The man was a loser. She wouldn't let him get to her. She was better than that.

But he grabbed her arm and stopped her.

'I think you need to be very careful what you do and say while you're in this city. This is my patch.'

Not for the first time, Grace wondered if the journalist was on the Steeles' payroll. She wouldn't put it past the snake.

'Take your hands off me.' She spoke calmly.

'Or else?'

'Don't flatter yourself that *you* can take me on. I'll knock you down before you can raise your hand. And then I'll have you in a cell before you can say "Sorry, I messed up, Grace."'

They squared up to each other, but he let her go just as she saw Simon drawing level with them.

'Everything okay?' Simon asked, catching the look on her face as Phil sloped away.

She smiled. 'Yes, I was after you.' She leaned forwards and kissed him, not caring now who saw her. 'How's Teagan?'

'She's subdued but she's with her friends now and—'

'Don't think you're forgiven after your earlier outburst,' she interrupted. 'I'm still annoyed at you.'

A hush went around everyone. Grace winked at him and turned to face the crowd.

THIRTY-FOUR

Grace kept her eyes on the small gathering behind Nathan Stiller. There were one or two teachers she had seen throughout the investigation and several pupils. To her left, she spotted Perry and Frankie standing together. To her right, Mr and Mrs Gillespie and Lauren's father stood in a group of older people she assumed were Lauren's family. Emma Gillespie was crying and making no attempt to hide her grief. Grace looked away from the intensity before it overwhelmed her.

Nathan cleared his throat. 'Ladies and gentlemen, friends of the school and the community, I really want to thank you all for coming out this evening, to show your respects to Lauren Ansell and her family. But it just doesn't seem right. Thanks shouldn't be given because a young girl has lost her life. So instead, I'd like to say a few words about Lauren.' He turned to the group of girls behind him. 'Same, too, of her friends. Even though her parents are here, I'm speaking on behalf of the family, and I know from talking to them earlier that anything you can do to help the police to find Lauren's killer they would be grateful.'

Not a murmur could be heard as he looked up while he took a moment to compose himself. Then he began again.

'I've been fortunate to know Lauren since the first year she started at Dunwood Academy. She was a bright little girl who had turned into an intelligent young lady. She excelled in a great many things, especially chemistry. Her teacher, Carole Mathers, enjoyed working with her and saw huge potential. It's so sad to see that it's been cut short. But we all believe Lauren will leave a legacy in the memory of her smile and her positive attitude, and we'll never forget her.'

A sob came from Emma and everyone's eyes fell on her. Alan hugged his wife to him, her shoulders shaking as she released yet more sorrow.

'Sophie, Teagan. Would you like to come forward and say something?' Nathan asked.

Grace stepped to her right so that she could see the girls better. Still holding her hand, Simon gave it a squeeze.

'We wrote a poem for Lauren,' Sophie said and began to recite.

Grace listened to the words. She was telling a story of a young woman who was loved by all of her friends.

'We want to pick up the phone and keep in touch.' Sophie paused. 'We love you, Lauren, and we miss you so much.'

It was Teagan's turn to talk. Grace watched as she took a deep breath and began. Like Sophie, she stood tall. Grace felt proud of her, even though she had yet to win her over.

'You'll always be in our hearts, my friend,' Teagan said, her voice cracking. 'And we'll never forget you until the end.'

A round of applause broke the silence and the girls moved back to the crowd, where they huddled together with their friends, tears flowing. Grace found herself wiping at her cheeks and saw lots of others doing the same as they lit candles in Lauren's memory. Music came on through an iPad connected to speakers and everyone stood in silence listening to it as a show of respect. It warmed Grace not only to be in the midst of the community, but to feel its beating heart. Here, people were hurting and yet they were coming together to grieve.

'You should be proud of Tee,' Grace whispered. 'It couldn't have been easy for Sophie and her to say those words.'

'I am,' he whispered. 'She showed me the poem this morning and I had a lump in my throat then.'

After the vigil had finished, lots of people hung around. Grace made her way through the crowd to speak to Nathan. He was with Jason Tranter, each with a woman by their side.

'Thank you for doing this,' she addressed Nathan.

'It's the least we could do. And it was for the kids, really. This is my wife. Toni, this is DS Allendale.'

'Hi.' Toni held up a gloved hand. She wore her blonde hair tied back in a ponytail, the collar to her coat up high. 'God, it's so terrible, isn't it?' she said, shivering slightly. 'I can't imagine how her parents must feel.'

'And now another one.' Jason joined in the conversation, his tone sharp. 'Do you have anyone in custody yet, Sergeant?'

'We're working on our enquiries.' Grace eyed the woman who was clinging on to Jason's arm. She had wide, bright blue eyes visible underneath a beanie hat, with a scarf wound tightly around her chin.

'This is Bethan, my partner,' Jason said.

Bethan nodded her acknowledgement. 'I hope you catch whoever is responsible soon. You never know what's going to happen next. It's very worrying for all of us women.'

Grace nodded, not wanting to get into that conversation right now.

'Your words were soothing,' she said, turning to Nathan. 'And there were some great anecdotes about Lauren. It was funny to hear about the time she played Baby Spice and then tripped on the stage. And that she made riffs up about lessons. It was good to know that she added a bit of humour to people's lives. I hope that brings some comfort.'

'I hope you catch whoever did this as quickly as possible – before there's a third victim,' Nathan said.

Grace eyed him. She thought he was being accusatory, but realised after a moment that he was just airing his thoughts. She nodded, moving away as other people came to speak to him.

It was heartbreaking to see everyone so upset, parents cuddling their own children close, friends embracing each other. Again, the outpouring of grief was devastating. Several times when she was talking to people she'd wiped away her own tears.

But no one had said anything about them being slow to catch the killer. It was as if there was some sort of unspoken truce called, a declaration of peace. Tomorrow might be another matter, but this evening was about Lauren Ansell.

Before she left, Grace went to speak to Lauren's family, chatted to a few people in the crowd and then she rejoined Sam, who was now with Perry and Frankie.

'Hear anything?' Grace asked.

'Nothing new.' Sam sighed loudly. 'I thought we might catch something.'

'People know we're here,' Perry remarked. 'It could stop some coming forward. We should get some calls tomorrow, though.'

'Maybe.' Grace stifled a yawn as Allie approached them.

'Anyone fancy a quick drink before heading home?' Allie queried.

'Oh, that's right,' a voice came from behind them. 'You all go out on the razzle while we look after the women of the city.'

They all turned to see a man in his mid-fifties, a menacing expression on his face. Grace recognised him from the residents' association; he lived at the top of the Bennett Estate. She was about to speak when she noticed his anger was directed at Allie. As head of the Community Intelligence Teams, Allie had stepped in to talk to the local residents that evening.

'Come on, Mr Sutton,' Allie replied. 'You know me well enough to know that I'm not full of bullshit. We want to catch this killer as much as you do. What makes you think we wouldn't be doing everything we possibly can?'

'It would be different if it was one of your own,' a man from the crowd joined in. 'But because it's a school on the Bennett Estate—'

'We're talking about the murder of a teenage girl! I can assure you that this case is being dealt with exactly as it would be on any street or estate in Stoke-on-Trent,' Grace responded. 'We have a duty to everyone and we will do our best to see it through.'

'Yeah, right.'

Grace was going to speak again, but the woman by the man's side pulled at his arm, an apologetic smile flashing on her face for a second.

'Lauren Ansell doesn't live on the Bennett Estate, so that's nonsense,' Allie addressed Mr Sutton. 'Just because the school is here doesn't mean we'll treat this enquiry any different to any other. We have a murdered schoolgirl—'

'And that woman in Hanley,' Mr Sutton continued. 'She's been strangled, too.'

'We're working hard to see if we can establish a link,' Allie said. 'Things don't happen as quickly in real life as they do on the TV. We have to wait for forensics, gather clues, interview people, which is what we're doing. So I can assure you this is not about where anyone comes from.'

Grace stepped forwards. 'Look, I know everyone is upset, but we have an innocent murdered child from the school that most of the children on the estate go to. It will affect a lot of people, so we need your help. Has anyone mentioned someone acting suspiciously lately?' She wasn't just speaking to Mr Sutton now – other people had stopped to listen. 'Did any of you see anything – no matter how small – that you could bring to our attention? Has anyone said anything to you recently that could be important? We need to find whoever has done this as quickly as possible. Can you help us?'

Mr Sutton visibly calmed then. Like everyone else, he wanted to do his bit. Finally with a nod of his head, he turned and left, the crowd dispersing around him.

Grace turned to Allie with a sigh. 'They make it sound as if we're out to get them, don't they?' She pouted.

'Living on the Bennett Estate gets you a reputation whether you want one or not,' Allie told her, battling to keep her long hair out of her face as the wind swept it away. 'Some of the residents will never like us – you know how it is. No matter what we do, they think we're heavy-handed.' She rolled her eyes. 'We're only like that when we're collaring one of them for something serious.'

Grace wanted to smile but she could see a couple of people out with their phones. She knew the vultures would spread the image if they caught it: two cops laughing after the vigil of a murdered schoolgirl.

In the distance she spotted Simon, with his ex-wife and daughter. His smile through the crowd told her she was forgiven for her earlier outburst. She smiled back.

'So, again,' Allie said, 'anyone want a quick drink before going home?'

'There's nothing I'd like better,' Grace replied. 'But I have to go to the morgue to identify our second victim.'

THIRTY-FIVE

Grace parked outside the morgue and switched off the engine. She took a few moments to remember the woman they had found this morning in Central Park. The last time she'd seen her, she had been battered and bruised, lying on a rug and dumped unceremoniously, waiting to be found. At least now she would see a glimpse of the woman that Diane had been, after the coroner had tidied her up for the viewing.

Inside the building, she found Steve Waybridge in the relatives' room with another couple. The room was a cream space with a navy-blue box settee and an armchair arranged around a rectangular coffee table. A set of three images of Stoke-on-Trent canals in years gone by adorned the wall to her right.

'Hello again, Steve.' Grace offered her hand to him.

He shook it and turned to the couple who were stood beside him. 'These are Diane's parents, Marian and Jeremy.'

Grace offered her hand to each of them in turn. As soon as Marian shook it, she burst into tears, squeezing Grace's hand hard.

'Find who did this to my daughter,' she sobbed. 'Please, I beg you.'

Grace nodded in reply.

'My parents wanted to come too, but someone needed to look after the twins,' Steve explained.

'It's best if most people remember Diane how she was before she died, Mr Waybridge. There will be a piece of glass in front of her. I know it's going to be hard for you, but as part of the formal identification, that's all I can do for you now. Do you understand?'

As Steve nodded, Grace reached a hand into the box of tissues beside her on the table and handed some to Marian. The woman nodded her appreciation and dabbed her eyes.

'Who will be accompanying me into the viewing room?' asked Grace.

'We all will – if that's okay?' Steve said.

'Yes, of course.' Grace cleared her throat. 'You will see Diane lying down. She will be covered in a white cloth. We've left her body beneath it. Her head and face will be on show, and there will be a bit of swelling as she has some cuts and grazes.'

Grace stopped for a moment as Marian sobbed. She let the older woman gain composure before starting again, clearing her throat. Grace was finding it hard, too.

'I'll be present for the identification, along with the mortuary technician, but you can have some time alone with her if you'd like that afterwards. Are you ready now?'

Steve took a deep breath. 'Yes.'

The technician showed them through to the viewing room. Marian almost caused a collision as her feet refused to work and she stopped outside the door. Jeremy reached for her arm and guided her in.

Diane Waybridge looked tiny on the trolley. The technician had hidden the harsh side of the bruising from the family by placing that part of her face to the wall. As Grace had been told to warn them, there was a cover over the severe bruising around her neck, but it was clear to see she had been a beautiful young woman.

Tears welled in Grace's eyes as she heard the wails coming from Marian, who had collapsed in Jeremy's arms, unable to look any more. Jeremy escorted her out as Steve stood there in silence. He stared at a spot on the wall above his wife's head for what seemed like an age. Grace was used to this – some people cried, some people said nothing, some people reacted angrily. Grief was never a one size fits all and today was no exception.

'Is this Diane Waybridge, date of birth the seventeenth of September 1991?'

Steve nodded. 'Yes,' he confirmed. 'It's her. It's my wife.' His face scrunched up and his shoulders began to shake.

Grace wanted to comfort him but knew that would need to come from his family. Still, she touched his arm to show she was there for him.

'What am I going to do without her?' he asked.

'Would you like some time with her?'

'No, I want to go home to the twins. Give them another hug and . . .'

He broke down and Grace waited patiently for him to grieve. Then she showed him back to the relatives' room, where he rejoined Diane's parents.

'Thank you,' Grace said after a few moments. 'I can't begin to imagine how hard that must have been. We'll be making an official statement to the press and the public in the morning now. I need you to be prepared for the interest this is going to cause. If you don't want to go home, Steve, might I suggest you stay with your parents for a while, or Diane's?'

'You're more than welcome, son,' Jeremy said.

'I don't know what to do right now,' Steve replied. 'I just want this – this killer caught.'

When everyone had left the building and Grace was back in her car, she let her tears flow. Taking in people's grief was a huge part of her job and yet each time, selfishly it reminded her of what she'd lost with Matt – her mum, too. Both of them had died far too young and she knew how Steve would be feeling right now; going back to an empty house, hoping it was all a dream, praying to wake up and find his loved one still around.

Grace knew it would take a while to sink in, and even longer before Steve might not hate going home to the house. But for now at least he had his children around him. They might upset him and make him sad, but they'd offer routine, stability. Life had to go on.

She started the engine and reversed out of the car park. Another murder, another long day and still so much to do that she was left with a feeling of getting nowhere. But she knew there would have been a slip-up by their killer. It was up to her and her team to find it.

She would do everything in her power to catch the person who'd done this to Lauren and Diane.

And pray that no one else died in the meantime.

THIRTY-SIX

Perry crept up the stairs, wincing as he hit a squeaky floorboard. He held his breath for a moment, but all was quiet. He didn't want to wake either Lisa or Alfie. They both needed their sleep.

After showering in the family bathroom, he quietly checked on his son. He was lying on his back, arms either side of his head, a breath of baby air whistling as he slept. Perry gazed down with adoration. Alfie almost seemed to be smiling. He was going to be a heartbreaker when he grew up, Perry was sure.

If I can protect him.

He gasped as his thoughts ran amok. Perry knew all about unconditional love for your own child, knew he would die to ensure his son's safety, but he also knew there would be a time in the future when he'd be out in the world on his own, and Perry couldn't watch over him all the time.

'Are you coming to bed, or do I have to wait for a cuddle all night?' came a voice from behind.

Perry turned to see Lisa in the doorway. She tiptoed towards him and he wrapped an arm around her shoulders, kissing her lightly on the forehead.

'How's your day been?' he asked, knowing that she would want to know the same of him but wouldn't ask unless he volunteered.

'Oh, you know. Kid's stuff, grown-up stuff. The usual.'

'My day was . . . bad.'

She hugged him tightly. 'Come to bed.'

He followed her into their room.

'Did you see Allie at the vigil?' Lisa asked as she pulled back the duvet.

'Yeah. Someone was giving her grief, but she's doing okay.'

'Did you ask her to arrange a date?'

'I did.'

Seeing Allie was always good, but much better under other circumstances. He'd wanted to remind her that she and her husband Mark were well overdue a night out with him and Lisa. He'd asked her discreetly. Allie had said she was all over it, but in reality he knew it probably wouldn't come off. Everyone was so busy nowadays.

'I'll get something sorted.' Lisa yawned most of the last word.

Perry leaned over and switched off the lamp. But even when Lisa was asleep in his arms, he couldn't settle. Seeing everyone that evening at the vigil was playing on his mind. He was supposed to have been working, listening for anything out of the ordinary, but he'd been close to tears a few times himself as the grief had rippled through the crowd. So many young lives affected by a mindless act.

He recalled one group of girls who had been inconsolable, their cries of pain hurting him. He'd chatted to them, not sure if it was helping or hindering. But they'd shared a few anecdotes and he'd made them smile a few times as they reminisced.

He'd spoken to the teacher who had told him that Lauren had excelled in her chemistry lessons. Perry laughed with her, saying it hadn't been his favourite subject at all. But apparently,

Lauren had loved it. The woman had said the class wouldn't be the same again as she'd fought to keep back her tears.

And then there was the group of boys who were trying to be all brave about things, when he could see they were finding it tough too, especially the speeches.

It had amazed him how well liked Lauren had been. Even if it was normal for the community to rally around one of their own, no one had a bad word to say about her. Usually, he'd catch a whispered derogatory comment that someone would make.

And now there was Diane Waybridge, too. He hadn't been able to look at the photograph of her children without sheer rage going through him. They were so young. He couldn't imagine what her husband would be feeling right now.

The CCTV footage had been a good find. How could there be two people involved? Was one their murderer and one an accomplice, or were they both in it together? Did one source out the women and one do the kill, or did they both carry out the attack?

He pulled Lisa in closer to him. She protested in her sleep but settled down again. He hoped she felt safe in his arms, prayed he could always protect her and his son.

He closed his eyes, trying desperately to rid himself of the images that were flooding it. He would be no use to anyone if he didn't get some sleep.

Somewhere out there in his city was a murderer and he wanted them off his streets.

THIRTY-SEVEN

Grace went straight home after her visit to the morgue. The lights were on, but she wasn't relishing seeing Simon. For once, she'd rather he had gone home to his own place. But, she supposed as she removed her key from the door, if possible it was better to go to bed on a good vibe rather than have unease lingering over them. She much preferred to clear the air. Because she was the one who'd overreacted and kept the argument going longer than it should. Guilt flooded through her. Life was too short for silly disagreements.

She and Simon had met in October last year. He had been reporting on the first murder case she'd worked after coming back to Stoke for promotion. Throughout the case, they had built up a rapport and even though she couldn't at first tell him who she was related to, they had drawn a line underneath it all when it had come out, and started again. It hadn't gone down well at the station, but so far they had made it work.

Simon was in the kitchen when she went in. He'd switched the kettle on and she could see two mugs waiting for hot water. She could also see his back, as he hadn't turned to greet her.

'Hey,' she said, putting her bag on the worktop beside him.

'Hey.'

The kettle was welcome noise in the prickly atmosphere. After a few moments of silence, Grace went to sit in the living room, unsure whether he'd bring her drink through and sit with her, or if he'd take his up to bed with him.

'I'm sorry about earlier,' she started as soon as he came to join her.

'I'm not really in the mood for arguing,' he replied, his voice calm.

She looked up at him sheepishly. 'Me neither.'

'I'm a journalist telling the news. You're a detective solving a crime and needing the public's help.' Simon sat down beside her on the settee. 'You should be asking me questions that I can pose to people.'

Grace knew he was right. Why hadn't she been working with him on this?

'I thought maybe you'd criticise,' she admitted, glancing across at him. 'But the reality was, I *had* been thinking about those kinds of things and hadn't wanted to ask you. I thought that you might have a go at me for hounding you, using your job as a journalist to get information.'

Suddenly they smiled at each other, realising at the same time what had happened. Too wrapped up in trying not to show each other that their jobs wouldn't interfere in their relationship, they hadn't been working together as they should. If she hadn't known Simon so well, she'd be using her charms to get to see him, have a chat, bargain with him over a cuppa and a piece of cake in the Spitfire Café-Bar.

If they hadn't been a couple, he'd most probably be asking her for a pint in Chimneys. They'd end up having a meal and sharing snippets of information – enough to keep each other satisfied but not tread over the line.

Instead, they had been pussyfooting around and not working

as a team. It made her realise how much he meant to her, how she didn't want to jeopardise their relationship.

But she did want to crack this case, and the others they would go through together in the future.

She rested a hand on his thigh. 'I guess we still have a lot to learn.'

'I guess we do.' He put an arm around her shoulders and pulled her in close.

'I would have chosen a better headline than the Stoke Strangler.' She pouted.

'Hey, I thought it was really good!' He gave her a quick squeeze.

'Teagan and Sophie's poem was lovely. It made me feel very emotional.'

'Me too. All I can see is Teagan whenever I see Lauren's photo. It doesn't bear thinking about.'

'How is she?'

'She actually gave *me* a hug earlier, asking if I was okay. But I think it's hitting her hard with Lauren gone.'

'It will. Friendships formed in our teens often go on for years, good or bad,' Grace replied. 'I'm sure you'll keep her safe, though.'

'What if I can't?'

'Then *we* will.'

She put a hand on his arm. He was hurting for his daughter – she could see that. He wanted to help Teagan to get through her grief.

'All you have to do is be there for her,' she added. 'You two have a fantastic relationship. Use it to your advantage.'

'Yes, boss,' Simon teased.

As they sat together, this time in companionable peace, Grace said a silent prayer. She felt stupid now – she had exaggerated earlier and it had been childish to snap at him the way she had.

She needed the press, Simon was good at his job, and even if he did have a boss who was hell-bent on causing trouble, maybe Simon would keep Grace one step ahead of Phil.

She smiled to herself.

Over their drink, they chatted through some neutral things that had happened during the day. Grace finally began to relax. Today had been a step forwards for them both in terms of where the relationship was heading.

She only prayed that today had been a day of moving forwards in more ways than one regarding their case, too.

THIRTY-EIGHT

Saturday

After morning team briefing, Grace was sitting at her desk going through her paperwork when Andy Fitzwilliam from the tech team came in. A bear of a man with an extremely infectious laugh, he had a huge smile on his face as he wheeled a chair over to her and sat down.

'I have some information for you,' he said.

'Oh?' Grace laced her fingers together, stretching out her arms.

Andy opened the manila file he'd brought with him, pulled out a sheet of paper and placed it in front of Grace. He pointed at a list set out in a spreadsheet.

'This has come from victim number two's phone,' he said, pushing his glasses up his nose. 'Diane Waybridge has been using a website called All Talk. There's a lot of –' he smirked '– talk on it, but mainly it's harmless. Just a load of people going on about sex and stuff, but no sharing of pornography or photographs. The idea is to share sexual fantasies.'

Grace's brow furrowed in confusion.

'I know!' Andy shook his head in mock exasperation. 'If you

want to get your rocks off, then download some porn or buy a magazine. But it seems this is set up so that users can chat about things they *want* to do rather than actually doing them.'

'And how do you know that?' She raised her eyebrows in a quizzical manner.

'Know what?'

'That they aren't doing anything afterwards.'

'Well, I don't, to be fair,' he admitted. 'But reading some of the messages, it just seems like a whole bunch of people talking about sex.'

'So some people clearly *are* all talk and no action when it comes to sex!' Grace grinned. In reality, she understood what Andy was saying, but she didn't comprehend why anyone would want to share that type of thing in public. 'And you think Diane Waybridge was a user of the site?'

'I know so. Members have to create an account with a username and their mobile phone number for a password.'

'That's extremely dodgy, don't you think? That would be really easy to hack into.'

'It is. I know I wouldn't do it,' Andy agreed. 'But it's good for us. So while I wait for the website to allow us access to their data, and we can get the IP addresses from Single Point of Contact, we don't need them owing to her phone records and the info on her phone. She goes under the name of WildWoman73 and she talks to someone called NightRider24 mostly.'

Grace wrote the two usernames down on her notepad. Maybe they were going somewhere with this.

'Do you have any credit card details?'

'There's no money involved in joining.' He raised his index finger in the air. 'WildWoman73 and NightRider24 live at the same address.'

'What?' Grace groaned as she worked it out. 'Mr and Mrs Waybridge both use the site?'

'Each to their own, I guess.'

Grace's heart sank. 'I really don't want to speak to him about it.' She grimaced before smiling at her colleague. 'Thanks, Andy. Great work.'

'I'll keep digging.' Andy nodded and left her to it.

Grace ran a hand through her hair and blew out her breath loudly. Would this be an enquiry that might lead them to their killer? Was there a possibility that someone on this site was doing more than talking? After all, the nature of the site alone could lead to someone being stalked indiscreetly. She shuddered at the thought.

Once she'd explained her findings to Sam, she asked her to cross-reference it with any mobile phone numbers they had collected at the school over the past few days as part of Operation Middleport. Anyone spoken to had been asked to give their mobile phone number voluntarily in case the police needed to contact them to clarify details. Anything else they needed would require a warrant.

Then she picked up her car keys. Sometimes she really despised her job, but she had to speak to Steve Waybridge.

Grace knocked on the door of the Waybridge home. She was shown through by Steve into a large family kitchen, children's paraphernalia everywhere but in the plastic box it should be. Lego bricks across the floor, a pile of books lined up in a row next to them and several toys scattered around. The worktops were clean but cluttered. Drawings she assumed the children had done were stuck all over the door of an American fridge-freezer. It looked such a happy place to be that Grace instantly felt a sense of apprehension again.

'My parents have taken the twins for a couple of hours,' Steve said. 'Although I'm sure if I hadn't got the kids I'd curl up in bed and not come out. Would you like a coffee?' He filled the kettle with water before she replied.

'Yes, thanks. I will.' Anything to put off the inevitable for a few minutes.

'Mr Waybridge. Steve,' Grace began when he handed her a mug. 'I need to ask you something personal about yourself and Diane. Anything you can tell us about it may help us with our enquiries.'

Steve's face had lost all colour as Grace continued.

'We've found details of a website that you and Diane have been using: All Talk. Tell me about it.'

He nodded, fighting back tears. 'We were members.'

'Go on,' Grace encouraged after he'd been quiet for a moment. She knew it was going to be hard for him but it needed to come out.

'It was a bit of fun. After the kids, our relationship had gone a bit stale, so I suggested spicing things up a little. Someone at work told me about this site called All Talk. We tried it out for a giggle, posing as if we didn't know each other.'

'And did you hook up with anyone else?'

Steve shook his head. 'But we didn't really want to, either. We chatted to each other on there all the time, sent each other messages. And it did the trick, because it certainly spiced things up.'

She paused, dreading the reaction from what she was going to say next. 'Do you think Diane ever used it to talk to someone else?'

'I hope not!' Then he hung his head. 'It was exciting enough to talk to each other. The messages on the forum were all steamy but it was purely fantasy.'

'And were these your usernames?' Grace didn't want to say them aloud for fear of even more awkwardness for him, so she showed them to him written down.

180

'Yes. I wish I'd never heard of it now.' Steve coloured slightly. 'Was Diane meeting someone that I didn't know about?'

'We can't be certain of anything yet.'

To be fair, it was one of the things Grace had thought of. Most killers were known to their victims. It could even be a case of a fantasy going too far, in which case she could no longer rule out that Mr Waybridge *was* involved.

But then, where would the death of Lauren Ansell fit in?

For now, Grace would put resources into looking into All Talk. Because something didn't add up.

THIRTY-NINE

Grace had been surprised when Kathleen Steele had asked her to call round. In the middle of a murder investigation, she could hardly pop in for a cuppa. Yet, she *had* said she might drop in, and a few minutes wouldn't hurt. So Grace sent a text message to Kathleen and took a detour when she left the Waybridge home. After all, she'd been worried about Megan.

Despite her eldest half-brother, Eddie, wanting her to play happy families, Grace hadn't got in touch with any of them since last year owing to the criminal activity they were known to be involved in. But she had a strange draw to the Steeles. Mostly she felt guilty for breaking up a family unit of mother and daughter, even though prison was where her half-sister Jade deserved to be after wreaking such carnage last year.

Her other half-brother, Leon, had been left for dead by Jade, too. You'd think he would be grateful to the police for finding him in time, but no. He'd been as hostile as ever. It had shocked Grace when he'd told her in no uncertain terms to stay away from him. Luckily, she didn't bump into him too often, which would have made things awkward.

Grace knocked on the door of her childhood home, trying

not to remember what had happened here all those years ago at the hands of her violent father. It was a sprawling pre-war detached house, set in four acres of land. Since she'd last been there, recurring nightmares had surfaced, but she'd eventually been able to push them away. She hoped this visit wouldn't start them up again.

Every time Grace saw her, Kathleen's hair was preened, make-up and clothes just so. Grace reckoned at times that you could easily put her ten years younger than a woman in her mid-fifties.

'Thanks ever so much for coming. Please, come on through.' Kathleen tottered away in heels amid small talk, showing Grace into the living room.

It still gave Grace the shivers to step into the house, all the memories rushing back to her. It never got any easier and she was glad she didn't have to visit on a regular basis.

'Isn't it dreadful what's happened to these women?' Kathleen started as soon as they were seated. 'Do you have any idea who it is yet?'

'We're working on a number of leads.' Grace could say the patter in her sleep now, always using it even when it wasn't quite true. 'You wanted to see me?' she pressed, looking at her watch purposely.

'You don't have time for a cup of tea?' Kathleen looked on eagerly.

'Sorry.' Grace shook her head. 'I need to be quick.'

'Okay, I'll come straight to the point, then.' Kathleen took a deep breath. 'I'm concerned about Megan.'

Grace frowned. 'Has she done something to worry you?'

'Oh, I worry all the time. She's very hard to control.'

'She's pushing new boundaries, I guess,' Grace reasoned.

Really, she had no clue what would be going through sixteen-year-old Megan's head. She'd be trying to find a place in her family, she assumed, now that her mother wasn't around to look out for her. Not that she'd done a good job of it before that.

Kathleen smoothed down her skirt as she sat back. 'She's secretive with her phone. She could be doing all sorts on there and I wouldn't know. She won't tell *me* anything, will she?'

Grace smiled. 'I expect not. I wasn't too keen to share at that age.'

'It's all hormones and tantrums,' Kathleen laughed.

It would have been easy to join in with the humorous banter, but Grace still wanted to keep a barrier up between them.

Kathleen went to speak, stopped and then decided to continue.

'She's been seeing this young man, Seth Forrester, and I . . . well, he's all right, but not the sort you'd want your grand-daughter to bring home, to put it bluntly. He's never come into the house, just screeches up in his car and then screeches off again afterwards. She clams up when I ask anything about him.'

'And?' Grace probed.

'Well, I thought . . . you would—'

'You're asking me to check up on Forrester?' Grace eyed Kathleen warily, wondering if this was her doing or Eddie's. Even if she *was* worried about Megan, she needed to stay one step removed from the family. They could lure her into a trap at the drop of a hat.

'No! I just want to . . .' Kathleen paused. 'Yes, if you will.'

'I can't do that.' Grace stood up.

'I'm sorry! I didn't mean to cross a line.' A slight pause. 'Can I ask you something else?'

Grace held in an impatient sigh.

'I know Jade let Megan do what she wanted, but I don't. I

184

try my best to discipline her and yet she still defies me. I . . . I wondered if you would talk to her.'

'Me?' Grace looked at her in disbelief. 'I haven't spoken to Megan since I saw her last year, and with Jade's trial coming up soon, I doubt she'd want to speak to me now.'

'Will you at least think about it?' Kathleen pleaded. 'I think it would be good for her to have someone to look up to.'

'She should be doing that with a member of her own family.' It was out before she'd thought about it.

'You *are* family, Grace, whether you like it or not. Megan's your half-niece.' Kathleen smiled shyly. 'Will you help me? Please.'

Grace had to laugh at the woman's audacity. But she could understand Kathleen's concerns, even if she didn't like her. After what had happened to Jade, Megan's grandmother wanted her granddaughter wrapped in cotton wool to protect her.

'Don't you think you should be asking Eddie to keep an eye out for her? He's particularly good at knowing what people are doing,' Grace said, a dig at him having her followed once she'd arrived in Stoke last year. He'd made it perfectly clear he didn't want her on his patch, as had Leon.

Kathleen smiled, giving a curt nod. 'It's nice to see you, Grace.' She touched her arm gently. 'It would be lovely if you could accept the family and come and visit every now and then.'

Grace said nothing, knowing that would never happen. As she was shown from the house, she wondered why it was that the Steele family mostly wanted something from her whenever they asked to see her. She wouldn't be used by them, nor anyone else, for that matter. But she did want to see how Megan was doing.

Once outside, she got back into her car and as Kathleen closed the front door, Grace had a quick check on her phone to see if anything had come in that needed her attention before she left. She was halfway through reading an email when she heard a noise. In her rear-view mirror, she could see a vehicle approaching. She sighed loudly.

She recognised the number plate of the black 4x4 immediately.

It was Eddie.

FORTY

Grace cursed: had she been led into a trap to get her to the house? Was it Kathleen's idea or Eddie's to get her here? But Kathleen hadn't tricked her about Megan. She had seemed sincere when she'd asked her to have a word with her grand-daughter.

Maybe it was bad timing on her part, being here when Eddie arrived.

Yeah, right.

Eddie parked beside her and turned his head to look at her through the side window before stepping out of the vehicle. Knowing that he'd want to speak to her, Grace reached for the door handle and got out again. If she stayed in her seat, he would lean in and tower over her. Not a good way to talk to him: he already intimidated her, although she'd never let him know that.

'Fancy seeing you here,' he said matter-of-factly.

'Yes!' Her reply was laced with sarcasm. 'What a surprise.'

Eddie couldn't hide his smirk.

In the light of day, Grace noticed how relaxed he looked, tanned skin showing the remains of a recent holiday overseas.

They stared at each other. It both unnerved and excited her at the same time. His eyes were fiery, curious even. They showed he still hadn't sussed her out yet.

A pigeon cooed in the background, garden birds singing a chorus all around them. The smell of freshly cut grass was in the air.

'Is there something you want?' she asked when there had been quiet between them for long enough.

'Jade wants to see you,' he replied, running a hand through his short hair.

'Does she?' Grace was about to shake her head and retort under no circumstances, but Eddie continued.

'Her trial's coming up and she doesn't know what to expect.'

'She'll go down for several things, I'm very sure of that.'

'That's not what I meant.' Eddie sighed. 'Don't you care a little bit?'

'I try not to.'

'After what happened to us all, I thought you might have a tad more sympathy.'

'After what she did, I'm sorry but I don't.'

Eddie scowled and Grace was instantly taken back to when she was five years old and her father was telling her off for something she hadn't done. Eddie looked so much like George Steele had when she was a girl, before they had left the house for good.

Even now, six months after Jade's arrest, none of them had sat down to discuss what had happened, but they each knew that George Steele had made the wrong impact on all of their lives with his cruelty and violence.

'Of course I care,' she admitted, watching a tractor bump along the lane outside the house. She turned back to Eddie. 'But I can't visit her.'

'Why not?'

'Because like it or not, I'm not her family. You are.'

'But you can be. She wants you to be, and so do I.'

'Your brother doesn't,' she said, knowing it was a childish dig.

Grace had probably saved Leon's life doing her job, but he'd refused to be civil to her afterwards, despite Eddie's best intentions to get them together as a family.

'I can talk him round.' He paused for a moment. 'Come for dinner, Sunday lunch, nothing fussy.'

'Stop asking me that. It's not ethical.' She opened her car door but he stopped her from doing so fully.

'It's nothing to do with your work.'

'It's still a no. I'm not sure I'd be able to be civil for that long, anyway.'

He smiled as he shook his head. 'You might not be a Steele but you have that stubborn streak we all have.'

She found herself smiling back, because he was right.

'Will you think about it?' he asked.

She shook her head.

'Do I have to beg?'

'It would be fun to see you trying.'

She held his eye for a moment, seeing the twinkle in it before he turned away. They had such banter between them that at times anyone listening might even think they liked each other.

As he got to the front door, she sighed. Why did she have to be drawn to this family?

'Okay, okay!' she shouted after him. 'Tell Kathleen to ask Megan if she wants to see me.' She didn't want anything sprung on her half-niece like the first time they had met. Jade had brought both her and Megan together without telling them they were meeting. It had been awkward, to say the least. 'And if so,' she added, 'tell her we can meet for a coffee.'

Eddie doffed an imaginary cap before continuing into the house.

Grace got back into her car and started the engine. As she reversed to turn around, she looked up at the house that she'd hated as a child. She knew some things would never change, no matter how much of a lick and polish it had. But at least from where she was, she couldn't see the garage with its hidden horrors that she had been lucky enough to escape.

Maybe that was what Megan needed. Someone different, outside the family, so to speak. If she could keep her on the straight and narrow, that would be a start.

It made her realise that she did care about her half-niece's safety, after all. Just like she cared about the safety of all the women in the city.

It wasn't her job to have every one of them on her conscience but, even so, she felt like there was a ticking time bomb in her mind.

190

FORTY-ONE

When Grace arrived back at the station, Sam had her head down at her desk.

'Found something interesting?' Grace asked as she slipped off her jacket and sat down.

Sam looked up, startled. 'If you give me a few seconds, I'm about to give you a link.' She pressed a few keys on the keyboard and then punched the air. 'Gotcha!'

'Tell!' Grace loved it when Sam reacted this way. It seemed they might have a lead.

'Now that we have data back from the All Talk website, I've been going through the numbers on Diane Waybridge's phone and I've come up with a match. One headmaster of Dunwood Academy, Nathan Stiller.'

'No!' Grace's jaw dropped. She held out her hand.

'It links him to the site, too.' Sam passed the printed spread-sheet across the desk for her. 'His username is KingSnow18.' She grinned. 'It's from *Game of Thrones*, isn't it? Jon Snow – King in the North.'

Grace smiled at the reference. 'The classroom that Stiller uses has that theme, too. So what does this mean? Diane

Waybridge only really used All Talk to chat to her husband. Or so we thought.' Grace ran a finger down the list, stopping at the name highlighted in bright yellow marker pen. 'Are there any text messages on their phones?'

'No. Just the one where they exchange phone numbers.'

'We'll need to bring him in and clarify if they met.' Grace nodded her approval. 'Great work, Sam.'

Andy Fitzwilliam appeared by Grace's side.

'We've got a lead from the list you gave to us,' she told him. 'One of the mobile phone numbers belongs to someone from Dunwood Academy. It's also linked to one of the users – KingSnow18.'

'Ah, a *Game of Thrones* fan.'

Sam and Grace shared a smile.

'Still,' Andy continued, 'wait until I show you what else I've found. All is not what it seems.'

Andy pulled up a chair and Sam came around to Grace's desk.

'Okay, All Talk is a site as you know that accommodates people's fetishes, for want of a better word.' He opened his laptop and entered the site. 'I set myself up as a user then got into the main system and dug a bit deeper in the background. There are groups set up that you have to get invites to. Obviously, I've been able to bypass them.' He turned the screen around so they could all see. 'Voilà.'

Grace looked at where the mouse was pointing. There was a list of linked forums to join. She frowned as he read out some of the names.

'For one night only. Dark and Nasty. True Crime Fantasies. Wife-swap.' He sniggered. 'I can't begin to imagine.'

'How many have you got into?' Grace asked.

'One or two. It won't take long to infiltrate them all.'

Once he'd gone, Grace tapped on the yellow highlighted line

again and glanced at Sam. 'It's just a thought, but can you check to see if Lauren Ansell's phone number is linked to the site as well?'

'You're thinking she might have been stalked by someone on there?'

'It's possible. Is there anyone else's name on the list that you can marry to the other list of phone numbers?'

'Not so far. But I'll run through it again now and double-check.'

Grace raised a thumb in thanks. 'Let's see what Stiller has to say for himself. At least it's a Saturday and we should probably find him at home. I don't want any more upset at that school.'

FORTY-TWO

Nathan Stiller had been put into Interview Room One. Grace went in with Sam and sat down across from him, flipping open her notepad. She cleared her throat and pressed record on the recording equipment.

'I'm Detective Sergeant Grace Allendale and this is Detective Constable Sam Markham. The time is eleven a.m. on the seventh of April 2019. Can you state your full name, please?'

'Nathaniel Michael Stiller.' Nathan cleared his throat, too.

'Good. You understand, Mr Stiller, that you are here under caution?'

'Yes. I'm happy to help with any enquiries.'

Grace looked at Nathan. He clearly had no idea why they wanted to question him. He must think it had something to do with procedure, as he'd been in charge of the school at the time Lauren Ansell was murdered.

'Do you know anyone by the name of Diane Waybridge?' she asked.

'No, I don't think so.' Nathan shook his head.

Grace showed him a photo of their second victim. It had been taken at her work's Christmas party. Diane was wearing a paper hat from a cracker, raising a glass of wine to whomever had taken the shot. Glitter sparkled on her skin and hair, matching the shine in her eyes.

Nathan shook his head again, clearly none the wiser.

'What can you tell me about All Talk?' Grace asked next.

His face coloured rapidly. After a moment, he spoke again. 'It's a website that I'm a member of.'

'And what do you visit it for?'

'Well, I chat to people online.'

'About?'

'Look, you know that I'm married – not that it's any business of yours. But I do chat to women online. Of course, I never act on it.'

Grace nodded. 'You have a right to a private life outside of your work. I just need to know if you knew Diane Waybridge.' She paused for a moment. 'Or WildWoman73?'

Nathan looked up at her pretty sharpish. 'I know that user-name, yes,' he replied. 'Why?'

'It belongs to the woman who was murdered yesterday, so we're trying to establish—'

'The woman who was left near to Central Park?' Nathan's eyes widened. 'Is it her?'

'We believe so.'

'Oh, no.' His body deflated slightly. 'I've never met her, though.'

'But you've talked to her in the chatrooms and one or two forums on All Talk?'

'She mostly talks to some guy called NightRider something or other. But yes, I've chatted to her a few times.'

'Have you ever met?'

'No. We were thinking of it and we exchanged phone numbers, but in the end we agreed it would be unethical. We're both in relationships. It isn't what we do, although I know a lot of people go on that site to pick up people for . . . extra-curricular activities.'

'So users chat to each other about their sexual fantasies?' Grace asked.

Nathan nodded, colouring again.

'And you categorically deny ever meeting up with Diane Waybridge?'

'Yes, I do!'

'But you can see my dilemma?'

'I can see how your mind's working, but you're wrong.'

'So you're not—'

'I'd like to go now, please.' Nathan sat forwards.

'It would be better if you left when we'd finished.'

Nathan stood regardless.

'For the purpose of the recording,' Grace said, 'Mr Nathaniel Stiller is leaving the room. This interview is terminated at eleven fifteen a.m.' She leaned forwards and stopped the proceedings.

'You're wrong,' Nathan snapped. 'I had nothing to do with either of these murders. And you'll realise that when you catch the person responsible.'

'I'm only doing my job, Mr Stiller,' Grace told him, standing as well. 'I have two dead women who won't be returning to their families. I won't apologise for any discomfort caused to others while we investigate matters.'

Nathan looked sheepish as Sam led him out of the room. Grace didn't know what to think about the conversation. She believed Nathan when he said he hadn't met their victim. His reactions told her so. But she wasn't sure that let him off the hook completely.

She rang Andy from the tech team. 'Are you in the building?' she asked when he answered the call.

'I am. Do you need me?'

'Did you get any further with the forums?'

'Yes, going into some of them now.'

'Great. I'm coming to you. I want to look at them too.'

After talking to Andy, Grace went back onto the open floor to find Perry there alone. She decided to take her chance to talk to him, as well as updating him about the case, and perched on the edge of his desk. Perry was leaning on his elbow, chin on a fisted hand and staring at his monitor. He seemed worn out; they all did.

'This website, All Talk, is quite disturbing,' she told him. 'The more I dive into it, the stranger it gets. It seems that on the side we can see, it's a site where people chat to each other, a bit like a blog. But if you log on as a user, it seems you get vetted by the site owner and then allowed to go into some pretty sick forums. I'm not sure it's all about fantasy, if I'm honest.'

He looked up at her and sat back in his chair. 'Who owns the site?'

'We're looking into it now. But I've a feeling we'll need to get a warrant and shut it down after our enquiries. It could be harmless, but . . .'

'We can only do what we can do,' Perry replied.

Grace nodded. 'Can I also have a quick word about something?' She moved in closer to him, took a quick glance around to see if anyone was in hearing distance and then dipped her head. 'Do you know anything about Seth Forrester?'

'Quite the little shit,' Perry said. 'He's twenty-two, been inside for petty theft and breaking and entering, but nothing for a couple of years. Why?'

'Megan Steele's hanging around with him.'

'Ah.'

Grace sighed. 'I know I have nothing to do with the family, but after what happened to her mother, I feel a moral duty to look out for her. Especially feeling it at the moment.'

197

Perry sat back in his chair. 'Do you see her much?'

'Not at all.'

'Would you like to?'

'Yes, but I know it isn't possible.'

'Why not?' Perry asked.

Grace paused. 'Don't you think it's a conflict of interest?'

'For the older Steeles, perhaps. But she's a child.'

'I know. Even so.'

'You could meet her for coffee somewhere neutral.'

'That's what I was thinking,' Grace admitted.

Perry sat forwards again and paused. 'Is this thing with Forrester serious?'

'A few weeks in at the most, I think. Kathleen Steele contacted me to ask if I knew of him.'

Grace wasn't about to tell him that she had met with Kathleen, nor mention anyone else in the family.

'Well, he's known to Leon. He's suspected of managing some of his runners.'

Grace pulled a face. Deep down, it was what she'd expected to find, but she wasn't too pleased at it being true. She very much hoped that Megan would take her advice now.

'Do you think he's being used to keep an eye on Megan?' she asked.

'Possibly. But if she's anything like her mother, she'll have a mind of her own and won't be easy to control. Take her for a coffee. No one needs to know.'

'We're in the middle of a murder investigation.'

'You're concerned about her because of that, too. You only need half an hour to ease your mind.' Perry's desk phone went and he reached for it. 'Hello, Perry Wright speaking.' He covered the mouthpiece with his hand. 'One coffee.'

Grace nodded, although Perry wasn't looking her way. She was pleased he didn't have any doubts about her now. He could so easily have been hell-bent on getting back at her because she was related to the Steele family.

One coffee, she could manage that. She'd see if she could arrange it for first thing the next morning, before she could change her mind.

FORTY-THREE

She was thinking about that visit, about when it had all started.

It was nearly a year ago. It had taken her longer to get there than usual. The traffic had almost come to a standstill on the motorway owing to an accident in the fast lane. She'd wondered if she was going to make it on the road at all when it had forecast snow. But the weather predictions had been wrong; instead, there had been torrential rain.

It wouldn't do for her to be late. She'd already had palpitations at the thought of missing the visit. There was no way she could wait a whole month before she could see him again. She had to tell him of her plans, how things were going, and keep him informed of what was happening on the outside.

Finally, she made it to the car park. The prison gates closed behind her with a clang fifteen minutes later. She jumped every time it happened, even though she was used to all the locked doors, the keys jangling, the oppression of the wing itself.

HM Wakefield was the largest high-security prison in the UK. It had been nicknamed 'Monster Mansion' owing to how many high-risk sex offenders and high-profile murderers were being held there. She hated that name. He wasn't a monster – not to her.

It had taken her a while to acclimatise, but with each visit she'd made she'd become more at ease. Once she was inside, when she was with him, she forgot about everything else: where they were, why he was in there. He wouldn't be out any time soon, so it would be a while before they could be together.

She moved along the corridor with all the other visitors, the dogs at the far end sitting to attention waiting to sniff out any drugs that someone might be attempting to smuggle in. She'd seen so many people being arrested as she'd waited to see him over the years. It was as if they thought they could do what they wanted. Everyone should abide by rules. Well, almost everyone.

She entered the visitors' room. There were about twenty tables, each having two chairs and most with a man sitting across from an empty seat. She knew a lot of the men by sight now; their families, too. Often, she'd notice when someone was missing and had maybe been released.

She scanned the room, waiting to see him, wanting to see him. And there he was. A huge smile broke out on her face and she waved as she caught his eye, almost skipping towards him.

She had made a special effort with her appearance. Her long blonde hair was immaculately washed and blow-dried, she wore red lipstick but not too much make-up, and a fitted dress, black stockings and high heels. A bit of fantasy in with the reality. Just the way he liked it. His smile of appreciation showed her it had been worthwhile.

She sat down opposite him and smiled. 'How have you been?' she asked.

'So-so. Time goes slowly in here. Tick-tock. Tick-tock.' He grinned. 'How's it going with J?'

'Slowly but good.' She nodded, noticing the same mirrored look of excitement on his face.

'What's he like?'

'He's very keen.'

'Would I like him?'

'Why does it matter?'

'I want to know.'

She nodded. 'I think so.'

He looked away from her for a moment and panic set in. What if she'd got the wrong one? Would he be okay? But then when he turned back to her, with a look of trust, she realised it was going to be fine.

'When can you start?' he wanted to know.

'It will take time – you know that. I need to gain his trust.'

The man and woman at the table beside them started to argue. Raised voices alerted the guards, two of them walking around behind them, and they pulled apart.

He shook his head and turned back to her, rolling his eyes. Then he smiled.

'So you think everything's going to plan?'

'Yes, I do.'

'Music to my ears. I feel so much better for seeing you, my love.'

At the time, that was what she had wanted to hear, what she needed. His words to reassure her. He loved her; he wanted her to do this.

Perfect, just perfect. And all part of her plan.

FORTY-FOUR

Sunday

A few minutes early for her meeting, Grace pushed on the door to Caffè Nero situated at the side of the three roundabouts in Smallthorne. She had texted Kathleen to ask if Megan would like to go for a coffee and had been surprised that she'd wanted to meet so quickly. Really, she wasn't sure she should be here at all, having so much to do, but she didn't want to let Megan down now that Kathleen had set a date.

The establishment wasn't too busy. Despite being early, Megan was already there. Grace caught her eye and walked over.

'Hi, Megan. Can I get you anything?' she asked as she drew level and spotted the empty glass of juice.

'I'll have a cappuccino, thanks.'

At the counter while she waited for their drinks, Grace glanced over at her half-niece. She had the makings of a beautiful woman and she reminded Grace of herself around the same age. Megan took after her mother and uncles for her looks, and they all had the same deep-set eyes that Grace had. Both Grace and Jade were dark, thin to the point of skinny, with long limbs and fingers.

Megan was staring out of the window, sitting back in the chair as if she hadn't a care in the world, her left leg swinging as it sat on her right. She didn't look too bothered about the meeting, whereas Grace for some reason was a bag of nerves.

Once their drinks were ready, Grace took them over.

'Thanks.' Megan added a sugar to hers and gave it a stir.

Grace offered her two packets of biscuits. 'I'm not sure if you like ginger nut or shortcake?'

'I'm not hungry.'

A silence fell between them. The three men at the next table laughed loudly at something one of them was showing the others on his phone. Grace wondered if it was an incident that had happened the night before, on a mad Saturday with friends. She hadn't had a good night out in a while.

'How are you?' Grace asked after a moment.

'Fine.' Megan gave a tiny shrug of her shoulders.

'So what have you been—'

'Look, I don't want to be here, but I'm doing it for my nan. She says you want to talk to me about something.'

Grace fumed inwardly. Kathleen had already put her on the spot.

'I was hoping we could chat about keeping yourself safe. After recent events, Kathleen's worried about you.'

'She wants you to check up on me?' Megan shook her head. 'I'm a big girl, you know.'

'Even more reason for her to worry about you.' Grace smiled – friendly does it.

Megan wasn't buying it, so Grace continued anyway.

'Your nan says you have a boyfriend.'

'Oh, *I* get it.' Megan's eyes were dark and furious. 'She's asked you to check up on him.'

Grace nodded. 'It shows she cares.'

'It shows she's sticking her nose in where it's not wanted.'

Megan folded her arms. 'She can't control me. I'm not a baby, and I'm nothing like my mother. I can look after myself.'

'I'm sure you can, but—'

'I won't get in trouble, or let anyone abuse me, if that's what she's after warning me about.'

Grace flinched at her hostility. It was clear that Megan had learned some of the finer details about why her mother went on a murdering spree.

'How is your mum? Have you been to see her?'

'Not since last month.' Megan glanced at Grace. 'If you must know, I was scared when I last saw her. I . . . I'm not sure if I want her to come out again.'

'She's under a lot of stress.'

'I mean that I don't want to go and live with her again if she does come out.'

'You won't have to.' Grace tried to put herself in the young woman's shoes. She, too, would be frightened of what might happen in the future, so she wanted to reiterate about the support Megan had around her. 'You have a family who will look out for you. Kathleen says you can stay there no matter what, doesn't she?'

'Yes, but Mum would have to move back in with us now that the house has been returned to the council.'

Grace paused, unsure what to say to appease her. Megan was right. Jade would have to move in with them, if they'd have her. But she hadn't the heart to say that with Jade's confession and the strength of the evidence there was no way she would be coming out any time soon. She was looking at more than one life sentence for her crimes. Grace decided to bring the chat around to what she was really here for.

'So, this boy you're seeing . . .'

'He's not a boy. He's twenty-two.'

'Okay, so this man you're seeing.'

'It's still none of your business.'

Grace thought back to what she had learned about Forrester earlier from Perry.

'I want you to be safe, that's all.'

'I'm safer with him than I am at school, by the sounds of it. How could that girl be murdered with so many people around her?'

Grace couldn't argue with that. 'It was nice of you to attend the vigil.'

'It felt right, I guess. I hope her parents sue the school for negligence. Surely they have a duty of care to look after her? Although now there are two women dead . . .'

Megan sounded so grown up – it was as if someone had put words into her mouth. She was clearly a very intelligent girl, which Grace liked, because it meant she might have her wits about her. Megan probably wouldn't let anyone get the better of her, not like her mother. But nonetheless, she still needed warning. She was only sixteen. Even now, Grace could remember how worldly she thought she'd been at that age.

After a moment's silence, Grace drained the last of her drink and put the cup back on the saucer.

'Just be vigilant, that's all I'm asking,' she said.

Megan shrugged. 'I'm not sure about that.'

'She wants to see you're safe, as do I.'

'So you keep telling me!' Megan sighed theatrically and stood up. 'I'm fine, really. You don't need to bother about me.'

'But—'

'I'm not likely to go off and do one like my mother,' she cried. 'If I was, I would have done it by now. She's damaged and I'm not. Why can't anyone see that? I used to live in her shadow before, but it's worse now she's in prison. It's all anyone talks about.' She prodded herself in the chest. 'Why doesn't anyone want to know about me?'

206

'They do!' Grace pointed out. 'But Jade's trial is coming up and people are worried about how it will go.'

'There you go again. It's always about her!' Megan held up her hand. 'I'm not the one in this family who lost her marbles.'

Grace stayed quiet. People were beginning to turn and look at them. It was no use. She wasn't going to get through to Megan while she was like this. Everything she said, she either twisted or had an answer for. This wasn't doing any of them any good.

But then Megan surprised her.

'Look, thanks for coming to see me, but I'm fine, really.' She smiled shyly. 'Despite what Kathleen thinks.'

'She worries about you, that's all.'

'At least she cares enough to bother about it.' Megan's smile widened.

'Maybe it's time to have a rethink about Seth Forrester?' Grace stood up too. 'You have a chance at a good future now. Don't ruin it with someone who doesn't value his freedom enough to stay out of trouble.'

Grace thought she might have overstepped the mark as Megan looked away. But finally, she turned back. There was a look of her mother about her, strong, defiant.

There was no answer to her question, though.

'Thanks for the coffee,' Megan said. 'See you around some time.'

'You will,' Grace found herself replying, realising how much she might like it.

FORTY-FIVE

Once at the station, Grace spent most of the morning going through forum records on the back end of All Talk. Yesterday evening she had sat with Andy again for over an hour as he'd shown her how to access it all. So far, they had found the regular users, but it was a tedious task to get through all the groups and messages.

She'd searched on Diane Waybridge's name, and her username, but found nothing more than they originally knew. There were links to a few people she had chatted to, but conversation had been friendly banter and nothing regarding meeting anyone else. Same too with Steve Waybridge. He had only ever interacted with his wife.

While she'd been searching online, the team were investigating both women's social media channels, their phones, Diane's bank records, and speaking to all of their friends. There had been several press releases and information coming forward of sightings that then led to nothing. They had yet to connect their victims. The women didn't seem to know each other. They didn't mix with the same people, no friends or friends of friends overlapping.

Even after her phone didn't come up on the site's registry, Grace had also checked to see if Lauren Ansell's name was on the All Talk site and came across nothing. Some of the names in the True Crime Fantasies room were familiar to her through work. She made a note of a few to check them out on their police system.

Nick came to his office door. 'Lunch next door – my shout?' he asked. 'My eyes need a break and I could really attack a roast right now.'

'Sounds good,' Grace replied, everyone around her echoing her thoughts.

The walk to Chimneys took all of two minutes. Sam, Perry and Frankie came too, and the five of them chatted amiably as they waited for their meals to arrive. Chimneys was the local hideout next to the station. Built around a bottle kiln used to fire pottery in years gone by, it had an 'old man's pub' feel about it, albeit it quite modern and airy. It was also busy owing to its reputation for a good Sunday lunch.

Grace glanced around, wondering whether or not to text Simon to see if he was still at work. He'd said he was going to spend some time with Teagan that morning, but had then sent her a message to say she had gone shopping with her mum. But Grace decided it was best to stick with her team.

'Oh, before I forget, forensics have come in to say that the blood found in the back of Diane Waybridge's car was her own, as we expected – but nothing belonging to anyone else,' Nick said quietly.

Grace's shoulders drooped.

Sam gave out a sigh of frustration. 'I thought there might have been a hair or something similar, although admittedly they probably weren't in the car long. I can't believe we're still none the wiser where she was killed.'

'Not yet, but—'

Nick held up his hand. 'I know we're working, but we need a break, too. No talking shop for twenty minutes and that's an order.'

Grace rolled her eyes at Sam, who pulled a face at her surreptitiously. It was hard to switch off when everyone was so involved.

'Did anyone see *24 Hours in Custody* the other night?' Perry asked. 'It was an operation similar to the one we had a few years ago. I swear someone must have been filming us, it was so close to our case!'

'At least there's one programme that shows how police really work,' Grace sniggered. 'If I do watch a detective series, I spend most of the time shouting at the TV.'

'I suppose if they made the programme too realistic,' Nick commented, 'it would be all paperwork and budgets, staff shortages and mind-numbing continual checking.'

'Ah, but that's why we're good at what we do,' Sam said.

'Hear, hear!' Nick raised his glass in the air. 'Let's get this down us before someone in here spots us and says something sarcastic about us not working the case . . .'

Grace smiled. You never could win with the general public.

After evening team briefing, Nick suggested they all go home and get an early night. Even with their impromptu lunch break, they'd been working flat out without any time off since the murder of Lauren Ansell. Everyone needed downtime to recharge.

Grace lay across the settee, her feet resting in Simon's lap. They were watching a series on Netflix, but if anyone asked her what this last episode had been about, she wouldn't have been able to tell them.

Her mind was still running over the things she had found out that day. It was so frustrating waiting for that piece of info that would give them what they wanted – what the women deserved, too. As usual, Nick did a great job of pulling the investigation in the right direction, but she could see that underneath his authoritative demeanour, he was flustered. It was clear that he was under pressure from the top. They had two murders unsolved and no one really being questioned in relation to either. She wasn't looking forward to team briefing in the morning.

As well, they'd had several assault cases come in that she'd passed to Perry and Frankie to work on alongside Operation Middleport. Two people had been attacked while getting cash from cashpoints. Reports suggested the suspects were teenagers, who then raced off on mopeds. It had been happening last year as they had investigated their last murder case, but it died down shortly afterwards.

'Penny for them?' Simon wiggled the toes on her right foot.

Grace stretched her arms above her head. 'Oh, you know me. Head in work when I'm in the middle of a case.'

'Understandable. It's been a few days since anything exciting happened.'

'It's not bloody exciting when someone's murdered!' she admonished.

'Sorry!' He held up a hand. 'I'm a journalist and yet even *I* use the wrong words. You know what I mean, though.'

'Sadly, I do.' She sighed.

'Is there anything more we can do at *Stoke News*? Run an article on, oh, I don't know, safety or something similar? Help out by getting in touch with Radio Stoke, Signal Radio, sharing more on social media?'

She pondered for a moment and then shook her head. 'I don't know. That's the problem. I hate it when I feel like this.' She stood up quickly. 'I need a drink. Maybe it will help me to sleep. Want one?'

'Yes, please.'

In the kitchen, she got out glasses and poured wine from the fridge. Then she found two packets of crisps and took them all through to the living room.

She dropped the crisps in Simon's lap and sat down next to him again. The frame had been frozen and he pressed play to resume the show.

She laughed inwardly as she snuggled up to him. He already had control of the remote for the TV. Then she caught herself. This was beginning to feel normal, without Matt on her conscience all the time.

If only everything in life could be so normal.

FORTY-SIX

As she came out of the house, Sophie Bishop wasn't at all worried that there was a killer on the loose. Of course, she was still upset about Lauren, but she was on her way to see her fella again.

She'd agonised for an hour over what to wear. She wanted to look sophisticated, not too tarty. She'd put a wave in her hair and wore her make-up in a vampy style that she had once practised on Teagan after they'd spotted it in a magazine. Speaking of which, she reached for her phone and dialled Teagan's number.

'Hi, babes,' she said when her friend answered.

'Hi, where are you?'

'Walking along Roberts Road.'

'Are you sure you're okay out on your own?'

'It's only half past eight.'

'What about your dad?'

'He's at work anyway, so no one knows I'm not at home.'

Sophie checked herself out in a shop window. She was looking good, feeling confident and very excited about the evening ahead.

'I wish my mum would let *me* out.' Teagan sighed. 'I can't believe I've been grounded for so long.'

'That goes with having a dad who's dating a cop.'

Sophie turned her head before crossing the road, running to avoid an oncoming car. She slowed as she got to the pavement in front of the Co-op, struggling to hear as she passed customers milling around in its doorway. There weren't many people ahead of her, so she quickened her pace to continue her chat.

'I can't help that,' Teagan said. 'You know how much I hate her.'

'She seems okay to me.'

'You only have to spend a few minutes at a time with her!'

'Ah, give your dad a break, Tee. He likes her, and it wasn't his fault your mum threw him out.'

'She didn't throw him out. They split up.'

'Whatevs.'

Sophie stopped when she heard a noise behind her. She turned to look, but there was no one there.

'You still there, Soph?'

'What? Oh, yeah.'

'What's up?'

'Just my imagination working overtime. I thought I heard someone behind me.' Sophie turned in to the walkway that would take her off the main road and through to Abraham Street. 'Anyway, I can't tell you – okay?'

A tut. 'Why all the mystery? We're supposed to be friends.'

'We *are* friends.'

'So tell me. If you don't want the others to know, I can keep it to myself.'

'He swore me to secrecy.'

'But you know I won't tell anyone.'

'He doesn't want *anyone* to know.'

'Why? He's not some sort of weirdo, is he?'

214

'Of course not.'

'Then why can't you tell me?'

Sophie sighed. She and Teagan had had the same conversation for the past few days, since Teagan had found her reading a text message and wanted to know who it was from. Sophie wasn't going to tell her. She couldn't. It was their little secret. She'd made sure she'd deleted all of his messages coming in since then, too.

A pause down the line. 'Omigod – you're seeing someone older than you, aren't you?'

Sophie giggled and then turned around sharply again. She was certain she'd heard footsteps behind her this time. She peered back into the dark but couldn't see anything. Jeez, her mind really was playing tricks on her. She blamed all the upset over Lauren and the stuff in the news. She didn't want to be sad and think of her friend this evening, though.

Moving forwards, she quickened her pace, walking towards the streetlamp in front of her. She was only a few minutes away from where she was meeting him. She checked her watch: she would be there before she knew it.

Suddenly someone came up behind her, grabbing her waist. A hand knocked her phone to the ground.

'Hey!' She turned round and sighed with relief. 'You scared me half to death. What are you doing creeping up on me like that?' She looked to the ground, trying to locate her phone. 'You'd better not have damaged the screen. That phone is my lifeline and—'

In one quick move, he grabbed her hair and pulled her towards him.

'What are you doing!' she cried. 'Stop it. That hurts.'

He kept a firm grip on her, pushing them both through a gap in the hedges into the building site next to the path.

'Let go of me!' she screamed.

He threw her to the ground and she landed heavily on her back, her head banging on the grass. She groaned, dazed momentarily. But as he straddled her, panic tore through her. What was wrong with him? She had never seen him act this way before.

'Please, stop!' she said.

He hit out at her then, slicing the back of his hand across her mouth.

She tasted blood as his hands then went around her neck, her eyes widening in disbelief and panic. She kicked out her feet and clawed at his gloved fingers, unable to speak as his grip tightened. Her vision faded but she fought to stay focused, watching him disappearing from her view.

Gasping for breath, she clawed at the soil beneath the grass. Maybe if she could throw some of that in his face, it might blind him momentarily. But it was hopeless.

She'd never seen his eyes looking so dark, evil. Fear coursed through her as she realised what was happening. That if she didn't fight, didn't try to help herself, she was going to die. And she wouldn't be able to tell anyone that she knew her killer.

FORTY-SEVEN

Grace's phone rang. Seeing Teagan's name flash up onscreen, she frowned as she answered it. Why would she be calling her and not Simon?

She sat upright and swivelled to put her feet on the floor quickly as Teagan started speaking down the line.

'Hey, slow down so I can understand you.' Grace listened carefully. 'Do you know where she was? And this was when? I'm going to disconnect this call, but I'm going to get your dad to ring you. Okay?'

Simon was looking at her intently.

'That was Teagan.' Grace stood up. 'She was on the phone to Sophie Bishop, who was walking to meet someone. She said one minute they were talking and the next she could hear funny noises. She heard Sophie scream and then nothing.'

'What?' Simon was up on his feet, too.

'She then disconnected the call and tried to ring her back.' Grace ran from the room and returned seconds later with her boots. 'But it keeps ringing out.' She pulled them on her feet.

'Fuck. You don't think it's a wind-up?' Simon was shaking his head. 'Someone grabbing Sophie but fooling around?'

'I really hope it was, but I don't think so. Not by Teagan's reaction. She was crying down the phone. She said Sophie's scream was real and she sounded terrified. I'm going to call the control room, get someone there as soon as we can.' Grace picked up his phone from the coffee table and handed it to him. 'You need to ring Teagan. See if you can get more details.' She dialled the control room's number. 'Shit! We were getting somewhere! I *knew* something like this was going to happen. I . . . I have to go.'

'Wait, I'm coming with you!'

Grace didn't have time to argue. Once she'd relayed the details and then alerted Nick, they got into her car and she reversed out of the drive quickly.

'Teagan says Sophie was on her way from home to the shops on Roberts Road,' Simon said as he came off the phone.

'Which is on the Bennett Estate?'

'Yes. She thinks she was on the walkway down the side of the Co-op.'

'Who was she meeting, did she say?'

'No. Sophie's been keeping the boy she's dating a secret from her.' Simon swore loudly and banged his fist on the dashboard. 'We won't get to her in time, will we?'

'We've got all available units on it.' Grace put her foot down as they came to a main road. 'We'll find her.'

They sped through the streets of Stoke-on-Trent towards the estate, Simon holding on to the handle above the door. Grace couldn't go too fast in her own car, but she took the quickest routes she knew.

Up ahead as they approached the Co-op that Teagan had mentioned, she saw two police cars, lights flashing, parked up on the car park. She quickly pulled in behind them and turned to Simon.

'Take my car and go and see Teagan.'

'No!' he cried. 'I know we have a fine line to tread, but I want to find Sophie as much as you do. She could be anywhere!'

Grace couldn't argue with that. She switched off the engine and almost ripped away her seatbelt. They ran past the stationary cars, where Grace could see officers tearing up and down the grassed area of a walkway in front of them.

'Someone heard screams from this direction but thought it might be kids messing around.' A uniformed officer ran up to her. 'I think this might be hers.' The woman held up a phone in between gloved hands, its screen smashed. 'I found it on the path.'

Grace followed the officer into the walkway. She'd brought a torch along with her from the boot of her car and could see several lights flashing in the distance.

'What's behind that hedge?' she asked.

'A building site. There's a new development of houses going up.'

'Sophie?' Grace cried as she searched the undergrowth, flicking through the hedges with her hands.

All round her she could hear the name being shouted, even though she realised it was probably useless by now. If this was the same killer, Sophie might not even be here. She could have been bundled into a car and taken anywhere. But she prayed they weren't too late.

Having no clear MO to go on made it doubly hard to make reliable guesswork. Although it went against the grain, as most serial killers were meticulously routine, this attack could be something totally different. She hoped Sophie would be alive somewhere – hurt but alive.

She raced up and down the path. Spying a gap in the hedgerow, she squeezed herself through and into the open area next to it.

Was she in here? She shone her torch ahead to see.

'Sophie?'

The grass was wet and in seconds her boots were soaking. In the distance, the shadows of half-completed homes loomed down on her.

She had only gone a matter of a few feet, when she tripped over something on the ground. She landed heavily on her hands and knees. Turning back to look at the obstacle, her torchlight caught her worst fears.

A young girl with long blonde hair swept away from her face lay on the grass. Her eyes were closed, bruising beginning to show on her lip. As Grace flicked the torchlight over the length of her body, she noticed a shoe missing from her left foot.

'Over here!' she shouted as she felt for a pulse, tears welling in her eyes.

She tried not to think about the girl she had spoken to only last week.

'No, no, no!' she cried. 'Over here! She's here!'

As torchlights came closer, Grace tried once again to find a sign of life.

They couldn't be too late.

They couldn't!

FORTY-EIGHT

Grace could tell that Simon wanted to go and see Teagan. Since she needed to speak to her too, she told him to wait and she would take him there as soon as she could. He moved behind the crime scene tape while she worked with her team to figure out what had happened to Sophie Bishop.

'Seal the entrance off either end and block off the road at the back,' she shouted to one uniformed officer while pointing at another. 'Can you inform residents nearby what's happening, keeping it as low-key as possible? Get as many house-to-house calls done as you can before it gets too late.'

Nick was on scene shortly after Grace had arrived. Their victim had been moved to the back of the ambulance, the doors shut while they worked on her for several minutes. At the last update, she had been alive but unconscious, her blood pressure dipping dangerously.

Grace was now waiting, fearing the worst but hoping for good news.

The doors opened briefly and the driver jumped out onto the pavement. 'We've stabilised her enough to move her to the Royal Stoke,' she said.

'Thanks,' Grace replied. 'I'll follow on as soon as possible. We'll notify her family, too.'

So many questions were running through Grace's mind as she went to find Simon. Why another attack so soon? Why was it someone else from Dunwood Academy? It was like going back in a loop. And why was it someone from the same group of friends? Was this a coincidence or a planned attack? Was Diane Waybridge a trick, a diversion, or chosen purposely?

Grace wondered who Sophie Bishop was due to meet and whether or not she'd actually met them. To her knowledge, no one had come to them while they were there to say she hadn't turned up. Was the person she was meeting their killer?

Simon was standing with a few people, notebook in hand. He came to her as soon as he saw her approaching.

'Are you okay leaving now, or do you want to stay?' she asked.

'I'm coming with you. I need to see my daughter.'

Grace nodded, glad he felt that way. After all, Teagan only had one dad and without being too unkind on Simon's career, anyone could report on the case. Besides, Teagan may turn out to be the last person to speak to Sophie before she was attacked, so Grace had a lot of questions ready to ask her, and she knew she wasn't Teagan's favourite person. Simon might calm his daughter enough for her to ask some vital things.

Simon's previous house was situated about a mile from the Bennett Estate, in a row of privately owned homes. Pulling up outside with him was a bit of a sticky situation. Grace had never been inside his marital home, but she had gone with him when he'd collected or dropped off Teagan a fair few times.

She gazed at the large property in awe, yet again wondering at the lifestyle Simon had left behind. How he must dislike living in his two-bedroom starter home. An ugly thought came into her head. She wondered if Simon was disappointed in her, renting a house in her mid-thirties rather than owning a palatial pad. She had made a bit of money selling her marital home in Manchester, but she was saving that for when she was settled enough to buy, set her store out in Stoke.

Then she chastised herself for thinking that of him. Simon wasn't like that. He, too, was starting again. That was all – nothing to it. It was just the events of the night, what had happened to Sophie Bishop, that were making her feel insecure. Whenever anything like this happened, it brought home to her how precious life was.

'I really don't want to go in there,' Simon said quietly as he got out of the car. 'Especially not in these circumstances.'

Grace knocked on the door and Natalie answered it moments later. She was taller than the man standing behind her, who Grace knew was her new boyfriend, Adrian. She had an elfin face that suited her short mousy hairstyle and bright blue eyes that were filled with tears right now.

Without hesitation, Natalie ushered them both inside. Grace admired her for that. They didn't really know each other, had only acknowledged one another on the odd occasion in which it had been polite, like the week before at Dunwood Academy when she had spoken to Teagan. And yet, here they were face to face under such extreme circumstances and it didn't matter. The only important thing at the moment was finding out who had attempted to murder Sophie Bishop.

Before someone else is killed.

Grace banished the thought the moment it entered her head.

'Teagan's in the living room,' Natalie said. 'I can't get her to stop crying. She's had a terrible shock.' She looked at Simon.

'It's not good, Nat,' Simon told her.

'Is she . . . is Sophie okay?' Natalie leaned on the island in the kitchen for support.

'She's in a critical condition,' Grace told her.

'Oh, no.' Natalie's hand shot to her mouth, tears spilling from her eyes. 'Is it the same man who's murdered the other women? Do you think she was meant to be killed?'

'It's too early to tell,' Grace replied truthfully.

Natalie looked to Grace for advice. 'What do I tell Teagan?'

'We need to inform Sophie's parents first. I was wondering if you had an address.'

'Yes. There's only her father,' Natalie said. 'Her mother died a few years ago. Jack works nights at Royal Mail in the sorting office. I'm sure he'll be there right now. I'll get you his number.'

Grace relayed the details to Nick while Simon continued to update Natalie and Adrian. When she disconnected the call, a voice came out from behind them.

'She's dead, isn't she?'

They all turned to see Teagan standing in the doorway. She had an ashen look, her eyes watery, her phone in her hand.

'No, but she's very sick,' Grace replied, not one to beat around the bush. 'It's touch and go at the moment.'

Teagan ran into Simon's arms. Simon held her close.

'We need to catch the person who did this, Teagan.' Grace spoke quietly. 'Can we speak to you?'

They all went through to the living room. Natalie sat next to Teagan and once she was calm enough to talk, Grace began to question her.

'Do you know where Sophie was going?' she asked.

'No.' Teagan looked up, her face blotchy. 'But she was meeting someone.'

'Did she say who?'

Teagan shook her head. 'I couldn't understand why she wanted to keep it to herself.'

224

'So you have no idea who it could be?'

'No.' Teagan wiped her eyes again. 'Her dad's on the night shift, so he doesn't know she snuck out. He's going to be so mad.'

Grace knew this would be the furthest thing from Jack Bishop's mind when he heard the news. 'And you haven't told anyone what happened?' she asked. 'Any of your friends?'

'I told no one. I was so shocked. I rang you, and then Dad rang me and then I told Mum. That's all I did, I promise.'

'Thank you,' Grace said. 'It's best we keep as many details as we can to ourselves for now. Speculation will be all over the city before morning, but . . . for the sake of the family . . .' She looked back at Teagan. 'So this person she was meeting, do you think it was a boyfriend?'

Teagan nodded. 'She was seeing Joel Nicholls last month – he's a boy from our school – but she only saw him a few times. I tried to find out who this one was, but she wouldn't tell me.'

'But you share most things,' Natalie jumped in. 'I'm surprised she wasn't bursting to tell you.'

'What exactly did she say about the dates?' Grace questioned. 'Did she say where they went? Or where they were going tonight?'

Teagan shook her head again. 'She's never been like this before. Now, I might never know.'

When Teagan burst into tears again, Grace thought it was time to go.

Once outside on the driveway, after saying goodbye to his daughter, Simon joined her.

'Can I give you a lift home?' she asked.

'I'll come with you, if that's okay?'

'I'm going to the hospital. Do you want to revisit the crime scene? I can drop you off on the way and collect you afterwards.'

He nodded. 'I feel the need to be working now that I've seen Teagan is all right.'

She gave him a faint smile. There were a few things niggling her at the moment. She needed to be alone, to give them more thought. But she wasn't going to get that any time soon.

FORTY-NINE

The Royal Stoke University Hospital was a little under six miles away from the Bennett Estate and was easy to get to at this time of night after she had dropped Simon off. Once there, Grace located the High Dependency Unit and waited at the nurses' station for further information. It was quiet, most patients asleep and visiting hours long gone for the majority of the wards.

She busied herself looking around as she waited. A poster showing how to sterilise your hands was on the wall beside her, next to a whiteboard split into boxes, writing in most of them. She wondered how much time she had spent in hospitals owing to her job, let alone the time with Matt. Waiting was a necessity in most cases she dealt with, patience a definite asset.

A few minutes later, Grace was shown into a private side room. A man wearing a uniform of navy trousers and jumper with a pale blue shirt was sitting in a plastic chair, his head in his hands.

'Jack Bishop?' Grace asked.

'Yes.' He looked at her expectantly. Then she saw him sag visibly, guessing he recognised she was an officer, not a hospital staff member bringing him news of his daughter.

He seemed to be in his late thirties as he looked up at her through watery eyes, the laughter lines at each corner redundant. She proffered her warrant card.

'I'm DS Allendale. Please call me Grace. May I sit down?'

'Yes – please.'

'I'm so sorry about what happened to Sophie,' she said. 'I want you to know that we will do our utmost to apprehend her attacker. How is she?'

'They're still looking at her at the moment, but for now she's in an induced coma. Her brain is still swelling from the attack.' He took a deep breath. 'Is this the same person who murdered those other women?'

'We don't know yet.'

'When will you know?'

'It could be a while.'

'Did he mean to kill her?' He pinched the skin at the top of his nose, closing his eyes momentarily.

'We don't know that either, but there's no point worrying about it now. The main thing is she's still with you, and safe.' She paused. 'We found a phone nearby. We believe it belongs to Sophie.'

'Are you certain it's hers?' His brow furrowed. 'How would you know?'

'The phone's locked but there's a screensaver of her and another girl. I spoke to them both last week as part of an ongoing investigation.'

'At school?'

Grace nodded.

'Who found her?'

'I did.'

As cries of grief burst from him, Grace let him have a moment.

Jack wiped his eyes with his handkerchief. 'What happened to her?' he said at last.

Grace's heart went out to the man. He needed to know, but he didn't want to find out either. She had to tell him.

'Someone attempted to strangle her,' she said quietly.

'I know that. I mean . . .' A sob escaped him.

'That's all I can tell you at the moment.' Grace pressed her hand to his arm. 'Do you know if Sophie was meeting anyone this evening?'

'No. She was in her room when I left for work. She must have slipped away after I'd left the house. My shift started at half past seven, so I always leave at seven.' He shook his head again, his shoulders shaking this time too.

'One of the things that can give us a lot of information about last known movements would be her phone. Do you happen to know the code?'

'She never told me.'

'That's okay, we can do it.'

Jack broke down again. 'I'm sorry. If I'd been at home, she wouldn't have gone out. Maybe I could have stopped . . .'

'This isn't your fault, Mr Bishop,' Grace told him.

Jack gathered himself again, wiping his eyes. 'What will happen now?'

'We're still looking for forensics at the crime scene and we'll look at Sophie's clothing as soon as we can.'

She wasn't going to tell him that Sophie's left shoe was missing. It may have been dropped at the crime scene in the struggle and the search team might find it later. All the same, it had been bothering her. Was this the first souvenir or had they missed something on the other two victims? She didn't think so, but she would double-check.

'We need to gather as much information as we can about what happened to her through policing the scene meticulously,' she explained.

Jack looked away for a moment, wiping his face.

'If there's anything you can tell us, Jack?' she pressed gently. 'Something you were worried about that happened during the past few weeks . . .'

Jack shook his head. 'There's nothing I can recall at the moment.'

'Okay. I'll arrange for someone to be waiting when you get home until we can allocate a family liaison officer.' Grace wasn't sure if another FLO would be available, as they had already got two officers out working the role with Lauren and Diane. 'You'll no doubt be here for a while, but do you have any family, or a friend or neighbour who can sit with you for a while?'

'I've rung my sister.' Jack's face crumpled again. 'She lives in Carlisle, but she's coming down early in the morning.'

Before she left, Grace took refuge in the restroom for a few moments – three women attacked in less than a week . . .

A feeling of unease enveloped her but she pushed it away quickly. This was *not* going to happen again.

FIFTY

Grace travelled back to the Bennett Estate in silence. Stoke-on-Trent's streets at night were nothing like the bustling nightlife of Manchester. She might pass cars on the road, and see the odd person heading home for the night, but most people would probably be tucked up in their beds, if not safe in their homes. Of course there would be pockets erupting every night, but right now the area she was driving through had a sense of calm rather than caution.

Her mind tripped back to a weekend away with Matt soon after they had met in their early twenties. They'd stayed at a hotel in Leicester Square, gone out for a drink and got lost on the short journey back. It had been well after midnight, but it had been as packed as Hanley would be in the Potteries on a busy shopping Saturday. There had been people everywhere, and the noise!

London would have intimidated her if she had lived in Stoke all her life, but Manchester had its busy places, too. She made a mental note to book a night away for Simon and her. She could take him to some of her old drinking haunts, introduce him to some of her friends. It was about time.

Driving along Ford Green Road, she tried to digest everything that had happened. This one was going to play on her mind for a while, especially since Sophie was the second teenager to be attacked. That poor girl, her poor father . . .

She stopped at a crossing as the lights turned to red and a drunken man staggered across the road. He waved his thanks as he reached the other side.

Before she drove off, a thought came to her. Had the killer left Sophie for dead? Would they assume they'd succeeded? Could they play on that in any way? She pressed her foot down and pushed the car up the bank, knowing they could never contain anything like this. Not any more. Days of blackouts from the press were typically long gone now that most people had a smart phone.

But no one apart from hospital staff would know Sophie had survived. Surely it was worth thinking about?

When she got to the crime scene, Grace parked as close as she could to the walkway and went to find her team. The area was now full of emergency vehicles, floodlights and people everywhere as the investigation got under way.

It was almost midnight and too late to do much investigation work. If they had persons-of-interest to speak to they could go to their homes, but if it was a business or organisation they needed information from, that would have to wait until the morning.

Perry and Sam were at the head of the walkway as Grace dipped under the crime scene tape. Nick was in the background, talking to Dave Barnett.

'How is she?' Sam asked as she drew level with them.

'Critical at the moment.'

'Poor kid.'

'Anything I need to know?' she asked them.

'Nothing else since you left,' Perry replied. 'No one has come forward to say they saw Sophie or anything out of the ordinary. At the few house-to-house calls we were able to carry out, people were more shocked than anything.'

'Something bothering you, boss?' Sam asked after Grace had stood in silence for a moment watching the ever-increasing activity.

'Has anyone found her missing shoe?' she asked.

'Not as far as I'm aware.'

'It's just that I recalled a name in one of the forums on the All Talk website. There was a man, Peter Bentley, who murdered four women and attempted to murder a fifth in Manchester, back in 2014. Some of Operation Middleport is similar, I think. If I remember correctly, one of the victims' shoes was never found.'

'I remember that, too. The Manchester Monster?' Sam paused as she stifled a yawn. 'I thought he was still inside.'

'He got four life sentences.' Grace nodded. 'I'm wondering if our killer might be aware of the case. Because if so, we might have a copycat.'

'Christ.' Perry shoved his hands in the pockets of his jeans, his shoulders drooping.

'Why don't you two go home?' Grace said. 'It will be an early start again in the morning. I'm going to find Simon and head off too.'

'Okay,' Sam said.

Perry nodded.

But they all stayed where they were, surveying the scene in front of them. None of them wanted to move.

Still, at least for now this victim was alive.

Once she was at home, Grace made something to eat while Simon took a shower. Her mind kept going over and over the case, the images of Sophie Bishop morphing into Diane

233

Waybridge and then Lauren Ansell. Was something going on at Dunwood Academy? But what connection would that be to their second victim?

'Are you okay?' Simon asked as he joined her in the kitchen.

'Knackered,' she admitted, kissing him as she passed. 'Dying for a cuppa, although what I really want is sleep. How about you?'

'It's getting to me. I've known Sophie as long as I've known Lauren. I hope she'll be okay.'

Grace gave him a hug and they stood in silence for a moment.

'I suppose the only thing I can do is report what I know,' Simon said. 'At least I can add a further layer of emotion.'

He yawned and stretched his arms above his head, the T-shirt to his pyjamas riding up to reveal his torso. Grace wished she had the energy to run a hand over it and pull him towards her. Some loving was what she needed, to feel wanted, alive. Instead, she let him go upstairs alone.

She followed him less than fifteen minutes later. After a shower, she slipped into bed beside him. Grace felt his body close to hers as he spooned himself around her, pulling her closer. She gripped his hand and tried to sleep. Even feeling protected by him didn't stop the grief seeping in, the frustration that it had happened again.

'It's another day tomorrow, Grace,' he whispered. 'You'll catch the killer soon.'

Grace squeezed her eyes tight as images of Sophie Bishop came at her. 'We will,' she whispered back. 'Hopefully before anyone else is murdered.'

She was out of bed again two hours later, still unable to switch off. At the kitchen table, she booted up her laptop to google Peter Bentley. For the next thirty minutes, she went over everything she could find.

Bentley's first victim was thirty-three-year-old Melissa Wyatt, strangled while out running. Then seventeen-year-old Vicky Cooke in a nature reserve, fifteen-year-old Cassie Rigby in a field, and twenty-two-year-old Petra Swindles by the side of a clock tower. Lastly came nineteen-year-old Mandy Shelley, who was the only survivor, owing to Peter being disturbed by someone out running.

Five women attacked in the open, four strangled to death. All within the space of ten days. It was weird that the Manchester Monster had been brought up on All Talk, and that there was a link to both Diane Waybridge and Nathan Stiller through the website.

Grace closed her laptop and went back to bed, hoping to catch a little sleep. She needed to update the team with her findings as soon as possible. There was something in this, she was sure.

More worryingly, if she was right it meant there was going to be another victim if they didn't find their killer – or killers – soon.

FIFTY-ONE

Monday

Grace arrived at work at seven a.m. and logged straight into her computer. As soon as Perry and Sam had arrived, she made them all coffee and asked them to gather round her desk.

'Something was bothering me from the research I was doing yesterday.' Grace turned the screen on her computer so that they could see what she had brought up online.

'This was the case I was talking about last night,' she explained. 'I didn't work it as a detective, but it happened when I was based in Salford. In 2014 Peter Bentley, thirty-seven, murdered four young women by strangulation over the period of ten days. Each woman was similar in looks to the three victims we have now: blonde, long hair, pretty. Each had been strangled, with no sexual assault. The first woman was killed in a field out on a run by herself, the second we found in a nature reserve and the third was in a field by the side of a walkway, with a shoe missing. The fourth victim was found by a clock tower.'

'How was Bentley caught?' asked Sam.

'Pure policing. Dotting the i's and crossing the t's, the usual legwork like we're doing now.'

'You mentioned he attacked a fifth woman?' Perry questioned.

'Yes, nineteen-year-old Mandy Shelley survived. And all three crime scenes are similar to ours as well. But I noticed something else last night. There's a pattern of days, too,' Grace continued. 'Two days after the first one was killed, the second one was murdered. Three days after the second one, the third was killed. Which means if it is a copycat killer, we have until this Thursday, the fourth day after Sophie Bishop's attempted murder.'

'Omigod!' Sam's hand covered her mouth.

'Hard to take in, isn't it?' Grace grimaced. 'But there may well be another murder once our killer finds out that Sophie's alive. It would have been great if we could have kept it under wraps but it's almost impossible nowadays with social media, and time is of the essence now. So instead it's essential we work with the press to keep the city on alert. And we need to be figuring out where the next crime scene is likely to be. Let's take a look at clock towers around the city.'

'I can do that for you,' Frankie offered as he joined them.

'Great. Just a list will do for now. Thanks.' Grace smiled momentarily and then leaned forwards, resting her chin on her hand. 'Peter Bentley is still in prison and isn't due out for parole until serving at least twenty years.'

'So if this *is* linked to him, who's helping him out?' Perry questioned.

'Or is this purely a copycat, with no actual links to him at all?' Grace responded.

FIFTY-TWO

At the team briefing, Nick had asked Grace to update everyone about her findings from the day before. She quickly ran through everything, her thoughts and conclusions.

Nick turned to the whiteboard. 'If we do have a copycat killer, what are the reasonings behind it? Who could be our prime suspect?' Nick opened it up to the floor.

'Nathan Stiller has to be in the running, as he's known to all three victims,' Grace said. 'We need to take into consideration his connection to Diane Waybridge, who is not to our knowledge linked to Dunwood Academy in any way. I'll question him further as a priority.'

'Do we need to be looking at anyone else who all the pupils might know? Someone who comes to the school on a regular basis?' Perry asked. 'I know we've checked out CRB references, alibis and staff complaints, et cetera, but could it be a visitor?'

'Or do we need to be looking at the pupils in the school?' suggested Frankie.

'We've already checked out the kids' records,' Nick told him. 'Most of the troublemakers have left and the odd few still there are doing much better.'

'Maybe that's because of the work Stiller has been doing,' Grace said. 'He seems to have turned the school around. I haven't genuinely heard a bad word about him yet.'

'The main thing is that Sophie Bishop's alive for now, which may have wrong-footed our killer stroke killers, if they're aware of it,' Nick continued. 'CCTV from the Co-op on Roberts Road shows Sophie going into the walkway at 20.25. Our suspect made off on foot to where? Anyone?'

'It's not clear yet, but more camera footage is being hunted out and is our top priority this morning,' Sam said. 'We'll also be asking for witnesses to come forward. Someone could have caught something, or remember someone running quickly past them at that time.'

'What do we know about Sophie?' Nick asked.

'She's in the same year as Lauren Ansell,' Sam went on. 'Apparently they were friends and spent a lot of time together in a group of five girls. So that's two of them attacked – we'd be looking at three murdered if our attacker had been more thorough.'

'She was one of Simon's daughter's friends,' Grace added. 'For anyone who wasn't there last night, Sophie was on the phone to Teagan when it happened. She rang me in a panic and I found Sophie.' Grace took a moment, trying not to bring up the image of the girl lying next to her as she'd tripped over her lifeless body. 'And that's why seeing Bentley's name in the chatroom came to me. It was the missing shoe that reminded me, because Bentley's third victim only had one when she was found too. We're going to warn the other girls in the group as soon as we can without scaremongering.'

Nick nodded his support. 'I can't tell you all how imperative it is that we're either seen to be pursuing someone or at least get the name of a lead. This is three women now and heads will roll soon – my own firstly – if we don't. I know you're all doing your best, so while we wait for forensics and CCTV to come through to us, let's get cracking on what we need to do for today.' He ran a hand across his chin before addressing them all. 'DCI Brindley's preparing a press conference in about an hour to let everyone know what went on last night, so we need some cover on the phones for that, too. Grace, can you look into paying Peter Bentley a visit?'

'I'm on it.' Grace spoke with authority.

The meeting broke up and they went back to their desks. But before she had the chance to sit down, Nick called across the office. 'Grace, can I have a quick word?'

Grace spoke under her breath before she went in to see him. She knocked and entered.

'Close the door behind you,' he said, sitting at his desk.

Grace's shoulders drooped. Why did those words always put fear into her? It was as if she was fifteen years old again and getting a telling-off, not that it happened often, as she was a swot at school.

She did as she was told and then sat down opposite him when he gestured for her to do so.

'You know when we spoke about Lauren Ansell and the fact that you knew, well, had been associated with her?'

'Yes.' She wondered where he was going.

'Well, now we have two girls as part of Operation Middleport that can be linked to Dunwood Academy, and Teagan Cole's friends with both of them, it means that Simon knows both of them too.'

Grace's mouth gaped. 'Meaning?'

'Meaning exactly what I say.'

'I don't understand,' she lied. Really, she knew exactly what he was implying – was someone out to get at Simon? – but wanted to hear him say it.

'I think you should dig a bit deeper and see what he can

find out. As the *Stoke News* are reporting it, he'll be close to the families. See what he's saying about them and—'

'You want me to be your mole again?' Her voice had risen an octave with incredulity.

'No!' He laughed nervously. 'Well, not as such. I don't suspect Simon of doing anything—'

'Well, that's good to know!' She folded her arms.

'I just want to know what the papers are saying before they report it, if you know what I mean.'

'Yes, sir. I do know what you mean. But can I ask you something first? What did you do to get inside info from the *Stoke News* before I came to work here?'

Nick frowned. 'I don't follow.'

'Which other member of staff got close enough to Simon to gather the information you require?'

'No one did.'

'So how did you work with the paper before I came here?'

He paused, her words sinking in.

'I don't think it's fair of you to use me for this. If you need information, either ask Simon or his boss – but don't you think I'd be doing that anyway? Simon and I have a good relationship because we work together on things like this, rather than work against each other.'

'Point taken.' Nick nodded. 'Still, see what you can find out for me, will you?'

Grace left the room, wanting to slam the door but equally knowing it would be childish to do so. She got back to her desk and sat red-faced as her team looked at her expectantly. She wasn't going to enlighten them as to her conversation. Instead she sat forwards, her back straight.

'Can you check in with uniform doing the house-to-house, Perry?' she asked. 'Liaise with their line manager and let me know if you find anything significant while I'm out?'

'Will do.' Perry nodded.

'Sam, can you carry out further research on Bentley, see if you can find anything else in the chat forums?'

'All over it, Sarge.'

'Thanks.'

Grace rubbed at her aching neck before moving to hide behind her monitor. She was so fortunate to have a good team behind her. They practically ran themselves.

And at least she felt she could trust them more than her DI. She wished Nick would think that about *her*, too. He didn't need to ask her to keep an eye on Simon. She was already on to it.

FIFTY-THREE

Through the police prison liaison officer, Grace found out that Bentley was out on a hospital appointment, so she arranged to see him at eleven o'clock the following day. Next, she made a mental note of people she wanted to speak to that morning while she was out, starting with Jack Bishop, who had left a message asking her to call to see him. He and Sophie lived on Milehouse Road, a few minutes' walk from Dunwood Academy.

Driving along Hanley Road to get to the Bishops' home took her past Central Park. It had been four days since the murder of Diane Waybridge and although the police presence was less now, the crime scene tape could be seen flapping in the distance. There were two mobile units there, officers busy canvassing the streets and visitors now that the park had been cleared for access to the general public.

It always saddened Grace to see things getting back to normal after such heinous crimes, especially when they had yet to bring someone to justice. And now she had another female on her conscience.

Once she'd found the house she was after, she walked up the path of a council-owned property, noting the tidiness, the trim hedges, and the rows of daffodils and tulips. Bunches of fresh flowers were appearing on the wall in front of the house. She wondered if this was appropriate considering there were two dead women and now the news had broken that Sophie had survived, but she knew it would be people paying their respects. Even so, she would have a word with Jack to see if he wanted them removed or not. Sophie was the only victim still alive, albeit in a coma.

After asking how Sophie was and hearing there was no change, Jack handed her a small book.

'Her diary,' he said. 'I haven't looked inside. Couldn't bring myself to do it. It didn't feel right.'

Grace found this endearing. Even though it might tell them what had been going on, Jack still felt like he was betraying his daughter's trust by going through her private things. She opened it.

'I'll put the kettle on while you look through it,' he added.

Grace sat down while he busied himself in the kitchen. Flicking through the pages, she could see a few entries over the past few weeks and the letter J referred to instead of a name, someone Sophie seemed to be infatuated by. She remembered Teagan mentioning the name Joel Nicholls last night but hadn't thought it appropriate to ask about it at the hospital.

The entry was blank for yesterday. Grace sadly realised Sophie might never fill it in now. She took out an evidence bag and popped the book inside.

'Anything?' Jack came in with coffee and sat down in the armchair across from her.

'Sophie refers to someone using the initial J. Do you know who this might be?'

A shadow crossed his face. 'Joel Nicholls. She started seeing him a few weeks ago now. I told her she had to stop.'

'Why was that?'

244

'I don't like the family he comes from, but I can't tell her what to do any more. Well, I can, but I can't always check up on her. She's sixteen, strong-willed. So much of her mother in her.' He pointed at a framed photo. 'Stephanie was taken from us three years ago – cancer.'

'Sorry to hear that, Jack.' She gave him an empathetic look. 'I lost my husband round about the same time through leukaemia.'

'Oh. Then you know what I've been going through.'

'I do.'

'And why Sophie is so precious to me.'

'Yes.' She smiled. 'But tell me, are there any other reasons you don't like Joel? Have you met him?'

'Only the once. He's not welcome at my house. He's a bad influence. Their father's in prison. I didn't want Sophie hanging around with him.'

'Do you know the last time she met him?'

Jack shook his head. 'Not for some time, not out of school at least. They only saw each other a few times before I put a stop to it. Then again, teenagers usually do completely the opposite to what their parents tell them. But I'd like to think I could trust her to stay away.'

There was a knock on the front door.

'That will be my sister,' he said.

As they were being introduced, Grace noticed immediately that the woman was an older version of Sophie, her blonde hair cut in a short bob, the same eyes and full lips.

'Oh Jack, I still can't believe it,' she sobbed, rushing into his arms as he broke down at the sight of her. 'Why our beautiful Sophie? Why?'

Grace stayed for a few minutes to answer what questions she could and then stood up.

'We'll keep in touch throughout this investigation as and

when we have anything to tell you,' she said to Jack as they got to the front door. 'If we can't get a family liaison officer, I will keep you informed. I'm afraid the press might become a little intrusive once more things get out as well. Our latest press release has just been issued.'

Outside in the fresh air, Grace walked to the car, relishing the silence. Dark clouds were moving in: she hoped it didn't rain on their crime scene. As well as making the day even more miserable for the Bishop family, it could wash away vital evidence.

Next stop was Dunwood Academy. But Grace couldn't get Nick's words from her mind. Annoyed by what he had asked her to do, she'd begun to wonder if Simon might be getting pressure from his boss, Phil, to show the police in a bad light.

Maybe it was time to double bluff both of them and start working together more thoroughly. She too could play games.

FIFTY-FOUR

At Dunwood Academy, Grace spoke to Nathan Stiller first. He'd just heard the news about Sophie Bishop.

'I can't believe this is happening,' he said, shaking his head in angst. 'Have you any idea what it means?'

'No, but I need to ask you a few more questions.'

Nathan's features darkened as Grace cautioned him.

'Where were you last night during the hours of eight p.m. and midnight?' she asked.

'Not this again. I was at home with Toni. We're in the middle of a garden makeover, so we were humping around slabs and soil until it was dark. I guess we'd have been cleaning ourselves up by then. I ordered a takeaway, too – Indian from the local. You can check all that, if you like.'

'I will.' Grace nodded, trying not to think that everything led back to him.

Even with an alibi, he could be an accomplice passing on information for their killer; they knew they were looking for a pair. Lauren Ansell and Sophie Bishop were pupils at his school, and he knew Diane Waybridge through All Talk.

Nathan paused. 'You have no evidence because there's none

to *find*! This isn't me being cocky, this is me being honest. I don't have anything to do with your case, Sergeant.'

Grace held his stare until he looked away. She wasn't put off that easily. She'd heard every lie and seen every deception to lead her away from the truth in her time. People fibbed to get themselves out of trouble. Inevitably, though, it landed them deeper in it.

'We also need to speak to one of your pupils, Joel Nicholls. Can you see if he's in school, please? And if so, find us a quiet spot to talk to him, now that the mobile unit has gone.'

'Of course.'

'I'll need you to stay while I'm with him too.' Grace knew this wasn't ethical as she was suspicious of him but she wanted to see if he said anything to Joel that could set him up in some way, lead her to doubt the young boy.

Nathan nodded. 'I'll find out for you. I won't be long.'

Grace took a moment to look around his office again while she waited. Stiller's desk was tidy, with a notepad open at a blank page next to his phone, and a framed photo of Toni and him to its side. She picked it up for a closer look. There seemed to be a lot of emotion behind their smiles; they were clearly happy to have been together when the photo was taken. Although that hadn't stopped him from messaging Diane Waybridge. She wondered if Toni knew Nathan was a member of All Talk. For all Grace knew, Toni herself was a member under a name they hadn't found yet. Grace made a note to check with Sam.

The door opened in the adjoining office. Grace moved back to her seat before the headmaster came through into his own.

'This is Joel Nicholls, Detective,' Nathan introduced. 'Sit down at the table, Joel, please.'

Grace could tell how any young girl might like his attention now she could see him close to. His hair was jet black and fairly long in a sexy bad-boy way, his eyes the proverbial smouldering, with clear skin and a strong nose.

She smiled as they sat at the table, hoping to put him at ease and wondering if he remembered her from the school assembly or the youth club.

'Joel, have you heard what's happened to Sophie Bishop?' she asked, realising he was probably in his first lessons as the news broke. 'She was attacked last night.'

'The girl everyone's talking about on the news?' Joel's hands flopped onto the table. 'No, it can't be Soph. Is she – is she dead? Those other women are. Is she?'

'She's in hospital in a critical condition.'

'What . . . what do you mean?'

'That's all I can say right now.' Grace gave him a moment before continuing. 'I'd like to ask you a few questions. You thought a lot of her, didn't you?'

He nodded.

'Have you been dating?'

'I went out with her a few times last month. But I haven't seen her much since then.' Joel shifted in his chair.

'Why?'

'Her old man stopped me seeing her.'

'Do you know why?'

'No. Bet it was to do with my dad being in prison.'

'Can you tell me the last time you saw Sophie?'

'The day after Lauren was killed. There was a bunch of us at Teagan Cole's house. We met there because we had no school.'

Grace chose her words carefully. 'Joel, it seems Sophie was meeting someone last night and I wanted to know if it was you.'

'It wasn't me.'

'So you were at home?'

He nodded.

249

'Were any of your family home, too?'

'My sister, Chantelle. She was asleep for most of the evening. My nephew, baby Billy, has been keeping us all up.'

Grace wrote the details down in her notepad before continuing.

'Do you know where Sophie would have been going last night, if she wasn't seeing you?' she asked.

'Not unless she was seeing someone else.'

'Do you think she was doing that?'

'I don't know.' He shrugged. 'But I don't think so. She's isn't a slag.'

'Tell me about Sophie,' she encouraged.

'She's fun to be around. I call her classy sassy. She always makes me laugh.'

'Where did you go when you dated?'

'Not far. We hung around by the shops on the Bennett Estate mostly, with everyone else.'

'Everyone else?'

'Me and my mates. Soph and hers.' He ran his hands over his face. 'Is she going to be okay?'

'She's in the best place,' Grace said, closing her notepad. 'I think I have what I want for now. Thank you.'

Once Joel had left the room with Nathan, Grace sat for a moment thinking about the morning. Sophie Bishop's diary referred to someone whose name began with the letter J. If she was referring to Joel in short, it seemed from what Sophie had written that she was very much still seeing him.

So either Joel was lying for some reason about when he had last seen Sophie, or Sophie was writing about someone else.

Which brought Grace back to a teacher.

FIFTY-FIVE

Grace went to find Jason Tranter. As it was midday, he was just finishing off a lesson.

'I need a word,' she said as she stood in the corridor, children streaming out around her.

She knew it wasn't ideal to keep speaking to everyone at the school, but while she was still there, she decided to take the opportunity and find somewhere quiet.

Jason beckoned her into the now empty classroom and closed the door behind them. As soon as he turned to her, she could see his look of uncertainty.

'I would usually do this kind of thing down at the station, but as I don't have time . . .' Grace cautioned him before she continued. 'I need to know where you were last night during the hours of eight p.m. and midnight.'

'You're joking, right?'

'You must have heard there was another attack. It—'

'Yes, on the news this morning. But there was no mention of a name.'

'It was Sophie Bishop. Details are being circulated at the moment.'

'Shit, is she okay?' Jason put a hand out to steady himself on the desk before sitting.

'She's critical at the moment.'

Silence encased the room while he gathered himself and then his demeanour changed.

'Are you suggesting I had something to do with it?' His eyes narrowed.

'New evidence has come to light.' Grace told him about the letter J referred to in Sophie's diary. 'The J could stand for Joel Nicholls, who she was rumoured to have been dating last month. It could stand for someone we don't know, or . . .'

'It could stand for my name,' Jason broke in. 'I can tell you that it doesn't.'

'I'm not saying it is you.' She held up a hand as he was about to protest further. 'But things might get unpleasant for you, as another pupil from the school you work at has been attacked.'

'That doesn't mean I had anything to do with what's been happening!'

'Yet you were the first to agree she had a crush on you.'

'Well, yes, but I told you I didn't do anything about it!'

'Who gave you that shiner?' Grace glanced at Jason's eye, green-and-yellow bruising still visible underneath. She couldn't understand why he wouldn't tell them.

Jason shook his head. 'I told you. I didn't see who it was.'

'May I remind you, you're under caution.'

Still he wouldn't look at her.

Grace tried not to let her impatience show. 'There's a lot of ill-feeling on the Bennett Estate since Lauren Ansell was murdered. It died down a little when our second victim wasn't related to the school, but now we're right back where we started because of Sophie Bishop. I don't want things to get unpleasant.'

Jason nodded. 'I can't believe this is happening to me. But those poor women.'

'So to clarify, where were you last night between the times I mentioned?'

'I was at home, alone.' He moaned. 'Which doesn't help me at all, does it?'

'Did anyone see you who can vouch for you? A neighbour? Were you out in your garden?'

'No, I was marking some work. My only friend was Jack Daniel's. Only the one, mind.'

Grace paused to put her thoughts into order.

'This is precautionary, but I think maybe you'd be better going home today, rather than being here.'

'I don't think so. That will make me look guilty and I haven't done anything!' Jason proclaimed. 'What about *my* best interests?'

'I'm just warning you that things might very well get nasty again. People will want to blame someone, anyone.'

'Because you haven't caught the right person!'

Grace glared at him. So far, there wasn't any evidence to connect him to the crimes. They had nothing to arrest him for, or even question him further about. But he wouldn't tell them who attacked him for some reason. He was lying to the police about that, what's to say he wasn't lying about something bigger? Right now, she could very well be looking at the murderer. And right now, she was pissed off as to why he wasn't playing ball.

'Who attacked you, Jason? We need to know. Now.'

Jason sighed. 'One of the dads had a go at me. Said he'd heard I'd been over friendly with the girls at the youth club. Called me a paedo and thumped me. That's the reason I didn't want to tell anyone. It would have pointed a finger at me and I didn't have anything to do with it.'

'Who was the parent?' Grace asked.

'Patrick Danson. His daughter, Andrea, is in Year 11. She comes to the youth club every Thursday. Andrea was another friend of Lauren's. I guess he put two and two together and made five. He told me to stay away from Andrea. I tried to explain that I would never do anything but he lashed out at me.'

'And you didn't want to press charges?'

'No.' Jason glanced at her, his cheeks coloured slightly with embarrassment. 'I'm really sorry, but I can't help you with your enquiry. I wish I could.'

Grace took out her notepad and wrote down the details.

'We might need you to come to the station for further questioning at a later date.'

'Fine by me. I have nothing to hide.'

Grace stayed straight-faced. Although not entirely convinced, she very much hoped that would be the case. Because an awful thought had crossed her mind.

Could Spiller and Tranter be in this together?

FIFTY-SIX

She switched on the TV and sat down to watch the news. The Stoke Strangler had stuck and she wasn't sure if she liked it or not. The name had been all over the headlines in the papers, too. It sensationalised the women's murders. But then again, wasn't that what everyone did anyway? It was always someone else's news to pass on after the story had broken.

She wondered if the police had come up with the moniker or if it had been the press, then decided she didn't care enough to think about it. Instead, she watched the detectives who were working the case. A tall male seemed to be the one in charge, a woman with long dark hair by his side. There were two other men, one with short blond hair, one auburn, and a female with long blonde hair. It was the last woman she was watching. Was she nervous? After all, she fitted the profile for the killer's preferred victims.

'Watching the detectives,' she sang the line from an old song and sniggered.

Minutes later, she threw down the remote and picked up her phone. There were no new messages, so she wouldn't be seeing him this evening by the looks of things. Maybe she should go online and see who was on All Talk. If she couldn't do anything with him, she could at least talk about it.

Talking was all she could do when he wasn't around. But, still, it whiled away the hours until their next interlude. Now that she was really looking forward to.

FIFTY-SEVEN

Tuesday

Yesterday afternoon had been another one going through evidence and forensics. With her team looking after the Stoke end of things, Grace was on her way to visit her old colleagues in Salford before she visited Peter Bentley in prison. She'd asked Frankie to accompany her. As well as an extra pair of hands, he'd be good company along the way. Being twenty-five and single, he always had an episode or two of a disastrous date to entertain her with. And he was an avid viewer of streamed TV sets, so kept her informed of the latest shows she should be watching if she ever got time.

'Do you miss working in Manchester, Grace?' Frankie asked as she was driving along the M6.

'Yes and no,' Grace admitted. 'I miss some of my work colleagues, but not all of them. I miss having the banter with a few people on the streets that I saw on a regular basis. I miss –' she glanced at him with a cheeky smile '– I think that's it, really.'

'So you don't regret coming back to Stoke?'

Grace had always had her doubts about returning, but felt

she had settled in and was here to stay. It had been tough to fit in at first, but now she had friends around her, and colleagues she could trust. She didn't say any of this to Frankie, though.

'Not at all,' she replied as she negotiated a lane change.

'Even with the Steele connection?'

'It is what it is, I'm afraid.'

There was a pause from Frankie. 'I'm glad you're here. I think you fit in well.'

Grace beamed. 'I'm glad, too.'

At the station in Salford, they signed in and were shown through by a duty sergeant Grace didn't recognise. But as soon as she walked along the corridor, she was greeted by shouts from everywhere. By the time she got to her old office, everyone was on alert and looking up at the door, and she felt as if she had never been away.

'It's Amazing Grace!' A man with a bald head and a three-inch grey beard walked over to them and enveloped her in a bear hug. 'Those Stokies are looking after you, I hope?'

'They are, Gus.' Grace smiled and turned to her colleague. 'This is PC Higgins. Frankie.'

'Ooh, get you, the big sarge.' A woman came towards them with two mugs of steaming coffee. She grinned at Frankie. 'I hope she's not too much of a slave driver. Even when she wasn't our boss, she used to rule us all with an iron rod.'

'I did not!' Grace cried.

'That's because you needed a rod up your arse to get some work done, Sandy,' Gus said.

The woman raised her eyebrows in jest.

'Sandy's the one who kept me sane while all around us went to pot,' Grace told Frankie.

'So what brings you here?' Gus asked.

'We've come for some info on Peter Bentley,' Grace explained.

'Oh, the Manchester Monster. He was a vicious bastard.'
Sandy wrinkled up her nose in disgust.

'Did you work the case?'

'Yes. He's a vile human being. He was homeless at the time
and always on some sort of come-down from whatever drug
he could get his hands on. When we arrested him, he gave as
many of us as he could a black eye, myself included – lashed
about before we could cuff him.'

'We used a taser on him as a last resort,' Gus said. 'Very
satisfying, to say the least.'

'I was in uniform then,' Sandy added. 'I was involved in the
case, brought into the Major Crimes Team. I helped with house-
to-house enquiries, being the eyes and ears of the communities.
At one time, there was even talk of me going undercover in a
blonde wig.' Sandy's eyes widened. 'It terrified me but I would
have done it. I had the backing of the team, and if it caught a
killer, then it would have been a job well done. My boyfriend
at the time hadn't been too enamoured when I told him, though.
I remember it causing an almighty row.'

'Wow, good on you!' Grace was impressed with her friend.
She wouldn't have liked to have done that.

'Cheers! Solving the murder as part of a large team gave me
a fire in my belly to get a promotion to detective. So anything
you want to know, I'm your woman.'

After ten minutes with her old team, Grace knew a lot more
about Operation Harriet. It was good to go over it, especially
with Frankie being there, as it brought him up to speed at the
same time. But really Grace wanted to look at things in more
detail.

Finally, they made their way downstairs to the basement,
where a PC let them in to the evidence locker after they had
signed in.

'This is what I wanted to look through,' Grace said as she

snapped on latex gloves and picked up sealed exhibit bag MP10S/14. She signed the time it was taken out and then cut the bag open. 'This is a notebook found amongst Bentley's possessions where he was sleeping rough. I was wondering if it might give us something to focus on, in case we do have a copycat on our hands. There might be a clue in here about our killer.'

'You think whoever is doing this knows Bentley?' Frankie asked.

'It's hard to say. There's a lot online about the killings. Even if they don't get everything down to the right details, the dates of the kills are there.' Grace looked at him. 'But we have to start somewhere. If it *is* a copycat, there will be something happening this Thursday, which gives us two days.'

FIFTY-EIGHT

Still in Salford, Grace and Frankie were in a free interview room. Frustration seeped out of Grace as she popped the CD into the machine. There had been nothing of interest found in the notebook, so she'd resealed it and signed the time it was put back again.

Mandy Shelley was Bentley's last victim, the only woman to survive his attack. Grace checked over the notes. Mandy's last known address was in a tower block in the north of Salford. Grace knew the area from her days in uniform. It was run down but had a good community spirit. If she remembered rightly, more people were willing to help a neighbour out rather than turn a blind eye when they were in trouble.

'Ready?' she asked Frankie. At his nod, she pressed play:

Interview with Amanda Shelley conducted at Salford Police Station on 12 April 2014.

Attending officers: DS Gus Banks and PC Sandy Princeton.

GB: *Mandy, I know this is hard for you to talk about, but as you know, it would be extremely helpful if you're able to tell us what happened to you.*

MS: I was coming home from work. It was still light, about half past seven in the evening, and I was walking through the park. [A sniff.] You think you're safe walking through a public place. I'd done it so often that I realised afterwards my routine had given him the timing to attack me. Stupid woman.

GB: I don't think that's the case. None of it was your fault, Mandy.

MS: But I keep thinking, if only I'd gone home another way. If only I'd taken the lift that had been offered to me by a work colleague. Anyway, I was walking along, watching some boys in the distance playing football. All of a sudden, an arm came around my neck. [A pause.] I was pulled off my feet and dragged into some nearby bushes. He . . . he pushed me to the ground as I screamed. And then he punched me, told me to be quiet or else he would hit me again. I've never been one to obey orders, so I screamed, louder this time. I got another punch for it, but I wasn't going to go down without a fight. But his hands went around my throat and before I knew it, I could hardly breathe.

GB: Take your time, Mandy. I know it's hard.

MS: I'll be fine.

GB: Thank you.

MS: I would have been number five if it weren't for that runner. He rushed behind the hedges to have a pee and found this man with his hands around my neck. The runner panicked him and he ran.

GB: And you remember what he looked like?

MS: Not really. It all happened so fast, and he was wearing a balaclava. But he seemed thin, and dirty. He smelt of unwashed clothes.

GB: Thank you, Mandy. It takes courage to talk about it so

soon afterwards, but it will really help us to bring him to justice.

MS: *I'm not brave. If it weren't for him being disturbed, I don't know . . . well, I wouldn't be here today, would I? I did what I did to survive.*

Grace retrieved the CD, switched off the machine and bagged up the evidence clearly again.

'I don't think there's any point in going to see her after hearing that. It would be unfair to bring everything up again.'

'You're sure she won't be in danger now?' Frankie queried.

'She'll worry about that, I guess.' Grace paused. 'It might be better to send someone round to see that she's extra vigilant for a while. You're right, Frankie, good thinking. She was a victim who got away. She could easily be a target for a copycat killer. I'll ask Sandy to pop in, just to be sure.'

Back in her car half an hour later, Grace checked her emails to find one with a subject header grabbing her immediate attention. It was from the police prison liaison officer at HM Wakefield Prison. She clicked on it, looked down the list and frowned.

'What's up?' Frankie caught her expression.

'Weird. I asked for a list of addresses for anyone visiting Peter Bentley. There are three names, all women: one of them is here in Manchester, one in Stafford, but there's another one in Stoke-on-Trent.' She glanced at her watch. 'We don't have time to visit now. Let's go and see what Bentley has to say for himself first, and then circle back.'

FIFTY-NINE

Grace could never understand the fascination of the serial killer to some women. Only last year, a woman from the city had married a man who was set never to come out of prison in his lifetime. Grace had read that she didn't believe he was an animal. Maybe she'd feel different if he had a release date of a few years. Would she feel safe then? Would she believe he hadn't committed these crimes, when he was in her home?

Perhaps it held a bit of notoriety for the women, being married to murderers. There were so many people fascinated by them. It was all very creepy.

Inside the prison, Grace and Frankie went through the procedure of getting booked in. They showed their warrant cards, were scanned and checked at the gate, and their phones removed from their possession. Then they were shown through to a side room, both sitting down at the small table on the same side.

'I've never been in a prison before,' Frankie said as he sat with his hands clasped together in front of him.

'It's quite intimidating the first few times,' Grace offered. 'You'll get used to it. As long as you stay on the right side.'

Frankie grinned at her.

A few minutes later, a man was brought in to see them. With his prison-pale complexion, dark hair flecked with grey at its roots and thinning dramatically at the top of his head, and shifty eyes, she couldn't understand how anyone would find him attractive now.

Dull, that's what she'd call him, especially in his prison uniform of navy sweatshirt and trousers.

Peter Bentley, the man her colleagues had put behind bars five years ago, sat down opposite them. Because of him, four women had had their lives cut short and one had been scarred for the rest of hers.

'Hey, babe, it's nice to meet you.' Peter sat back in his chair with a grin.

'It's DS Allendale to you.'

'Whatever. You're very pleasing to the eye.'

'Well, you still look like the weasel you are,' she replied.

His laugh made her blood boil and she frowned at him. There were no signs he was nervous: no wringing of the hands, no jigging knees, no restless eyes. Which gave her the distinct feeling that he knew what she was here for.

'Who's the monkey?' Bentley turned to Frankie.

Grace ignored him, thankful for the silence that came from her officer. Frankie was clever enough not to retaliate.

'I want to talk to you about a case I'm working on,' she continued.

'They're calling him the Stoke Strangler, I see.'

As Bentley leered at her, waiting for her to speak again, Grace thought back to the press calling him the Manchester Monster. She hadn't liked it, but whatever big case it was that was going on, the journalists loved to make up these names. To her, it gave suspects power, which often led them to kill again before they were caught. It was stupid and irresponsible, and even though she may have overreacted at the time, she still couldn't believe Simon had used it.

'So he's following in my footsteps, is he?' Bentley said.

'He?'

'Well, that's obvious if you think you have a copycat killer.'

'Not necessarily,' she snapped. 'Did he know the killer was male? Or was it a guess?

'If you're here, you must think he's male,' Bentley added as if reading her mind. 'It's quite an honour to be copied.'

Grace swallowed her disgust. 'As you're aware from the media, we have two murdered females and the attempted murder of a further female.'

'Is the third one still alive?' he asked.

Grace didn't answer his question.

'The similarities are enough to warrant us coming to see you,' she continued.

'Why both of you? And what do you expect me to do in here?'

'I know very well how easy it is to manipulate someone on the outside.'

'I haven't had any strange men visiting me,' he declared. 'Only beautiful women, pretty like yourself.'

'Cut the crap, Bentley. I want to know of anyone likely to copy you.'

'I have a few fans.'

She scowled at his choice of words. They sat in silence, Grace hoping he would elaborate. But when he didn't, she realised with an uncomfortable feeling that she shouldn't have come to see him. If he was coercing someone to do the killings for him, it gave him the upper hand. Worse, if someone was going to finish off what Bentley had started by going after his surviving victim, they might have forewarned whoever it was.

She leaned forwards, wanting to look him in the eye and say one final thing to him.

'You touch Mandy Shelley and I'll rip off your balls with my teeth and shove them down your throat until you can no longer breathe.'

Bentley lounged in his chair. Then he sat forwards so quickly that he made them both jump.

'No one's going to touch her.'

'And you know that for certain, do you?'

'She's damaged property.'

'To you, maybe.'

'And besides, isn't this killer having far too much fun in Stoke?'

Grace stood up to leave, Frankie too.

'Best leave the detective work to us, Peter,' she replied. 'It might escape your notice, but you're not in a position to do anything about it in here, anyway.'

'So one minute you accuse me of setting up someone to do these crimes and the next you say I don't have the ability?' He shook his head slowly. 'You disappoint me.'

'I disappoint myself at times,' she muttered, turning to leave once more. She'd practically put Mandy Shelley's life in danger with her threats.

But he'd clearly heard her.

'Bye-bye, Detective.' He sneered at her. 'And remember, the clock *is* ticking.'

SIXTY

It took Grace an hour to get back to the first of the addresses
she had been given in relation to Peter Bentley's visitors from
the police prison liaison officer. By this time it was mid-
afternoon. The house she parked outside of was a middle
townhouse with large bow windows upstairs and downstairs.
It was in an area of Manchester that she'd visited often and
always felt safe in.

Grace knocked and a man in his early thirties opened it. He
was carrying the tiniest of babies dressed in blue clothing,
resting on his chest. Grace groaned inwardly before holding up
her warrant card. She might be about to break up a happy
home.

'Mr Barber?' she asked.

'Yes.'

Grace introduced herself and Frankie.

'Is Mrs Barber home?'

'My wife?' He looked confused. 'Yes, but—'

'Who is it, Martin?'

A woman came into view and when Grace held up her
warrant card again, it was as if she shrunk into herself.

'Could we have a word with you, Mrs Barber?' Grace stepped inside as the door was held open for them.

'What's this about?' Martin asked as they moved through into a large living area.

The room had pale walls and whitewash floorboards. A striking orange rug was in the back area, a pine table seating six standing on top of it. On the wall in front of it Grace saw two large portraits, which she assumed were of the newborn.

'Do you want to settle Isaac down upstairs while I sort this?' Denise said to Martin.

Wishful thinking on her part, thought Grace. It was obvious the woman knew why they were here.

'What's this about, first?' Martin asked as the baby wriggled around in his arms. He held him closer to his chest.

'It will be something to do with work.' Denise wafted a hand in the air. 'I'm sure it won't take long.'

Martin stood his ground. 'I'd prefer to listen, especially if you're in danger.' He looked at Grace. 'She's a probation officer. She had a real idiot stalking her for a while a few years ago. Until he got locked up again.'

As she glanced surreptitiously at Frankie, Grace couldn't believe what she was hearing. Denise Barber was in gross negligence for what she'd been doing. She shouldn't be visiting someone she used to work with while he was in prison. She was supposed to look after her client's welfare, not take advantage of it.

'It won't take a moment.' Denise was insistent.

But Martin was, too. 'I'll wait, then.'

As they decided between them, Grace got out her notepad and pointed to the table.

'Shall we sit and get this over with?'

'What do you mean?' Martin looked on. 'Can someone tell me what's happened?'

Grace waited until they were all seated, sitting purposely across from Mrs Barber. Martin was glaring at Denise, who kept her eyes from his.

'Mrs Barber, we're investigating a series of murders in Stoke-on-Trent. I'm sure you will have heard about them. The case is quite newsworthy right now. As there were a few similarities with these and some of the murders carried out by serial killer Peter Bentley, we visited him in prison before coming to speak to you.'

Tears began to spill from Denise's eyes and she wiped at them frantically.

'It's come to our attention that you've been visiting Bentley once a month in prison for the past two years. Now, I'm fairly certain it's not job-related, so can you tell us your reasons for this?'

'I . . . what the fuck is going on?' Martin held on to the baby's head as he turned sharply to his wife. 'Denise?'

'I . . . it started a while ago. I wanted to do some research about serial killers for a book I was thinking of writing and I . . . I decided to visit Peter in prison.'

'Peter?' Martin gasped. 'You're on first-name terms with a serial killer?'

'Martin, I'm sorry. I should have told you—'

'Too fucking right you should have.'

'But I couldn't find the words.' She looked at Grace. 'I wanted to tell the police too, but . . .'

Martin looked to Grace now. 'What's he done exactly, this bloke?'

'He murdered four women by strangulation and attempted to murder a fifth,' Grace told him.

Martin's mouth dropped open this time.

Grace turned back to Denise, who had gone the colour of putty. 'Denise, why did you visit him?'

'I – I don't really know.' Denise stumbled over her words.

But Grace kept looking at her. She had no sympathy, couldn't understand the reasoning behind what she'd done. She did need to stay professional, however, and garner her trust.

'After reading about everything he'd done, I wanted to understand why,' Denise continued once Grace had stared at her enough to make her feel she should talk. 'I was only going to go for a few visits. But in the end I felt sorry for him.'

'You felt *sorry* . . .' Martin stopped mid-sentence and shook his head.

'Denise, you last visited Peter two months ago,' Grace continued.

'Six weeks before Isaac was born,' Martin muttered.

'Can you tell me what you discussed?'

She visibly coloured. 'We were just talking about stuff.'

'Stuff?' queried Martin, almost as if he were choking on the word.

'What exactly?' Grace leaned forwards.

'Nothing in particular!' Denise turned to Martin in panic.

'How can I trust you?' he seethed. 'It seems you have a whole different life besides the one you have with me.'

'He was lonely, that's all.' Denise shrugged. 'Maybe it was my hormones, I don't know, but I felt—'

'You were seeing him long before you became pregnant!'

'Mr Barber, can I ask you to remain calm, or leave and let us talk, please?' Grace said. 'I know this must be stressful, but we need to ascertain information as quickly as possible.'

Martin put up a hand before returning it to rest on the baby's head.

'I won't be visiting him again now.' Denise looked at Martin. 'I swear! I'm sorry.'

'I thought I knew you.' He shook his head in disdain. 'But I don't, do I?'

'Martin.' She placed a hand over his.

'No.' He shrugged her hand away and got up. 'I'm putting Isaac down now and then I'm going out.'

Grace let out a breath of air as they left the house and walked down the path.

'Wow, that was awkward,' Frankie said, airing her thoughts. 'I didn't know what to say!'

'That poor man. He hadn't got a clue what was going on, had he?'

'So you don't think she has anything to do with our case?'

'Well, we never rule anyone out, but I'd have to say with a newborn baby she'd be pretty pressed, wouldn't you?'

Frankie opened the car door and got into the passenger seat before speaking again.

'How do you get over the trust element of something like that?'

'I'm not sure you ever do.'

Grace started the engine.

SIXTY-ONE

Grace ran across the field, knowing he was close behind her. She thought she'd be able to outrun him, but he was too quick. She screamed as he put his hands around her and pushed her to the ground. The pavement beneath them scraped along her palms, stinging them, but she couldn't think about that. He turned her over onto her back.

She kicked out with her feet, lashed out with her fists, but he punched her to silence her. While she was dazed, he grabbed both of her arms and put them above her head. Sitting on top of her, there was no way she could push him off. He was too strong.

'You're an idiot to come after me,' a voice said.

She looked into the eyes of Peter Bentley and screamed out as his hands came around her neck. He squeezed harder as she—

'Hey,' Simon said as he woke her. 'Grace, it's me! You're safe here.'

She sat up quickly, screaming again as she scrambled away from him. A lamp went on. They both blinked as their eyes accustomed to the light.

Grace's breathing began to calm as she looked around, realising she was safe, at home and with Simon.

'Allie Shenton told me she dreams as much as I do.' Her laugh was nervous. 'I guess we take too much of the victims' energy in when we're involved.'

'It's natural, I suppose,' Simon replied. 'I only report it all, not see it as you do.'

She scooted back across the bed and into his arms. He lifted his head to catch the time on the alarm clock.

'I'm sorry to wake you,' she said quietly.

'It's fine.'

'I wish my body would make up its mind. One minute I can't sleep and the next I'm having nightmares.'

They lay together in silence while her breathing returned to normal. How had she allowed that man to invade her thoughts, her dreams? She couldn't believe he had got under her skin so much.

But she knew why really. It was because they hadn't caught the killer and, now there was a third victim, it felt as if it was their fault. She knew the people in the city would be blaming the police for their incompetence, but they didn't realise what was going on behind the scenes. Nor did they understand how much torment they were in, as well as the families of the victims. Each person murdered stayed with them eternally. It felt as if they should have done more, worked harder, been smarter, when in fact they had done as much as possible. Sometimes getting the evidence in was a long and tedious job.

But she wouldn't stop until Operation Middleport was complete.

She heard Simon sniff; she thought he might have sunk back into sleep.

'Fancy a brew now we're awake?'

Downstairs, they sat in the kitchen drinking tea.

'How has Phil been with you today?' Grace asked, cursing herself for not checking before now. She really should think about Simon more, she knew, but once on a case, it was all-consuming. Matt used to hate it at times, but he was always there for her when she had come out of the fog. He gave her time to come back to herself. She was sure Simon would do the same, given the nature of his job. Especially with a sleaze-ball like Phil for his boss.

Grace had been right when she'd wondered if Phil was putting pressure on him, like Nick was doing with her. Simon had told her that ever since she and Phil had had words at the vigil, Phil had been making digs at Simon for sleeping with the enemy. Simon had laughed it off at first, but he'd been putting more pressure on each day.

'The loser suggested I should try to find dirt on you and the police in the station today.'

'What!' she cried.

'I categorically refused.' He grinned. 'But he threatened me with my job, said I was being insubordinate.'

'He can't do that!' She paused. 'Can he?'

Simon shook his head. 'In the end, I turned the tables and said I'd go to Chris, the editor-in-chief, and let him know of his plans. He soon backed down then.'

'Good for you!' Grace shook her head. 'Does anyone even like him at the *Stoke News*?'

'Not that I know of, but he's old-school. He'll retire soon.'

'And you'll be promoted into his role.' She smiled. 'I'm sorry I didn't ask you earlier. My bad.'

Simon waved her comment away. 'I think you've had more important things on your mind.'

Grace shivered as she picked up both of their mugs and stood up. Before she got to the dishwasher, Simon reached for her hand and drew her onto his knee. Kissing her on the lips, he yawned.

'As much as I love spending time with you, I need some sleep, too. Let's go back to bed.'

She laughed as she ruffled his hair.

'Wow, you old romantic, you.'

SIXTY-TWO

Wednesday

Grace pushed the speed up on the treadmill and ran the last minute of her half-hour run at full pelt. Arms pumping, sweat pouring down her face, she ran as if her life depended on it. She'd set a tough, high-intensity programme. Getting to the end was a challenge, but she could do it.

It was six a.m. After her nightmare last night and her chat with Simon, she'd been unable to sleep once they'd returned to bed. Images of Peter Bentley had come to her every time she closed her eyes. Him with his hands around the victims' necks, one after the other; then him with his hands around her neck as she struggled to push him off. In the end, she'd got up and headed for the makeshift gym.

Her workout finished, she took a shower and went back into the bedroom. Simon was awake but still in bed, so she snuggled in next to him for a moment. He pulled her into his arms without opening his eyes.

'You smell nice,' he acknowledged. 'Did you manage to sleep at all?'

'Not really, but I'm glad you did. Sorry about that.'

'It's not a problem. Really.'

Grace ran a hand up and down his torso. 'Maybe we should do something now that we're both awake.'

'What do you have in mind?' Simon's eyes were still closed but she could tell he wasn't fully asleep.

'A cooked breakfast?' she joked.

One eye opened. 'Is that all you fancy?'

'If only there were more time.'

'Let's live dangerously.'

She giggled. 'What, again, so soon?'

Grace rubbed at her neck as she got out of the car. Hours of driving over the past two days was playing havoc with her joints. Luckily, the second person on Bentley's visitor list lived in Bucknall, less than two miles from Bethesda Police Station.

It was her first visit after team brief and she'd taken Frankie with her again. At a small row of terraced properties, she squeezed her car into a space and hotfooted back several houses until she found the number they were looking for.

'I wonder what this one's going to be like,' Frankie said. 'After seeing the first woman on the list, I bet she'll be adamant Bentley was innocent. How can he manipulate anyone into believing that?'

'Sometimes they believe what they want,' Grace said. 'Ours isn't to reason why but to catch the bastards.'

Grace, too, was curious to know what a person who would visit a convicted serial killer on a monthly basis was like. Even more curious was the fact that Bentley had three women coming to visit him. He wasn't a charmer and, to her, didn't seem the type to be stringing one woman along, let alone three.

But then, it could be a fascination thing that did it for the women. Surely they would never be interested in Bentley if he was loose to kill again? If it were Grace, she'd be afraid to overcook a meal in case his hands were around her neck. How anyone lived a life like that she'd never know.

'Susan Bailey?' she asked the woman who came to the door.

'No, I'm her sister. Can I help?'

Grace held up her warrant card. 'We'd like to speak to Susan, please.'

'She's popped to the shop.'

'Do you know when she'll be back?'

'Sometime in the next ten minutes. It's only on the next street. What's this about?'

'It's imperative we speak to her.' Grace pointed to her car. 'We'll be over there . . .'

'You can come in, if you like.'

They followed the woman into the living room and sat down when offered a seat. The house was tidy and clean, functional but not exactly modern. Outdated furniture, including a settee that had seen better days, and a slight smell of damp filled the room.

'Sorry about the mess.' The woman pointed to the wall. 'We've been asking the landlord to do something about it for months now. There're a few tiles missing on the roof and it's raining down that corner. But he hasn't come out so far. I don't expect he will.'

'Is it the two of you that live here, Ms . . .'

'Dawn Brodie. Susan lives with my husband and me. She's been here about a year now. She's okay, just a little lonely. That's why I keep her close. Derek doesn't like it so much, but he works away mostly so he doesn't see either of us often.'

Grace smiled at Dawn, warming to her. It seemed everywhere she happened on, family came first. It grated on her; was someone trying to tell her something?

She heard a key in the front door.

Dawn got up. 'Ah, here she is now,' she said, heading out of the door.

'I can't even imagine what this one will be like,' Frankie said, glancing around the room as they were left alone.

Grace didn't know what she was expecting when she saw Susan Bailey, but recognising her immediately took her by surprise. She glanced at Frankie, wondering if he knew her. By the looks he was shooting her way, he clearly did.

The woman standing before them worked in the school canteen at Dunwood Academy.

Susan Bailey was nothing to write home about. Her greying hair was tied away from her face that was free of make-up, her clothes various shades of beige. Flat brown shoes sat beneath a long coffee-coloured corduroy skirt. The pink buttons on her cardigan were the only hint of colour.

She didn't look Peter Bentley's type at all. Not that Grace would ever know his type.

Blushing slightly, Susan came into the room without saying a word and sat on the settee, legs together at the knees, hands in her lap, back ramrod straight.

'We meet again, Ms Bailey,' Grace said. 'Quite a surprise, I must admit.'

'What is it that you want to speak to me about?' Susan asked, looking at her feet.

'I believe you've been visiting Peter Bentley in HM Wakefield for the past three years.'

'That's right. There's no law against that, is there?'

'Of course not,' Grace replied. 'I wanted to know how you found him at the last visit. Did he seem agitated in any way?'

'He's in prison. I'd expect that might upset a lot of people.'

Grace nodded, wondering how best to play this. 'I understand that you—'

'No, *you* need to understand. Peter's locked up for something he didn't do. I go and visit him to keep him company until he can come out and join me. And then—'

'Has it escaped your mind that there is evidence that he murdered four women and attempted to murder another?'

'All lies.' She put a hand up in the air as if she didn't want to hear anything else. 'Peter wouldn't hurt a fly.'

Dawn, who had been standing in the doorway, tutted. 'Oh, would you listen to yourself, Susan. The man's a convicted killer. He won't be coming out any time soon and he's making a fool of you.'

'No, he's not. He loves me.'

As Susan continued to look at the floor, Grace and Dawn shared a glance. Grace couldn't help but feel sorry for her. Dawn was trying to hold her sister up, when really she didn't want to be held. Susan didn't believe Bentley was guilty. Grace wondered what stories he'd been concocting for her while he was inside.

But the other thing she was querying was why Peter would want to see Susan in the first place. Unless he got off on the adulation, she couldn't work out the relationship. Did he just see her for company? Denise Barber, she could understand, was a power trip. Did he love Susan? And did he love his third visitor as much?

'Did he ask you about any of the girls at Dunwood Academy when you visited him last week?' Grace went on.

'No!'

'What do you talk about?'

'That's none of your business.'

'But you see, it is our business, or else we wouldn't be here.'

Grace watched Susan's skin redden. They could all see it, but Susan wouldn't raise her head to look at them again.

'May I have a look around your room?' Grace asked.

Susan got to her feet. 'No, you may not.'

281

Grace stood up too, Frankie following suit.

'We'll come back with a warrant, then. I'm sure you have your reasons, but a judge might not be so lenient if we find out later that you've been aiding and abetting a known criminal.'

'Okay, you can look! As long as you leave afterwards.'

Grace was back downstairs ten minutes later. Dawn was right. All it suggested was a lonely woman, living with her sister and her husband. Life didn't seem to have turned out well for her. But then she shook her head to rid herself of her judgemental attitude. Hers was not to wonder why. Even so, Susan Bailey needed to be questioned further.

'I'd like you to come to the station with us,' she told Susan.

'You're going to arrest me?' Susan stood wide-eyed.

'We need to take a statement from you about what we've discussed, Ms Bailey.' Grace took her by the arm. 'And ask a few more questions.'

'He's innocent.' She glared at Grace. 'I know him.'

Grace didn't reply. There was so much that she wanted to say. Besides, unless there was a crime committed, it was none of her business. If Susan chose to be in a relationship with a convicted killer, then she could do nothing to stop her, unless she had evidence to suggest she was involved.

During her earlier years in the police, Grace had been fooled the odd time or two by weak people who then turned out to be devious and manipulative. Now, she suspected the same of Susan. She seemed headstrong. There was something in that alone. Whether it was good or bad remained to be seen.

Once back at the station, Grace showed Susan Bailey into a side room.

'There will be someone along to speak to you soon,' she told her before turning to leave.

'It won't be you?' Susan asked, pulling a chair out.

282

'I have something else to check first. Unless you'd prefer to wait and speak to me when I get back?'

Susan shook her head vehemently and sat down.

'I'll bring you a drink and a bite to eat. Have you informed the school you might not be in today?'

'Yes.'

'Good. Now, is there anything else you'd like to tell us at this stage?'

Susan shook her head, choosing to look at the floor again.

Grace left her to it. Maybe Sam could get it out of her. She had told her to keep Susan waiting for as long as possible before releasing her. Let her stew. She was hiding something, she was certain. And if they got it out of her, they could arrest her and keep her for longer.

'How do you think that went?' Grace asked Frankie as he walked beside her back to her car.

He shook his head. 'I can't understand her logic. But we have nothing else to ask her, do we?'

'Apart from her hanging on to our every word while she served us refreshments in the school canteen?'

'Ah.' Frankie nodded. 'Still seems strange why someone like her would be visiting a man like Bentley in prison.'

'Indeed. She's very different from Denise Barber.' Grace rubbed her neck again. She could feel in her gut that Susan Bailey wasn't one of the killers. 'But for now, it's back in the car. Let's go and see what visitor number three, Elizabeth Shelby, is like.'

SIXTY-THREE

In Stafford, Grace pulled up outside 5 Warwick Street. The woman who came to the door was in her late fifties. She wiped floury hands on a tea towel and then ran them through short grey hair. Grace glanced surreptitiously at Frankie. Had Bentley got a thing for older women? Maybe he found them easier to manipulate.

'Hello, I'm DS Allendale and this is PC Higgins.' Grace held up her warrant card, Frankie following suit. 'We believe this to be the address of Elizabeth Shelby. Is that correct?'

'You mean Lizzie.' The woman stiffened immediately. 'My daughter doesn't live here any more. What's this about?'

'Do you know where she is now?' Grace continued. 'It's imperative that we find her and speak to her as soon as possible.'

The woman held open the door. 'I think you'd better come in.'

Grace and Frankie stepped inside. Immediately, the smell of baking wafted at them. Grace breathed in, realising it was lunchtime when her stomach growled its complaint.

She smiled. 'We won't keep you long, Mrs . . .'

'Mrs Shelby. Please, call me Lesley. My cupcakes are due out of the oven in about two minutes. I bake them to sell, so I don't want to burn them.' She pointed to a door. 'If you pop yourself in there, I'll switch on the kettle.'

'Not for us, thanks!' Grace shouted after her.

She and Frankie went through and found themselves in a pleasant living room. It seemed very ordinary, similar to the women's homes they had already visited. She turned when she heard Lesley behind her.

Once back with them, Lesley sat down, indicating for them to do the same.

'What's she been up to now?' was her first question once they were all comfortable.

Grace watched Frankie sit forwards in anticipation as he got out his notepad. Grace took hers out, too. She wanted to make sure they didn't miss anything.

'We need to ask her a few questions,' Grace explained, not wanting to give too much away. 'Can you tell me when you last saw your daughter?'

'I can't recall exactly. She pops by every few months. We usually end up arguing and she leaves. It isn't good for either of us, really. I dread the knock on the door.'

Grace was shocked by how resigned she was but stayed deadpan. Lesley had clearly been through a bad experience and Grace would need to get to the bottom of it.

Before she could ask anything else, Lesley spoke again.

'She was such a happy child until she was five. But when my husband died suddenly of a heart attack, she was distraught and became uncontrollable.' Lesley reached for a tissue in the box by her side, but instead of using it, she wrung it in her hands. 'She was at school when it happened, and when she was old enough she blamed me for not looking after him properly. Threw the remark at me all the time. But it was so sudden. I

285

didn't even have time to say goodbye to him. Marvin was only thirty-two.'

'So sorry to hear that,' Grace said, her tone sincere.

'She was such a daddy's girl,' Lesley continued. 'I don't know why, but she blamed me for his death. The older she got, the nastier she became about it. "Why hadn't you noticed he was ill?" she kept saying, as if it was all my fault.' Lesley managed to look at them for a millisecond, a faint blush tingeing her cheeks.

'She was always a strong-willed – I guess you could say spoilt – child, but it became much harder to control her when there was just me. She never seemed to listen. I tried my best to discipline her. She got into trouble at school and eventually they assigned a social worker.'

Grace stayed quiet, intrigued to hear what she was going to say next. Lizzie Shelby seemed a likely candidate for Peter Bentley, perfect to mould into someone he could find useful to gather information from. But then, was he using Susan Bailey to do that?

'She started going out with friends, staying out late, taking drugs, drinking alcohol. I was so ashamed of her at times – I didn't even know my own daughter.' Lesley looked up at them, humiliation written all over her face. 'So whatever she's done, it's my fault. I couldn't control her.'

'You mustn't blame yourself.' Grace's gut feeling was to believe Lesley. There didn't seem to be any reason why she'd make up all of that. And she had volunteered the information without pushing to find out why they wanted to question Lizzie.

'But I do!' Lesley sounded distraught. 'My young daughter was grieving and I couldn't help her through it because I missed Marvin so much myself. I suffered from anxiety and depression after his death.'

'Do you know where she's living now?' Grace asked.

Lesley got up and went over to a side unit. She took out a notebook and wrote a few words in it. Then she ripped out a piece of paper.

'This is the last address she gave me, about six months ago.' She handed it to Grace. 'I don't know if she'll still be there, though. She moves around such a lot.'

Grace looked at the note. It was an address in Manchester. She handed it to Frankie who wrote it down in his notepad.

'Do you have any photos of her?' she enquired.

'I have a few, but only up until she left home at sixteen.' Lesley sighed. 'Despite our differences, I still can't part with them.'

She went into the side unit again and pulled out a box, handing it to Grace.

Grace removed the lid and sifted through its contents. There were photographs of a young girl – on a swing, sitting with a man on the settee, one with Lesley opening Christmas presents. On the back of one of them was a surname she didn't recognise.

'It says Lesley Whiston here. Is that you?' Grace asked.

'Yes, that was my maiden name. There are no recent photos, I'm afraid, but she does look a bit like me.'

'Have you ever visited her?' Frankie asked.

'No. I don't think I'd be welcome. And besides, I haven't been out in years. Agoraphobia,' Lesley explained. 'My doctor thinks it's something to do with feeling safe indoors. That's why I don't like Lizzie visiting. But she *is* my daughter, I suppose. I can never make amends, but I still send her a monthly allowance. It's from a fund that Marvin set up for me and I give her a bit of it, too. She'll always be my little girl.'

Grace felt pity for the woman who was sitting in front of her, especially after getting her so wrong and assuming it was her who had been visiting Peter Bentley.

'Could . . . could you give me details on why you're looking for her?' Lesley asked. 'Is she in trouble again?'

'We need to speak to her, to help with an investigation. We can't say for certain that she's involved until then.'

'Oh, dear. I hope she hasn't caused anyone any harm.'

'Do you think she would do that?' Grace probed.

'I – I don't know. She's always been very mixed up.'

'Do you have anyone to help you?' Grace said instead, to ease the fact she hadn't answered her earlier question.

Lesley smiled then. 'My parents aren't too good healthwise but they're very supportive. I don't know what I'd do without them. Would you believe, I used to have my own accountancy firm hiring seven staff? It collapsed when I could no longer cope with Lizzie. Losing Marvin spiralled me into a black hole I have yet to find a way out of.'

Although Grace was strong, she knew first-hand how grief was all-consuming. She closed her notepad and stood up.

'If you ever need to talk, perhaps there's someone I can refer you to.' She gave Lesley a contact card.

Lesley took it from her and showed them out.

'You didn't have to stay deathly silent,' Grace told Frankie as they walked down the path.

'I didn't! I was gobsmacked and unable to speak.'

She smiled at him briefly then shook her head. 'It's essential we find Shelby right away. See what she has to say for herself. Which won't be easy without an up-to-date image. We need to do some digging.'

SIXTY-FOUR

Grace got Frankie to ring the station to see if anyone wanted to order lunch. She stopped at the chip shop on the way back and at her desk, dished the food out. She and Frankie updated everyone about their findings as they tucked in.

'How's Sophie doing?' asked Sam.

'There was no change the last time I spoke to Mr Bishop.' Grace wiped her greasy fingers. 'But that in itself seems to be good news. I might pop in to see him later, seeing as we have no FLO available and he's okay without one.'

The rest of the day was taken up with paperwork as Grace and her team worked on cross-referencing and double-checking everything. Every time a story changed slightly, or they gathered more information, both statements and records had to be gone through again. It was meticulous and tedious, but it had to be done.

Susan Bailey was interviewed, but she wouldn't say anything to implicate either herself or Peter Bentley. They'd had no choice but to let her go for now. It was frustrating to say the least, but without evidence, they couldn't keep her there.

On her way home, it hadn't taken more than ten minutes of

her time to visit Jack Bishop. From what he said, Sophie was very much the same, still in a medically induced coma, but the consultant she was under was keen to try to bring her out of it soon.

It was nearly half past seven as she walked back to her car outside the Bishops' house. She'd been on shift for over twelve hours and was in desperate need of some downtime in which to digest everything and get her thoughts in order. So much was running through her head right now, none more so than the visit she'd had with Peter Bentley.

As she clicked off the car alarm, she heard someone shout. A young man approached her.

'Oi, I want a word with you.'

Grace didn't have time to react before he pushed her hard in the chest. She found herself backed up against the fencing of the house next door.

'Leave my brother alone,' he said, the snarl on his face matching the darkness in his eyes.

'Hey, back off!' she warned.

'He's done nothing wrong. And if you were doing your job properly, you'd have caught the murderer when the first girl got killed so Sophie might not be lying in a coma. It was your fault – yours!'

'I get that you're upset –' Grace tried to calm the situation '– but this isn't helping.'

'I don't care what you think.' He pointed at her. 'Just keep away from Joel and my family. This is nothing to do with us and—'

While he'd been talking, Grace had kept her eyes locked with his. In one quick move, she placed her hands on his shoulders and kneed him in the groin.

He groaned and dropped to the pavement.

'No one threatens me, have you got that?' She stood over

him, letting him catch his breath as she studied his face in the streetlight. 'You're Dean Nicholls, Joel's brother, aren't you?'

'My balls!' he moaned.

'Oh, stop being a baby. It was your own fault anyway. Come on, get to your feet.' She pointed to a low wall a few houses away. 'We can sit down there.'

'Why are you so mad with us?' she asked once they were seated.

'I know you lot. You'll set my brother up for it all just to get another one of us off the streets.'

'Now you're really talking nonsense.' She shook her head. 'If Joel has nothing to do with any of it, then you're here wasting my time when I could be looking for the killer. Had you thought about that when you pulled your big-man routine back there?'

He went quiet.

'You think I'm a pushover and I'm not,' she told him. 'If I wasn't so knackered, you would have earned yourself a night in the cells for assaulting a police officer.'

The fight had gone out of Dean now, to the point that Grace almost felt sorry for him. But he had to know he couldn't go around threatening whoever he wanted, not even to protect his family.

'Want to tell me what that was really all about?' she asked.

'I'm looking for Joel. That's why I came round here. I thought he might be trying to find out how Sophie is.'

'He isn't inside the house, if that's what you mean. I've just come from there. Would he have gone to the hospital?'

'I don't know, but I doubt it.' Dean shrugged. 'I'm tired of everyone blaming my family for everything all the time.'

'No one held a gun to your dad's head and demanded that he did what he did. And because *he's* done something, it doesn't mean we all tar you with the same brush. And you're lucky that you're not nicked yourself.'

'He's not my real dad.'

He wouldn't look at her, just kept his eyes to the ground. Grace fished a contact card from her pocket and handed it to him.

'The next time you want to speak to me, do it the official way. Now, push off before I change my mind.'

He took the card from her and got up to leave.

'I'm sorry,' he said. 'It's just that I'm the eldest man in the family now and I'm trying to keep them all together. It's a bloody nightmare at times. My sisters are the worst.'

'How old are you, Dean?'

'Nineteen.'

'And your sisters?'

'Twenty-two and twenty. They're not my real sisters, either. Gary and Sharon, that's my adoptive mum and dad, were their real parents. It's only me and Joel who are adopted.'

'You're blood brothers?'

'No, we have different parents, but we took the Nicholls' surname. I was nine when I joined the family and eleven when Joel came along. My parents were druggies and could barely look after each other, let alone me.' He glanced away for a moment as if painful memories were too much to bear. 'Joel's dad murdered his mum in front of him when he was six, and he was put into care. Then he came to live with us, adopted before Sharon died. His real dad's still in prison, too. We were doing all right until Sharon's death and Gary got in a lot of debt.'

'You had no idea of anything?' Grace had checked out the Nicholls' background once back at the station after speaking to Joel. She'd found out that Gary Nicholls had been sent down for robbery.

'No, it all happened so quickly.'

Grace understood him now. He'd come from a broken home

292

and was determined to keep everyone in this one as close as he could. He was also hurting, having too much burden for someone of his age.

'Even so,' she told him, 'your adopted sisters are both adults. You should all be looking out for Joel.'

'I know, but they can hardly look after themselves. The only thing they're good for is mouthing off at people. So who else will do it if I don't?'

He got up then and Grace stayed on the wall as he walked off. She thought about his words. It was a breath of fresh air to speak to someone who was actually bothered about keeping their family together. It made her think of her half-siblings again, and Megan.

Which is why when she got to her feet, she was surprised to see a black Range Rover pull out of a space a few feet in front of her.

The engine started up and the car sped off. But she didn't even have to check the number plate to recognise it was Eddie's.

Was he following Dean? Or was he following her?

SIXTY-FIVE

She swore loudly and kicked out at the table. It was all closing in again – no! She wouldn't let it happen.

The phone call had taken her completely by surprise. She'd even thought of not answering it; she hadn't spoken to her mum in such a good while. But she was glad now that she had, because it had put her and Peter one step ahead.

She'd met Peter Bentley during a particularly volatile time in her life. She had been kicked out of her squat in Rochdale and had travelled to Manchester, hitching a lift from a good man. She'd been a mess; she was surprised anyone had picked her up, but the old man had seemed no threat. It had turned out to be a good move, as he'd felt sorry for her and had dropped her off after treating her to something to eat.

Arriving in Manchester, she'd trailed around the usual places, sleeping in shop doorways, dossing in subways that didn't look too dangerous. After two nights, she'd been punched around the head when she was accused of pinching someone's patch and told to move on. She hadn't retaliated – it wasn't on, not in her circumstances. She didn't need to create enemies. But she had gone back a day later and threw a can of piss all over the man's sleeping bag.

She waited impatiently for her fifth day there to come round, then she'd looked for somewhere to stay. She couldn't stop anywhere permanently until then. Finally, she came back to the arches. It was where the homeless congregated – not as bad as tent city around the corner – tucked almost underneath a disused railway line.

It was a rubbish dump really. For refuse and people.

She approached a man with dreadlocks, who was warming his hands on a makeshift fire. He told her his name was Tommy. She'd chatted to him for a while and, after being invited, stayed the night. She drank some booze, took the drugs she was offered. In the morning, when she awoke still in one piece, she decided to stay.

Peter Bentley was the fifth man she met under the arches. They got to know each other slowly, as friends. Theirs was never a passionate love affair. They spent the odd night together but realised there was no desire. Even pissed-up junkies needed that.

Over the next few weeks, they had chatted a lot. There wasn't much else to do and it was good learning about people when she arrived at a new place. She'd been honest with him about her past. Eventually, they had spoken about their hopes and dreams for hours. Then they'd confessed the dark thoughts they had.

Now, she screamed out in anger, throwing her glass against the wall. Why had this one been so careless, leaving that last girl alive? Stupid, stupid idiot. She had thought of everything, double-checked, triple-checked to ensure they'd get to number five this time.

She couldn't be this close again.

She had to finish what she'd started.

SIXTY-SIX

Thursday

Grace had made arrangements to meet up with Sandy in Manchester at ten a.m. She wanted to see if she could find any information out about their missing woman. But the day was playing heavily on her mind. If her theory was right, it was the day for the next victim and as yet, they were no closer to having a suspect in custody.

As she was about to leave the station, her desk phone rang. She picked the call up quickly.

'I thought you might like to know that our Dean was in a right state when he got home last night.'

'I'm sorry, who is this?'

'Dean Nicholls' sister, Chantelle. He was beaten up. Set upon by two people.'

'Where did this happen?'

'He was walking home from the pub.'

'Did he see who it was?'

'No, but I know it has something to do with you.'

'Me?' Grace sounded aghast.

'Blaming our Joel for something he hasn't done started it off.

And then our Dean wanting to put things right. His card with your number was in the pocket of his jeans, so I know he's been to see you.'

'Did Dean tell you he assaulted a police officer?'

'Only because you goaded him! Our Dean wouldn't hurt a fly. He's the only sane one in the family. And now he's in a right state. I've a good mind to complain to your—'

'How bad is he?' Grace interrupted. There was no way she was responsible for Nicholls' attack, but she still wanted details, especially after seeing Eddie in the vicinity. She wondered if he was aware she had spotted his vehicle.

'He's got a black eye, a split lip and all the skin scraped off his cheek where they pushed him into the pavement. He was punched in the stomach too.'

Grace sighed. 'Why doesn't *he* report it?'

'Because our Dean doesn't want any trouble. He said he was told to keep away, but he doesn't know who from. I'm not letting some low-life get away with that.'

'Let me have some details –' Grace reached for her notepad '– and I'll get someone to come and see him.'

'It had better not be you, because you've caused our family enough damage so far.'

'I want to help, Chantelle. Did Joel come home last night?'

'Stop hassling us!'

'All I need to know is his whereabouts on Sunday evening, between—'

'He was at home with me all night.'

'You're certain of that?'

'Yes!'

'So—'

'Just keep away from us!'

The phone went dead. Grace cursed loudly. Sam was already looking over.

'What was all that about?' she asked.

'Dean Nicholls took a bit of a pasting last night.'

'And that's your fault because . . .?'

'He was waiting for me when I came out of the Bishops' home. Said I shouldn't have had a go at Joel. Says his brother isn't a troublemaker.' Grace wasn't going to tell her everything, not about the assault by Dean or the fact she'd seen Eddie hanging around. Not at least until she'd looked into things further.

'Really?' Sam shook her head. 'Does Chantelle know who it might be?'

'No, but she's blaming me for his injuries. And Joel's gone AWOL and that's my fault too, apparently.' Grace looked across at Perry. 'Did you ever wonder if the Steeles had anything to do with it?' Rather than look at him, Grace fiddled with her lanyard as it twirled around a few times. She straightened it out again.

'Couldn't prove anything either way,' Perry replied. 'I liked Gary, though. I was a PC through some of the family's fostering days. Spent a lot of time cautioning troublesome kids and taking them home. I've kept an eye on the family ever since. Dean tries to keep everyone together, which is no mean feat.'

'I can imagine!' Grace replied.

'Want me to pop in on my travels later?'

'I suppose it won't hurt. And reinforce he can't go around assaulting us cops without consequences.'

'Leave it with me,' Perry told her. 'I've got some things to go through and then I'll sort it out.'

Grace nodded, then grabbed her car keys and headed out of the building. But as she drove along the A500 towards the M6 with Frankie, the fact that she had seen Eddie's car the night before was worrying her. Had he got something to do with the attack on Nicholls? Had he seen Dean have a go at her and given out a warning beating?

Was he still having her followed?

Eddie wanted her on side. Maybe this was his way of saying he was taking care of her.

She pinched the bridge of her nose. No, that was ridiculous.

Wasn't it?

SIXTY-SEVEN

In Salford, Grace parked her car in Manchester Way and killed the engine. She pointed across the road to an arch underneath a disused railway track.

'There's Sandy waiting for us. Come on.'

'Hey.' Sandy smiled at them both as they drew level with her. 'That address you gave me yesterday was a boarded-up property about two miles from here.'

Grace sighed, annoyed at another dead end. 'So why have you asked to meet us here?'

'You've been here before, I assume?' Sandy was speaking to Grace.

'Yes. Several times when after people.'

'Shelby seemed to have been a rough sleeper on occasions, so I was wondering if she'd been here. Did you meet Tommy, the gaffer?'

'I think so, but it was a while ago.'

'I'll take you to him.'

They walked in step together, the traffic from the road almost drowning their conversation. Sandy pushed open a door into a building nearby and stepped inside.

'This used to be offices, built under the arch,' she explained to Frankie. 'There are about ten individual office shells left, so we have lots of homeless people staying here. It's not ideal, but as quick as the council move them on, they come back. Even so, some of them have lived here for years.' She wafted a hand in front of her mouth. 'It stinks and it's a bit grim, but I guess it's marginally better than sleeping in tent city.'

They watched where they trod as they stepped through and over newspapers, food and drinks cartons, the odd bag of clothes, discarded shoes and a pyramid of rubber tyres. They looked in a couple of rooms but there was no one there.

In the third they found two young men. They were awake, sitting up in sleeping bags, smoking. Grace recognised the cloying smell of cannabis; ignored it, knowing she had bigger crimes to solve.

'Do either of you know where Tommy is?' Sandy asked.

'Not seen him this morning, but he was in Room Eight last night,' the nearest one said.

'Room Eight?' Sandy muttered as they left. 'They make it sound like a bloody hotel.'

Room Eight was empty, so Sandy pushed open the fire exit at the end of the corridor and they stepped out into a small yard. There were a group of people sitting around a fire in an old burner. Some were in plastic white chairs that had seen better days and a few on boxes, whatever they could find.

'Is Tommy around?' Sandy asked.

One of them pointed to the man by the fire.

She smiled. 'Ah, I didn't recognise you! You've had your dreadlocks shorn off.'

Tommy ran a hand over his number two crewcut. 'Well, a man has to keep himself smart and make an effort.' He smiled a gap-tooth grin.

'This is Grace and Frankie, detectives from Stoke.'

'Hey, Tommy,' Grace said. 'Remember me?'

Tommy gave her the once-over. 'I do. Haven't seen you in a while.'

'I moved to Stoke six months ago.'

'Poor you.'

She laughed. Anyone could see that Tommy had been on the streets for a while. They could tell not only by the state of his clothes, but also his manner. Grace often found the longer someone had been sleeping rough, the more edge they had about themselves. Tommy wasn't fazed by them calling at all. Indeed, he even had a smile for them.

'What brings you here?' he asked, shooing some of the people out of the chairs.

Sandy sat down. 'We're after information on someone named Lizzie Shelby – or Elizabeth.'

'It would have been around 2014,' Grace added, perching on a seat across from him. 'I know it's a long time back, but we're investigating—'

'You're after that killer, aren't you? The papers say you have a copycat in your city.'

'Yes, we think so.' Grace nodded.

Behind her, she could feel the others listening in. She nudged Frankie and nodded in their direction. Frankie got up and went to talk to them.

'We know Peter Bentley stayed here,' Sandy said. 'Did he ever have a woman with him?'

'There used to be several around him, but he only had eyes for the one when she arrived.' Tommy rolled a cigarette as he spoke. 'She came here on her own, befriended him. I'm not sure they were a couple as such, but they got pretty close.' He licked the top of the paper and rolled it up. 'Bentley had been here about a year before she came. They were sharing Room

Five until he got caught for murdering those women. People like him give us a bad name. Bastard.'

Grace admired his loyalty: he wouldn't let Bentley use the excuse of being homeless as a reason to have hurt those women.

'Do you know what happened to Lizzie?' she enquired.

He shook his head, lit the roll-up and took a long drag. 'She and Peter were pretty tight at the time. She disappeared, so I thought she'd been banged up with him. I never trusted her. She always went out of her way to cause or make trouble for people here. It was as if she wanted to self-destruct, but she needed to make others do it to her. And she had this thing about room number five. She was weird.'

'Can you recall what she looked like?' Grace asked. 'We don't have any recent photos of her.'

'My memory isn't how it used to be,' Tommy said. 'But she did have long blonde hair. And she used to go mad if any women sniffed around Pete.'

Grace ran a hand through her hair. There were plenty of women out there fitting this description. It seemed they were at another dead end. She stood up to leave.

'You could always try the hostel in Curzon Street.' Tommy looked up at her. 'She used to hang around there a lot. Always one of the first for a bed.'

'We will, thanks.' Sandy stood up too. She handed a ten-pound note to Tommy for his troubles.

'Don't spend it all at once, mind,' she said.

'I won't. I promise!' he shouted as he took it from her.

Back out on the side of the road, Grace breathed in fresh air, even if it was full of fumes from the nearby road.

'Do you have time to come to the hostel in Curzon Street with us?' she asked Sandy. Although she remembered the place and the woman who ran it, with Sandy still being local, maybe she would get intel from people there more easily.

303

SIXTY-EIGHT

The hostel was within walking distance, in an old townhouse set over three floors. Its black front door was windowless and mostly void of paint, blinds at the windows open slightly. Grace almost mourned its lack of love, but knew that money would be tight for the homeless unit, and inside its people would be glad to be there rather than out on the streets.

'It's me, Helen,' Sandy said when the buzzer was answered. 'I need to talk to you about someone.'

'I'll let you in. Can you wait in the hallway for a minute and I'll come to you?'

The three of them went inside. A door had been left open to one of the downstairs rooms. Grace could see two worn settees that looked as if she'd be better off sitting on the floor than perching on one, and a coffee table with several mugs and an overflowing ashtray.

'Sorry to keep you waiting.' Helen flew down the stairs wearing yellow marigold gloves and holding a plastic bag out in front of her. 'One of them has been sick and I've had to clean it up. Not in my job description but, equally, I couldn't stand the smell, so had to do something about it. Grace! How are you? I won't be a moment.'

Grace smiled as Helen went through into the room at the back of the house. She had visited the hostel several times during her previous role. Many a time Helen had found her a bed for someone at the last minute, got them off the streets. Often, she had turned lives round by doing this, but if you said that to her, she'd brush the comment away.

She appeared in the doorway a few minutes later and beckoned them into the kitchen to join her.

'So, what brings you back to Manc?' she asked Grace.

'We're after picking your brains.' Grace went through what she could tell her about Peter Bentley.

'I remember him. And her, too, come to think of it. Long blonde hair and the bluest of eyes.'

'When was the last time you saw her?' Sandy asked.

'Oh, it must be a few years ago now, not since he was jailed.'

'Are you able to describe anything else about her? Has she any distinguishing marks?'

'Not that I can recall.' Helen paused for a moment and then got to her feet. 'Wait a moment.' Across the room was a corkboard crammed with photos. 'Ah, yes, here you go. This is her, with Peter Bentley. They always came as a pair until he went to prison.'

They crowded around the corkboard while she removed the photo. It was of a man and a woman sitting on the low wall at the front of the building. Both of them appeared to be under the influence of some kind of drug addiction. The man was Peter Bentley. The woman was a wreck, her hair matted as if it needed a good wash. Her skin was sallow, eyes dark, and she had several scabs on her chin. Grace had a spark of recognition, but nothing concrete.

'Oh, I remember her!' Sandy cried.

'You do?' Grace couldn't help the glee in her voice.

'Yes, she was arrested for shoplifting a few times, on her own and once or twice with Bentley.' She nodded. 'If I'm right, we should have her prints on the system.'

'Yes!' Grace and Frankie said in unison, then grinned at each other.

'Is it who you're after?' asked Helen.

'We hope so,' Grace said. 'We didn't know what she looked like until now, so this is a great help. Do you have records of who stays overnight? Going back to 2014?'

'Yes,' Helen replied. 'It might take me a while to go through them, though.'

'Why don't you leave this with me?' Sandy suggested. 'I'll let you know if I find anything.'

Driving back to Stoke, Grace's mind went into overdrive, trying to figure out what this woman's role was in everything.

'You've had an email from Sandy, Sarge,' Frankie said as he looked up from his phone. 'She's copied me into it. We have the woman care of the hostel address, but with the name of Beth Whiston.'

'That surname!'

'Yeah, and the photos match with what's on record.'

'So she's done a runner.' Grace gnawed at her bottom lip as she raced down the motorway. 'We need all hands on deck to find out where this woman is.'

Grace pulled into the service station at Knutsford to use the bathroom forty minutes before Junction 16 would take her back to Stoke. As Frankie went off to find coffee for them, she checked out the image of Beth Whiston attached to the email. Suddenly, she felt she had seen her before. In her line of work, she met so many people that she'd often go face-blind. But there was something about the woman that she recognised.

306

Back in the car, she gave Sam a quick ring to update her.

'I want everything you can find out about Whiston,' she said. 'Her social media profiles, try the different names she's used – plus, see if she's a member of All Talk.'

Grace disconnected her call and removed the lid from her coffee.

'I don't know about you, Frankie, but I think Whiston could know our killer. We have to find her.'

Frankie pinched the screen on his phone to make the image larger and stared at it.

'She could be totally different if she's cleaned herself up after this was taken, you know?'

'I'm going to check on social media myself.'

Grace ran the name through Facebook. There were four Beth Whistons: two of them were dark-haired, one was a redhead and the fifth had the image of a number five as her profile picture. She wondered, was that a clue?

She clicked on the image of the number five straight away and onto another profile page, astounded by the lack of privacy settings, leaving the content for anyone to look at. Grace didn't use Facebook often, but her security settings were set very tight.

All of a sudden, she stopped scrolling down and went back up again.

'There's an image here of a few people together. I can see Nathan Stiller!'

Frankie leaned across the seat to look as she scrolled down the screen.

'There! Oh, no, it can't be!' Grace cried excitedly as she enlarged the screen. 'It is. It's her, isn't it?'

'I'd take a bet on it,' Frankie agreed.

The woman they were looking at was sitting on the knee of someone they both knew. Her head was thrown back in laughter, her blonde hair hanging down like a curtain.

Grace scrolled down further to be certain. There were several selfies of her. As Frankie had indicated, she'd cleaned up her act as her skin wasn't as sallow. Her hair was lighter and she'd put on weight. Yet even having only met her briefly, Grace could now see who it was.

Those vivid blue eyes.

It was Jason Tranter's partner, Bethan. The woman he had been with at the vigil for Lauren Ansell.

Grace started the engine while she waited for her call to connect.

'Put Nick on speaker when he answers.' She gave her phone to Frankie, her need to leave imperative. There was no time to waste.

She raced towards the motorway again.

308

SIXTY-NINE

Perry located the Nicholls' address and pulled up outside a council-owned property. There was no gate on the driveway and he could see straight through to the back garden, covered in grass a few inches in height. A large dog in next door's garden was tied to a chain. It began to bark ferociously as he walked up the path.

The front door was opened before he got to it. A woman in her early twenties stood there with folded arms. Caked in make-up, her embarrassingly thin black leggings seemed two sizes two small and her jumper would have looked better on a larger man.

'You come to see our Dean?' She took a drag from her cigarette and blew out smoke.

'Yes, is he in?' Perry replied, recognising the elder sister, Chantelle.

'He's only just come back. He's been out looking for our brother.'

'Has he found him?'

'No, I haven't.' Dean appeared in the doorway next to his sister.

Perry clocked the injuries to Dean's face. 'That's some bruising there. Are you okay?'

'I'm fine,' Dean said, but he wouldn't look at Perry.

'Dean.' Perry tried again to get his attention.

'I got jumped, that's all.'

Perry gave up for now. The dog continued to bark.

'Will you pipe down, Barney!' Chantelle yelled. 'I can't hear myself think.'

Behind them came the sound of a baby crying. Chantelle sighed.

'You've woken Billy now. It took me ages to get him down.' She disappeared inside.

Perry refrained from saying it was probably her big mouth that had frightened the little one.

With resignation, Dean opened the door. 'You'd better come in.'

In the living room, Chantelle had picked up the baby and popped him on her chest, his head resting on her shoulder looking their way.

'It isn't like Joel to stay out and not let us know,' Dean said. 'We've been calling him and texting him, but nothing.'

Chantelle frowned. 'Has something happened to him and you're too afraid to say? Because if so, you'd better put us out of our misery or—'

Perry held up a hand for her to stop. He could understand her hostility towards them in some respect. Despite her father committing the crime, she and her siblings had probably been left to carry the can and look after Joel. But she didn't have a right to know anything. Besides, his copper nose had been twitching for a while and he wasn't leaving the house yet.

'I came here to speak to you, Dean, but if you're that worried, let's take a look at Joel's room.'

'What for?'

'Maybe you'll notice if anything is missing – clothes, et cetera.'

Dean nodded. Perry followed him upstairs.

'This is ours.' Dean opened a door and entered. 'It's not much.'

The room was cramped, two single beds and two old wardrobes fighting for floor space. Perry searched in Joel's wardrobe first. Underneath a pile of clothes at the bottom, he found several shooting and true crime magazines.

He bent down and looked under the bed. There was something wrapped in a towel. He pulled it out. It was a tatty shoebox.

Perry lifted the lid. Inside, he could see two balaclavas and two pairs of black gloves. His mind went into overdrive even before he picked up a large notepad. Inside, there were pages of handwriting, talking about sexual fantasies and graphic doodles. Words written in thick lettering. SexyBear5555. LoverBoy6912.

Suddenly, he stopped and went back a page. There in black handwriting was a list of names. They were all familiar to him:

1. Lauren
2. WildWoman
3. Sophie

Their first three victims.

There was a space next to number four.

Perry glanced at Dean, who was staring wide-eyed in alarm.

'Out of the room,' he ordered. 'Now.'

'What's happening?'

He shoved him in his haste.

'Hey, don't push me about!'

Perry ignored him and closed the door. His phone rang before he had time to make a call. It was Grace. He sat on the bed as he listened to what she had to say about Lizzie Shelby, who they also knew as Beth Whiston.

'Whoever is doing this with her, they had to plan meticulously to get everything the same as Bentley,' Grace told him. 'I think Shelby's being told what to do by Bentley. She seems vulnerable enough to manipulate. And then she's getting help from the outside.'

'I think I know who from. I'm at Joel Nicholls' house and there's stuff here, Grace.' He told her what he had found. 'It's one thing to be morbid and write a list of the women who have been attacked, and I might have thought nothing of that on its own. But with balaclavas and gloves, Joel's got to be part of this.'

'I agree. Can you get to Tranter's while I arrange backup to meet you there? You're the closest; we'll make our way to you after we've been to Lizzie's flat.'

'Yes, boss.' Perry stood up again.

'I'll update everyone and put an alert out for Nicholls, too, as he's a minor. Be careful, Perry. We don't know who might be with Shelby if both men are working with her, nor what state of mind they'll be in. She could well be at Tranter's house.'

Perry disconnected the call and opened the door. Dean was standing on the tiny landing. Behind him, Chantelle was in tears.

'Joel wasn't in the night Sophie was attacked. I lied. I'm sorry,' she sobbed. 'I would have told you if I thought it might be him.' She took a breath. 'It isn't him. It can't be!'

Perry had more things to think about than Chantelle obstructing their enquiries but he was as mad as hell.

'You could have stopped this!' he cried. 'What you've done is irresponsible.'

Dean pointed to the box on the floor. 'I don't want him to get banged up. But this is . . . sick!'

'Where do you think Joel will be?' He glared at them both.

'I don't know.' Dean shook his head.

'You must know where he's been hanging around lately. Think!'

'I've dropped him off in Waterside Road a few times lately. He said he had a mate in one of the four-block flats.'

'What's his friend called?'

'He never said!' Dean was close to tears.

'Which flat did he go to?'

'I'm not sure, but it was definitely in the first block on the right.'

Perry marched across the room, already ringing Grace back to update her. He'd need to request assistance from other officers too. Someone would have to take these two to the station for further questioning.

They wouldn't be getting away with this scot-free.

SEVENTY

Teagan was off school. She'd been so distressed after seeing Sophie the night before that she'd had trouble sleeping. Mum had come in to her during the night and held her while she'd sobbed. Eventually she had fallen asleep, but her eyes this morning were so swollen she'd barely been able to open them. Mum had taken pity on her and given her the day off. It was a rare treat; usually she'd be sent to school no matter what.

Her dad had called earlier, and had a quick coffee with her. Said her mum had rung to tell him how sad Teagan was. It was nice to see they both cared so much about her, even if she knew they were never going to get back together.

She dropped the magazine she'd been trying to read on the coffee table. All she could think about was Sophie and Lauren. Having two friends who had been harmed in such brutal ways was always on her mind and although she was trying to be brave, like last night it got to her that bit more every now and then. Without Sophie, she was lost.

Courtney and Caitlin were coming over at six. There had been no need for her parents to ground Teagan this time. She wasn't going out by herself again until things were safer. They were going to order in pizza once they were all here. It was a treat from her mum.

Yet, it worried Teagan in a way that things had begun to get back to normal after the death of Lauren. Even though her killer was still at large, she knew Grace and her dad were working flat out.

It was also distressing that she was part of the gang where Lauren had been murdered and Sophie attacked and left for dead.

Sophie was still in a coma, but she was stable now rather than critical. It had been really upsetting last night to see her best friend with tubes and machines attached to her. Her mum had spoken to the doctors. They said that Sophie might have damage to her brain, but they wouldn't know until she was brought out of the induced coma today. She might never recall what had happened to her, either.

Never normally stuck for words, Teagan hadn't known what to say. So in a way, she was pleased to get back to routine, do normal things, go to school and see some of her other friends. Even if she did feel guilty about it. She didn't want to think about what would happen if she lost Sophie.

A message came in on her phone. It was from Joel.

Are you okay? Heard you were ill?

She tapped a reply:

I'm fine, a bit upset. Will be in school tomorrow.

Up for visitors? Can we come and see you?

Her heart leapt into her throat. Maybe he was with Lewis. She typed back quickly.

There was a knock on the door. Opening it, she found Joel on the doorstep.

'Right now?' he said.

'I wasn't expecting you so soon!' She smiled, looking behind him and trying not to show her disappointment that he was alone. He was in his school uniform, yet she was sure there was a tang of aftershave in the air.

'Is Lewis not with you?' she said as casually as she could muster.

'Sorry, I wanted to come on my own.' The toe of his right boot bumped on the step. 'You don't mind, do you? I just need someone to talk to. About Sophie.'

At the mention of her friend, Teagan's eyes brimmed with tears again.

'No.' She opened the door. 'Come on through.'

'Your mum isn't in?' he asked as he stepped inside. 'I'm not good with parents.'

'She's at work; Adrian is, too. They won't be home for a while yet.' She walked through into the kitchen. 'Do you want a drink? A cup of tea, or juice?'

'Juice, thanks.'

Joel stood with his back to the worktop. His cheeks were flushed, she noticed. She reckoned he must have run most of the way here. It was lunchtime. They only had an hour for lunch so he'd have to get back to school soon.

'Are you okay?' she asked him even so.

'Yeah, but I have something to tell you. You know when Soph's old man stopped us from seeing each other? Well, we were still meeting.'

'It was you!' Teagan gasped. 'She wouldn't tell me.'

'I swore her to secrecy.' He stepped towards her. 'Besides, he didn't like who I was anyway.'

'Oh, Joel.' She nodded, mistaking his manner for melancholy. 'So you were dating in secret?'

'Yeah.'

'Well, I know she wasn't happy about what her dad said. She thought a lot of you.'

'Did she tell you that?'

'All the time!'

He shrugged, which she thought was weird. Then she frowned.

Wait a minute!

Was Joel saying *he* had attacked Sophie? That *he* had been going to meet her and then tried to strangle her? Because if he was, then he had killed that other woman. And *he* had murdered Lauren.

No, it couldn't be him. He was supposed to be their friend – not killing their friends!

'So, it was *you* she was meeting on Sunday?' she said, her voice faltering.

Joel took another step towards her, a strange look on his face. 'Yes, it was me.'

Teagan froze for a second. Then she ran past him towards the kitchen door.

He pulled her back by her hair and covered her mouth with a cloth. Her voice muffled as she tried to scream, breathing in some kind of sickly smell. She breathed in more as she panicked.

In desperation, she clawed at his hands with her own. But it was useless. Helpless, she felt her limbs going weak, feeling the world slipping from her.

SEVENTY-ONE

Grace had been on the A500 heading towards Stoke when Perry called. Waterside Drive was on the Bennett Estate. She turned off at the exit to Tunstall. Sam rang next.

'I've checked the phone records for SexyBear5555 and LoverBoy6912 and they're both members of All Talk. Shelby's phone has been used in Stoke about an hour ago. She's been in contact with both Joel and Jason. Triangulation puts her in the right spot for Waterside Drive. While I was doing that, I asked Allie to check in with the council housing department. She came back to me to say that Lizzie Shelby lives at—'

'Don't tell me. Number five,' Grace finished for her, glancing at Frankie as she drove. 'She seems to be obsessed by the number, but I don't really know why.'

'All numbers have a significance,' Frankie said, getting out his phone. He googled the meaning of the number. 'Here you go. "You've either completed or are about to complete a cycle, and everything is falling into place, physically and emotionally." I'm not sure how that fits into her remit, though.'

'Me neither. Thanks, Sam. Great work.'

* * *

After screeching up in Waterside Road, Grace and Frankie raced across the green. They found the side door to number five and banged on it. When there was no answer after trying twice, Grace knocked on number seven.

'Who is it?' a voice enquired from behind the door.

'Staffordshire Police. We're looking for Lizzie or Elizabeth Shelby.'

'Lizzie? She's the flat above.'

'Yes, we know that. I'm wondering if you know where she is? Or do you have a key?'

'I'll need to see ID.'

'If you can open the door, I'll show you.'

The door opened a fraction with a chain. An elderly man popped his head around it. 'Sorry about that, you can never be too careful.'

Grace smiled as she held up her warrant card. 'Have you seen Lizzie today at all, Mr . . .'

'Jerold. Arnie Jerold.'

The chain was removed and the door opened wider as he came into view. Grace rather wished he hadn't as the smell of cat pee assaulted her nostrils. She took a step back.

'I saw her going out this afternoon. Not sure if she's back yet, though, as I fell asleep.'

'I'll try the door again,' Frankie told Grace.

'She didn't even say hello when I spoke to her. She seemed in a rush to get to somewhere.'

'Do you know if she has any regular visitors?' asked Grace.

'Only the one recently. A young boy. Tall lad, he was. She told me she was teaching him maths lessons.' He chuckled. 'Maths lessons, indeed. I'm not going senile yet.'

'How old would you say he was?'

'Fifteen – sixteen maybe. He mostly comes in his school uniform.'

It was all fitting together. Jason Tranter and Joel Nicholls were in this together.

Grace looked to Frankie. 'Can you shoulder it open?'

'My dear, I have a key if you need it,' Arnie said.

Grace sighed then smiled at him. Eager public were always an asset but sometimes they were a little too slow in a crisis.

'Thank you, that would help.'

She hoped her impatience wasn't showing as she waited for him to return.

'I can trust you with it?' he asked when he came back, handing it to her. 'It would take me until tomorrow to come with you and climb her stairs.'

'You certainly can. Thank you, Mr Jerold. You've been a great help.' Grace took the keys from him. Frankie stepped aside for Grace to use them.

'Police!' Grace cried, going into the flat and up the stairs. 'We're coming in! Stay where you are!'

They checked the few small rooms to find them all empty. A laptop was still switched on. After flicking latex gloves on, Grace pressed a button to wake it up. The browser was open on the *Stoke News* website, details of their case and an image of Sophie Bishop on show. There was a pile of printouts on the table about their current case.

She looked around again, expecting to confirm her notion: five framed photos on the wall together; five coasters spread out in a row on the coffee table.

'Sarge,' Frankie said from behind her.

Grace turned to see him pointing. In the corner of the room was a black shoe, caked in mud. It was like the one Sophie Bishop had lost. Then she noticed something else that looked familiar. Moving a crime novel from a pile of books, she saw one of the books was a notepad. She held it up for Frankie to see.

'Isn't that the same notepad as—'

'The *exact* same as Peter Bentley's,' Grace interrupted him in her eagerness.

She flicked through the pages. There was a list similar to the one Perry had told them he'd found in Joel Nicholls' bedroom:

1. Lauren
2. WildWoman
3. Sophie

Then she paled, blood rushing to her feet. She steadied herself for a moment before crying out.

Grace thrust the book at Frankie and almost fell down the stairs in her haste to get out and back to her car.

The next name was Teagan.

SEVENTY-TWO

Joel Nicholls let Teagan go loose in his arms, then he laid her out on the floor. Inside his hoodie pocket was a roll of duct tape he'd brought with him. With no care, he bound Teagan's hands and feet together. Then he placed a strip across her mouth. She was still out for the count, but he needed to keep her quiet if she woke too early.

Getting his phone out, he sent a text message:

She's all yours.

He glanced around the room while he waited. He'd always liked spending time at Teagan's house – not that he'd been there much, but every time it had felt like what he imagined a home should. And it was always warm and clean, biscuits ready with the coffee. Coasters to put the mugs on.

His stomach rumbling, he opened the door to the fridge and looked inside. It was full to the brim. Would he have time to make a sandwich?

He was just about to reach for a pack of cheese but, hearing his name, he turned his head towards the door.

'In here,' he shouted.

Lizzie Shelby stepped into the kitchen, trying not to look annoyed. She hated the fact that some people lived like this, well-off with all mod-cons, warmth and comfort.

'Impressive, isn't it?' Joel caught her eye. 'We should have a place like this one day.'

'We will.' Lizzie walked to him and pressed her lips to his. 'Where's the girl?' she asked afterwards.

'Quiet for now.' He pointed to behind the kitchen island.

She took a step towards it, spotting a pair of fluffy socks first. The girl was out for the count, so she turned her attention back to him. She ran a hand through his hair, kissing him deeper before reaching for the buckle on his belt.

'Let's do it first this time,' she whispered. 'While she's in the room.'

'Her olds aren't due home any time soon.' His hand cupped her breast.

'That's not a problem, anyway.' She pulled Joel to the floor. 'If anyone comes back, we can say we found her like this.' She pressed a finger to his lips. 'We can save the day.'

'She saw my face!'

'She was confused. I'll say you were with me. We arrived here together – or we can run away like Bonnie and Clyde.' Lizzie straddled him, hitched up her skirt and whispered in his ear. 'Come on, lover boy. You know you want to.'

She undid his zip and reached inside for him, smiling when he groaned. His hand found her waist as he sat up. She let him kiss her for a moment before pulling down his jeans and guiding him inside her.

'It's my turn to give you the pleasure.' He grinned and then flipped her over onto her back.

It took her by surprise.

'No!' She tried to push him off, but he grabbed both of her hands with his own. 'There isn't much time!'

'You're *stalling*!' He held them either side of her head. 'You're still not sure you can go through with killing her, are you?'

She struggled beneath him, but she didn't show him in her facial expressions. As his hands went to her throat, she took the opportunity to flip him over onto his back again. She squeezed her thighs to keep his legs together this time.

He laughed. 'Okay, I surrender.'

She laughed, too. Her hands went to his throat this time and she squeezed just as Peter had shown her all those years ago. She moved up and down, slowly at first, then faster as she squeezed harder.

His face contorted as he reached his orgasm, but this time she kept on squeezing. Harder. Harder. She wasn't going to have a sixteen-year-old boy get the better of her.

Joel pawed at her hands when he realised what was happening, that hers was the last face he would ever see. It was extremely satisfying as she watched him taking his final breaths, gasping for air as he tried to throw her off him. But she was strong and in control. That was the side of her she had never shown him before.

See, she could do it when she had to.

It was a shame not to get to number five with him, but he'd messed up with the third one. He had served his purpose so he had to be included now, to ensure she got further than Peter with his victims. As soon as she had done what she'd set out to do with the Cole girl, she'd be long gone. No one would find her. She was used to running at short notice and going to ground. She'd survived on the streets before; she could always start up again somewhere. There was always a Number Five bus out of a city she could catch. They'd never find her.

When she was done, she sat for a moment. She looked down at his lifeless body while she caught her breath. It had been fun with Joel while it had lasted, but he'd been stupid. He had failed her.

A loud groan came from the other side of the room. Lizzie smiled: the girl was awake. Quickly, she got off Joel and righted her clothes. Then she pushed his arm nearer to the side of his body with her foot, making sure he couldn't be seen behind the island before standing.

'Teagan?' She rushed over to her. Gently, she removed the tape from her mouth. 'My name's Lizzie. Are you okay? What happened?'

'I . . . I'm not sure.' Teagan burst into tears. 'One minute I was talking to Joel and then I . . . I can't remember.' She looked up. 'He put a cloth over my mouth.'

'Oh, you poor thing! I gave him a lift because he said he wanted to talk to you. When he didn't come out, I came to see. Your front door was open. Do you know where he is?'

Teagan could only shake her head in response. She glanced around the room, eyes widening.

'He must still be in the house!'

Lizzie rushed across to the kitchen units, opening drawers until she found the cutlery tray. She picked out a small sharp knife.

Teagan shied away as she came towards her.

'Don't be scared! I'm going to cut you free.'

Lizzie began to slice at the tape around her feet. Soon, Teagan was free from the binding, but when she went to stand, her legs gave way.

Lizzie held on to her. 'Let's get you out of here, just in case he's still around. Where are your shoes?'

'In the hall. I want to ring my mum.'

'We can do it on the way.' She took her by the elbow. 'Hurry!'

'But . . . my dad . . ?'

'Where's your phone?'

Teagan paused. 'It was in the living room.'

'Wait here.' Lizzie was there and back in a matter of seconds. 'I have it in my pocket. I picked up a jacket for you, too.' She placed it over Teagan's still-bound hands. 'Come on, I'll take you somewhere safe.'

'My mum works in Hanley.' Teagan began to shiver. 'Can you take me there? I want to see her.'

'Of course I can.' In the hall, Lizzie helped the dazed teenager to pop her feet into a pair of boots and then led her by the arm to her car.

Perry raced to Tranter's address, sirens blazing. Backup had been called, but if they weren't there before him, he was going in. Shit, how had they missed that Tranter and Nicholls were working together, and that Shelby was the conduit!

Minutes later, he pulled up outside the house and ran up the driveway, flicking out his baton. In the distance, he could hear sirens approaching. With no sign of anyone else, he wasn't waiting.

'Police!' he shouted. 'Open up.' When no one came to the door, he banged again. 'Police.'

He moved to the bay window and looked inside. Tranter was lying on the floor, blood visible from a wound on his head.

Behind Perry, a marked car double-parked, blocking off the street, lights flashing. A couple of uniformed officers ran to his aid as he shoulder-barged the door. With the help of a kick from the burlier of the two, it gave way and they piled inside.

Rushing through to the living room, Perry dropped to his

knees, ignoring the shards of glass everywhere as he desperately searched for a pulse.

Glass was embedded in the side of Tranter's face, too. His eyes had glazed over. Perry had seen those signs before. Bruising was already appearing on either side of his neck.

Perry cursed as he fought to find a pulse.

SEVENTY-THREE

Grace rang Teagan's phone, but there was no answer. At the same time, Frankie was updating Nick and putting everyone on major alert. After a third failed attempt, she had no choice but to ring Simon.

'Where's Teagan?' she cried, sounding breathless as adrenaline took over her fear. 'Will she be at school?'

'No, she's stayed off today. She's not feeling too good. I called to see her earlier. Why?'

'Do you still have a key to the house?'

'Yes, but why, Grace?'

Grace tried not to sound too emotional as she said the next words.

'I think she might be in danger. Our suspect may be going after Teagan next.' She gave out a sob. 'We're on our way to the house now.'

'What? How?'

'There's no time for questions! I—'

'Fuck! I'm on my way, too. I'll ring Natalie.'

'No,' Grace shouted. 'Please, not yet.'

'But—'

'Trust me, Simon.' She knew she wouldn't be able to stop him from following her, so she wasn't even going to try. 'Come alone.'

'I'm on my way.'

With Frankie by her side, Grace rushed across the city towards Teagan's address. Frankie put Nick on loudspeaker as he liaised with the control room, arranging backup.

'Get an Enforcer, too,' Grace said, suspecting they'd need the battering ram to get in the house.

No sooner had he disconnected that call than the phone rang again.

'It's Perry,' Frankie told her.

'Keep him on speaker.'

'Tranter's dead,' he told them. 'He's been hit with a bottle and then strangled.'

'No!' Grace cried as she turned a corner. 'Thanks, Perry. Get CSI in and seal it off.' She glanced at Frankie. 'We don't know who killed him, do we? It could have been either Joel or Lizzie at the moment.'

Finally they arrived at Teagan's home, screeching to a halt in the road. Grace switched off the engine and rushed to the front door. She banged on it, hoping that Teagan would come to answer it, that it was all a false alarm. That she would be fine and in no danger.

But no one came.

Frankie peered through the front window. 'I can't see anyone and nothing looks out of place.'

Grace banged on the front door again, and with still no answer, she kept Control informed.

'We're heading around the back now. Is the Enforcer on its way?'

She didn't wait for a reply as they ran around the side of the house. They tried the kitchen door, finding that locked, too. Her breathing becoming raspy, she took a moment to calm herself. She would be no use to anyone if she began to panic.

'There are some French doors here that lead into a conservatory,' Frankie shouted from the back garden. 'But they're UPVC.'

'Any windows open?'

'A tiny one at the side. Looks like it might be a utility room. I can try to get through. Can you give me a leg up?'

Grace went to him, laced her fingers together and pushed up when Frankie put his foot inside them. She wasn't sure he would fit through but admired him for trying. As she held on to his feet, he disappeared.

'Okay, let me go,' he whispered loudly. 'I'm in. There's a key in the back door.'

Within seconds, Grace was inside the house too. They were indeed in a utility room. She pressed down the handle on the door in front, finding herself in the kitchen.

'Police! Stay where you are!' she shouted, her baton raised as they progressed through the room. 'Teagan? Are you here?'

She took in the scene: strips of duct tape and the small knife on the worktop.

'Someone's been tied up and then released,' she stated, pointing at the debris.

As they moved round the island in the middle of the floor, a boot came into view. It was followed by another, then legs covered in navy trousers.

'No.' Grace took a further step nearer. Joel Nicholls was lying on the floor, his mouth wide open. His eyes bulging, dead and staring up at the ceiling.

Grace dropped to her knees, searching to find a pulse, but she couldn't. She rang for an ambulance, but a lump caught in her throat as she sensed there was nothing that could be done for him.

'No!' she cried, banging the palm of her hand on the floor.

Once they'd checked to see if anyone else was in the house, the first backup had arrived. A couple of uniformed officers rushed in through the front door.

'Seal off the house, and either end of the street, then stay outside.' Grace barked her orders as another car arrived. 'This is a crime scene and needs to be preserved. No one touch anything until the paramedics and CSI arrive. And don't let anyone in either, nor come back in yourself.'

'Is everything okay in there?' An elderly man appeared in the open doorway.

'You need to move away from the property, sir,' Grace told him.

'But, I—'

'It's fine, sir. We can handle it.'

She nodded in the direction of an officer, who escorted the man out of the way. Neighbours were already starting to congregate in doorways and at gates as she spotted Nick arriving.

Grace explained what she knew.

'If Shelby was here, we don't have much time. Frankie –' Nick turned to him '– what did you find out about local clock towers?'

'There are four nearby: Burslem, Hanley Park, Victoria Park and Tunstall.'

'They're all within a couple of miles of here,' Grace cried. 'It could be any of them!'

She thought back to Bentley's fourth murder victim, Petra Swindles. She prayed that they wouldn't be too late.

'We'll send units to each one.' Nick reached for his phone.

'You two head over to Burslem and I'll arrange the rest. I'll be right behind you.'

Grace quickly tried Teagan's mobile number again. Still there was no reply. A commotion to her right caught her eye. She turned to see Simon. An officer was holding him back from the house. She ran to him.

'You can't go in there,' she explained. 'It's a crime scene.' As much as she could, she quickly explained what had happened.

'I don't understand.' Simon held her at arm's length. 'Where is Teagan?'

Grace couldn't tell him what she knew. 'Wait here,' she said instead. 'We're going to find her.'

'I'm coming with you!'

'The situation has changed!' Grace was adamant. 'You need to stay here. In case – in case Teagan tries to contact you.'

'She'd ring my mobile!'

'You can't come with me!' Grace took both of his hands in her own. 'Please, let me do my job.'

Simon looked her in the eye, pleading with her to say more, but she couldn't.

'Do you know who the killer is?' he asked, his voice wavering.

'Yes.'

'And are you sure Teagan is the target?'

She nodded, hating herself as she watched tears pour down his face.

Simon gasped and his face crumbled. 'Find her for me, Grace. Bring her home.'

She nodded, wanting to draw him into her embrace, feel his heart beat against her chest, bring her lips to his to comfort him. But there wasn't time.

It almost broke her heart to leave him there, but she wasn't sure even *she* would cope if they were too late to save his daughter.

She beckoned to a uniformed officer who was guarding the door.

'Make sure he doesn't follow us,' she said, nodding towards Simon.

Then she raced to her car with Frankie.

SEVENTY-FOUR

Teagan's teeth began to chatter as they drove along Leek New Road towards Hanley. She glanced over at Lizzie, whose hands were clamped at ten to two on the steering wheel, eyes wide and alert. Who the hell was she? And had she really been waiting for Joel outside her home? Because if so, why?

'What happened to Joel?' she asked.

'I told you. He ran when I saw him. I don't know what he was going to do to you, but luckily I came in. He seemed in such a good mood, too.'

Teagan stayed quiet. That wasn't what she told her when she first came into the house. She said he'd disappeared.

The sounds of Ariana Grande burst into the space once more.

Teagan glanced at Lizzie. 'That's my phone again. Can I answer it? It might be my mum.'

'I'm driving,' Lizzie snapped. 'I'll get it for you once we stop.'

'But—'

'I'm concentrating!' Lizzie threw her a sideways glance. 'What's the rush, anyway?'

'You forgot to untie my hands.' Teagan raised them in the air to show her.

'Oh, yes, silly me!' Lizzie laughed this time.

Something made her decide not to say anything else. That didn't seem a valid excuse.

Lizzie turned off at the slip road that would take her up and onto Hanley Road. At the junction, she turned right instead of left.

'You've gone the wrong way,' Teagan said, trying not to show the tremor in her voice.

'We're just nipping to somewhere else before we go there.' Lizzie pressed down on the horn, making Teagan jump. 'Move out of the way, you idiot! I want to get there today, not tomorrow.'

Tears welled in Teagan's eyes as she tried to grasp what was happening. Because she had worked out where she knew the woman from. It was Mr Tranter's girlfriend. She'd often been at the youth club with him.

'Where do you think Joel went?' Teagan asked.

'I don't know and I don't care. You shouldn't, neither. He was going to kill you.'

'Wh . . . what?' Teagan blinked profusely. 'Stop it. You're scaring me.'

Lizzie's foot went down on the pedal, sending Teagan's head back against the seat with the force. She decided she would stay quiet until she figured out why this woman had taken her in the car. Because she wasn't taking her to her mum, was she?

Panic tore through her. She tried to think what Grace would do. Grace would stay calm. Grace would try to talk to Lizzie. Grace would look for something she could use to defend herself.

Discreetly her eyes travelled around, but there was nothing in the footwell, nor on the dashboard. Maybe there would be something in the glove compartment, but she wouldn't lean forwards and have a look yet. Even with her hands tied, it would be useless and might even prove dangerous. One move from her could send Lizzie off the road and they could both end up dead if they crashed into something.

They were driving along High Lane now. Lizzie was singing along to the radio as if they were on a day out. Teagan began to think about why Lizzie had turned up as she had. Something must have happened to Joel. After all, it was him who had put the cloth over her mouth, making her pass out.

It was all starting to come back now.

'I want to go to—' she started.

'Shut the fuck up!' Lizzie screamed. 'It's all your fault everything's gone wrong and now you must pay the price. Five! I have to get to five, don't you see? But, oh no, everyone had to interfere! And now look what they've made me do!'

Instinctively, Teagan reached for the door handle. But Lizzie swerved the car as she pressed down the automatic door lock on her side, locking them both in. Teagan sobbed. She knew she'd probably be able to open it from the inside regardless but she didn't dare try again.

Lizzie leaned over and punched Teagan in the stomach with the back of a closed fist.

'I told you, no funny business,' she screamed, keeping her eyes on the road.

Teagan's head hit the side window as they bumped over a speed hump.

'Please! Slow down!' Tears pricked her eyes.

'We're here!' Lizzie pulled the car into the side. 'Keep that jacket over your hands while we go into the park.'

'But—'

Teagan gasped as a knife appeared beside her cheek. The tears she'd tried desperately to hold in began to pour down her face.

Lizzie reached for her chin and squeezed it hard, turning

Teagan's face towards her own. She held the blade next to her skin.

'Say one word or shout out to anyone and this knife will go into your stomach, do you hear?'

Teagan nodded.

'Good.' Lizzie let go of her and got out of the car.

As she came around to her, Teagan knew her idea to look inside the glove compartment for something to use as a weapon wasn't going to work.

'Come on, poppet.' Lizzie opened the door and smiled sweetly at her. 'The clock's ticking.' She grabbed Teagan by her bound hands and pulled her out onto the pavement. There were people around but she didn't care now. It would be too late before they realised what was happening.

'We're going to walk into the park and you're going to behave yourself, aren't you?' she said calmly, the knife down by her side.

Teagan nodded, willing to do anything to buy herself time to figure out a way to escape. Because if she didn't, she was sure she was going to die. Lizzie had hurt Sophie, killed Lauren and another woman.

Ahead, she could see the clock tower coming up in the distance. There were a few people in the park. They passed a woman with a pushchair, staring at the knife, mouth dropping open. Teagan pleaded with her eyes, willing the woman to help her, but Lizzie dragged her past.

'What are you looking at?' Lizzie roared over her shoulder. The woman scurried off quickly.

The path was clear in front of them. Teagan could see an elderly man with a dog in the distance, and nearby there was a park worker. There was a lawned area between them, which looked like it doubled as a bowling green. Teagan thought he hadn't seen them, but then he shouted.

'Hey, you!'

Lizzie turned back with a sigh. 'What?' she protested.

'What's going on? Is she okay?'

'She's fine!' Lizzie held the knife up in front of her. 'Now, back away, because I'm not afraid to use it.'

The man stayed where he was. Teagan could see someone behind him with a phone to his ear. But so could Lizzie.

'Put that away!' Lizzie screamed, holding the knife up to Teagan's chest.

Teagan gasped and tried to wriggle from her grip, but Lizzie squeezed her arm to stop her. The men weren't close enough to help. Lizzie could slit her throat in an instant.

Lizzie marched off, pulling her along.

Grace, where are you?

'Please, let me go.' Teagan jogged to keep up with her. 'I won't say anything, I promise.'

'Oh, shut up whining,' Lizzie sneered at her. 'Come on. Nearly there.'

SEVENTY-FIVE

Grace pushed the car as quickly as she could through the traffic as Control relayed the details via Frankie. But she could barely hear him over the beat of her heart.

She had to get there in time.

She wouldn't have it on her conscience that Teagan had died on her watch.

'All available units,' a voice came over the radio. 'Several calls coming through of a female in Victoria Park wielding a knife. Suspect matches the description of Elizabeth Shelby, also known as Beth Whiston and wanted in connection with the kidnap of sixteen-year-old Teagan Cole.'

'Assign us to it, Frankie!' Grace shouted to no one in particular.

At Smallthorne, she flew over the three roundabouts and onto High Lane. Past a few more streets and she turned into Greenbank Road. Tunstall Park was on the right, almost in the town centre, still a couple more minutes' drive.

'We're going to be too late,' she cried, slowing to go over yet another speed hump. 'Can you locate the clock tower in the park?'

'No need, it's right by the entrance.'

Turning into Victoria Park Road, Grace could see it coming into view. Despite the craziness of the situation, something that her mum had told her as a child flashed up in her mind. The tower had been named in memory of William Adams, a well-known manufacturer in the area, erected in 1907.

It looked to be less than a few hundred feet inside the park. Through the railings, it was audacious and imposing, set in a triangle of grass surrounded by a hedge, but she didn't have time to admire its elegance as it loomed over them.

She screeched to a halt outside the gates and they scrambled out of the car before running through the entrance, along the main path.

Teagan almost tripped as Lizzie dragged her towards the clock tower.

Lizzie pulled at her hands, righting her. 'Watch where you're going,' she tutted, continuing to pull her along.

Teagan thought again about what Grace would do. Could she try to talk Lizzie down until help arrived? She chanced a quick look behind her. The man who had shouted over was still on his phone.

'Please,' she said the first thing that came into her head. 'I won't say anything if you let me go.'

Lizzie laughed. 'You won't tell anyone that I've killed two people today?'

That stopped Teagan in her tracks and she whimpered.

'You wanted to know where Joel went?' Lizzie added. 'Well, I left him dead on your kitchen floor.'

'Wh-what?' Teagan faltered. Lizzie must be lying. She hadn't seen anything, but then again, she had been bustled out of the room. Seeing the knife in Lizzie's hand, she had to assume she was telling the truth. And who was the other person she had killed?

They were at the top of the steps now, the clock tower in front of them.

'He was good, you know.' Lizzie pushed Teagan against the side wall. 'Still, he had to go in the end, because he was careless. He didn't do things properly. He led the police to me, so I had to end it for him.'

Teagan squirmed as Lizzie's face came within inches of her own, and she turned away, dropping her eyes. But Lizzie grabbed her by the chin again so that she had to look at her.

'You'd never think he could be so violent, would you?' Lizzie tittered. 'I must admit, he had such charm about him, no one would have guessed. But he had a really dark side. He kept it well hidden. It was so much fun having him fawn all over me. I pick them out, you see, the lost souls.'

Teagan said nothing, too scared to speak, even if she could think of something to say. Listening to Lizzie, it seemed as if she was enjoying telling her what she had done. She didn't seem to care who she hurt.

She began to lose hope of ever getting away. But she wouldn't give up, because she knew Grace wouldn't, either.

'You won't win,' she told her. 'Grace will find me and you'll be locked up and—'

'I *have* to get to number five! Don't you understand?' Teagan screamed.

'Be quiet!' Lizzie sliced a hand across her face.

Teagan cried out again. Still bound together, her hands were caught between them. She couldn't help herself in any way.

She really was going to die.

341

SEVENTY-SIX

Teagan's scream travelled through the air towards them. Every hair on Grace's body stood on end as it pierced her ears.

Please don't let me be too late.

'This way!' Frankie shouted and she followed him.

Rounding a corner, she saw two men pointing in the direction of the clock tower. In the distance were Teagan and the woman Grace now knew was Lizzie Shelby. Lizzie had a knife in her hand. They *were* going to be too late.

'We have eyes on our suspect!' Grace told Control over her phone. 'Police! Stop!'

As they moved closer, Lizzie wrapped her arm around Teagan's neck, drew her close to her chest and placed the blade against her stomach.

'Back off!' she screamed.

They slowed. Shelby was in control here. Grace would have to keep her talking until further help arrived.

'Elizabeth, or would you prefer I called you Lizzie? Or Bethan, even?' she said.

'My name is Lizzie.'

'Okay, Lizzie, I just want to talk to you.' Grace braved a step forwards, hoping to take more as she went. 'We have your DNA all over Joel Nicholls and Jason Tranter,' she said, not knowing if it was true yet but not caring either as she moved another step closer. 'You killed them; you can't deny that. Let Teagan go.'

'No! She's number five.'

'And I have way more than five officers surrounding you,' she fibbed. 'So there'll be no happy ending.'

Grace looked straight into Teagan's eyes, willing the young girl to stay calm and quiet. She watched as Lizzie tightened her grip around Teagan's neck. Teagan screamed.

'Shut up, will you!' Lizzie shouted.

'Let's calm it down.' Grace held up her hands.

She glanced at Frankie, who was still by her side. Neither of them could move without Lizzie seeing them. It wasn't even safe for other officers to come up behind the clock tower. It was too open.

'It's over, Lizzie,' Grace continued.

'I didn't kill any of them,' Lizzie said. 'It was her – Teagan.'

'No,' Teagan sobbed.

'Oh, come on, that's not going to wash. We know she isn't involved.' Grace changed tack. 'So why these young blonde women?'

'Why do *you* think? You're obviously going to tell me.'

'I think they reminded you of you, or what you could have been. Clean, happy, loved.'

'You can't prove that.'

'Not yet we can't, but I can connect you to Peter Bentley in 2014. You were both charged with theft two months before the killing spree. You gave us false information when we charged you. You were homeless and living under the arches but spending a few nights in the hostel on Curzon Road. Went by the name of Beth Whiston. That's your mother's maiden name, isn't it?'

It was fun to see Lizzie begin to squirm as the net closed in, but there was a fine line to tread between being pushy and antagonistic.

'I suppose you're going to say that Peter Bentley made you do it,' Grace continued.

'Peter didn't make me do anything. He loved me.'

'Really? Did you know you weren't the only woman he saw regularly while he was inside? He had three female visitors every month.'

Lizzie's eyes locked with Grace's at this revelation. 'You're lying.'

'I'm not.'

'Who were they?'

'You know I can't tell you that.'

'Then how do I know you're not trying to trick me?'

'You don't.' Grace paused for effect. 'You're not sure you can trust me. But Teagan is. She knows me well enough to realise that while all this is happening around her, she's clever enough to use her head. Isn't that right, Teagan?'

Grace stared at the young girl, flicking her chin up ever so slightly, hoping she'd catch her meaning. Teagan looked back at her, fear clear in her wide eyes.

Do it, Teagan.

She wasn't sure she was going to, but then Grace watched as Teagan drew back her head. She heard the crack as it caught Lizzie's chin. Lizzie stumbled backwards, dropping the knife to the ground and giving Teagan the opportunity to run.

'No!' Lizzie screeched, reaching to grab her, just missing her shoulder.

Teagan raced away from her and Grace prayed she wouldn't stumble.

'Run, Teagan!' Grace thundered towards her. She was almost there, another second. In the background, she saw Lizzie running in the opposite direction.

'Grace!' Teagan cried.

Grace pulled the girl into her embrace. She squeezed her eyes shut, burying the relief she felt deep inside. She wanted to hold on to her, keep her close, but she needed to catch Lizzie.

She let go of Teagan, handing her over to Frankie. 'Get her to safety and then follow me.'

A uniformed officer in the background was running towards them.

'I'll be right behind you,' Frankie reassured her.

Grace took off, running round the back of the clock tower, scanning the grounds for signs of Lizzie. There was so much foliage around the edges that she struggled to see past it. But there! A streak of blonde hair.

She kept going. Now in the open park, Lizzie had nowhere to hide. Grace was gaining on her second by second, but she was also losing energy.

Come on, Grace, you can do this.

She was almost close enough to bring Lizzie down. As she glanced quickly over her shoulder, she saw two uniformed officers running to catch up with her, Frankie close behind them.

She dived at Lizzie's legs in a rugby tackle, knocking them both to the ground. They rolled around on the grass. Grace tried to keep control, but Lizzie was strong. Grace slapped away her hands as they reached for her throat, grabbing one of them and bending Lizzie's fingers backwards.

Lizzie screamed in anger and lashed out at Grace with her free hand balled in a fist. It caught Grace on the cheekbone, but not enough to make her loosen her grip on Lizzie. She flipped the woman over onto her stomach.

Lizzie wriggled beneath her, screaming. 'Get off me, you mad cow!'

'I'm not the mad one, you evil bitch.'

Grace got out her handcuffs, wrestling to snap them shut around Lizzie's wrists. When she at last managed, it was with great satisfaction.

'Elizabeth Shelby, I'm arresting you on suspicion of the murders of Lauren Ansell, Diane Waybridge, Jason Tranter and Joel Nicholls, the attempted murder of Sophie Bishop, and the kidnapping of Teagan Cole.'

After she'd completed reading the rest of the rights, Grace looked up at Frankie.

'What kept you?' She grinned.

Frankie bent over and put his hands on his knees, breathing heavily. 'I'm going to call you Forrest Gump from now on,' he wheezed.

As other officers drew level, Grace pulled Shelby to standing and passed her to them. 'Take her out of my sight.'

They marched off with Lizzie. Grace wasn't through with her yet, but there was something she needed to do first. She got out her phone and with shaking hands, made a call.

'We have her, Simon,' she told him, turning away from everyone while she wiped the tears that rolled down her face. 'We have Teagan and she's safe.'

SEVENTY-SEVEN

Back at the station, Grace was sitting with Teagan in an interview room. They were waiting for her parents to collect her. Grace had made her a hot drink and told her to eat some chocolate while they waited for the station doctor to arrive. As far as she could see Teagan was shaky, and her wrists were sore where the tape had chafed, but she seemed in particularly good spirits now she was safe again.

'That was a great move you made with your head,' Grace said as she sat opposite her. 'I'm glad you understood me. It was very brave, too.'

'I only did it because you told me to.' Teagan grinned at her shyly before sipping on her drink. 'You know, Sophie wants to join the police. I used to laugh at her but I'm not going to any more. I hope she gets better so she can follow her dreams, too.'

Grace smiled. She really wanted Teagan and her to become friends now. It had been an experience for them both, but they had come out of it together.

Teagan went quiet for a moment. 'Lizzie told me she'd killed two people this morning. Is that right?'

'You don't need to worry yourself about that.'

Forensics would have to be analysed, but everything suggested Lizzie Shelby *had* killed both Jason and Joel. It added up – number three and number four, after their two murdered women. Thank goodness Teagan hadn't been number five.

'But—'

'Yes, there are two people dead, if that's what you mean.'

Grace thought she deserved to hear the truth after what she'd been through.

Teagan gasped loudly, tears welling in her eyes.

'It's okay, you're with me.' Grace reached over and squeezed her hand. Even though Teagan knew both victims, she couldn't tell her who they were until their next of kin had been informed. It was going to be another blow to the school. And with both suspects deceased, they may never know exactly how much each of the men knew.

There was a knock on the door. Frankie appeared with two people behind him.

'Someone here to see you, boss.' He moved aside to let Simon and Natalie through.

'Teagan!' Natalie cried.

Teagan stood up and raced into her mum's arms. She hugged her fiercely. 'I'm fine,' she said. 'Grace has been looking after me. She's so cool.'

Simon raised his eyebrows at Grace.

Grace threw him a knowing smile. 'I'll leave you to it,' she said as Teagan gave Simon a hug too.

'Thank you,' Natalie acknowledged as Grace was leaving the room.

And then, suddenly, Teagan was in Grace's arms.

'Thank you from me, too.' Teagan hugged her tightly.

'Thank *you* for being so brave.' Grace hugged her back, excited by the show of affection. 'We'll speak more to you about this soon.'

'I'll see you later?' Simon asked.

'Yes, I should be finished at a decent time this evening.'

'Could I come and see you, too?' Teagan asked.

'I'm sure your mum will—'

'It's fine,' Natalie replied. 'As long as I know she's safe now.'

Back at her desk upstairs, Grace sat for a moment. The hustle and bustle of the station went on around her, but she needed to be still. It had been emotionally draining dealing with Teagan's kidnap, but the main thing was that she seemed okay. She could be in shock, or even suffer from delayed shock, but she was alive. No doubt what had happened would hit Teagan when she had a quiet moment.

Grace had told both Natalie and Simon to keep an eye on her. It hadn't been a good experience for someone at such a young age, but there were people she could connect Teagan with if she needed help, or someone to talk to.

And Teagan seemed to have changed her mind about Grace. She smiled to herself, hoping it would last and they might become friends. Although, knowing teenagers and their moods, it could possibly be a few days and they'd be back to normal. But she would take the few days and run with them. Anything was better than what they'd had before. She would just cherish whatever she could while it lasted.

Nick came over to her. He had been fine since her outburst about Simon. She hoped the matter was closed now.

'What's your plan for interviewing Shelby?' Grace asked. 'Can I come in with you?'

'Plan?' Nick shook his head. 'You don't need me. Go and do your thing, Sergeant.'

'By myself?' She was a little intimidated at the thought. But there was excitement too.

'Why not?' Nick said. 'I think you'll do a great job.'

349

'Well, if you're sure.' She was pleased with the vote of confidence. 'I'll take Frankie in with me. It'll be good experience.'

'Yes. He's doing okay with us. I'm going to suggest he takes his detective's exams. In readiness, in case we can ever fill our vacancy.'

'That's a great idea.' Grace nodded. 'I think he'll fit in well.'

'Just like you have.' Nick smiled warmly. 'That was some awesome work you did these past few days.'

She smiled. 'All part of a colossal team effort, even if we were too late to save everyone.'

Nick looked away briefly before turning back to her. 'And sorry for what I said about Simon the other day.'

'I won't be a mole, sir.'

'I know, I know. It was way off the mark. Frustration getting to me, I guess.'

She didn't reply, but she did nod in acceptance. She wouldn't say it was okay because it wasn't, but at least he'd apologised.

Once he'd gone, Grace glanced across her desk to see Sam with her head down checking through a spreadsheet. Perry was on the phone to someone and Frankie was making coffee in the background.

What a great team she had around her.

SEVENTY-EIGHT

A few minutes later, Grace took a deep breath and pushed on the door to Interview Room One, Frankie following behind her. Upstairs, the rest of the team were watching on the monitors.

Grace was keen to see if she could break Shelby, but at the same time she hoped that having a man by her side might calm their suspect down, give her the advantage over a female predator.

Lizzie Shelby was sitting next to the duty solicitor. Grace had met her a few times now and liked that she kept in the background as much as she could. The solicitor nodded when they sat across from her.

After setting up the recording machine, Grace introduced herself and Frankie, then read out the necessary details to start the interview: time, date and who was present. Then she cleared her throat and began.

'Lizzie, I'd like to talk to you about—'

'You're barking up the wrong tree. I didn't kill those women and you have no proof,' Lizzie interrupted.

'I'm confused,' Grace admitted. 'If you didn't kill them, tell

351

me, what was Jason Tranter's part in all this? I'm still not clear.'

'He wasn't involved.'

'So it was Joel?'

Lizzie yawned and looked away, as if bored with the whole conversation.

'I know you're trying to trick me. But I'm not lying.'

'I agree. I think that Joel carried out the murders, after you gave him the information from Peter Bentley. You're all in this together.'

'You have no idea.'

'Care to enlighten me?'

'No!' she giggled. 'Care to enlighten *me*?'

'Well, I also think you used Tranter to get close to Dunwood Academy, and you introduced Joel to All Talk.' Grace paused for effect, as if getting her thoughts in order. 'That was our link, you see.'

Lizzie glared at her.

'So I'm thinking now that maybe Diane Waybridge's phone was dropped by accident. Did one of the men do that? Because it gave us vital evidence to link her to the website. And from there we worked most of it out.'

Silence invaded the room once more. Grace sat forwards.

'You like to manipulate your men, don't you, Lizzie? First Peter and then Joel. But this time it backfired. Did Joel get too energetic for you, after he'd killed for you?'

'What planet are you on?' Lizzie laughed. 'Those men didn't do anything for *me*. They did it for themselves. They're the ones who are sick in the head. Joel was a natural-born killer.'

'Joel was a child!' Grace reined in her temper. 'Did he see you as a mother figure when his adoptive father had abandoned him, too?'

Lizzie pouted. 'I was his lover, you idiot.'

'So after Diane Waybridge was killed, you had sex. And that was the reason why there was forty-two minutes between you leaving Diane Waybridge's body near to Central Park and returning to the car. Someone had his reward from you.'

'And I rewarded him well,' Lizzie smirked.

'Who?' Grace cried, wanting her to say a name. 'Who did you reward well?'

'Well, it would hardly be Jason, would it? He was so wet. And at least the boy had a lot of energy.'

Grace was slowly reeling her in. 'How did you get him to kill for you?'

'I've told you! He didn't kill for *me*.' Lizzie rolled her eyes. 'I let him see he had it in him.'

'Oh, come on!' She turned to glance at Frankie, rolling her eyes. 'This is all lies! Next you'll be telling me that Joel and Jason were in this together – you were just the information provider. The men didn't need you.'

'They didn't.'

'But *you* still had to show them who was in charge.'

'I didn't need to show them that.' Laughter again. 'I *was* in charge.'

'So you're not blaming Joel?'

'Of course I am!'

'I suppose it's easy to implicate dead people, isn't it? And now neither of them are able to defend themselves, so you could say Joel had forced you into it, coerced you into –' Grace shrugged '– all of it?'

'He knew exactly what he was doing!' Lizzie yelled, making her jump. 'Joel did the kills, but I was the one in charge.'

Grace watched colour rush to Lizzie's face. Still, she held in her elation for a while longer.

'And Peter?' she urged.

'What about Peter?'

'When we arrested and charged Bentley, we weren't looking for anyone else in connection with the murders. Just him, a man acting on his own. But after what's happened these past ten days, I've realised it was all your idea, wasn't it? You coerced Bentley into murdering those women, and then you walked away when he got caught and you weren't.'

'All lies.'

But Grace could see she had rattled Lizzie as she continued. 'By killing Joel and Jason—'

'You don't know that I killed Jason. That could have been Joel!'

'It could have, but I doubt it. And the forensics will tell us once they're in. Going back to my line of questioning, I'm sure you were able to kill those women, but instead you let the men do it for you. How did you do that?'

'I'm a femme fatale.' Lizzie laughed.

Grace tried to hide her disgust. 'What did you do, Lizzie? Say they were your heroes every time they killed? Did you like them killing for you? Is that why there was no sexual assault on your victims? Did you get jealous and not let them take it any further? Or did you want them to stay pure because they reminded you of yourself, of how you could have been if you were happy?'

'Oh, what do you know? He hated you lot. He said you never looked out for him.'

'*He* was found guilty of four murders and one attempted murder, so I don't care how much he hates *us lot.*'

'I'm not talking about Peter!' Lizzie sighed. 'Joel! He hated you. First, you took his dad from him and put him in prison.'

'For murdering his mum,' Grace said.

'And then you put him with a family and jailed his stand-in father, too. Imagine all that anger festering inside his head. He was raging, so he made mistakes. And *you* stopped me from

354

getting to number five, *again*. I was seeing the number five *a lot*, and I was so sure I'd make it this time, but you ensured I didn't get my happy ending.'

'You don't deserve a happy ending after what you've done!'

Lizzie looked at Grace again. 'You think you're so smart, don't you? Yet you missed tons of things.'

Grace looked at Frankie, smiled and then back at Lizzie.

'You're entitled to your opinion, I guess. But I didn't miss the most important thing.' Grace sat forwards. '*You* might have had your men fooled, Lizzie, but you didn't fool me.'

SEVENTY-NINE

Two Days Later

Breakfast that morning was courtesy of the Quarter cafe. In Hanley's Piccadilly, it was a regular haunt for Grace and Simon, being close to where they both worked in Bethesda Street. But they hadn't been able to visit for the past fortnight, being so consumed by the case. Something they were still talking about.

'How's Sophie doing?' Grace asked Simon as they waited for their order. He'd told her he was going to ring Jack Bishop first thing. The last they'd heard was that Sophie had been brought out of the induced coma as planned and been supporting herself ever since.

'She's doing okay. It's early days but she needs further tests.'

Grace sighed loudly. 'I still don't understand why Shelby did it all again when she'd already got away with it the first time.'

'Yes, she could have walked away and no one would have been any the wiser.'

'I thought maybe she loved Bentley at first. But now, I don't think she knew what love was. Maybe that was the problem; she mixed up love, hate and true passion, and made those men kill for her.'

'So you think she was obsessed with killing people?'

'No. In her eyes someone took her father away from her and she blamed her mum. So maybe she was killing females who looked like her. Maybe she thought they had a happier family life than she did. She was obsessed with the number five, and then murdering five people. Perhaps she'd been so traumatised at that age by her father's death that she associated it with the last age she'd been truly happy.' Grace took a sip of her coffee before continuing. 'That's why I think she never killed men until the end; she just latched on to their pain. Joel Nicholls had lost not one, but two father figures.'

'And she was willing to let both Bentley and Joel take the blame for everything.'

'Yes. I think she never intended to kill anyone. She let the men think they were manipulating her, but in fact it was the other way around. So if Joel *had* got caught, I'm sure she would have been saying it was all his idea. That he'd told her to kill, that it was all his doing. But Joel idolised her.'

'Well, someone had to!' Simon joked.

Grace grinned. She'd met some devious women in her time, but Lizzie Shelby had been one of the worst. Susan Bailey had surprised her, especially how she'd been so trusting. She had finally confessed to helping out Peter Bentley. She had been the one to provide him with information about Joel Nicholls. She'd told Bentley that Joel's father was in prison, and that his adoptive father had landed himself a jail term too. At Bentley's request, she had watched him on Facebook, and at school, and told him what he was like, and about the other men at the school. It had meant that he could pass the information to Shelby, who'd then been able to get close to both Joel and Jason.

Chantelle Nicholls had been charged with providing a false alibi. Grace could understand her protecting Joel in a way. She'd thought he was in trouble for something far less serious and had been remorseful when questioned. Dean Nicholls had done nothing wrong as far as they could find.

There were still a few loose ends to tie up in terms of who else would be charged, and with what. Even though three women had been visiting Bentley in prison, it wasn't against the law. It would be up to them to put together a case to prove that Susan Bailey, and perhaps Denise Barber, had been willingly providing information to Bentley, rather than being tricked.

Grace reckoned Shelby must have visited the youth club every now and then, although she had yet to admit that. So she had been right – everything led back to Dunwood Academy, even if her initial thoughts had gone off-kilter.

'At least I don't have to put up with any more of your silly headlines right now,' Grace teased.

'Hey!' Simon faked a sad smile.

She giggled.

'I'm glad you caught them,' he said. 'And that Teagan's okay. I don't think I can ever thank you enough.'

'Just doing my job.' Grace waved off his comment.

'You saved my daughter's life, and I for one will always be grateful.'

'She was brave in her own right,' Grace acknowledged. 'I must admit, it's nice that she's at least talking to me in a civil manner. I don't seem to be the arch enemy now.'

'You're her heroine!'

Grace didn't think that was a fair comment. But Teagan had surprised them both when she'd appeared with a huge bunch of flowers and a box of Grace's favourite chocolates last night. It was early days, but it was good that they were getting on better. Not just for her, but for Simon too.

'Grace, I have something to ask you.' Simon cleared his throat.

She glanced at him quickly.

'Everything is so good between us,' he said, reaching for her hand. 'Do you think we could make it more permanent?'

'Oh!' She froze, not at all ready for that.

The noise around them intensified; teaspoons stirring, cups dropping into saucers, chatter of customers and staff taking orders.

'If you'll have me, I'd like to move in with you,' he continued.

'That's only because you like my home better than your own.'

Her laugh was hollow, but she didn't know what to say. She loved Simon, without a doubt. But was she ready for full-blown commitment? Living together would take their relationship to a whole new level. There would be things to be split, money to be shared, two people's dishes in the washer all the time.

Then again, would it really be much different than what they were doing now? She smiled. Simon spent so much time at her house already.

She couldn't give him an answer, mainly because she hadn't got one yet. It needed a bit of thought.

'It's okay, I sprung it on you.' Simon waved a hand in front of his face. 'Forget I said anything.'

'No, it's fine!' She sat forward a little. 'I need some time, that's all.'

He nodded and looked into his cup. He was hurt, she could tell. But if he wanted her, he'd have to wait until she was ready.

Although she wasn't quite sure what she was so frightened of.

'So, what are you doing for the rest of your day off?' Simon changed the subject as they waited for their food to arrive.

'Not much, really. I might pop to the shops, have a mooch around.'

'Whereas I get to cover the cases coming out of court today.' He glanced at his watch. Nearly half past nine. 'At least I have time for an oatcake breakfast.'

Grace smiled. Simon was good for her, she knew. And she wouldn't keep him waiting for long. But she had secrets that she couldn't share with him, and that worried her.

She didn't want to be deceitful, but she also couldn't tell him what she was really doing later that day.

EIGHTY

Grace left Hanley and drove down Bucknall New Road, turning left at Limekiln traffic lights. She parked up at Steele's Gym ten minutes later and went inside the building.

It was weird going back there after so long, especially under the circumstances. Grace had thought she might never go there again, even on official police business. Even though the force were keeping an eye on the Steele brothers, things definitely seemed to have gone quiet since last October. Grace would like to think it was because of her, but she wouldn't dream of being so presumptuous.

There was no one on the tiny reception desk, so she pushed on the swing door and went through to the gym. It hadn't changed at all since she'd last been there. The air was filled with the smell of sweat and rubber, a couple of teenage lads sparring in the boxing ring. The music blaring out was enough to blow her ears. It had never been this loud before. She wondered if Eddie was out for the day: if Leon was back yet.

She noticed a teenager in a vest who was pumping iron. 'Is Eddie in?' she shouted over to him.

The youth nodded to the back. 'In his office.'

361

Grace made her way across the room. She knocked authoritatively on the door and waited.

'Yeah?' Eddie's voice rang out.

She braced herself before she went in. Would he be expecting her or not?

'Ah, Grace, how lovely to see you!'

He sounded genuinely pleased, but she knew it was laced with sarcasm.

'This isn't a social visit, Eddie. I'm on business.' She sat down across from him uninvited. 'Do you know anything about Dean Nicholls being attacked the other night?'

'Not sure I know him.' His brow furrowed in concentration and he shook his head. 'What happened?'

Again there seemed genuine concern, but Grace wasn't fooled. She remembered what Chantelle Nicholls had said on the phone. Dean had said he'd been told to stay away, but he wasn't sure who from. Could it be Grace he was being warned against? She'd only met him that once, but he had threatened her, and Eddie, if he really was driving the car, had seen him do it.

'He was beaten up,' she continued.

'Oh, what a shame. I must remember to send him some grapes.'

'Cut the crap. What are you playing at?' Grace wanted to know.

'I have no idea what you're talking about.'

'Why were you outside the Bishops' home the same evening? I saw you when I was with Dean.'

'So you should know who beat him up then!' Eddie sniggered.

Grace refrained from rolling her eyes, staying silent so he would continue.

'I was collecting a takeaway and my phone rang,' he said. 'I stopped to answer it.'

'You expect me to believe that? I can check.'

'Why does it matter? The attack on that Nicholls fella has nothing to do with me. Although it does show you need to watch out for yourself.'

'You said you'd leave me alone,' she said.

'I have.'

She eyed him with disbelief. 'I *can* look after myself.'

'Really?' Eddie raised his eyebrows but said no more.

'So did you have anything to do with the assault?' she asked again.

'I saw him push you in the hedge. And then you gave him a great doing over before he was done over.' He laughed at his own joke.

Grace didn't laugh back. Yet again, she couldn't prove he was involved.

'We'll be checking CCTV carefully to see what we can find.'

'Good luck with that.' Eddie sat quietly for a moment before speaking again. 'If you must know, I do follow you every now and then. I just want to keep an eye on you.'

'To see what I'm doing at work?' She frowned at him.

'No, because I want to keep you safe.'

'I'm a big girl. I don't need your help.'

Eddie looked away for a moment, as if wondering whether or not to speak. Then he turned back to Grace.

'While you're here, perhaps you might help me out?'

'It doesn't work like that.' Silence invaded the room. 'What?' she snapped after a while.

'First, I'd like to thank you for whatever you said to Megan. She's ditched that fella, Seth. Kathleen's delighted, too.'

Grace said nothing, although secretly pleased her words had had the desired effect.

'I'd like to know more about him, though.'

363

She laughed, knowing there would be some catch.

'*You* already know him, don't you?'

'Whatever gave you that idea?'

'Well, I'd have thought you'd find out all you need to know from your sources.'

'I lost my source last year, remember?'

'I thought you denied working with DC Alex Challinor.'

'Who said it was Alex?'

Grace raised her eyebrows. 'I can't tell you any more than you know.'

'Not even to keep your niece safe?'

'Not even that.'

She was lying. After what had happened with Teagan, she wasn't sure what she would do if Megan was in trouble. But she wouldn't tell anyone that.

'Look, rumour has it that while he's inside, Trent Gibson's still arranging those stupid cash-and-grabs that were happening last year. Seth Forrester is supposedly running it for him, recruiting the lads from round the city.'

'How do you know this?' she demanded.

'I can't tell you everything.'

Grace opened her mouth to say that she already knew what he thought of as new information but closed it again. Trent Gibson had been jailed last year for the murder of Elliott Woodman, a young father who had been beaten to death. Eddie volunteering information about him had thrown her. Even though they were on different sides, he still wanted to help her. This was something she could pass on to the team who had been investigating the case last year.

She was about to speak again when the door opened. Grace bristled immediately as Leon appeared in the doorway. The two brothers together were intimidating, their similarities unnerving, almost replicas of each other.

364

'What's *she* doing here?' Leon asked his brother without looking at Grace. 'She's not welcome.'

'*She* came here to see Eddie,' Grace replied. 'But it's good to see you, Leon. How are you – good holiday?'

'What do you want?' Leon replied, ignoring her sarcasm.

'Chasing up on an assault. Dean Nicholls.'

'I hope you're not trying to stitch me up like the last time you tried, for Elliott Woodman's murder last year? I wasn't around then, either.'

She glanced surreptitiously at Eddie, who shook his head in the same furtive manner. She got the feeling he didn't want his brother knowing they had been discussing Trent Gibson.

'That was down to one of your friends, not me,' she replied.

'Whatever.' Leon glared at her. 'Are you going to be long, only I have business to sort out with Eddie? *Family* stuff.'

Grace stood up. 'I'm glad to see you've been behaving yourself since last year too.'

'We weren't doing much wrong, anyway,' he muttered.

Grace realised he was talking about the illegal parties her team had shut down last year. Parties in which young girls were brought in to entertain sleazy old men.

'Oh, really?' she barked, unable to contain her emotions. 'Well, for your information, one of the girls was brutally raped after being made to service eight men in one evening, and then not getting paid for it. Some party it turned out to be for her!'

'What?' Leon sat up straight. 'No, there was nothing like that going on. They were respectable guys. I would have known.'

'There were allegations that—'

'Allegations are nothing.' Leon cocked his head to one side and raised an eyebrow.

'I couldn't follow it through because the girl decided not to press charges.' She paused for effect. 'Plus, he was one of the men who had been murdered. Dale Chapman – the one who molested your sister when she was a child. You get the picture?'

'It was him?' Leon shook his head. 'Shit. I had no idea.'

'Well, now you know.'

'Come on, you two.' Eddie sighed loudly. 'Can't we at least try to be civil to each other? No one needs to know if that's better for you, Grace?'

'No one needs to know what?'

'That you're in touch with your family every now and then,' Eddie said.

'But I'm not!'

'And I don't want her to be!' Leon protested.

Grace rolled her eyes before leaving the room, cursing under her breath at herself. She had lost her cool for a moment back there. She shouldn't have said that about the parties. But Leon deserved to know what had been going on. And at least they had come to an end.

But she was damned if she was going to play the sister role for them. Even if deep in her heart it was what she might have wanted.

366

EIGHTY-ONE

Peter Bentley lay back on his prison bed, a hand behind his head, listening to some whacko outside his cell shouting the odds at the wardens. Other prisoners joined in, banging on doors, kicking the balcony walkway that overlooked the ground floor and watching no doubt as some unfortunate was dragged away to solitary.

He thought of Lizzie and laughed. She would probably be sitting in her cell now. He hoped she'd rot in there, because he rued the day he'd met her.

When Lizzie had said she wanted to kill someone, and he'd realised she wasn't fooling around, she had told him about her plan: to kill five women. Would he want to join in? They discussed how they would do it, as if they were going to prepare a Sunday lunch. He'd wanted her to find the women for him to kill, but she said they'd choose which ones together.

She'd told him it had to be by strangulation, and he was to have no sexual contact. She'd said she didn't want him sleeping with anyone else. Which was fine with him. He might be a sadistic bastard, but he wasn't a rapist.

He knew it had taken her by surprise when he'd killed the

first one. She didn't think he would go through with it. She'd stood in the bushes and watched. Knowing she was there gave him the thrill to continue.

After that first one, always high on something or other, they had walked around and sought their prey. They'd wake early after a restless night and go out at the crack of dawn. They'd hold hands, trawling for women. But it had all come to an end when she'd betrayed him by letting him take the blame. And she was supposed to have killed too, instead of leaving him to do everything.

He'd tried telling the police that he hadn't acted alone but he was told no one could find Beth Whiston. No wonder if she was using a false name.

He wondered if Susan or Denise would still visit. He doubted it; he'd bet his life on the police poisoning them about what he'd been up to. He'd had fun with Denise, fancying her when she'd been his probation officer, before he'd landed himself back in prison again. He couldn't believe his luck when she'd fallen for his charms. She had nothing to do with anything but keeping his ego alive.

And Susan had been useful, telling him all about her work at the school. Good old Facebook – although he hadn't been able to gain access to it on a regular basis unless he'd borrowed a phone that had been smuggled in. And she didn't have a clue he'd been after information for Lizzie to act upon when he'd first become her friend. He thought about how he'd got out of her that Jason Tranter would be perfect for Lizzie to get close to, that Joel Nicholls would be a good target.

It hadn't taken long to find out about Nicholls' real father through the prison system after Susan had told him about the boy, Joel. Paul Tring had served a few years of his sentence for murdering the lad's mother.

It had been hearing about Joel that had put the idea into his

368

head when Lizzie first asked him about setting up a copycat killing to get back at the police. Tring's young son was perfect for turning if he was anything like his father, even if a little young. And he knew Lizzie would like the power, the adulation she would receive if it worked.

Lizzie had been foolish. She should never have run when he'd been caught after that bitch Mandy Shelley got away. He'd found out she'd disappeared from Manchester to escape capture. It had festered inside him for two years until all of a sudden Lizzie had started visiting him again. Once she mentioned copycat killers, he knew what he had to do.

But he hadn't wanted to help her, and he would never have helped the police. He just wanted to make sure she was caught this time, for leaving him in the lurch. It had been a game, a bit of fun to while away the time.

Stupid Lizzie.

He picked up a pen and notepad and began to write. There was always some weird woman who would become infatuated with him.

AUTHOR NOTE:

To all my fellow Stokies, my apologies if you don't gel with any of the Stoke references that I've changed throughout the book. Obviously, writing about local things such as *The Sentinel*, Hanley Police Station and Central Forest Park (or Hanley Forest Park as it's more locally known as) would make it a little too close to home, and I wasn't comfortable leaving everything authentic. So, I took a leaf out of Arnold Bennett's 'book' and changed some things slightly. However, there were no oatcakes harmed in the process.

A LETTER FROM MEL

First of all, I want to say a huge thank you for choosing to read *Tick Tock*. I have thoroughly enjoyed writing about Grace and her team and I hope you enjoyed spending time with them as much as I did.

If you did enjoy *Tick Tock*, I would be forever grateful if you would leave a review on Amazon. I'd love to hear what you think, and it can also help other readers discover one of my books for the first time.

Many thanks to anyone who has emailed me, messaged me, chatted to me on Facebook or Twitter and told me how much they have enjoyed reading my books. I've been genuinely blown away with all kinds of niceness and support from you all.

You can sign up to my newsletter and join my readers group on my website www.MelSherratt.co.uk or you can keep in touch on Twitter @writermels and Facebook at MelSherrattauthor.

Thanks, Mel

Some secrets should stay in the family...

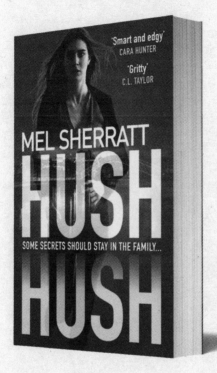

The first Grace Allendale novel, out now